THE SHEPHERD SLEEPS

By Wallace F. Brown

Writers Exchange E-Publishing
http://www.readerseden.com/
http://www.writers-exchange.com/

THE SHEPHERD SLEEPS

Writers Exchange E-Publishing
PO Box 372
ATHERTON QLD 4883

Cover Art by: RJ Haas

Published Online by Writers Exchange E-Publishing
http://www.writers-exchange.com
http://www.readerseden.com

ISBN Electronic 9781921314698
Print 9781921314193

- 1 -

The heat came to the lowlands early that year. It hung over the Gulf of Mexico like a malevolent vapor that blurred the edges of things and smothered the wind. It invaded people's lives like an uninvited guest and became the starting point of every conversation. For Paul, it was just another obstacle to deal with. Keesler Air Force base in Biloxi, Mississippi was mainly a training facility. It was like a half-way house for eighteen-year old kids, trying to recover from the trauma of basic training. They didn't scream in your face twenty hours a day and tell you what species of vermin you were, but there was still way too much spit and polish and too many stiff-assed NCOs. It had become Paul's permanent duty station so they cut him some slack, but he spent as much time as he could away from the place. Just off the base, following the rim of the Gulf, was route 90. It was an eighty-mile run to New Orleans. Not a great distance measured in miles, but so far removed from the drab reality of his life that it was like the opposite pole of a magnet, tugging at him every waking hour, and often invading his dreams.

He had duty that Saturday morning until noon and then he changed into his civilian clothes and headed out to the highway. After a few minutes, a rusted old Ford pick-up pulled over and he climbed in next to the driver. He was an older man with hair that was mostly gray and a face that had seen too much sun. He smiled at Paul and extended his hand.

"Charlie Wilkes, how y'all doing today?" The gears growled as he jammed the floor shift into second and the old truck bucked when he let up the clutch. "Watch that door. It don't always latch on the first try."

Paul opened the door again and then slammed it closed. "I'm fine. You?"

"Good as I'm gonna be. Where you headed, son?"

"I'm going down to New Orleans. You going that far?"

"I'll be runnin' by north of it, if that helps you any."

"Sure, I usually get out around there anyway and take the bus the rest of the way."

"You stationed there at Keesler?"

"Yeah. For the last six months."

"You a pilot?"

"No. I tried out for it but my eyes aren't good enough."

"Just as well. They'd probably be sendin' you over to that damned jungle and they'd be tryin' to shoot some holes in ya. I can't figure out what the hell they're tryin' to do over there anyway. It don't make no sense to me."

"It doesn't make any sense to a lot of people," Paul said.

"Ya know I was in the big war. Now that one made some sense. Those bastards attacked us and we give 'em hell for it. Seems to me this country's tryin' to get too big for its britches. I had a friend once told me when the only tool you got is a hammer, every damn problem starts lookin' like a nail. You go around this world hammerin' on everybody and pretty soon people gonna get pissed off."

Paul laughed. He sat back in his seat and relaxed, looking out over the water. Sometimes it was awkward trying to make conversation with the strangers that picked him up along the road, but Charlie had the gift and Paul just let him ramble on. The time went by quickly and after a while he felt like he had known Charlie all his life. It was likely they would never meet again, but that was what he liked about hitch-hiking. It was like reading a little bit of a story about someone without finding out what happens in the end. It was great entertainment making up your own ending. When they were getting close to the city, he asked Charlie to pull over at a bus stop, and thanked him for the ride.

"You watch your back down there in the Quarter, son. Some of them people's just rats with britches on."

The bus-stop sign had long since rusted beyond recognition, but the place was marked by an ancient bench of concrete and rotting wood that was in the process of returning to the earth. The look of it did not inspire confidence, but he had waited at this place before and eventually a bus had come along. Paul was not someone who could sit patiently on a bench. Instead he leaned against the side of it to indicate his intentions, without committing himself to the wait. Shielding his eyes, he peered down the highway to where the bus had materialized before, as if directing his impatience in its direction would help hurry it along. He wiped his brow with his hand and then ran it back through his short brown hair.

After a few minutes he heard someone come up behind him and he turned. He was startled to see a beautiful young woman looking back at him. She immediately looked away. Her skin was light brown but there was a paleness about her, like someone who did not like the sun. Her hair was auburn and long, with a slight wave to it. She had it gathered in the back with a carved wooden clasp. Her eyes were dark, almost black, and features were fine, except for her lips, which were full and wide. She wore no makeup that he could see. The fine wrinkles at the corners of her mouth and eyes spoke of someone who liked to laugh but her expression was serious, maybe even a little angry. The plain white dress she was wearing clung to her thighs in the humid air. She clutched her tattered canvas bag against her chest like a shield. He held his glance a little too long and finally she glared back at him with a look of contempt that startled him for a moment.

"My name is Paul," he said, by way of apology.

She swatted at an imaginary fly with a bible she was holding in her hand, but said nothing. They stood at opposite ends of the bench in silence, intruding on each other's thoughts.

After a few minutes, a tired-looking bus pulled up in front of the bench and let out an exhausted hiss of air. The door folded open, and a heavy-set black man in a gray uniform shirt and hat looked down at them impassively. The girl hung back so that Paul would have to board first and declare his seat. He dropped some coins in the box, then moved toward the back so that she would sit somewhere in front of him. He had no plan to talk to her further. Over the years he had learned not to force it. It would happen at its own pace, if at all. It was better to let it find its own drift, like the slowly turning tumbler of a lock. He had a strong feeling about this one though, and no urgency of time. She took a seat near the middle. The bus moved off, making its way into the city a few miles at a time, stopping now and then like a runner trying to catch his breath. It was late afternoon and the air pouring through the open windows felt too thick to breathe.

He thought about how he might spend his evening. New Orleans was a house with many locked doors. Most of those doors opened readily with money. He needed other means. He had spent many weekends wandering around the French Quarter, watching. He learned early on that Bourbon Street was not the French Quarter. It was like a boardwalk where people could dip their toes into sin without being swept away by the tide. It was the other places he wanted. The labyrinth of hidden courtyards leading to unexpected rooms, the sound of a woman's laugh behind a closed gate in a wall topped with broken bottles cemented into the stone, a casual glance through a closing door and the sound of jazz, and ice in glasses, couples in dark alleys, making love against a wall. It was a place that existed only in the night.

The bus came to a stop and two men boarded. The first one was big and slow in his movements. He dropped his change on the floor and had difficulty picking it up with his thick, blunt fingers. The driver waited patiently. The other one was wiry and mean-looking. He cursed at the big one and gave him a shove. All the while his gaze darted about like a snake, tasting the air for an opportunity. He saw the girl and his face distorted into a malicious grin. The big one lumbered down the aisle, looking down at the floor and then he turned back, not knowing where he was supposed to sit. The other one stopped next to the girl, as the bus moved off. He said something to her that Paul could not hear. She snapped back at him and then turned away. He said something else but she ignored him. Finally he grabbed her by the hair and pulled her up so that she was forced to look into his face.

"Don't you turn away from me, nigger. I know what you are. You ain't foolin' me. You damn sure ain't no white girl. Move your black ass to the back of the bus."

It was not that Paul had made some carefully considered decision to intervene. Some other part of him had taken control and he became a detached observer of his own movements. His body surged forward, while somewhere lost in the back of his consciousness, a voice was going on about consequences. The big one looked confident. Now that his friend had started doing something familiar, he knew what he was supposed to do. He was there to keep anyone from spoiling the fun. Paul came up behind him. He turned and glowered at Paul with that smug confidence that comes from never being challenged. Paul stepped forward, knees bent and thrust his fist into the center of the man's chest. The big man slumped forward, unable to breathe, a look of shock and fear washed over on his face. There was no need to hit him again. Paul pushed him into a seat.

Paul now had the other one's full attention. He dropped the girl like a used napkin and his eyes widened with fear. Slowly, a look of hatred came over his face. He reached into his back pocket and flicked open a knife, slashing the air in front of him like the tail of a lizard. Paul moved toward him. He watched like Andre had taught him all those years ago. In a fight a man might do any number of unexpected things, but a man with a knife will tell you exactly what he is going to do. How he holds it. How he stands. What his eyes say. It was not the first time Paul had faced a knife. This one just wanted to scare him off. Paul kept moving toward him and he saw panic growing in the man's eyes. The knife-wielding man lunged forward wildly. Paul shifted his weight, avoiding the blade and, at the same time, grasping the man's wrist, pulling forward and twisting until the knife fell onto the floor. He released his grip and pushed the man backward.

Out of the corner of his eye he saw the girl open her Bible and he laughed to himself thinking that she was about to pray for him. Something fell out onto the girl's lap. Then, in a flash of white fury she was on her attacker's back, a straight razor pushed against his throat. A small drop of blood appeared on the man's neck and he went still, his eyes wide with panic. The driver had stopped the bus and he came up behind the girl. Paul watched fascinated, as the line of blood under the blade grew wider.

"Now you put that thing away, Lucinda," the driver said. "I'm sure this gentleman will be happy to take himself and his friend off my bus."

The injured man was shaking now and when he spoke his voice was a high-pitched wail. "Get her off me. Oh, my God, please. Get her off me."

"I think I'll just cut your ugly head off and take it to town in my bag," she said.

The driver gently reached around, grasped the girl's hand and pulled it carefully away from the man's throat.

The man immediately reached up and clutched at his bloodied neck. "She cut me. The bitch cut me. I'm gonna kill you, you fuckin' whore."

"You ain't gonna do nothing, mister," the driver said, "except get you and your friend off my bus and be happy you still got your damn head on your shoulders. Maybe you ain't heard, Jim Crow is dead around here."

The man looked at the girl still holding the razor and then at Paul. "I'll find you," he said to Paul. You gonna see me again."

The girl raised the razor in the air and he had no more to say. He turned and hurried toward the door.

"You, too," the driver said, looking at the big man still slumped over in his seat.

The big man got up slowly, clutching his chest, and walked toward the front, sliding sideways past Paul like he was afraid of being burned. He did not make eye contact. The two men jumped off the bus and the driver turned toward Paul, as if considering whether he should go too. He apparently thought better of it.

"I don't allow no trouble on my bus," was all he said. He got back into his seat and released the brake.

The girl turned to Paul, still angry. "I don't need no help from you," she said, and sat back down.

Her voice sounded hollow and distant, like she had shouted it from the other side of a wall. He stood there in the aisle for a moment trying to gather himself, a little surprised by the girl's reaction. His body felt heavy, like it was being pulled toward the center of the earth. In a few seconds, he started to shake as the adrenaline left his system. His eyelids began to twitch and pretty soon his whole body was throbbing. He closed his eyes and clasped his arms across his chest. There was nothing to do but to let it run its course. After all the scrapes he had been in, it surprised him that it never went away. His thoughts drifted back to the years he had spent in the neighborhood. It was like his mind was rerunning the lessons he was supposed to have learned to keep him out of things like this.

* * *

The memories always started at the door of his grandmother's house in Pittsburgh. His father had died in an accident at the mill when Paul was six. His mother died of a stroke a few years later. He was watching television with her one night and she turned to him slowly and looked at him like she didn't know who he was. There was confusion on her face for a moment, and then she slumped over and slid onto the floor. He didn't remember much of what happened next. At the cemetery he watched the dirt fall from the blade of the shovel and he screamed for them to stop. But they didn't stop, and he began to feel like he was falling, too. A part of him had been falling ever since, utterly alone in some formless void. It was like his connection to the world had come undone.

He went to live with his grandmother. His two sisters moved in with an aunt who lived in Johnstown. She had a daughter of her own and thought the girls would be company for her. She said she didn't know how to raise no boys. His grandmother's neighborhood was almost all black by then, except for a few blocks where some old white people were going to hang on until somebody carried them out on a stretcher. He was thirteen years old and the new kid at school with no friends. The older kids beat on him until he learned to fight back. The beatings he took made him tough, but his grandmother kept him from becoming hard. She was the kindest person he had ever known and it made him feel protective of her. He knew it was hard on her raising a kid at her age and he didn't want to do anything to cause her any hurt. Still, he was spending more and more time on the streets, trying to find a place for himself. Mostly he was just alone. Andre changed all of that.

The first time he met Andre was down at the rail yard. It was one of those late fall evenings at the end of a warm day. The heat rising from the ground created a layer of mist about knee high, like walking through smoke. Smoke that smelled of soot and tasted like steel. It was a place alive with possibilities. He imagined the tracks reaching out into every corner of the world. Sometimes he put his ear down on the cold steel rail and listened to the distant trains, singing their secret songs, like whales in some far off ocean. He was looking for a slow moving freight to hop a ride downtown when he came across a bunch of black kids stealing radios from a boxcar. He stopped for a while and watched them, amazed by their audacity. Suddenly, there were cops everywhere. He ran in front of a commuter train and nearly got clipped, but it gave him enough time to slide under a boxcar and climb up onto the truck. The flashlight beams stabbed under the cars like bolts of lightning but they passed him by. He crawled under the train, flattening himself to slide under the axels until they were far enough away, and then he ran. There were two squad cars on the access road but no cops. As he passed them, he noticed a black kid sitting in the back of one. Without even thinking he opened the door and let the kid out. They bolted up the access road together. The kid was cuffed behind his back but he was fast and, before long, he had turned the corner and vanished. Paul figured that was the end of it. It was just the beginning.

A few weeks later he was coming home from the store with some groceries when he ran into a gang of black kids. The kid from the rail yard was with them. They had Paul up against a wall and were going through his pockets when the kid recognized him. Everything changed. They gave him his money back and then turned their backs and walked away. All of them except the kid, who picked up the bag of groceries and gave it back to him.

"Name's Andre," he said, holding out his hand.

"Paul. I guess that makes us even."

"Hell, no, we ain't even. We ain't close to even. You think those bulls back at the yard were goin' to take me in? Hell, no. They were goin' to beat the shit out of me. Maybe break my legs. Maybe worse. That's what happens round here if you ain't white."

Paul didn't say anything. It was the first time he had considered that the world might be different for a black kid. He wondered what they would have done to him.

"It's cool. I'm gonna tell my boys to let you slide around here. But just the same you don't need to be around here at night unless you with me. You dig?"

"Yeah, I get it."

"Hey, what you doin' later?"

"I just figured on takin' this stuff home and stayin' in."

"All right, that's cool. But if you feel like it, meet me down at the school in about an hour. I got something goin' on."

That was the beginning of Paul's abbreviated life of crime. Andre wasn't into violence and he didn't do stickups, but he was good with locks and could climb anything. He started out tagging walls in places where the competition was too afraid to climb. He learned that people weren't too careful about locking windows high up. At first Paul mostly stood lookout, but he learned fast and soon he was almost as good as Andre at getting into buildings. It was all penny-ante stuff. They got beer from the VFW regularly, until a couple of guys surprised them one night and they had to jump off a two-story roof into a dumpster full of garbage to get away. They got a lot of petty cash and some typewriters and adding machines. It wasn't a lot of money but that wasn't the point anyway. It was the rush. Doing things they shouldn't be doing, taking risks and getting away with it. Andre taught him other things besides picking locks and walking high ledges. He taught him how to handle himself in a street fight. How to hit a guy so that he wouldn't get up, but he wouldn't die on you either. How to go up against a guy with a knife. How to walk down the street when the cops were looking for somebody. "It ain't never about how tough you are," Andre always said. "It's about doin' what you gotta do to save your ass and get away. Guys who fight for the fun of it are just assholes and sooner or later they end up dead, or worse."

They ran together for a few years. Eventually, their luck ran out in a record company warehouse. They were caught climbing in through a ventilating duct, but since they hadn't taken anything yet, the cops just made his grandmother come down to the precinct to get him. He couldn't stand the look on her face. He didn't see Andre for a while after that. Not until the night he told Paul he needed him just one more time. Paul didn't want to do it. It was an office on the fourth floor of a building on the Pitt campus.

* * *

He had almost drifted off to sleep when he felt someone sit down next to him. He opened one eye, just in case it was someone he needed to pay attention to, and saw the girl looking back at him with a quizzical expression. The shaking had stopped but he still felt a little nauseous.

"Are you okay?"

"Yeah, I'm fine," he said, managing a weak smile.

"Thanks for helpin' me. Sometimes I don't know how to act, you know. I was pretty mad."

"I could tell. I thought you were going to cut that guy's head off."

"Nah, you just can't get the attention of a cracker like him without drawin' a little blood." She smiled at him and her eyes became transparent, like smoked glass.

"My grandmother had a bible like that except I don't remember it having a straight razor in the binding."

"Yeah, well I guess your grandmother never worked in New Orleans. My name is Lucinda by the way, but my friends call me Lucky. You can call me Lucky."

"What did you do? Win the Irish Sweepstakes?"

"The what? No. They call me Lucky because I'm lucky to be alive with everything I've been through." She laughed again, like a child, full of joy and mischief.

"Like what?"

"Like never-you-mind what. What are you doin' around here anyway? You sure as hell don't come from Louisiana."

"How do you know?"

"Because none of these Louisiana boys move that fast. You a football player or somethin'?"

"I played in college. I wasn't big enough for the pros. I'm in the Air Force, stationed over in Biloxi."

"Biloxi? Then what were you doin' back there at the bus stop?"

"I hitchhike into the city almost every weekend, but it's easier to get downtown if I take the bus from there."

"Oh, I get it. Goin' into the Big Easy to get yourself a girl and have a good time."

"Yeah, something like that, except I really haven't found my way in yet, if you know what I mean. I walk up and down Bourbon Street like everybody else and the locals put on a show for you. But I know that's not all there is to the French Quarter."

"You got that right. But you better watch out, it can be a dangerous place for somebody don't know their way around."

"Yeah, I can see that. But you know everything that's really worth doing has a little bit of danger in it. Don't you think?"

"Well my Aunt Jess used to say 'be careful what you wish for, cause you might get it and it's the worst thing you ever got.'" She studied his face for a moment. "What color are your eyes anyway? They look like a different color every time I look at you."

"Well, they're sort of blue-green-brown."

She chuckled and a knowing smile crossed her face.

"What?" he said after a while.

"Oh, nothin'. I was just thinkin' you ain't the type to stay out of it."

It was his turn to laugh. "I guess that's true. I've survived so far though."

"Yeah, well the night is just gettin' started and you already made two enemies."

"Yeah, but I made one friend. You see, that's what I mean."

She smiled. "Yeah, for what it's worth."

"It's worth plenty."

They were silent for a while. The bus was now on the outskirts of the city and starting to get crowded. The passengers stared straight ahead, avoiding conversation, preferring instead to look inside themselves, at the random images of their solitary lives. When Paul spoke, it was as much to himself as to the girl.

"You know what I'd really like to find is a good place to eat dinner that doesn't cost me a week's pay."

"There are plenty of places like that. You just have to know where to look."

"How about you take me to one. I'll buy."

She smiled at him. It was a softer smile that quickly faded. She turned away and didn't say anything for a moment. Finally she looked back at him and seemed to study his face for a moment. "Okay. I know a place we can go, but we gotta go as soon as we get into town. I got things to do."

"Great. What things?"

"Private things, and anyway I'm buyin'."

"I can't let you do that."

"You ain't lettin' me do nothin'. You don't have no other choice."

* * *

It was a small place on Rampart Street just off Canal. A half dozen tables and a row of booths along one wall. The light reflecting through the plate glass windows from the sidewalk was swallowed by the brown, hammered metal ceiling and dark paneled walls before it could penetrate the room. It was as if the visual distractions were being held to a minimum so as not to compete with the seductive aromas emanating from the kitchen. A votive candle in a transparent green glass holder marked each table, like a lonely island in a dim sea. The menu was loaded with exotic-sounding dishes that he knew nothing about.

Paul glanced at her over the top of his menu and watched her come to a decision. "How about you order for me," he said.

"Okay, how about some prawns?"

"That's like shrimp, right?"

"It ain't like shrimp, it is shrimp. Anyway it ain't what they are, it's about what Baby does with them."

"Baby?"

"That's who owns this place. His real name is Beauregard St. Michael, but everybody calls him Baby. He's the best chef in New Orleans, I swear. He was the chef over at Dauphine's until he chased the owner three blocks with a meat cleaver for puttin' salt in the Gumbo." She giggled at the thought of it and her face lit up again, like a little girl opening a Christmas present. "Anyway he likes ownin' his own place. He lives upstairs."

Paul smiled. He noticed there were no salt and pepper shakers on the table. "So, how did you meet Baby?"

"Oh, hell, I don't know. I've known him forever."

"Is this where you usually eat?"

"I eat here a lot but I haven't been in for a few weeks. It just didn't work out, you know?"

A waitress brought over some silverware and water. She nodded to Lucky but didn't say anything.

"Where's Baby tonight?" Lucky asked.

"He's in the back," the waitress said. "Y'all want to talk with him?"

"No, just tell him I'm here when you pass him by. I want him to meet somebody."

The waitress gave Paul a curious look and raised what used to be her eyebrows before she decided to shave them off and draw them higher up on her forehead. She turned and went back into the kitchen. A few minutes later a large black man came waddling through the kitchen doors. He had on a stained white apron that looked like a lobster bib on him. He was about as wide as he was tall, and his features were tucked in between rolls of fat wrinkles that cascaded down his face and neck and presumably kept on going.

"Well, hey, Miss Lucky," he boomed with a voice as large as his body, showing a big gap-toothed smile.

She got to her feet and gave him a big hug, almost disappearing behind his huge arms. "I want you to meet my hero. His name is Paul."

Baby offered a huge ham of a hand and Paul shook it, just managing to get his own hand around the fingers.

"Hero, huh? Well, it ain't every day a body gets to meet no hero."

"Well he is one, Baby. He saved me from a couple of crackers on the bus today." Lucky reseated herself, beaming at him.

Paul smiled. "I'm not sure who saved who."

Baby laughed. "Lord, lord don't you know I believe that. Nobody wants to go messin' around with Miss Lucky. She ain't as helpless as she looks."

"I found that out."

Baby turned back to the girl. "Where you been, honey? I ain't seen you in a month, it seems."

"I know, Baby. I just been runnin', you know."

He leaned over and whispered something in her ear that Paul couldn't hear.

"No, no that's okay, I got that fixed up, Baby."

"You remember what I told you, honey. That's some bad news there. You need to be lookin' around, if you know what I mean."

"I know, Baby. I will."

"So what did you kids order today?"

"We're havin' some of those prawns, Baby. You still doin' them up the same?"

"Well, you know I never mess with something that works so good. You tell me, Mr. Paul, if these ain't the best damn prawns you ever tasted."

"Lucky says they are and I don't want to argue with her. I've seen her Bible."

Baby laughed and his whole body shook. "He learns fast, else he's known you for a bit."

"Oh, I think he ain't too stupid," she said, smiling.

"Okay." He laughed again. "Let me get back to my kitchen. You be well, Miss Lucky, and its fine to meet you, Mr. Paul."

After he left, they didn't talk for a while. She was looking down at the table but her eyes were focused far away, like there was something troubling unfolding in her memory. She quickly smiled when Paul looked at her. Suddenly unable to hold her glance, he looked around the room, taking in the place. It felt comfortable, like somewhere he had known about all of his life. Finally, he looked back at her and caught her studying him. He held her eyes this time and he saw something change in her. There was no shyness there, but she had a wall around her that he guessed would be difficult to get over.

"So, are you going to tell me what you do down here in the city? I would have guessed you were down here preaching and saving souls until I saw what you use for a bookmark."

She chuckled and looked away for a moment. When she looked back she was serious again. "Look, I like you, Paul, and I really am thankful for what you did today, but I don't want to talk about what I do. I don't want to talk about my life or anything like that. I just live for the moment, you know what I mean? I try to be happy with what I'm doing and who I'm with. I think the past is the past and it don't matter anymore. Let's just have a nice dinner okay? Don't spoil it by askin' a lot of questions about things I don't want to talk about."

"Okay, I'm sorry. I didn't mean to make you uneasy."

"I'm not."

There was an uncomfortable silence. She took a compact out of her bag and studied her face in the small mirror, turning it to get the light.

"Well, maybe you can tell me about some places I can go in the French Quarter."

"That all depends on what you're lookin' for. You can find anything you want down here if you know where to look. So the question is…" she snapped her compact closed and looked at him. "The question is what are you lookin' for, Mr. Paul? Hey, what's your last name anyway?"

"Its Greene. Paul Greene."

"Pleased to meet you, Mr. Greene."

"What's yours?"

"I don't have one anymore. I gave it up. So tell me what you're lookin' for, Mr. Greene."

"I guess I'm not sure."

"Well, you see, that's your problem. You need to know what you want before you have any chance of getting it."

"I know that's true."

"Are you lookin' for a woman? You don't seem the type that's looking the other way."

"Well, sure, I mean I'm always looking for a woman."

"So are you lookin' to get a ride or are you looking for something real."

He smiled. "Well, both I guess. I mean I'm not looking to do it with someone that I don't care anything about."

"You mean like a whore."

"Well, yeah. I mean I've never done that."

"Why? You scared?"

"No, I mean it's just that it seems so cold to do that with someone you don't even know. Somebody doing it just for the money."

"How many women have you been with?"

"I don't know, a few."

She leaned forward and looked him in the eye. "Bullshit. I never met a man yet who didn't know how many he had and what he liked about this one or that one."

He was speechless for a minute. She sat back against the booth and smiled at him, watching him squirm.

"Okay, so how many?"

He laughed. "Exactly eighteen."

She grinned at him. "Okay, and which one was the best?"

"Well, that depends. They all had their good points, you know?"

"Oh, yeah, I know. But the thing is you didn't stay with any of them, right?"

"Well, no."

"Why not?"

"Well, I don't know. For all different reasons."

"Were you in love? Did you get your heart broken?"

"Only once, that was enough."

"No, it wasn't. You got to get your heart broken lots of times before you understand."

"Understand what?"

She leaned forward again and took him by the hand. "Look, honey, I don't want you to think I don't believe in love, because I do. I've seen it myself. Felt it myself. But most of what is going on out there don't have nothin' to do with love. Most men need to get laid just to feel like a man once in a while. Most men are getting beat up all of the time. Beat up by their boss, beat up by the bill collector, beat up by the tax man. Some men just turn mean and they go home and beat up on their wives and scream at their kids. Most men get beat up by their wives, too. I don't mean punched and bloody. I mean beat up in their souls. When the excitement goes away, and it grinds down to livin' every day, there just ain't that much love out there, honey. The good ones stick around anyway. Sometimes they go lookin' for a whore and everyone thinks how horrible they are, but those are the good ones. That's when you know it's love. When she's too miserable to make it through another day and too tired to put on her makeup and he can't keep his belly from fallin' out of his belt but they kiss each other good night and make love anyway. The bad ones just take off. Young ones like you think they're lookin' for love but they're just lookin' to get laid. In the beginning you bring flowers and take her out to nice places, buy her jewelry. Anything to keep her happy so she'll do what you want in bed. After a while, when you start getting it regular, you forget about the flowers. Pretty soon she stops lookin' so good to you anymore and you start lookin' around. Sooner or later, you find one who looks back and you start doin' it on the sly. After a while you don't want to look at the old one anymore and all you want is out. Mostly, the only marriages I know about that work are the ones put together on purpose, for money or power and stuff like that. People like that screw around like crazy. Usually they don't even try to hide it. They keep the marriage together because it's a society thing and ..."

The waitress brought their food and Lucky began eating in mid-sentence. Paul took a mouthful and discovered immediately what she meant about the prawns.

"Wow, this is the best shrimp I have ever tasted." He was happy to change the subject.

"Told you so."

The conversation ceased completely while they ate. Lucky cleaned her plate and then stood up abruptly. "I'm sorry, Paul. I really have to go. Baby will just put this on my tab. If you want, you can go over to the kitchen and tell him what a good cook he is. He likes that. Oh, and leave a couple of bucks for Loretta."

"Wait. I mean, let me walk with you a little."

"Not tonight, honey. I've really got to run."

"Well, will I see you again?"

"You might. I'll be around. Listen, if you're lookin' for a place to hang out there's a bar called the Seven Seas back on Ursulines Ave. There's a bartender there named Louis. He kinda looks like that Beatle, John Lennon. He knows me. Go over and introduce yourself to him. Louis can find you almost anything you need."

She reached down and kissed him on the cheek, touching him tenderly on his neck. A shiver ran up his spine. She stood back from him and smiled for a second and then she was out the door. He looked around and suddenly felt like he didn't belong there. All he wanted to do was leave. He put a few dollars on the table and went over to the kitchen door. He peeked his head in.

"That was the best meal I ever had, Baby." He felt awkward saying the name.

"Didn't I tell you? You come on back any time, Mr. Paul. I got lots of good things cookin' back here."

- 2 -

On a Saturday night, Bourbon Street was a river of humanity, washing in and out of the bars and strip joints and carrying wide-eyed tourists downstream, like debris caught up in a flood. Occasionally, a few would drift into some of the less hospitable tributaries of the Quarter and wake up missing some of their possessions. For the most part they survived with their lives, if not their consciences, intact. Floating among the innocent and the gullible were the sharks. They were generally in disguise, except that they could never seem to erase that look imprinted on their faces. It was at once, a declaration of their bad intentions and a roadmap to the darker places in their souls. They could spot a fish a mile away, but if they caught you watching, they darted away to the safety of deeper waters. In the middle of it all was the Orange Julius. To Paul, it was a small island of sanity where you could anchor yourself for a while and get a feel for the flow. He usually started his nightly forays there, hanging around in the recessed doorway when it was too early to go to the bars. They made a drink with orange juice, powdered sugar and a raw egg. It was enough to get him through the night. In the early evening there were a lot of young families with kids patrolling the street. The parents were as wide eyed as the kids, who didn't know what all the fuss was about but were pretty sure it was fun. The adults were mostly blank faced, but if you smiled at the kids they would always smile back, especially the babies.

Paul was entertaining himself by making funny faces at the kids to see if they would laugh. He struck up a conversation with a guy who had been watching him play the game. He was on the short side with thick, curly black hair and a full moustache that curled at the ends, making him look like a diminutive pirate. His name was Spencer Dupree and after a rambling conversation about everything in general, Paul went with him to pick up his girlfriend whom he referred to as the countess. They ended up dropping some mescaline together and doing a Technicolor tour of the Quarter. Spencer had a plan to retire by the time he was thirty. He had been hired right out of college by the Times Picayune as a society page reporter, owing to the blueness of his blood. He came from one of those old Louisiana families whose lineage reached back into the fog of history, and whose wealth, though dubiously acquired, had accumulated respectability over the years like a snowball, rolling down a hill.

Having been born with a deformed foot, Spencer was sadly ineligible to serve his country and protect its good citizens from 'those vicious little men in pajamas who inexplicably wanted us to remove ourselves from their homes'. That was how he put it anyway. The infirmity gave him a slight limp, which, combined with a penchant to occasionally speak like a cultured southern gentlemen, made him irresistible to the ladies. He owned a collection of ornate canes and walking sticks and considered them as ordinary an accessory as a wristwatch.

Spencer's beat was the social life in the Crescent City, much of which revolved around the Carnival krewes. His real talent, however, was as a repository and purveyor of sensitive information. The lions of New Orleans society had a talent for finding themselves in compromising situations, and there was Spencer, ever so discreet and all too happy to keep them out of the paper in exchange for promises owed. It was a growth industry. The trick, Spencer told him, was to never make it seem like you were blackmailing anyone. You just leveraged a few favors for a few introductions to a few social functions where you met more people who might end up climbing out the back window of a whore-house. He was twenty-seven, and already owned six acres of land on the bend of the Mississippi out by Baton Rouge. Spencer couldn't tell most of his friends about what he was doing because he understood what a dangerous game it could be. All the same, he felt the need to share his exploits with someone and Paul was a good listener. He was an outsider with nothing to gain by telling tales. Besides they liked the same music.

Spencer's acquaintance list wasn't limited just to the high rollers. He also knew his way around the Quarter. He knew every bartender by name and every cop on the beat. He exchanged information with the police on certain unsavory characters he knew of, in order to ride along on drug busts. He only ratted out the ones who didn't play by the rules, for instance by eliminating their competition and leaving bodies lying about for the tourists to trip over. He considered it his civic duty. The police allowed him to take crime scene photos and while documenting the evidence, he would often find a small amount of some contraband substance, miraculously overlooked by the officers on the scene. He ran on a twenty-four clock, mostly taking half-hour naps a few times a day with a big crash every three or four days when he would sleep all day. He was a library of the city and its history. He knew about secret passageways and hidden rooms. He knew most of the players, or at least he knew who they were. He knew who inhabited strange places behind closed doors and shuttered windows. He knew which doors to whistle past in the night.

Paul found him at a little watering hole called the Limbo back in the Quarter. It was a favorite of the local, intelligentsia, and the owners did everything they could to make it unattractive to the tourists. Just beer and bourbon, and no little umbrellas. Spencer was reading the newspaper as usual in his favorite booth at the back. No one escaped his notice. He spotted Paul as soon as he came through the door.

"Well our brave warrior returns from the fray. On a quest for beer and conversation, one presumes."

Paul shook his hand. "What's up, Spence?"

"Bartender, a libation for this fine gentleman. I think a Pabst Blue Ribbon will suffice."

The bartender rolled his eyes.

"Everything is in play, sir! I find myself overcome with opportunity."

When Spencer got excited he stepped out of character, and Paul could tell he was really keyed up. Spencer lowered his voice and reached across the table, putting his hand on Paul's sleeve to emphasize his excitement.

"I mean I've got so much shit going on, I'm starting to lose track of it all. It's scary. The other night I was hanging out on my couch listening to Santana, and I started to see how all the pieces fit together. You know, how the politicians and the lawyers and the upper crust interact with the dealers and the street. The whole thing is like a living, breathing organism with everything more or less in balance. And that's what it is, man. It took me so long to figure this out."

He stopped while the waitress delivered a beer to the table, setting it down on a cardboard coaster.

"Ya'll want something to eat?"

"No, thank you, dear lady. My confederate and I will simply imbibe this evening."

She smiled at Spencer and posed for a minute for him to appreciate her assets. He winked at her and she wiggled back to the bar.

"It isn't about eliminating crime and corruption. It's about maintaining a balance and making sure you get yours. If you push too hard in one place, it starts to fall apart in another. The real crooks in this city will never be arrested. If they ever did rid this city of corruption, it would turn into Cleveland in a swamp."

"So you're not on a crusade to expose the scandalous graft and corruption in The Big Easy?"

"Hell, no. I love this stuff. This is the best spectator sport in the world. We must fight the good fight against these long odds to rid the city of the work of the devil! Are you kidding me? I write for the society pages. Sometimes I know ahead of time that something is going to go down without anyone even telling me. Besides, why would I screw around like that with my livelihood?"

Paul looked at him and laughed. "I think you need to go pass out somewhere for a while and shut your brain off."

"Yeah, I'm out of here after this one," Spencer said. "What about you, man?"

"Same shit, different day. It's about balance for me, too. Do what you need to do to stay out of trouble, but try not to let it interfere with your life."

"Sounds like all measure of a good time. I don't know how you abide it."

"Well mostly during the week I just put my brain in my pocket and sleepwalk through it. You don't really need a brain to do what I am doing anyway."

"Which is what?" Spencer asked.

"For the most part, I take reports from one pile, check to see if they can be safely ignored, and then move them to another pile."

"Well, see that. You, sir, are qualified to be mayor of our fair parish. I suggest you begin a campaign immediately. I shall insure you receive the full attention and endorsement of my fine publication."

"Yeah, well I'm not nearly devious enough for that job. Sounds like you might enjoy it, though."

"Heavens, no. Much too high profile. That much attention would surely atrophy my entrepreneurial spirit." Spencer stood and poured the remainder of his beer down his throat. "Well, I've got to pick up the countess and if I'm late she will no doubt punish me in some new and hideously creative way. By the way, do you need anything?"

"No thanks, Spence, I don't want to be carrying anything around with me tonight."

"As always, the soul of discretion. Well then, I will take my leave of you, good sir. And may you be of good cheer and grace."

"Hey, Spence, did you ever hear of a girl in the Quarter they call Lucky?"

"Is she one of our fine ladies of the evening?"

"I'm pretty sure."

"She has the name for it. Anyway, I don't know her, but I can ask around for you. Give me a call later and I'll see what I can find out."

"Later? I thought you were crashing."

"Yeah, but I'll be up by midnight. I've got things to do."

Paul sat for a while and finished his beer. It was futile to try to search the streets for her. He decided to check out The Seven Seas. On the outside it looked like just another bar. It was tucked away between some nondescript buildings around the corner from the Preservation Hall where the old Dixieland musicians played for the tourists. What was going on inside was more barely controlled chaos than he had ever experienced. It was like a perpetual Halloween party, except that the masks were not so obvious.

The French Quarter in 1969 was a witch's kettle where all of the experimental ideologies, life styles and obsessions of the decade were churning and grinding against each other, slowly brewing into some as yet unknown reality. There was not a lot of overt conflict. It was as if everyone had gathered at a landing on the stairway between the past and the future, catching their breath, waiting to see what was going to happen next, and desperately hoping they would find a place in it. The peaceful demonstrations of the anti-war and civil-rights movements had dissolved into anarchy, and the government had taken a hard turn to the right. The student protests in the United States, in Paris and in Prague had been beaten back by the truncheon or by the tank, and the heady feeling that young people were going to change the world overnight had evaporated into a kind of deep-seated anxiety for the future. A few slogged out of the mud at Woodstock and headed for the commune. Most dropped back in, disillusioned, resentful, and alienated from the society that had nurtured them.

The Seven Seas was the epicenter of this strange little universe. It was such a freak show, that they had installed bleachers along the wall in front of the bar just so people could gawk at it. The bar was usually three deep with hippies, bikers, gays, suits, society types, college kids, cult members, self professed wizards and actual witches. There was also no small number of dark souls lurking in the corners, staring at the crowd through hollow eyes. For Paul it was like finding an oasis in the desert. He spent some time on the bleachers just watching, trying to sort everyone out. He located Louis but he did not introduce himself right away. Most of it he understood well. It was just young people hiding their insecurity and self doubt behind some persona they dressed up in on a Saturday night like a well-worn pair of jeans. In the groups of males you could pick out the alphas and the betas from the mere hangers on. The women were not as easy to decipher. There were the usual groupie types, competing for the attention of the most desirable males of their particular cult. There were the beautiful ones out to crush as many egos as possible before midnight. But then there were the opaque ones, usually in small groups, talking intently, laughing occasionally and basically ignoring everything else going on around them. He could never figure if they were just not interested in meeting guys or if they were waiting for a guy with enough balls to break into their little coven and steal them away. Or maybe they were interested in girls.

It was the dark ones he paid attention to. It was a self-defense mechanism he had learned over the years. Fights often broke out in places like this but it was normally just between a few drunks and didn't go very far before the bouncers took out the trash. This was not a GI hangout where the whole place could erupt in casual head breaking for lack of anything else to do. In a place like this, if anything dangerous was going to happen, it would be around the players. There were dealers and pimps looking for customers. You could spot them if you looked hard enough. And then, like out on the street, were the ones looking for victims. They hung around the edges and sometimes followed drunks out the door. After a while he had identified the people he wanted to keep track of and plotted what he thought was the best course up to the bar where Louis was serving. It took a while to get his attention. It was pretty loud and he wasn't sure he would be able to have a conversation.

"What'll ya have?"

"Lucky told me to look you up."

"Who?"

"Lucky."

"Oh, yeah, how's she doin'?"

"I was goin' to ask you. Have you seen her lately?" Paul asked.

"No, man, I haven't seen her in a few weeks."

"Do you know where she hangs out?"

Louis took a long look at him before he answered. "So who's asking?"

"My name is Paul. Paul Greene."

"Okay, I'll tell her you were asking about her next time I see her. I don't know where she is."

"Ok, just give me a Jax."

Louis pulled one out of the cooler and took two bills off the bar. When he came back he tossed a quarter on the bar and motioned to Paul to lean closer.

"Listen, I don't know who you are, man. You understand? When I see Lucky I'll ask her about you. If you check out, I'll see what I can do for you. Lucky doesn't like letting people know how to find her."

"Sure, I understand."

"In the meantime there's a courtyard in the back of this place, through that door next to the restrooms. It's a better crowd back there, you know what I mean? Not so nuts."

Paul pushed his way back through the crowd and found the door. It looked like a closet. He opened it and immediately felt like he was walking onto a different planet. There was something like a cocktail party going on. The crowd looked upscale and relaxed, not to mention better dressed. Several people turned and looked at him but didn't take much notice. It was a warm Spring evening but there were no stars and it smelled like rain. In one corner an old black musician was wailing on a clarinet. He guessed these were people who lived in the Quarter. As he scanned the crowd, he noticed one group of well-dressed people sitting at a table by the outdoor bar. There was an animated discussion going on between two of the suits. They didn't look angry exactly but it looked like it might turn that way. The women sitting with them were beautiful and they didn't look happy about what was going on.

As Paul studied them he began to get an uncomfortable feeling, like a tingling on the back of his neck. He turned and found that he had gotten someone's attention. The man was tall and slim and dressed entirely in black. His long dark hair was gathered in a ponytail and he had a sharp-featured, weathered face. He was leaning against the courtyard wall in the shadows opposite the table Paul had been watching. Their eyes locked and something subliminal passed between them. Not exactly hostile. He wanted Paul to know he had been noticed. Paul went back to watching the argument. Out of the corner of his eye he saw the guy moving in his direction. He didn't react. The guy stopped in front of him, but he didn't challenge Paul nor did he look him in the eye. He stood with his back to Paul, blocking his view of the table. Paul smiled and nodded his head slightly; he had just been given a message. Whatever was going on at that table was none of his business. There was nothing to be gained by pushing it. He turned around and went back through the bar and onto the street. It had been enough for one night, but he would be back. Here at last was a door he could open.

It was ten o'clock when he got back to Bourbon Street and the crowd had changed noticeably. There were fewer family types and no kids. It was noisier and everyone was a lot drunker. Groups of people were singing and swilling beer. Women, some to their delight and some not, were being groped. Everyone was being jostled but there were few complaints. He came to a corner and found a group of guys who had two girls more or less pinned up against the side of a building. The girls had reached the point where it wasn't fun any more and there was some shouting going on. Paul stopped. One of the girls was Lucky, only she wasn't wearing a plain white dress. She was dressed in a red, sequined evening gown and red high heels. She looked beautiful, not like she belonged on the streets. It was something that came from inside of her. One of the guys was trying to put his hand up her dress. Paul walked into the middle of the group, grabbed her by the arm and walked away with her. Her friend also took the opportunity to escape and caught up to them, taking his other arm. The group followed them for a while cursing and trying to start something, but Paul just ignored them and walked on. Lucky was looking up at him, trying to judge his mood. The other girl looked back and waved at their pursuers. One of them threw a bottle, but it flew wide and broke against the curb.

"This is him, Ginger," Lucky said, finally.

"Who?" Ginger smiled at Paul.

"My hero. Remember, I told you? His name is Paul."

"Oh, yeah, well I guess you're my hero, too, ain't you, Paul? How did you know those pecker-heads weren't goin' to jump you?"

"I could see they were afraid of Lucky."

Lucky stopped. "Hey, Ginger, I think me and Paul here need to have a conversation. Would you mind?"

"Not at all, honey. See you later. Good-bye, Paul. Thanks for the rescue."

Lucky took his arm again and they walked along in silence for a while. "Cat got your tongue?" she said finally.

Paul smiled at her. "I guess I don't know where to start."

"There's a place I know near here. Let's go have a drink."

"Sure, lead on."

- 3 -

It was a warm evening with just a slight breeze out of the northwest but Ernesto shivered as the boat pulled away from the dock.

"A journey like this one should begin under the bright sun, with a woman waving to you from the shore," he said, to no one in particular.

Miguel laughed. "Si, Ernesto, and also a band should be playing."

They were both young, but Miguel already had the weathered skin and rough hands of a fisherman. Ernesto still looked like a boy, even though he had reached his twenty-fifth year. He was not a large man, but he was athletic and intelligent. He had the wavy dark hair and light skin from his Spanish blood. His mother and father had held positions of importance in the Batista government, before the revolution. For most of his life, he too had paid the price for their loyalty. This would be the most dangerous part of the passage, he knew. Most of the gunboats would be out in the Florida Straits, looking for escaping refugees, but they patrolled the Windward Passage also. If you were boarded and could not account for yourself, it was said they would burn your boat under you, and shoot you if you jumped into the water.

The captain headed south a little, hoping to find a freighter or perhaps a cruise ship so that he could cut into its wake and avoid becoming interesting to the coastal radar. He soon turned east southeast and ran at full throttle into the darkness. Luck was with them and they reached mid-channel with no pursuit. The captain switched on the running lights in case there were other crazy men running dark on this night. He would douse them again when he came within sight of the coast. The wind, smelling of salt and the things of the sea, pushed against Ernesto's face as he looked up at the stars. He had been in a boat before, but never at night and never out of sight of the island. The vastness of it made him uneasy. He felt as if he were on a lonely streaking comet, moving through the black void of space.

Ernesto had been so sure this was the path he wanted. Now, lying on the deck of the darkened boat next to the spare drums of diesel fuel, with the damp salt air seeping into his clothes, he wondered how he could have been so stupid. He thought about his home in the mountains. The little blue house with the veranda full of flowers and the bee hummingbirds probing them for their sweet nectar. Especially he thought about the sugar cane fields at Christmas with their white-flowered tops extending to the horizon, and the wind as it rippled across them until the land looked like a beautiful woman in a white gown, writhing in pleasure beneath the hot sun.

He believed Cuba to be the most beautiful place in the world, even though he had never been anywhere else. Still, he knew there was no future for him on the island. The future lay north, in that land so rich that it was beyond imagination. He was not naïve. He knew it would be difficult to find his way in a strange country. Still, just stepping onto that soil gave him a chance. They would not turn away a Cuban who made it to shore and claimed asylum. There would be friends there. Friends of those who sent him on this journey to begin with, and then many others who had already found freedom. That, plus the money he would be given for successfully completing his mission would be enough for a start. What else could any man ask for? His mother had cried bitterly when he left. She knew in her heart that, at her age, she would likely never see him again. He remained strong for her as he waved to her through the back window of the battered old Hudson that would take him to the Punta del Maisi on the eastern shoulder of his island. But alone in the back of the car, he too had cried quietly as he summoned all of his will to keep from screaming for the driver to stop so he could leap out and run home.

The drone of the engines and the rhythmic rocking of the boat soon put him into a fitful sleep. He was wakened by Miguel who pointed over the bow to a string of lights on the horizon. Ernesto lit a match, cupping his hand around it in order to see his watch. He had been asleep for nearly two hours.

"No lights." The captain hissed and then pointed off the starboard bow. "Mole St. Nicolas. Haiti." When they were a few hundred yards out, the captain lit three lamps on the mast. Green, green, red. He cut the motor and waited. After a few minutes they saw a white light flash three times, a pause and then steady. The captain gunned the engines and made for the signal. They pulled into a dock that looked like it had been destroyed in a storm. Ernesto looked at the ladder doubtfully but Miguel pushed him up and wished him good luck. Two men waited for him on the dock. They did not speak. He followed them out to a dirt road where an open jeep was waiting.

Ernesto climbed into the back seat and the jeep headed out into the night. As they drove, the man in the passenger seat turned and handed Ernesto an envelope. Inside was a forged Nicaraguan passport in the name of Juan Diaz, along with a plane ticket for Puerto Cabezas departing Santo Domingo at seven the next morning. It was too dark to get a good look at his picture. He hoped they had been given the right one. They crossed the boarder into the Dominican Republic at an unattended border post and sped off through the jungle. Ernesto tried to sleep but the road was filled with ruts and potholes and he was being thrown around like a rag doll. Occasionally they drove through small villages, noticed only by the dogs and the land crabs standing belligerently in the headlights, oblivious to the spinning tires.

They were still driving when the sun rose, and Ernesto asked them to pull over so that he could urinate. The two men decided to join him and they stood there side by side pissing into the jungle, listening to the insects, and not uttering a word. He felt uneasy to be in a foreign country with men who hardly spoke to him and at the edge of a wild jungle filled with things he did not wish to see. He was exhausted when they dropped him at the airport and drove away without even a good luck. To his relief, the customs and immigration officers hardly looked at the passport. If he had not been so exhausted by the journey, his nervousness might have betrayed him. He had never flown before and he stared out of the window of the departure lounge feeling larger than he had ever been. *I have finally become someone*, he thought. He intended to enjoy every second of the flight, but as soon as the well-traveled 707 climbed above the clouds, he fell asleep.

In Puerto Cabezas, he fought for a taxi and told the driver to take him to the bus station. He purchased a ticket to Vera Cruz. Ernesto did not expect any trouble from this point and for the first time he began to relax and feel a little pleased with himself for undertaking such a risky mission. He looked out the window of the bus at a foreign land, which nonetheless looked a lot like home. The bus stopped occasionally to pick up some dust-covered people, sometimes with a pig or a chicken in a cage. At the Honduran border the bus was boarded by two immigration officers. He had been told to look bored, to make only brief eye contact, then to hold out his hand for them to return his passport to him. Not to speak unless asked a question. To remember the address he had been given and the names of the people he had been told about. He would not have a problem if he remembered all of this.

* * *

He was fifteen years old when the revolution came and it was exciting to see the rebel soldiers firing their guns into the air and all of the people dancing in the streets. It all changed when the men came one day and took his father and his uncle. Castro had organized his Committees for the Defense of the Revolution all over the island. Their job was to spy on their neighborhoods and report "unsympathetic acts". Often an unsympathetic act was having a better car than they did.

They called his father a 'gusanos' - a worm. He did not even know what they were accused of. His father was dead now. He died in a cage like an animal and Ernesto didn't know why. As the son of a political prisoner, he could not be admitted to the university, but his mother knew how to speak English and she insisted he learn to speak and to read it well. He also learned how to fix cars, and he was good at it. Still, there was not much work and less money. He didn't know what his future would be. He only knew that he hated what life had become on his beautiful island and he hated Castro because of it. He told them he would do anything to help overthrow the communists and now he was looking out the window at Honduras on a mission that would take him to the United States, for a reason he did not know.

The trip up through Mexico was just a blur to him. The scenery changed little except when they were in the mountains. He felt like he had eaten a bucket full of dust. He waited for almost a week at the safe house in Matamoros, staying alone in his room above a smelly, garbage-strewn back alley and watching cowboy movies on the old black and white television. His food was delivered twice a day by a toothless old woman who looked at him each time as if he were stealing it from her. He was happy when they told him it was time.

* * *

There was a just a fingernail of the new moon, but to the men drifting toward South Padre Island it seemed as bright as the sun. Ernesto swore it felt hot on his back. They were running dark. Anyone listening to the throaty rumble of the twin V8 engines, even at idle, might have guessed this was no ordinary fishing boat, in spite of its appearance. The men crouched along the gunwales as if it would make the boat less visible. They were taking a chance coming ashore in the more heavily settled part of the island, but it was a calculated risk. There were drug patrols along the more desolate stretches and a boat coming close in to shore was hard to miss. Ernesto had wanted them to go two days earlier at the new moon, but the captain said he needed at least a little light to show him the surf line. He would not risk running aground, and he reminded Ernesto that he could risk it least of all. Anyway, it had worked before. More than once.

He traveled light. Two changes of clothes, toiletries, some tour books, an ancient camera, and sewn into the padded strap of his backpack, an envelope wrapped in plastic and containing something important. What it was he did not know, and did not want to know. They told him it was better that way. On the trip out of Cuba, the backpack had also contained a large rock. If they were stopped he was to drop the backpack overboard, as quickly and as quietly as possible. He had forgotten about it and was half way to Vera Cruse before he realized why it made such an uncomfortable pillow. He dropped the rock out the window of the bus, much to the amusement of his fellow passengers.

Now, entering the US, the danger was not as great. He would be just another wet-back trying to reach the promised land. He had to complete his mission in order to be given the documents that would prove he was a Cuban citizen and eligible for political asylum. If they caught him, he would be sent back to Mexico and they would try again in a couple of weeks.

The bow broke low as the captain throttled back and the sea flooded the deck through the forward scuppers. The water was relatively calm but he could hear the breakers close in. The wind blew on shore and he felt the salt on his skin. Ernesto already had his shoes stowed in the backpack and his trousers rolled up as far as he could manage. Up on the beach road, about one hundred meters north of their insertion point, a Tex-Mex roadhouse was lit up like carnival. The music reached them when the wind paused, but the wet gulf air smeared the colored lights. The captain hauled the boat hard over to port and the engines growled as he added power to push against the surf. Paolo put his hand on his shoulder.

"Que le vaya bien, amigo!"

Ernesto went over the side and dropped into the surf, holding his backpack high over his head. He cursed as the cold water drenched him to his chest and he struggled against the shifting sand under his feet up onto the dark beach. Behind him the boat roared to life and the wake almost pushed him over. Once he reached the beach, he crouched at the water line until the boat was well off shore. Finally he stood and slung the backpack over one shoulder. He was now just another faceless turista enjoying a late night stroll on the beach. He walked south until he was behind a gas station and then turned toward the highway. The restroom door was open and there was no bulb in the fixture above the sink. The floor felt slimy and he hoped he had not cut his feet. He quickly changed into some dry clothes and washed each foot in the sink before putting on his shoes. He threw his wet clothing into the trash can. The attendant didn't bother to look up as he came around the front of the building and headed north toward the roadhouse.

He walked through the parking lot keeping his eyes forward and ignoring the couples going at it behind misted rear windows and in open convertibles, oblivious to everyone around them. At the door the bouncers searched his backpack and patted him down. Once inside, the noise and smoke curled around him and joined him to the crowd. He picked a spot along the back wall and ordered a beer from the waitress, being careful not to make eye contact. He nursed the beer as his gaze moved across the crowd, looking for anyone showing more that a passing interest. It was unlikely, he knew, but his training, brief though it was, had taken control. He was having a hard time trying not to smile. He had made it to the United States and his fear had not betrayed him. His confidence was high and some of the girls smiled at him.

When he had finished the beer he went up to the bar and indicated to the bartender for a new bottle. When the bartender returned, Ernesto leaned over to him.

"Has Jesus Guzman been here tonight?"

"Who wants to know?"

"I'm his cousin, Juan."

The bartender shrugged his shoulders. "Everyone is Juan. I don't know any Jesus Guzman."

"Well, if somebody asks for Juan, I'll be over in the corner. Juan Diaz."

The bartender shrugged his shoulders again, as if he couldn't care less, and Ernesto guessed that was the case. He went back to his waiting place and after an hour he was starting to worry. They had given him no information past this point. He didn't even know where he was going, much less how to get there. He was wondering where he could spend the night when a man wearing a white cowboy shirt, boots and a string tie moved in next to him. The man did not look at him but appeared to be surveying the crowd. Ernesto saw right away that he was Cuban.

"There are many beautiful women here tonight," the man said, finally.

It was the signal.

"Yes, but they only want a man with a fat wallet."

The man turned his back to the crowd, still not looking at Ernesto. He spoke quietly.

"I am going to walk over to the bar. I will wait ten minutes and then I will leave. Wait ten minutes after I leave and then meet me in the parking lot. I am parked under the large sign by the highway. It is a black '58 Chevy. Do you know what this car looks like? Nod your head if you do."

Ernesto nodded and the man walked away.

It was the nicest car he had ever sat in and it was a convertible. The engine purred like a jungle cat as they pulled out onto the highway. Again there were two men in the front. They were friendlier than the two in Haiti and they made him feel relaxed. The driver's name was Ramón and the passenger was Hector. They asked him about his journey and he felt proud telling them the story. He told it as if it were something routine, but being careful not to seem to brag. Finally he asked them where they were heading.

"It is a long ride, Ernesto. We are going to New Orleans in Louisiana. You can lie down and sleep if you feel tired. We will wake you in time for breakfast."

At first Ernesto was too excited to sleep. Ramón and Hector treated him like a brother and he asked them so many questions they had to tell him to slow down. He decided he would like his new life in the US. For the first time he was sure he had done the right thing. They laughed when he asked them if they would be passing Miami on the way. He did finally sleep and he dreamed again of his home in the mountains. When they shook him awake, the car had stopped at a place called the Waffle House.

"Where are we? Is this Louisiana?"

"No, Ernesto, this is Houston Texas."

He looked around the parking lot, almost expecting to see cowboys riding up on horses. Instead, he saw the largest highway he could have ever imagined and buildings that looked like mountains. As they left the restaurant, Ernesto turned to Ramón.

"Ramón, I have never been in a convertible before. Can we put the top down?"

Ramón looked at Hector and they both laughed.

"Sure, Ernesto. Maybe for a little while. Perhaps we will not look so conspicuous that way."

- 4 -

It was just another off-Bourbon taproom except that the clientele was more racially mixed than at Spencer's hangout. Lucky ordered a martini but Paul just asked for coffee. The only light came from an assortment of neon beer signs placed strategically around the room and the back-lit liquor rack behind the bar. Etta James was singing "I'd Rather Go Blind" from a jukebox in the corner. A black couple stood clutching each other on the small dance floor, but it was hard to tell if they were dancing or just trying to keep each other from falling over.

Paul stared into his coffee. Lucky studied him from across the table, her long fingernails tapping restlessly against the side of her glass.

"So, you gonna lecture me about bein' a bad girl?"

There was a challenge in her voice, but he didn't want to make her defend herself. "Why would I do that?"

"Well, I hear you heroes have your high moral standards."

"You can stop calling me that."

"Ok, Paul. So tell me, did you know or were you shocked when you saw me tonight?"

"I guessed, but not right away."

"So would you have jumped in to save me back there on the bus if you had known about me."

"It wouldn't have made any difference."

He had answered right away, but it took him a few seconds to decide if he really meant it. He decided he did. Lucky seemed like a completely different person now. It wasn't just the clothes. It was more that now that he knew about her life, she didn't have to be coy with him any more. She was looking him squarely in the eye. It took some getting used to.

"I guessed that about you. That's not very smart, you know. Sweet, but not very smart."

"Why? Don't you think you are worth saving?"

"Sure," Lucky said. "But most men wouldn't think so. And most of the girls would have thanked you by tryin' to take your wallet."

"I guess I don't make the distinction."

"Well, most guys figure we deserve it. That we're askin' for it."

"I never thought about it really. I never knew..."

"You never knew a whore before?"

Paul just looked at her, once again at a loss for words. Sometimes when he looked at her, he saw her as just a young, beautiful girl, dressing up to look sophisticated. But when she came back at him like that, she was a totally different person. He kept trying to sort out which of the images he was talking to.

"If it makes you feel any better, I'm not one of those street corner hookers out there on Bourbon street. I'm what they refer to as a call girl."

"What's the difference?"

"Not much really, except we usually get classier clientele."

"Do you have a pimp?"

"I used to, until I wised up. I work for a service now. It's run by what you would call a madam."

"Don't you worry about it? I mean, how do you know what kind of guy you are with?"

"It's the luck of the draw, honey. It's why I keep my bible."

"Have you ever had to use it?"

"A few times. I try not to cut a john so bad he's goin' to run to the cops. It's bad for business. Usually all you need to do is shove it between their legs and they get real peaceful."

Paul took a drink of his coffee and looked over at some people talking at the bar. He was pretty sure he knew where the conversation was going.

"So are you going to ask me how I got myself into such a nasty business?" Lucky asked.

"No."

"Why not?"

"I guess if you had another choice, you would have taken it."

"How do you know I don't just like it? How do you know I don't just want it all the time and I don't care who I do it with?"

"Is that the way it is?"

"Do you think it is?" she countered.

"No, I don't believe that."

"Why?" she asked.

"Because you're sitting here talking with me like this."

She was quiet for what seemed like a long time. He was trying to think of something to say when she stood up and slid over beside him. She kissed him on the cheek and slid her arm around his. She didn't say anything. She just held on to him with her head against his shoulder. He felt her warm body against him and smelled her perfume. He wanted to make love with her, but he wasn't sure how to ask. Actually it was more that he didn't know who to ask. The prostitute in the hot, red dress, or the pretty, young woman he had shared dinner with and tried to get to know. He wondered if he should offer her money. The whole thing seemed absurd. She started talking and he was so absorbed in his dilemma that it took him a second to catch up.

"Last week, there was a story in the paper about this guy who had just got some kind of big degree from Tulane," she said finally. "He was thirty-two years old and had been in school just about all of his life. On his way home from the graduation, a car crossed over and hit him head on. Killed him dead. The other guy was just some drunk asshole from Storyville. He got out of it with just a few cuts and a broken arm. He said in the paper that it was okay 'cause he could drink with either hand."

"So why are you telling me that?"

"I live for today, Paul. I live for right now. I've seen things. Too many things. This is a one-way trip, you know. Nobody gets out alive."

"Just tell me this. If you had some other way to make a good income, and make a life for yourself, would you do it?"

She looked at him for a while, as if trying to decide how much the answer would mean to him. "I don't waste my time dreamin' about things that ain't gonna happen, baby. I told you, I just live. One day at a time."

He realized he didn't really care what the answer was. He had seen enough of life not to judge people, and he wasn't going to judge her. The whole time they had been talking, he was thinking about what part, if any, he wanted this woman to play in his life. He already knew he didn't want her as a lover. The thought of her being with other men, and especially the chance of her being hurt, would not be something he could live with. Still there was some part of him that wanted her to be in his life. She had reached something inside of him and he wasn't sure how, or what it meant. He only knew it was important and not something he should ignore.

"Tell me about what it was like growing up" he said.

"What do you want to know that for?"

"I don't know. I guess I'm just trying to get to know you."

"Ok, if you want. I grew up back in the Bayou. They tell me my daddy was a good man but I never got to find out. He made his living crawfishin'. My granddaddy was white. Anyway, my daddy got shot one night playin' cards or something. I was just a baby at the time. I had two brothers, too, and they're both dead. Reggie got killed by a Cottonmouth when he was seven. Willie was born real sick and he never was right. He died at the hospital when he was twelve. Something to do with his kidneys. I have a sister. I think she's still alive, only I don't know 'cause they split us up after my momma died. She killed herself. Not on purpose. She started puttin' that stuff in her veins with a needle. I was ten years old. I went to live with my aunt Stella and my Uncle Luke. They were real nice people but they were poor as dirt and I had these big dreams, ya know? When I got to be fifteen, I ran away with this boy from the city. He told me he had all of this money and he was gonna buy us a restaurant and we would be livin' the high life. Turned out he didn't have a dime. After he was done with me, he just ran off. I was on my own. I started turnin' tricks to make enough money to eat. After while I met this pimp and he gave me a place to stay. I worked for him for a couple of years...Do I need to go on? You get the picture, right?"

"I'm sorry."

"You mean you're sorry for me or you're sorry you asked?"

"I mean I'm sorry you had it so tough."

"Why should you be sorry? You didn't have nothin' to do with it. Besides, I'm not complaining. I'm alive and I've got some money and I'm not sick. I've got it a lot better than some of those other girls out there on the street."

"So what now?" he said finally.

She squeezed up against him and whispered in his ear. "You gonna sit here and talk all night baby, or you gonna fuck me?"

He threw some money on the table and they walked out onto the street. The rain was coming down harder now, but he didn't care. He didn't keep track of the streets, only that there were fewer streetlights and it was quiet except for an occasional disembodied laugh, bouncing down the street like an empty beer can. She was telling him a story about her friend Inez, who had been found in a kneeling position in the back of a congressman's limo by his eight-year-old daughter.

"He told his daughter it was just a nurse giving him an examination. Now she's afraid to go to the doctor's office."

He laughed, but he was only half listening. He felt her body against his, touching him. Every time she brushed against him, it sent shivers of anticipation through his body. He felt the heat of her and the smell of her hair. Every look, every laugh, the shape of her legs as she climbed a curb. It was turning him on just walking with her.

They stopped in front of an old hotel. There was a skinny white guy in a garish plaid sport coat and a pork-pie hat, leaning against the steps. He looked at Lucky with raised eyebrows and she nodded, letting him know it was okay. Before Paul could ask her about the place, she grabbed his arm and pulled him up the staircase. They passed the second floor landing and continued up to the third floor. There was a long, dark corridor lit only by the spill of an outside light on the fire escape at the end. She towed him down a few doors. The wallpaper was old and peeling and the air reeked with the odor of stale tobacco. A tattered old rug ran down the length of the hallway. In places there was nothing left of it except a few threads, and a pattern imprinted on the wood floor underneath. She took what looked to be an old-fashioned skeleton key out of her purse and opened the door.

The room looked lived in. The bed was made and he noticed her bible on the table under the lamp. He sat down on the bed and tested the springs.

"Is this where you bring them?"

"No, honey, this is just were I stay. They don't ever come here." She sat down on the bed next to him and then leaned back with one arm propped up under her head. He looked at her body and she stretched for him. "See anything you like?"

He smiled and ran his hand down the length of her side. She rolled over onto her stomach.

"Unzip me, will you, honey?"

He pulled the zipper down slowly and then placed his fingers against the small of her back, touching her lightly and feeling the silkiness of her skin. She slid out of her dress like a serpent shedding her skin, and then knelt behind him and started to open his shirt. As each button slowly came free, she moved against him, telling him with her body what she was going to do with him. He ran his hand along her thigh and she bit him on the ear, and then whispered something that was more heat and breath than sound. She wasn't wearing a bra, and there was nothing under her short red slip. He pulled her firmly against him and buried his face in her full, firm breasts.

"You like that, baby? Is that what you've been dreamin' about?"

He had no more words. The pleasure seeped through his skin like a vapor. It worked its way into his being, dissolving the tension that barred the doors to his dark places. He fell into a void, where nothing remained but her body and the sound of her breathing. He surrendered himself to her completely and she took him to places he had never been and never wanted to leave. Her breath on his neck felt like fire. They danced to the sound of the rain beating against the window and the thunder that seemed to come from deep inside of him. At last he felt her will begin to dissolve, as her body melted against him, and her breath cried out to him in short desperate gasps. He took control of her then, making her feel the power of his body. Holding her on the edge of pleasure and pain until she cried out and dug her nails into the flesh of his back. Their souls touched, and they erupted together like an exploding star. Outside the storm raged, as his body drifted slowly back to the earth like so much dust. They lay together unable to talk, hardly able to breathe. Gradually he became aware of her lying next to him and he cradled her in his arms, tenderly until he could feel her warm tears against his chest. He reached out and pulled her to him, kissing her face, and cradling her like a baby in his arms. In a while she spoke, her face still buried against his chest, in breathless words, almost a whisper.

"I never felt like that before. I didn't know it could be that way. Why did you come to me?"

He answered by holding her a little tighter and burying his face in her hair. He could have held her forever, but it wasn't to be. In the next second the whole world seemed to crash in around him. At first he though the building had been hit by lighting. The walls shook, and then the door exploded off its hinges. An enormous black man, still wearing half of the door frame, crashed into the room. He was enraged and cursing at the top of his lungs. He kicked the debris aside, took two steps and grabbed Lucky by the hair, flinging her into the corner as easily as if she were a pillow. He glared down at Paul.

"Get your ass out of here, honky, before I kill you."

He turned back to Lucky and grabbed her again, pulling her to her feet. She screamed He must have assumed Paul would run, like any john in his right mind would have. He was wrong. Paul grabbed the lamp next to the bed. It had a brass base and a long solid neck. He ripped it from the wall, plunging the room into darkness. The hot bulb seared his arm and shattered against his skin as he slammed the lamp down on what he thought was the guy's head. The guy cursed and staggered. Paul couldn't see him, until the lightning flashed. He wheeled and came at Paul. There was a knife in his hand and he knew how to use it. The blade sliced down and diagonally across Paul's body. Paul managed to jump back but he tripped on something and staggered into the wall. The guy reached out with his hand, blindly trying to find Paul's throat. Paul dodged sideways but he wasn't quite quick enough. The lightning flashed again and this time the blade found flesh, imbedding itself in Paul's shoulder. A searing hot pain ripped through him and his arm went dead. At the same instant he saw Lucky come up from behind. Her hand brushed across the guy's forehead like she was wiping his brow. A cascade of blood erupted from a gash that opened across his face from temple to temple. The blood ran down his face like a waterfall, blinding him. He screamed and staggered, letting go of the knife. He was rubbing his hands across his eyes, trying to clear the blood out of them.

"Run, baby. He's gonna kill us."

The guy staggered, cursing and flinging himself around the room like a bear. Paul saw Lucky leap through the doorway wearing nothing but her slip. The maniac swung wildly, still not able to see. He was between Paul and the door. Paul grabbed a wooden chair with his good arm, and slammed it against the guy's head, knocking him sideways, then ran for the door, somehow having the presence of mind to grab his jeans on the way out. He ran down the stairs naked, stopping at the bottom just long enough to put his pants on. He couldn't use his left arm. He looked at the wound and found the knife still protruding out of it. He almost laughed at the absurdity of it. He pulled it out, letting it fall to the floor. It felt like it was tearing his stomach out with it. The blood started to pour out of the wound in impressive amounts. His arm was blood-covered and dripping in an instant. He ran out into the rain, not stopping to look behind him. There was no sign of Lucky or the guy who had been guarding the door. The rain was coming down so hard it hurt and he could barely see. He ran across streets and up alleys, feeling like the guy was right on his heels. He dodged cars, the drivers honking at him angrily. Some people were scurrying to get out of the rain. A woman screamed. Finally he started to feel the energy draining out of his body and he staggered until he could no longer walk.

The world was starting to fade. He didn't know where he was, but it didn't matter, he wasn't going any farther. He slumped down onto the curb, shivering, his arms clutched across his chest. Everything started to close in around him. Just before it went dark, he became aware of a black shape moving in front of him. It was a limousine. A door opened and in the spill of the dim interior light, a slender, disembodied woman's arm reached out to him. The last thing he remembered was taking hold of a jeweled hand and wondering if this was what it was like to die. And then everything went black.

- 5 -

It was the kind of room that inspired whispering, like the nave of a great cathedral. The polished oak walls extended up two floors, interrupted by a balcony that encircled the room on three sides. The fireplace looked like the entrance to a tomb, and even though the fire roaring enthusiastically inside it was large by any measure, little of the heat and light escaped the charred gray stone. Tapestries depicting medieval scenes adorned the walls, and above the huge slab of granite that formed the mantle, hung an ancient wooden relief depicting a wheel, a cauldron and a sword. A thick, red Persian rug covered all but the edges of the hardwood floor.

An enormous, leaded-glass window dominated the south side of the room. The late- afternoon sun cast a dappled shaft of light obliquely onto the floor. It marked time like a crimson sundial, ending just short of the large round table that occupied the center of the room. The table was covered with an elegant cloth of blue and gold, and set with crystal goblets and decanters in shades from honey to dark brown. Although it could have accommodated twice their number, seven men of various ages, but none younger than forty, sat at the table. They represented a variety of ethnic backgrounds. The eighth, a tall man who appeared to be in his middle fifties, stood and addressed the group. His manner was relaxed and gave the impression that he was perhaps not so much the leader, but first among equals. Despite his graying hair, he had a youthful bearing and a strong voice that was able to fill the room without sounding overly loud. His name was Marc Francoeur.

"I would like to thank Mr. Chou for his assessment of the Peoples Republic of China. I believe we all share his belief that there is little to fear at this point; that any significant economic or military cooperation with the Soviet Union will develop in the next decade or beyond. To the contrary, the recent border clash at the Ussuri River was particularly vicious. It is, however, believed that the Soviet Union will continue to show restraint. They have no desire to deal with a two-million-strong Chinese army surging across the border, especially having so recently crushed the rebellion in Czechoslovakia, and further raising the hackles of NATO. China, as we have discussed, has enormous economic and military potential, but it seems likely that it will take decades before its internal political restraints will permit the dragon to be unleashed. It is a problem, I believe, for the next century. The one remaining question is whether any of us believe there is the potential that China will intervene more than covertly in the current American adventure in South East Asia. For that analysis I will invite Mr. Thomas to share his thoughts."

The man who stood now was tall, but slightly bent at the shoulders, like someone practiced at looking inconspicuous. He was thin, with pale blue eyes, sparse gray hair and a face that spoke of an arduous life. He took a long pull on his cigarette and then stubbed it out before he spoke. His voice was deep and his first words were exhaled in a cloud of smoke.

"Thank you, Marc. I am just back, as you know, from a visit with our friends in Virginia. Although there is still of cadre of true believers that think the war can be at least fought to a standstill, albeit with a fairly substantial commitment of additional troops, most concede in private that the war is lost." He looked at the faces around the table and noted their silent affirmations. "The American public has long since lost its stomach for the war, and Nixon is desperate to find a face-saving exit. We have it on good authority that the administration has been in secret contact with the North Vietnamese as the first step toward negotiating a suspension of hostilities. There is a rumor they have threatened the use of nuclear weapons, but I cannot verify this. It is a foregone conclusion that the US will begin drawing down its troop presence, perhaps as early as this summer. US bombing attacks in Laos continue and we have learned that Cambodia is now secretly being bombed as well, in a further attempt to cut off supplies to the south.

"As to the question of Chinese intervention, the American leadership has misread this aspect of the conflict badly, no doubt due to the prevailing paranoia over communist expansionism, along with a tendency to fight the current war as if it were the same as the last one. The Korean experience is very fresh in their thinking. The Vietnamese people are not the North Koreans, however. They have been fighting the Chinese for a thousand years and would no doubt fight them again if they came across the border. The Chinese, as well as the Russians, are supplying arms of course, but this is of little strategic political significance at this point, with the US already determined to withdraw. It merely allows the North to keep the pressure on until Saigon crumbles. All of this, as well as the current and projected financial impact on our enterprises related to South East Asia, is detailed in my report."

Francoeur spoke again, remaining seated this time. "What do you see as the immediate and near-term impact of the fall of the Saigon government on the remainder of the region, Peter?"

Mr. Thomas hesitated for a moment, taking time to gather his thoughts. "There are few certainties, although it is likely that the communist elements in Laos and Cambodia will succeed in throwing over the current regimes. In Cambodia, Shianouk is weak and there is intelligence that the CIA is funding his ex-PM, name of Lon Nol. Everyone expects a coup, sooner than later. It is generally agreed, however, that it is only a matter of time before the Khmer Rouge take over the country. It is also commonly assumed that a blood bath will follow and that the region will be in turmoil for at least the next decade. Once the Americans pull out of Vietnam, they will turn away from the region and allow it to go through its death throes alone. The CIA will continue to throw money at the region but likely to no avail. Laos has pretty much been bombed into non-existence already, especially in the north at the Plain of Jars. It is estimated that fully one quarter of the population are already refugees.

"India, although the government is currently left-leaning, has a firmly developed social system that makes a serious communist uprising unlikely. They seem to be getting cozy with the Soviets, but it will be a self-limiting exercise. From a strategic point of view, the economic impact, at least as it pertains to our interests, appears to be very limited."

"Thank you, Peter. Unless there are any further questions or comments regarding our Asian interests, I now would like to turn our attentions toward this hemisphere and, in particular, to the influence of Cuba on the current regimes in Central and South America. Mr. Santiago, would you provide us with a synopsis of your findings?"

The man who stood was somewhat short and fastidiously dressed, with oiled hair that had turned gray at the temples, a thin moustache, and a red silk handkerchief in the breast pocket of his Armani suit. He spoke English with a slight Hispanic accent but his command of the language was excellent, suggesting an education in the United States.

"Yes, thank you, Marc. Gentlemen I have listened to your presentations with great interest and, as usual, I have learned much. As always, I am deeply impressed by the depth of knowledge and understanding of this troubled world we inhabit, by those present in this room and those in our organization who support us. The report I have given you today is largely speculation I am afraid, since I believe we are just beginning to glean the forces working beneath the surface in our region.

"Let me begin by saying that all of us here, and in our family, believe in democracy, especially as it permits the exercise of free-market capitalism. Unfortunately, there is little understanding, particularly in the United States, as to the vital elements required to grow a democracy from the peasant and, may I say, even feudal social systems that currently exist in Central and South America. We all know that it is not possible to form a democratic model without the existence of an established and propertied middle class. The peasant will not fight for the land that is not his. To him, a new government means only a different hand on the whip. As economic forces sow increasing unrest among the peasants, the communist model begins to look not only appealing but inevitable. For years, they have listened to empty promises of land reform but they know it will never happen without violence. It is just a matter of time before they come over the wall.

"Indeed, we have begun to see the communist model as an interim solution, though certainly not an end in itself; we are all well aware of its tragic limitations. It may serve, in the near term, to tear down the existing institutions and, we hope, fertilize the earth in such a way as to allow the seeds of democracy to sprout at some future time. Unfortunately, the earth is too often nourished with the blood of the peasant, and I believe this will be the case again.

"As we all fervently hope and believe, the current impasse between the Soviet Union and the West has passed its critical point. Having held the blade to each other's throats and peered into the abyss together, it is believed that both sides will continue to glower at each other from a distance. It will become an economic war, which we all believe the Soviets must ultimately lose. It may well take several decades for this to occur but it will occur. In the interim, both sides will use client States to push their agenda and exert influence in the developing world. Which brings us to Cuba. Although it is widely agreed that the United States won a great victory in the missile crisis earlier this decade, what is lost on most is the agreement this country made with the USSR that they would not invade Cuba. In making this agreement, the United States has been forced to allow a permanent irritant to function more or less freely in this hemisphere. Although the military juntas in South America will be difficult to displace, the weak governments in Central America are, if you will excuse the metaphor, ripe for the picking. We are beginning to see the start of a long struggle which will have at least some consequence on the regional economy and therefore on our interests."

"Thank you for that very lucid overview of the situation, Carlos. I know you have detailed some of the anticipated economic repercussions in your report. Perhaps you would give us a brief overview of this as well, especially as pertains to the family's interests."

"Certainly. First and foremost is the risk to the Canal. Although any overt attack on the Canal is highly unlikely and would be extremely foolish, it is quite feasible that, for instance, a ship could be scuttled in one of the locks and effectively close the canal for weeks, if not months. This would, of course, have a major impact on our world-wide shipping interests, as well as the plantations and mines in the region in which we are invested. The successful coup d' e-tat by Senor Torrijos last year has not helped clarify the situation. It is still a feeling-out process.

"The most significant impact, although hard to quantify, is the overall political changes that increased US attention to the area could produce. We've known for many years how to do business profitably in this region. We know who is to be paid and how much, in order for our interests to be protected. Any significant communist insurgency, followed by an American response, even if clandestine, will change this equation in largely unpredictable ways. I am sure I do not need to remind you all that maintaining predictability is why we are here. We are a strong family. We have shown that we can flourish within all political models. It is the periods of transition from one political model to another that create the most difficulty."

"So what do you feel is our wisest course at this time, Carlos?"

"We must, I'm afraid, try to maneuver the middle road until the situation stabilizes. There is little doubt that, in the long run, some variety of the democratic model will prevail. In the short run, we may need to work with both sides to insure our interests are protected."

Marc stood and addressed the group. "Thank you, Carlos. Gentlemen, I would like to echo Mr. Santiago's sentiments regarding your contributions here today. I do not believe a finer group of political and economic analysts exists anywhere in the world. It has been a long day and I know you are all tired. I would invite you to enjoy the remainder of the afternoon. All of the facilities of my humble house are available to you. We will meet for dinner at eight. Before we adjourn, are there any questions you would like to address to me or to any of the council?"

A portly, dark-skinned man with distinctly Arabic features stood. He spoke with no discernable accent. "Yes, Marc. I would like to ask the council if they have projected the near-term consequences of the escalating violence between Egypt and Israel. As you are aware there has been a steady increase in artillery exchanges between the two sides as well as some aggressive, covert operations."

Marc spoke again. "Andrew, perhaps you would like to venture a response."

The man who spoke now, without standing, was blond, athletic and young looking. He was the only member who did not wear a tie and he spoke with an upper-class British accent.

"I'm afraid I've left my crystal ball at home on that one, old boy. I don't believe anyone at this table foresees a peaceful resolution in Suez in any of our lifetimes. The best thinking seems to be that there will be another bash-up, sometime in the next decade and probably sooner than later. With apologies to Mustafa, we believe the Israelis will again prevail. Aside from causing more misery for the Palestinians and yet another redrawing of the borders, the world economic impact will be minimal. That is, as long as the Saudis stay neatly out of it. The only thing of any value that comes out of that bloody sand pit is the oil. We do not anticipate any curtailment of production as the result of a new war. The canal would, of course, be closed for some period of time, which will result in a short term spike in price-per-barrel on the world market. The major oil companies already have work-arounds, or should I say sail-arounds, at the ready. As I have discussed previously, the real danger is not from a war, but from the increasing reliance by the West on oil from the region in toto. It is just a matter of time before someone decides to throttle the valve to see how loudly we can scream. Other that that, there is too much at stake for the US to allow the region to flash over and they can be expected to keep the Israelis from pushing it too far beyond their existing patch. If there is war, we expect it to be short and violent, with the emphasis on short. As in the past, it will resolve nothing."

Marc stood again. "Thank you again, gentlemen. Tonight after dinner we should have a chance to exchange ideas on some of the opportunities that have been suggested today and how we may best take advantage of them. If you need anything, just dial 444 from the phone in your room."

After the guests had departed. Marc went over to a small desk next to the fireplace and pushed a button on the phone. Almost immediately, a man in a black uniform entered the room.

"Charles, please take these reports to my study. Oh, and make sure the door is locked and the alarm system armed. Also would you find Mr. Taylor and ask him to join me?"

He was standing at the fireplace absently prodding at the logs with a poker when a large, muscular man entered the room, closing the door behind him. His hair was blond and close-cropped over a square and rugged-looking face. Despite his bulk, he moved with a graceful stride and seemed to balance on the balls of his feet, making for a very light step for a big man.

"Hello, Bruce. I hope you've been able to entertain yourself while you were waiting."

"I always have plenty to do, Mr. Francoeur."

Marc walked over to the table. "Let's talk a bit shall we." He pulled out a chair and pointed to it. "Would you like a drink?"

"No, thank you, sir."

"I understand you have had a further conversation with the Shepherd."

"Yes, sir, I spoke with him last night," Bruce said.

"I take it he was still in the city then."

"Yes, sir. He was leaving this morning."

"So bring me up to speed."

"Well, sir, he acted disappointed in our counter-offer, but it was just part of his act. I have watched him work before."

"So you think there will be no problem with the terms?" Marc asked.

"Not with the payment. I got the impression that they would be prepared to pay a good deal more if they could avoid getting involved in any commitments to our other requests. He as much as said so."

"Precisely. Of course the money is really not the primary object here. It merely offsets our expenses in obtaining the item and establishes an acknowledgement of its value. What is of true value to us here are the specific action items we have detailed. Was there any particular comment on any of these?"

"He just said that these were being carefully considered, but he could not predict the outcome," Bruce answered. "He will be returning to the Lodge later this week for further discussions."

"How did you leave it with him?"

"I told him that we needed an answer within the next two weeks or our window may close."

"Excellent. Although time is not yet a critical factor, we don't want them kicking this thing around until it starts to look too expensive for them."

"Yes, sir, that's what I thought."

"Did he question you on our progress at this end?" Marc asked.

"Only that he was concerned about the chain of possession. They prefer a single hand-off. I told him that would not be possible in this case, but that we would maintain control of the item at every step."

"Yes, this is my concern also, but I am confident we will have all of the pieces assembled when needed. Have you arranged for your next session?"

"Not yet," Bruce replied. "He will contact me through the usual channels when he is ready to meet."

"Excellent work as always, Bruce. Please let me know as soon as you are contacted."

"Yes, sir."

"Also, it is vital that our watchers maintain a high level of vigilance at this time. Have them report anything that might be of interest. Even if they think it is trivial."

"It's already done, sir."

"Oh, and Bruce."

"Yes, sir?"

"Make sure the Shepherd does not stray from his flock. Do you understand?"

"Loud and clear."

- 6 -

Paul woke up in a room that looked like the inside of a palace. There were no windows and he didn't know if it was night or day. At first he didn't remember what had happened, until he moved his arm and was rewarded by a sharp stab of pain. There was a bandage on his shoulder. He lifted it up and saw that someone had stitched his wound. Other than a vague headache, he felt okay. He started to get up but his head began to spin and he thought better of it. His thoughts turned to Lucky and he wondered if she had managed to get away. Exhaustion overtook him and he fell back to sleep. When he revived again he was startled to see a woman standing next to the bed. She had a tray with a cup of coffee and some kind of pastry.

"How do you feel?" she asked.

There was a subtle accent in her voice, which he couldn't place but he could tell she was from money. She was tall and slender with long, dark hair and eyes that were a deep, piercing blue. Her skin was very white, like milk, he thought. She had on a long, blue dress that covered her to her ankles. She was smiling at him with her mouth, but not with her eyes. They were not cold eyes, just somehow detached. He could not tell how old she was. She looked young but she seemed too mature to be less than thirty or so.

"Okay, I guess. Where am I?"

"You are in a house on Barracks street. You are quite safe, there is no need to worry."

"Who are you? How did I get here?"

"We found you last night in the rain. Don't you remember? We brought you here and tended to your wound. We gave you something to help you sleep." She handed him the coffee cup and he took a sip.

"Why are you helping me? Who are you, anyway?"

"Do you always ask questions in pairs?" She smiled. "My name is Katherine. As for why we helped you, there are many answers to that question. Let us just say that we saw you were in trouble so we did what we could."

"Do you always go around helping strangers?"

"We help when we are able but, no, to answer your question, we do not help everyone. That would not be possible or even beneficial. We help whom we choose to help. Last evening we chose to help you."

"But why me?"

"The simple answer is that you were of concern to us. An innocent man, half naked in the rain, bleeding and lost, a victim of violence."

"I'm grateful for your concern, but I don't know if I would have stopped to help. How did you know I was innocent? What if I had been a murderer?"

"We know this city very well. Let us just say it was obvious to us. To answer the second part of your question, you clearly were in no condition to do us harm, even if you were so inclined."

"You keep saying we. Who is we?"

"We are a family. A society, let us say. We are active in many areas in this city and others. I cannot explain more at this time. I will return shortly. Please eat, and drink your coffee."

Without another word she turned and left the room. He watched her glide across the floor. The pastry was delicious and he realized that he was starving. He finished it and the coffee and then started to get up, until he realized he was naked. He could not see his jeans anywhere in the room. A few moments later she came back in carrying a shopping bag.

"I have brought you some clothes. I hope they fit you. Try them on. There is a bath and shower through that door. Try to keep the dressing as dry as possible. Everything you need should be there. I will wait for you in the next room."

It was the most elegant bathroom he had ever seen. The fixtures looked like they were made of gold. He showered. On the sink, wrapped in a clean hand towel were a razor, tooth brush and comb. Shaving cream and toothpaste were in the cabinet. He dried himself with a plush white towel that looked too good to use, and then opened the shopping bag. There was a pair of gray slacks, a light blue pullover, underwear, socks and a pair of casual shoes. Everything fit like he had bought the clothes himself. Even the shoes. The tags were removed, but he could see that they were too expensive for his budget. He walked over to the door and then realized he didn't have his wallet. It wasn't on the nightstand either. He couldn't remember if he had it in his jeans when he bolted from the room. If he had lost his ID, it was going to be a hassle. He wondered again what had happened to Lucky.

The woman was waiting in the next room, which was a small parlor. There was a couch and a chair and a coffee table between them. He recognized his wallet lying on the table. He picked it up but didn't look inside. She was sitting on the sofa, looking at him with those cool eyes. There was no expression on her face. He heard some voices coming from another part of the house.

"I see I guessed well. You look quite presentable when you are not drowning in the rain and bleeding. I am sorry about your jeans. I threw them away."

He smiled. He still did not comprehend what was going on. "Thank you again for helping me, but could I ask you something?"

"Of course."

"Why didn't you just take me to an emergency room and leave me there?"

"This is what we thought to do originally, but then, in our attempt to find out who you were, we found your military identification. We thought treatment in a public hospital might cause some problems for you. We had our physician attend to you. I am sorry for going through your wallet but it was necessary. Nothing was removed that was not returned."

Paul was a little dumbfounded at the turn of events and still a little bit in shock after everything that had happened. "Well, thanks for helping me. You probably saved my life. How can I repay you?"

She waved her hand as if to dismiss the question. "There is no need, there is nothing to repay."

"But these clothes, the doctor's fees. I have to pay for something."

She ignored the question. "I am afraid we cannot offer you transportation at the moment. Do you know your way around these streets?"

"Sure, pretty well. I'm sure I can find my way."

"Do you think you are strong enough to walk on your own? Otherwise I can have someone escort you, or we could call a taxi."

"No, I'm sure I'll be fine."

"You may go then, Paul. Please be sure to change the dressing on your wound when you get back. If you see any signs of infection or if you start running a fever, go to a doctor. The wound is not too serious. No major blood vessels were damaged, but it must be taken care of, and you have lost a considerable amount of blood. I think it will ache quite a lot for a while and you may experience some fatigue and thirst."

He was startled to hear her call him by name. He stood there for a moment not knowing what to say.

"You wish to ask me something more?"

He hesitated, not able to form the question.

"You wish to know if you will ever see me again or find out who we are who have helped you."

"Ah, yes. I guess."

"That is up to you. In your wallet you will find a number where I can be reached most of the time. If I am not there you may leave a message. Whatever happened to you last night is not our concern but if it was due to some recklessness on your part... well, let us just say it is not our interest to protect people from themselves. This city has many attractions, but also many dangers. You have no doubt learned what can happen, sometimes with little provocation. We are not the police, but if you find yourself in need of help, you may call and we will consider helping you if we can. Now that we have done this service for you, we feel, let us say, some connection with you. You are not obligated in any way to repay this service we have performed for you. We wish you well. I will only tell you that our family has many members and many levels of involvement. Part of how we function is to provide help to each other. Our members take it as a matter of personal honor to provide help, or service, to others in the family as they are able and as the need arises. Nothing is demanded; often services are requested. To be fair, I must tell you that, considering your current obligations to the military, it will most likely be better for you in your life if you do not try to become involved with us at this time."

A moment later he was standing out in the street. He just started walking until he got his bearings and then he headed out toward Canal Street. He was still a little dizzy. It was early afternoon but he had had all he could handle for one weekend. He decided to go back to the base. He opened his wallet. All of his money was still there along with his I.D. Also there was a card, like a business card. The only thing written on it was the name Katherine and a phone number. There was some kind of strange symbol up in the corner, which he did not recognize. It looked like a letter from some ancient alphabet. He studied the card for a while and then put it back in his wallet. The events of the previous evening were playing back in his mind in an endless loop. It was like a sine wave. Pleasure and pain, joy and fear, despair and redemption. He hardly remembered the trip back to the base.

Paul had mixed feelings about Keesler as a duty assignment. It was like being at a boarding school for delinquent boys. He was looking forward to an assignment on a normal base where everyone pretty much just did their job and the bullshit was kept to a minimum. On the other hand, it was a lot better than being in Vietnam, which would likely be his next tour. Being so close to New Orleans made it tolerable most of the time. He had enlisted in the Air Force after receiving his draft notice. No matter what they asked him to do, it was going to be better than humping through the jungle with an M16. He hadn't grown up feeling that way about the military. The war, this war, had changed him. It had changed a lot of guys. He had a college degree, but had chosen not to go after a commission when he found out how many years they would want out of him. He couldn't relate to the kids very well, and he couldn't fraternize with the young officers because of his rank. It was just an unavoidable pause in his life, and he did his best to endure it.

The week after the incident passed quickly, and Paul had every intention of going back into the city to see if he could find Lucky. He told his first sergeant that the wound was the result of a fall. No one really believed him, but since it hadn't interfered with his duties, they weren't inclined to make an issue of it. Too much paperwork. The last thing they wanted was another report to fill out. His top sergeant didn't like Paul's attitude much, but Paul did his job well enough and wasn't normally involved in any trouble. The sarge looked the other way. The incident had taken its toll on Paul, however, and the pain in his shoulder was intense at times, making it difficult to get a good night's sleep. He was tired and he had to admit, a little traumatized by the incident. He woke up one night in a panic. The vision of that knife-wielding maniac had lodged in his mind. He guessed it would be with him for a while, alongside some of the other terrors in his memory. By Friday he realized he was in no condition to go back into the city and he just hung around the barracks.

As much as he wanted to know what happened to Lucky, he was also intrigued by Katherine and the society she was involved in. He knew about groups like the Rotary and the Elks. Civic-minded organizations that supported charities and community activities. This sounded more like what he knew of the Masons, except he knew what the Mason's symbol looked like and it was nothing like the symbol on Katherine's card. After running it around his brain for a few days, he decided it was just another peculiar and mysterious face of New Orleans and decided to let it go. He was having trouble getting Katherine out of his mind, though. He had never met anyone like her before. By the middle of the following week he was feeling much better, and on Saturday morning he walked out to Route 90 and thumbed a ride into the city.

It was the same bus stop where he had met Lucky, but it was no longer just an anonymous place along the highway. He stood by the bench and played back in his memory everything that had happened since the day he met her. Every few minutes he glanced down the road where he had first seen her, hoping to see her materialize again, like a genie out of a lamp. The bus came along. It was a different driver and there were not many passengers. He spent the ride into the city trying to center himself. There was not much sense in going over everything endlessly in his head as he had been doing, but he couldn't help but wonder where it was all leading. There was a persistent voice telling him to just let it all go. She was a prostitute, and not someone he was going to get deeply involved with. Still he liked her, and felt somehow responsible for her, even though he knew none of what happened was any fault of his own. Most of all, he just needed to know if she was all right.

He knew the hookers wouldn't be out until later in the evening, so he just walked around the Quarter. It was a different universe during the day, like a picture postcard of itself. Not exactly inanimate; there were plenty of people. It was just lacking something. Like a ballroom before the party started. It was a beautiful day. The humidity was down for a change and it wasn't too hot. He wasn't going to do it, but in the end he found himself walking by the house on Barracks street. There were no signs of life. The place looked abandoned. He wondered if the phone number on the card rang at this address or somewhere else in the city. He stopped for dinner at Baby's. Baby was in a good mood and he insisted Paul should try his jambalaya. He hadn't seen Lucky and Paul sensed he was a little concerned about her. He didn't ask Baby about the maniac, whom he figured had been Lucky's pimp. After dinner he went over to the Julius and hung out for a while. The hookers came out almost as soon as it got dark. The transvestites came out first. They needed to work harder to find a trick. The girls came out a little later. He asked a few of them if they knew Lucky. One or two asked if he wanted to get lucky with them. One girl named Tammy said she knew Lucky, but hadn't seen her around for a while. He took it as a good sign that nobody knew where she was. If anything had happened to her, the girls would probably have known about it. He didn't want to ask any questions about the pimp. He thought some of the girls might be working for him. Paul was sure he would recognize him if he saw him again. He guessed his forehead looked like a zipper after how she had cut him. Anyway, Paul didn't want to tangle with him again. He gave up and went over to the Seven Seas.

It was still pretty early when he got to the bar. There was already a good-sized crowd inside and it was rowdy for so early in the evening. There was nothing going on in the courtyard. He got a beer and took his favorite spot on the bleachers, about half way up near the door. He had learned by experience that it was better to avoid being too close to the bar where the likelihood of having beer or anything else spilled on you was pretty high. There was also a pretty good possibility of catching a stray elbow or fist, especially later in the evening. Being near the door was also a good thing. He had also learned when trouble did erupt, the crowd tended to push toward the back of a bar. You could usually slide out the door behind whatever was going on. On this particular night there was a pretty large group of roughnecks off one of the oil rigs out in the Gulf of Mexico. They were already pretty well sauced and there was a lot of good-natured pushing and shoving going on. The rest of the crowd was wisely giving them their space. It was pretty good entertainment.

When he had been there for an hour or so, a group from a motorcycle gang called the Pagans came in, sporting their colors and chains and malignant attitudes. They pushed past the roughnecks and there were some hard looks exchanged. There was going to be trouble. It was just a matter of time. The roughnecks kept getting louder and the pushing and shoving was looking a little more edgy. Any female foolish enough to get near them was being seriously groped. One well-built blond seemed to be into it and they were pouring beer on her blouse. Some of the guys picked her up and sat her on the bar. The Pagans were getting more and more pissed-off. They did not like anyone stealing the show from them, especially if they were not shown the proper respect. Finally one of the roughnecks got shoved into one of the Pagans and the whole thing flashed over. In an instant they were squared off against each other. Some beer bottles were broken against the bar and some knives were drawn. Paul started easing his way down toward the door.

A man appeared out of the crowd and walked into the middle of it. Paul recognized him as the guy who had stepped in front of him in the courtyard. He turned to the leader of the Pagans and spoke to him. The Pagan stepped back and stared. He had a wild look in his eyes. The guy then turned his back on the biker and addressed the group of roughnecks. Paul heard him say they would either have to behave themselves or they would have to leave. A couple of the roughnecks laughed out loud, but the ones closest to him looked confused. For a few moments it looked like a painting of a bar fight. The whole place was suddenly as quiet as a tomb. A bottle fell off the bar and rolled across the floor. All at once the Pagans put their weapons away and just walked out of the bar. Paul had never seen anything like it before. The roughnecks stood around mumbling to one another. They stayed for a while, but they were mostly just standing at the bar and talking quietly. After about twenty minutes, they walked out as well. The empty space they left behind was quickly filled with a different assortment of characters, more interested in preening and posturing than in fighting. It was like smoke rushing in to fill a vacuum.

Paul was curious about the guy who had stepped into the middle of the conflict. He assumed he must have been a bouncer, although he was not built like one. Or maybe he was one of the owners of the place. It also occurred to Paul for the first time that he had never seen anyone like a bouncer in the bar, which was strange considering the craziness. The guy had gone into the courtyard after the roughnecks left. Paul walked out back. Some musicians were setting up and the crowd was drifting out.

The guy was standing near the back wall talking to some other people and Paul worked his way over, trying to be inconspicuous. Leaning against the wall close to where they were talking he pretended to be interested in the band. He picked up bits and pieces of the conversation, but nothing that gave him a clue to who the guy was. He decided to let it go, but as he started to walk away he noticed that the guy had a tattoo on the side of his neck. He hadn't seen it on their first encounter. As Paul passed him, he got a good look at it and what he saw startled him. He walked straight through the bar and out onto the street. He opened his wallet and pulled out the card Katherine had given him. The tattoo was the same as the symbol on her business card. A shiver went up his spine.

Paul decided to see if Spence was around. He walked over to the Limbo. Spencer was sitting at the bar watching a basketball game. He turned when Paul came in and motioned for him to come over.

"Once more the gallant warrior returns. How goes the battle, lieutenant?"

"Right now I appear to be losing." Paul showed Spenser the bandage and explained what had happened. Spencer seemed shocked by it all.

"Well, I am impressed. You, sir, have managed to find the center of the cyclone in record time. I shall have to keep better track of you in the future. The pimp's name, for your information is Jackie Davis, and he is very bad news. The word on the street is that your friend Lucky had a falling out with him and went somewhere else. He has a reputation for keeping his girls in line by any and all means. The rumor is that a few have disappeared altogether after crossing him. The worse news is that he is paying someone off big-time. The cops aren't going to touch him unless he kills a john or something."

"Yeah, well he almost killed me."

"Why don't I make a few phone calls and see if there is a way to get this thug distracted a little?"

"No thanks, Spence. I'd like to see him get what's coming to him but, until I find out what happened to Lucky, I don't want to make any more waves."

"Listen, it's none of my business, man, but are you sure you want to stick your neck out for this girl? I don't mean to insult you or anything, but she is a prostitute. I don't see this developing into a long-term relationship. Of course, I could be wrong."

"No, it's not like that. I just want to make sure she isn't hurt somewhere and needing help. I guess I feel responsible for her. I like her, but that's all there is."

"Okay, if I hear anything I'll let you know."

"Something else strange happened."

"Well as I told you, captain, this is the Big Easy. Strange occurrences rise like a miasma from our low places. The tourists find it amusing. We denizens generally hold our noses and scurry back to our familiars."

Paul explained about being rescued and about Katherine. "The weirdest thing is that I saw the symbol I told you about tattooed on a guy's neck over at the Seven Seas. He is some kind of a heavy. He seemed to wield a lot of influence, at least in that bar." Paul showed him the card Katherine had given him.

"It looks Celtic or maybe even Sanskrit. I've seen this somewhere. Where the hell was it? It wasn't a tattoo. Give me a minute."

Paul went to use the bathroom and picked up a couple of beers at the bar. When he got back, Spencer was looking pleased with himself.

"Once again the prodigious intellect of Spencer the Unparalleled prevails. I remember where I have seen this. It's on a lintel above a doorway on a building on Royal. If memory serves, that structure is one of the oldest in the Vieux Carre."

"Where?

"Vieux Carre. It's the real name for the French Quarter. We don't let the tourists in on it. Anyway the building is nearly 200 years old."

"Do you know anything about it?"

"Sorry, not a thing. There are scores of secret organizations in this city. Most are just a bunch of rich people acting out their fantasies. A lot of them are Carnival krewes. Some of them are extremely secretive and very old." He lowered his voice for emphasis. "Some of them are so well connected that they fly under the radar, as you might put it, and under the law. Some are rumored to be evil, aligned with the devil, that sort of thing, if you are the superstitious type. It has also been rumored for years that there is some shadowy enforcement organization, of unknown origin, that more or less keeps a lid on things to maintain order and protect its own interests in, shall we say, under-the-table activities. I've never really seen any evidence of it. Some even say that the government of this city and of the entire state of Louisiana is just a straw dog for some invisible power structure. But then, some say that about the federal government as well. Who knows?"

"Well, I hate to ask, but do you think you could find anything out about this group?"

"Anything for a gallant warrior defending my city from the barbarian horde. Seriously, I love this kind of crap. You have no idea how much useful information I run across while mucking around in the shadows. If this is some fifth column working in the city it could be a goldmine for me. It implies, at least, that a lot of the illegal activity in the Quarter is being controlled by some single entity. The possibilities are endless. You, sir, much to my delight, are far more interesting than I first supposed. Forgive me for underestimating you."

"Well, at the moment, I'm on a personal quest to become less interesting for a little while."

"An exemplary strategy, my good man. Seriously, Paul, you need to be careful. There are people in this rat's nest that can make you disappear. Do me a favor and don't contact this organization until I have some time to do a little digging."

"I'm not expecting to contact them at all. I'm just curious, I guess."

"Yeah, well that's what you said about your friend Lucky, remember?"

Spencer had to leave to meet some people. Paul thought he would make one more attempt at getting some information about Lucky. He went over to Bourbon and walked up and down for about an hour. He was about to give it up when he felt a tug on his elbow. It was Lucky's friend Ginger and she looked scared.

"Keep walking, okay?" She walked a little behind him and pretended not to be having a conversation with him. "Lucky is over in that flophouse on Dauphine street. That pimp beat the crap out of her. She's hurt pretty bad. Somebody told me she almost died. He's holding her there, making her work off some money he says she owes him. I think he's going to kill her."

"Why don't you call the cops?"

"Don't be stupid, man. Do you think the cops down here give a shit about some whore? That fuckin' pimp is paying them off plenty. Word is he's looking for some white dude who was with Lucky when he got cut. I don't even want to know if that was you and you didn't hear any of this shit from me." She turned on her heel and walked away.

He was beginning to feel paranoid, like there were eyes watching him. He tried to tell himself that it was none of his business and that Lucky was just somebody he met and he didn't have any responsibility for her. He thought he had himself convinced, but he found himself walking toward Dauphine Street. After all, she had saved his life. She could have run and left him there. If she hadn't cut that maniac, he would be dead right now. He had to try to help her. He wasn't expecting a good outcome.

Fortunately the street was pretty dark. He walked by in the shadows on the other side. There were a couple of guys hanging around in the entrance. Neither of them was Jackie Davis. Still, he wasn't going to risk just walking up to them and telling them he was looking to get laid. He walked down a few houses and then crossed over. He doubled back and walked toward the old hotel. The bouncers, if that's what you called them, were not paying any attention to the street. There was a narrow alleyway between the two houses next to the hotel. He turned into it and made his way cautiously along, keeping contact with the brick wall. He couldn't see a thing. The rats scuttled out of his way, but just long enough for him to get by.

There was an ancient gate at the end with iron spikes on the top. He looked over. The lot in the back was strewn with trash. There didn't seem to be any dogs. He managed to get over the gate by holding on to a drainpipe. It was pitch black. He walked behind the buildings until he came to the courtyard wall behind the hotel. It was about six feet high with rusted barbed wire on the top. He listened for a few moments, but didn't hear any noise from the other side of the wall. There were some old crates in the yard, and he managed to drag a few over to the wall and make a kind of stair by stacking them. The wire was rusty and sharp. He looked through the debris for a while and finally found an old mattress. He carried it up the crates and dropped it onto the wire and then went over on his stomach, landing in the courtyard.

There was a fire escape in the back. He jumped up and grabbed the ladder to pull it down. It was rusty from lack of use and at first he couldn't budge it. He was hanging from it with his entire weight when it gave way. It sounded like a train wreck. He scrambled back into the shadows, feeling like his heart was going to burst out of his chest. His shoulder was beginning to ache and it felt like it might be bleeding again. The voice in his head was telling him what a dope he was and how he was about to get sliced into a thousand small pieces. He waited for what seemed to be a long while before starting to climb. He had no idea where they might be holding Lucky, but he thought he would try the room they had been in that night. The fire escape was at the end of the long central hallway on each floor. When he reached the second floor he could see a guy standing at the end of the hallway near the stairs, smoking a cigarette. It was too far for him to make out who it was, but he didn't think it was Jackie. A john came out of one of the rooms. He was zipping up his pants and looking satisfied. Paul climbed up to the third floor. There didn't seem to be anything going on. He waited again.

Finally he tried the window and it opened. He listened but didn't hear anything. After climbing in, he stood frozen in the shadows. His heart was pounding so loud he thought it would shake the entire building. He wanted to make his way down the hall but his legs didn't want to work. Finally, he forced himself to move. The floorboards were creaking under his feet. He couldn't remember which room it had been but then he saw one with a new door. He put his ear up to it and listened. There was some soft moaning coming from inside, but he wasn't sure. It could have been a couple going at it. He tried the knob and it turned. His hands were shaking. He opened the door a crack and looked in. Lucky was lying naked on the bed. He opened the door wide enough to put his head in and take a quick look around and then he stepped in and closed the door quietly behind him.

Lucky was beat up pretty bad. Her eyes were black and almost swollen closed. Her lips were swollen so badly that she could hardly speak. His first thought was to get her out of there but he saw she was handcuffed to the bed frame. When she saw him she started to cry. He put his head down next to her.

"How did you get in here, baby? Can you get me out? Can you help me? He beat me so bad." She reached down to her chest with her one free hand. "I think he broke my ribs. There's blood when I cough."

Paul went into the bathroom and filled a glass with water. He lifted her head and let her drink. The anger was washing over him. He wanted to go and get a gun and come back and kill all of them.

"Do you have a hair pin?"

She pointed to the bureau. He walked over and found one in a glass bowl. After straightening it out, he slid one end between the door and the frame and bent it over so that it made a small hook. He started working on the handcuffs. The hairpin kept bending and he couldn't quite get it. He heard some footsteps outside of the door and dove for the floor, rolling under the bed as quietly as he could. The door opened and Paul saw a pair of snakeskin boots walk into the room. The man spoke and he knew it was Jackie. He fought against his fear and his rage. He knew there was no way he could take him one on one, especially as good as Jackie was with a knife. Still, he felt like a coward lying under the bed. He had to keep telling himself it wouldn't help Lucky if he got himself killed.

"You talking to yourself again, you ugly fucking whore?"

Lucky didn't say anything. He must have reached down and pushed on her because the bed moved and she cried out.

"Don't worry, bitch. I ain't going to mark you any more now. I'm gonna let you heal up real pretty and then you're gonna fuck every scumbag I can find until I get my money back. You don't need to worry about how fucked up you look, just as long as you still got that sweet little ass."

Paul heard a slap and a soft cry, and then Jackie turned and walked out of the room. Paul waited for a few minutes and then he slid out from under the bed. Lucky was crying. She had her head turned away from him. With Jackie somewhere outside, there was no way Paul was going to be able to get her out. It didn't look like she was well enough even to walk. He had to find some other way.

"I'm going to get you out of here, Lucky."

She didn't respond. He took her hand and held it. Her grip was weak.

"You just hang on, I'm going to figure out a way to get you out."

She turned to him then and she was angry. "You just get your ass out of here, white boy. You ain't nothin' to me nohow. You don't know what you're fuckin' with. Go on, go. I don't want to see you no more."

"Just hang on, Lucky, I'm going to get you out."

She turned her head away from him again and wouldn't look back. He walked over to the door and listened for a moment before opening it a crack. The hallway was clear. He went out into the hall, closing the door behind him and walked quickly down to the end. He slid the window open, expecting Jackie to spring out at him at any minute, but he made it and out onto the fire escape. Back down in the courtyard, he managed to get himself over the wall where he had left the mattress, pulling it down behind him. At the end of the alley he looked toward the entrance but didn't see anyone. The anger was raging inside of him. He knew what he needed to do.

- 7 -

Marc Francoeur's library was not as imposing as the conference room, but it was impressive nonetheless. Hundreds of books, arranged by topic and by language, lined the walls in row after row of inlaid mahogany shelves. Another large fireplace dominated the north wall and was surrounded by a setting of brown leather sofas and loungers. An enormous globe sat in the corner and maps of the world covered the walls. There was a reading table at the far end of the room with a green-shaded lamp that gave the room the feel of a university library.

As Bruce entered the room, Marc looked up from where he sat and placed his book on the end table. He motioned to Bruce to join him.

"Good morning, Mr. Francoeur."

"Good morning, Bruce. I trust everything is well."

"Yes, sir

"May I assume you have some information for me?"

"We haven't heard back from the Shepherd yet, sir, but I have some news regarding the other package we have been waiting for."

"Bring me up to speed, won't you."

"Well, sir, the package has arrived in the city and they're waiting for us to set up a meeting. They seem a little nervous about this one. They want to get it off their hands as soon as possible."

"Understandable. Tell me, Bruce, you've dealt with this organization in the past. What can you tell me about them?"

"Well, as you know, sir, there are a number of anti-Castro groups operating in the US. The RECE is one of the more militant organizations. It is rumored that they have performed some wet work for the CIA. Not here, but in some of the Latin American countries. They don't have a particularly large presence in New Orleans, but they are well represented in Miami."

"What is our relationship with them?" Marc asked.

"I don't know if you would call it a relationship. We have a few contacts in the organization. They knew enough to approach us when the package became available."

"Why not go directly to the CIA with it?"

"I get the impression that they do not trust their existing conduit. They have suspicions he may be available to the highest bidder. Also, they try to avoid any direct contact with the agency because they do not want it looking over their shoulder."

"Will your personal contacts be involved in the hand-off?"

Bruce shook his head. "Not likely, sir. Generally they recruit a mule on the island and he keeps possession until the mission is complete. That way few, if any, of the resident operatives are exposed if things go sour. Probably the mule and a driver would be at the hand-off."

"For your information, Bruce, the package consists of a list of thirty or so identities and code names of Castro's DGI operatives, currently active in locations throughout Central and South America. I've recently learned that the Cuban government may be aware of this security breach. We have intelligence that a general roundup of suspected sympathizers has taken place on the island in the last few days, and there are rumors of people being put up against the wall and shot. We suspect they may know the list is out and are desperate to get their hands on it. If this is the case, it would explain why the RECE is so nervous. Havana will likely have notified the pro-Castro elements in this country to be on the lookout for it."

"Yes, sir. I guess in that case we should procure it as soon as possible."

"Yes, time is of the essence, but let me run an idea by you. It may be to our advantage to make it appear that we never took possession of the list."

Bruce frowned. "I don't know if I follow you, sir."

"This is an extremely valuable piece of information. The CIA is not yet aware of its existence as far as we know. They certainly don't know it's been offered to us. In any case, they would be inordinately grateful to have it in their hands. Let us suppose, and let me stress I consider this unlikely, that something goes wrong in our dealings with the Shepherd. The list would be an excellent card to be holding. It is of immense value to both sides. Eventually, after the item has been safely delivered, we can offer the list to the CIA as planned. In the meantime, it would be extremely important that no one suspects we have it."

"That might be difficult, sir. If the RECE were leaned on, they would certainly give us up."

"What if they thought we never received it? What if some third party operatives intercepted the package before it could be delivered? If they could be made to think Castro's agents got the list, we would be in the clear. We could play the jilted lover and make them understand how unhappy we are with them and that they owe us some consideration in the future."

"Yes, sir, I see what you're driving at."

"I believe you've seen their handy-work before. Do you think you could put together a team, intercept the package, and make it look like a DGI operation?"

"Yes, sir. I can do that. They like to let their enemies know who hit them. I know what their calling card looks like."

"In your opinion, do you think there is any chance they might suspect we were behind it?"

"I seriously doubt it, sir. All of these groups are paranoid about spies in the Cuban community. They would most likely assume there was a mole in their own organization."

"I don't see any obstacles then. Do you?"

"Sir, you do understand that we would not be able to leave any witnesses?"

Marc's eyes narrowed and his reply was more like a challenge. "Do you have a problem with that, Bruce?"

"No, sir. Not at all."

"Very well, I'll leave the details up to you. After the operation, wait at the drop-off location for one-half hour and then call your contact at the RECE. Demand to know why they missed the hand-off. It might be useful to suggest they're holding out for more money or in some way playing us. We want them on the defensive. Once you're sure they don't suspect us, bring the package to me immediately."

"I will see to it, sir. In the meantime, would you like me to try to contact the Shepherd to find out what progress has been made?"

"No, let him come to us. We don't want to appear overly anxious about that project at this stage of the negotiations."

* * *

The black limousine pulled into the long driveway, and Katherine lowered the car window to take in the scene. Ancient Magnolia trees, standing one hundred feet tall, were covered in white flowers. A warm breeze filled the car with their fragrance and the scent of newly mown pasture. Beyond the trees, horses grazed behind a double white fence that extended as far as the eye could see. Katherine relaxed. This place had a calming effect on her, no matter what else was going on in her life. The driveway divided around a circular plaza with a fountain at its center, then looped under a portico at the front door of the mansion. The driver got out and opened the door for her. As she entered the house, she was passed by a large, blond man whom she knew but always tried to avoid. He was Marc's chief of security and she thought him a soulless thug. He nodded to her and she acknowledged him but quickly looked away. It gave her the chills just being in the same room with him. She walked into the library.

"Sorry I'm late."

Marc came over and kissed her, draping his arm lightly over her shoulders. "How are you, Katherine? You look stunning as always."

"I'm fine, Marc. It's such a gorgeous day!"

"Would you like to go for a ride with me later? I'm looking at an Arabian this afternoon and I want to try him out."

"Thank you for asking. I'd really love to, but I must meet with Angelina this afternoon. The donor committee meets on Monday and there is still some disagreement as to the naming of the addition."

"How can they object? I'm underwriting the entire cost of the construction. It'll be the largest pediatrics department in the city. The least they can do is let me name it."

"Yes, I know, but they say the equipment they'll be purchasing will cost almost as much as the construction of the wing. There are some other large donors who want to just call it by a generic name with a list of contributors on a plaque in the lobby."

"Well, I don't suppose I can withdraw my offer at this late stage. Try to find out who's raising most of the fuss and perhaps we can come to some agreement."

"That was my objective."

"If worse comes to worse, I'll throw in a couple of medical school scholarships for intercity students who want to be pediatricians. If that doesn't do it, nothing will. Don't put that on the table yet, though. I still think we can win this one."

"I'll do my best."

"You always do, darling." He kissed her again. "I understand you performed a mission of mercy of your own the other night. You never could resist a stray dog left out in the rain."

"Yes, I felt for him for some reason. But I think you may find this one of interest to you."

"How so?"

"His name is Paul Greene. He's a sergeant on the Air Force base in Biloxi."

Marc seemed momentarily stunned. "That's extraordinary. Did you know this when you picked him up?"

"No, not at all. But once I found his identity card, I decided to take him back to the apartment rather than to the hospital. I called Douglas to come treat him."

"Was he badly injured?"

"A knife wound in the shoulder. This one is lucky, I think. Douglas said it missed the subclavian artery by a millimeter. He likely would have bled out before we found him."

"What did you think of him?"

"It's hard to say. I don't think this was some kind of drunken brawl he was involved in. There was no alcohol on his breath. He's well spoken and has a rather pleasant manner about him. He's also quite athletic looking. I would say he is above average in intelligence, but not very sophisticated. Of course he was in pain and, I am sure, not himself."

"So how did you leave it with him?"

"I felt it better not to say anything for now. I gave him my card. My instincts say he will be in contact with me. If not, we know how to reach him. You have always told me to let them come to us."

"Indeed, but do not allow too much time to pass. Our need is pressing. If he has not contacted you by the end of the week, see if you can reach him by phone, on the pretense of checking on his injury. Invite him to have dinner with you in the city."

"As you wish."

"In the meantime, I will have our people make some discreet inquiries to make sure there is nothing to make him unsuitable to our purpose."

- 8 -

There was a pay phone next to the Julius. Paul took the card out of his wallet and dialed Katherine's number. The phone rang seven times before someone picked it up. It was a man's voice.

"Vincent."

"Ah, yes. I'm trying to reach Katherine."

"Who shall I say is calling?"

"Tell her it's Paul Greene."

"Just a moment."

He waited a long time. He wondered if she was going to take the call. Finally he heard someone pick up the phone.

"Yes, Paul, what can I do for you?"

"I'm sorry to bother you, I really am, but I need to ask for your help with a problem."

"So soon? Are you somewhere bleeding again?"

"No, nothing like that."

"Where are you?"

"I'm on Bourbon Street at a pay phone."

She told him to go to the corner of Charles St. and St. Louis and to wait there until he was contacted. It took him about ten minutes to get to the corner and after about a half-hour the black limo drove up. The back door opened and he got in. Katherine was alone. She was wearing a black evening dress with a pearl necklace. It occurred to him that she was probably the classiest woman he had ever been this close to.

"Thank you for coming," Paul said as the limo pulled away from the curb. "I'm sorry if I took you away from something."

"We try to help when we can. Are you well? Is your wound healing?"

"Yes, it's doing fine, thank you. They did a good job of sewing me up."

"So what is it that you are in need of?"

As the limo cruised the city streets, he told her about Lucky. About how he had met her and about the night in the house on Dauphine Street, emphasizing that he was not paying her for her services. He told her the circumstances leading to the fight. He told her how he had been wounded and why she had found him standing out in the street half naked. He told her what had happened since and how he had found Lucky chained to her bed and badly beaten. She listened impassively and said nothing. When he finished, there was a long silence. Finally she spoke.

"Are you in love with this woman?"

"No, nothing like that. I just… she's in bad trouble and I don't know who else is going to help her."

"You realize this woman is a prostitute and that she has no love for you."

"Yes, I know."

"You know there are dozens of such woman in this city and many of them will die a violent and untimely death, or will succumb to disease at an early age?"

"I know, but..."

"You know all of this and yet you would risk your life to save her?

"I…somebody has to do something."

She reached over and pushed the switch to open the window. "Look out there, Paul. All of the lights in all of the windows. What do you think is behind them? Do you think they are filled with happy people loving each other? Are you so naïve to think this? There may be some like that, but most are not. Most are filled with miserable human beings desperate in their lives, fighting a war within their own souls. Some of them try to live good lives. Most have given up even thinking of it. Those windows are filled with human suffering, with people doing unspeakable things to each other, physically perhaps but certainly psychologically. Do you understand this?"

"Yes, I mean I guess so. I never thought about it that way."

"And so you come here from your sheltered world, you're shown a glimpse of this horror and you decide you must act."

"Something has to be done."

"No, you are wrong about this, Paul. Nothing has to be done. If you save this one woman, if you are somehow able to rescue her and avoid being killed, do you imagine that she will quit the life she has chosen and find a job as a missionary or a school teacher? Do you imagine that after learning how to make money by giving pleasure, she will somehow be able to be happy with some tedious subsistence, with hard work and barely enough money to survive, let alone find some enjoyment in her life? Many of these women are forced into this life by terrible circumstances, it is true. Nonetheless, very few are ever able to return to a normal existence even if provided with an opportunity."

"I think she will probably just go on doing what she is doing."

"Of course she will. She will go on being what she is until the next pimp beats her or she takes money from the wrong man and he takes her life from her. Imagine that you manage to save this woman, but are killed in the effort. Is this an equitable exchange in your view of the world? Do you value your own life so cheaply?"

He didn't know how to reply. It even sounded stupid to him when she explained it out loud. He felt suddenly foolish for even talking to her about it. There was a long silence. She studied his face as he struggled with his thoughts. Finally he spoke. "Look, I know this doesn't make any sense to you. I'm really sorry I bothered you. You've been kind to me. I was being stupid. I won't bother you again. You can drop me off anywhere."

"You will not ask for my help again in this matter, but you will persist in your attempt to rescue this woman by some other means?"

"Yes, I don't know how, but I have to try."

"Please explain this to me. I know you are not a stupid man. You tell me you do not love this woman and yet you would risk all for her. I want to understand you."

He was silent again, trying to find the words. "I guess it has to do with what I believe. I think that most people see life as a series of random events. People pass in and out of your life and you hardly get a chance to know them. I believe that every encounter with another person is important. I can't explain it. It's as if we all are here trying to put together a puzzle and everyone has a handful of pieces. When we meet someone, we need to see if any of the pieces fit, even if there doesn't seem to be any other reason to interact with that person. But it's more than that. It's like for a brief instant in time you are responsible for the people you encounter. If they stumble in front of you, you instinctively reach out and catch them. Sometimes there is only you and no one else standing between another person and a tragedy. It's too easy to turn your back and walk away, believing it's not your duty to save them. You told me when you picked me up that night that you could not help everyone, but that you helped those you chose. Maybe it was because I had the same questions as you about Lucky's life that I spent time with her trying to understand it. Something about her got to me. She is a prostitute, that's true. It's how she survives; it's not a measure of the value of her life. Not to me anyway. There's no one else in this world who's going to lift a finger to help her. I know what that feels like. There's only me. I can't walk away. I couldn't live with myself if I did."

She looked at him for a long time, waiting for him to say more. Finally she reached over and kissed him lightly on the cheek. "I told you when we saw you injured in the rain that you were an innocent and you surely are this. You are also a terrible fool, but you are young and have not seen very much of this world. Perhaps there is a time in every life to be foolish and to risk all for what you believe. In spite of this, I like you very much, Paul. I don't find many like you in my journey. Before I offer my help to you, there is something you must understand. We have helped you once and have required nothing in return. You have now asked us to help you again. We are a family. We help each other. If we perform this service for you we may ask for a service in return."

"What kind of service?"

"I don't know, except that it will be in proportion to the service we render to you and that we will not ask you to do anything that is illegal or which runs contrary to your ethical beliefs."

"What if I were to refuse what you asked me to do?"

"You may certainly refuse any request we make of you if you are not comfortable with it. In this case we may make a different request at a later date, or we may simply decide to sever our ties with you. One of our missions as a family is to help advance civilization toward its perfection, even if perfection is ultimately not an achievable goal. You'll find that there is great benefit to be realized by working with us, both personally and for those we serve. Do you understand this?"

"Yes, I suppose."

"Knowing this and knowing that we may request a service from you in exchange, do you still seek our help?"

"Yes, I do."

"Very well then, Paul." She pushed a button on the armrest. "Vincent, please stop here." The car pulled over to the curb, and she opened the door. "Do you recognize this place?"

"Yes, its Jackson Square."

"Will you be all right from here?"

"Yes."

"I will say goodnight to you then. We'll see what we can do for your friend. Will you come to the city next weekend?

"Sure."

"Contact me when you arrive. I will inform you of our progress."

The turmoil he had been feeling inside gradually subsided, like the tide running out to sea. It felt as if he had placed his problems in the hands of some higher authority. He knew they would take care of it. As for the whole business about performing a service, he didn't take it too seriously. She had said they would not ask him to do anything that violated his ethics. With that kind of assurance, what could they ask him to do that could be a problem? He decided not to worry about it.

* * *

He was becoming more and more distracted at his job. It was like the week crawled on in black and white while he waited for the burst of color that was the weekend. He was starting to make mistakes and his sergeant was beginning to notice. He didn't really care what they thought about him. He just needed to avoid ramping up the bullshit level, especially if it prevented him from having his weekends in the city. He had resolved to cut his ties with Lucky in any case. Life had been like a roller-coaster ride almost since the moment he met her. Paul felt like he needed to take a step back now and try to figure things out. Katherine was right about her for the most part. She was not going to get out of the life and he would never be able to have a relationship with her unless she did. In spite of what he had told Katherine, he wondered what it all meant. Why had he met her in the first place? Perhaps it was just chance and nothing more. Or perhaps his part in the encounter was to save her for some larger purpose that only God knew. He was tired of puzzling over it.

As the weekend approached, the anticipation became unbearable. He needed to know how it had turned out. He left for the city right after duty hours on Friday and got into the French Quarter by about eight. He called Katherine. Vincent answered.

"I'm sorry, Mr. Greene, but Katherine is unable to see you this evening. She has left instructions that you may use the apartment on Barracks street this evening. She will pick you up there at nine tomorrow morning. Someone will be at the apartment to let you in. You will be provided with a key and you may use the kitchen and the bar as you require. Can you find your way there?"

"Yes, I know where it is."

"Do you have any questions?"

"No, I don't think so."

"Good evening, Mr. Greene."

He walked over to Barracks Street and found the house. It was amazing how much it looked like any common brick warehouse, with thick wooden shutters on the windows. No one would ever guess what it was like inside. He knocked on the door. After a few seconds it opened and a thin black man appeared. His hair was done up in an enormous Afro. There was a black comb stuck in it, as if he had stopped in the process of combing his hair and forgot he had left it there. He looked Paul up and down and then pursed his lips slightly. He had on a button-down, blue business shirt but the shirttail was pulled up and tied in the front over his stomach. He wasn't being at all coy about his sexual orientation.

"Who is it?" he asked, looking right at Paul.

"I'm Paul Greene."

"Oh, yes, Mr. Greene. I've been expecting you. My name is Eugene. I hope you find the accommodations acceptable. I've done my very best to tidy things up."

"Thank you, I'm sure everything will be fine." Paul wasn't homophobic, but he was fervently hoping that Eugene was not going to be sharing the place with him.

"Miss Katherine, that girl is such a doll. Can you believe her eyelashes? Anyway, she told me to tell you to use the master bedroom." He reached out and touched Paul's arm. "She said you would know which one it was." He gave Paul a wink.

"Yes, thanks, I know where it is."

"I'll just bet you do."

Eugene stuck out his hand like Paul was supposed to kiss it. Paul gave it a shake. It felt like warm Jell-O.

"Well, I guess I'll be leaving now, unless there is anything you would like me to do for you. Anything at all?

"No, thank you, Eugene. I'm sure everything will be fine."

"All right then." He feigned disappointment. "Oh, goodness, I almost forgot." He reached into his pocket and pulled out a key chain. There were two keys on it. "Now this big one here opens the front door. And this little tiny one opens the bar in the cabana out back. It is just lovely back there on a pleasant evening like tonight."

Paul thanked him again, wishing he would leave as soon as possible. Eugene walked over to the door as if he were modeling his outfit and then made a dramatic turn showing off his profile.

"I do hope you enjoy your stay." He smiled and stepped outside.

Paul locked the deadbolt behind him. The apartment was like a palace. He really hadn't seen it on his previous visit. The foyer was two stories high with a crystal chandelier. All of the windows were backlit so that it appeared that there was light coming through them even though they were shuttered. There were three other smaller bedrooms, each with a bath, and a huge living room with a brick fireplace. One room had nothing in it except a grand piano and some very expensive looking paintings that he guessed were originals. He roamed around the place for a little while, taking it all in. The kitchen was also large. The appliances were all stainless steel like in a commercial kitchen. He opened the refrigerator and found a beer. There were also some prepared dinners in foil trays with cardboard tops. Each was labeled with it contents, how long to cook it and at what temperature. He picked one out and put it in the oven and then sat down at the kitchen table and worked on his beer. Somewhere in the back of his head a little voice was telling him this was too good to be true and that he just didn't have luck like this. He thought again about this family and what they were into. Whatever it was, it generated a lot of money. Maybe too much.

He remembered that Spencer was going to look into that symbol for him. He found a telephone and called his number. No one answered. After dinner he grabbed another beer and went out back to the courtyard. There was a beautiful, kidney-shaped swimming pool and real palm trees, not to mention every other kind of tropical plant imaginable. It looked like there was some kind of retractable roof over the whole courtyard and they probably kept it heated in the coolest months of the winter. The pool looked inviting but he didn't have his bathing suit. Then he realized it didn't matter. There wasn't anyone else there anyway. He stripped off his clothes and went in. He sat there in his dog tags, drinking his beer and looking up at the moon. Not bad for a kid from nowhere, he thought. Not bad at all.

The alarm was set for eight but he was awake by seven. He had a shower in the same elegant bathroom he had used before and then dressed and made the bed. There was some cereal in the cupboard and he had a light breakfast. At eight-thirty there was a knock on the front door. Paul opened it and found Eugene standing there with a big smile and a grocery bag with a baguette protruding from it. He was wearing sandals and short shorts with what looked like a halter-top. He still had the comb stuck in his head and Paul decided it was a fashion accessory. He rushed passed Paul and headed for the kitchen.

"Good morning, good morning, I trust you slept well. I didn't expect to find you awake at this beastly hour. No matter, I'll have breakfast for you in a jiff." He stopped in the kitchen. "Oh, you naughty man, you ate already. Well, you are just going to have to eat again. Miss Katherine will be here and she'll be wanting her breakfast. Don't you dare tell her you had your breakfast. I'm sure a big, strong man like you could eat all morning."

At precisely nine o'clock there was another knock at the door.

"I'll get it," Eugene yelled. He trotted out to the foyer and opened the door.

A man Paul didn't recognize entered, followed by Katherine. She smiled at Paul. Eugene gave her an air kiss and then stepped back.

"Let me look at you, dear. My God, you are just more beautiful every time I see you. How do you do it?"

"Thank you, Eugene. You're looking quite chic yourself today."

Katherine glanced at Paul and he returned her smile. She turned to her companion who was carrying several packages. "Please put those in the guest room, Vincent, and then would you come back for us in an hour?"

"Certainly." He turned to Paul. "Good morning, Mr. Greene."

Katherine had on a light, summer-print dress. She wasn't wearing much make-up and she really didn't need any. Her hair was done up on the top of her head, and Paul noticed her long, elegant neck. She walked as if she had been trained as a model. Everything about her said class. He didn't feel like he belonged in the same room with her.

"We'll have breakfast by the pool, Eugene."

"Oh, that will be lovely. This is such a sparkling morning."

Paul followed her out into the courtyard.

"Did you use the pool last night?" she asked.

"Yes, it was beautiful." He wanted to add 'and so are you' but he held himself in check.

She sat at a glass-topped table, decorated with a centerpiece of fresh flowers. "So, I trust you're well and were comfortable last night."

"Well, it wasn't quite as nice as my bunk back at the base, but I suffered through it."

She smiled at him again. Maybe it was just that she was dressed less formal but her smile seemed more genuine. She looked younger than the last time he had seen her, by years. If he had just met her, he would have guessed that she was not over twenty.

"How is your shoulder?"

"Oh, it's great. I took the bandage off last week."

Eugene came out with a tray. There was a carafe of coffee, two glasses of orange juice and two covered plates. He put the plates down in front of them and lifted the covers with a flourish. "Voila, eggs benedict ala Eugene."

"Oh, this looks lovely, Eugene. You are such a find. Please eat, Paul. I have some news for you. What you have asked of us has been done. I will take you to see your friend this morning."

"Is she okay?"

"Well, frankly, no, but she is better I think than when you last saw her and she should be able to talk to you. I think she will recover fully, although there may be some scarring."

"I don't know how to thank you. How did you do it?"

"I will not speak of this now, but I will explain later after I have taken you where we need to go"

"Where is that?"

"Several places, if you agree to what I will request from you now."

"Sure, what is it?"

She smiled. "You give yourself so readily. There will be a dinner and cocktail party tonight in the city. It's a formal party. I would ask you to accompany me."

"Well I would love to, but I left my tuxedo back in my locker."

"That is one of the errands we will run today. You have no other plans for the weekend?"

"No, not at all."

"Wonderful. Then you will be my guest this evening."

The conversation ran to other things, mainly about the city and its history. He was becoming more and more intoxicated every minute he spent with Katherine. If she was leading him into trouble, he didn't want to know about it. They finished breakfast, and Vincent returned with the limo. The street-sweepers had done their usual efficient job. The cobbled streets were still wet but quickly beginning to steam in the late morning sun. It was amazing to him how quaint and benign the Quarter looked in the morning. It wasn't just the daylight. There were, he thought, kinder spirits afoot than in the night, under the Cajun moon.

They pulled up in front of what looked like a small clinic. Katherine reached over and touched him on the arm. "She's inside. Take as long as you like, Paul. I'll wait for you."

Paul went in and stopped at the front desk. "I'm looking for Lucky, I mean Lucinda. I don't know her last name."

The woman gave him a long look. "Yes, she's in room three, down the hall."

Lucky was partially sedated and had an IV drip in her arm. She didn't look a lot different than the last time he had seen her. When he walked over to the bed she recognized him and the trace of a smile crossed her face. She raised her arm weakly.

"How are you, baby? I was worried about you. You look out for that bastard. He wants to kill you."

"How are you doing, Lucky?"

"Not so good. But you got me out of there. You said you would. I didn't believe you. I'm sorry for what I said to you. I can't believe you saved my life again. You must be my guardian angel. They said I'm going to be fine, but I sure don't feel like it. I don't want you to see me this way."

"Don't worry about it. You'll be back, just as beautiful as ever."

She took his hand. "I ain't goin' back to that life again, Paul." She started to cry. "Those people, who are they? They said they would find a job for me if I wanted it."

"Don't worry about that now, Lucky. Just work on getting well. I'll come back and see you when I can."

"Come back soon, baby."

Paul sat with her for a while, holding her hand. She seemed to be going in and out of consciousness. He leaned down and kissed her on the forehead. On the way down the hallway it occurred to him that he might not see her again. He wasn't sure how he felt about it. Some part of him was telling him he had done what he could and it was time to walk away. Katherine was waiting as promised.

"So how was she?"

"I guess she's doing well, considering. She told me you were going to find her a job."

"You asked us to save her. Making her free from that place only saves her for the present. We'll offer her a chance to change her life. It will be up to her to take advantage of it. We shall see if she is worthy of your efforts on her behalf."

"How will you do that?"

"I've told you, Paul, our family has many members. Many own businesses. We will, of course, not ask anyone to take on a non-productive employee. When she has recovered, we will assess her skills. If she needs some additional training, we will arrange it for her."

"You would pay to send her to school?"

"Yes, of course. This is a small thing. We nearly paid a much higher price to honor your request."

The limo was moving again. They crossed the bridge over the Mississippi and into what looked like a factory district. Katherine pointed out some of the landmarks along the way. He started to feel relaxed. Something he did not think he could pull off in the presence of this woman.

"Where are we?"

"This is Algiers. There is something I must show you here."

They were driving along the river in front of a row of warehouses. Vincent pulled up to a large door and beeped the horn. The door opened and they drove inside. The building was huge and dark. It seemed completely empty. They drove to the back wall and Vincent pulled the limo up next to a long packing table. There were two men there. They both had the tattoo on their necks. They did not look at him. There was a long wooden box on the table. Katherine opened the door and asked him to get out. She got out behind him and nodded toward one of the men.

"Please open it."

The shorter of the two men stepped over and took the top off the box. There was a body inside. A large black corpse with a mean looking scar across his forehead. Paul stepped back. He turned to Katherine.

"You killed him?"

She looked at him, her eyes impassive. "Is this the man who attacked you and hurt and imprisoned your friend?"

"Yes, that's him."

"So you see now he is no longer a danger to either of you." She nodded to the men and got back into the limo. Paul looked at the body one more time. It wasn't that it bothered him to see Jackie dead. He just felt like somehow he had ordered his execution. Katherine reached out to him from the car. He remembered the first time she had reached out to him.

"Get in now please, Paul."

He got back into the limo and Vincent started the engine and drove out of the warehouse. Paul was silent for a while. Finally Katherine spoke.

"This has disturbed you, what you've seen."

"It's just a shock is all. To see a man like that."

"Have you not seen death before?"

"Yes, my mother, but not like that. What will you do with the body?"

"He'll be put into the river when the tide is changing. He will not be seen again."

"Everything is so easy for you."

"You imagine this is easy? Do you think we are killers who just go and take a life when we want to? I assure you it is not this way. It was not our intention to kill this man. We sent our people to get the girl. The others who were guarding the house were reasonable and they walked away. This one was not reasonable. He fought very fiercely. One of our family was badly wounded and nearly died. We have paid a high price to grant your request."

"I understand."

"No, Paul. I don't think you understand. Did you think this man would just let us take the girl? How did you think we would save her? Did it cross your mind at all that there would be violence and that maybe someone would be killed?"

"I guess I didn't think about it."

"Yes, this is how it always is. We want the result. We don't consider the method or the price to be paid."

"I'm sorry, I didn't mean to anger you."

"I am not angry. I just want you to understand properly. Tell me, if you had determined to rescue this woman yourself, would you have gone there with a gun perhaps? And if this man attacked you as he has once already, would you have been prepared to kill him to save yourself and your friend?"

"Yes."

"Do you feel now that this man's death is on your conscience?"

"I don't know."

"You do know, Paul. You feel responsible for this man's death and I am glad that you do. It tells me that you are a good man and that you recognize that this is a human being, no matter how evil and degraded he has become. We are not the Mafia. We do not kill to achieve our ends. We do not take a life lightly, as you do not. I want you to know this about us. There is great sadness that this has happened."

"I understand. I'm sorry."

"There is no reason to be sorry, but let us agree never to speak of this again."

They drove back over the river and into the city. Vincent pulled up in front of some very exclusive stores on Royal Street.

"Now we will attend to more pleasant duties. Come with me, Paul."

He followed her into a tailor shop. Everyone seemed to know Katherine. The manager came out to greet her. He kissed her on her hand.

"We need to provide Mr. Greene with some formal attire for an evening engagement. Black tie and cummerbund please, and black studs on the shirt."

"Oui, Madame. Would you follow me please, monsieur?"

Paul followed him to the back of the shop. They had him strip down to his shorts and then they measured what seemed like every part of his body, including each foot individually. It was all done very quickly.

"Thank you, you may get dressed, sir."

"Do you have one that will fit me?"

"Excuse me? One what, sir?"

"A tuxedo. Isn't that what you are measuring me for?"

"Of course, it is, sir. We will have it for you by five this evening. It will be delivered to you."

"Don't you want me to try it on?"

"That will not be necessary, sir. I assure you it will fit perfectly."

"I could try it on now while I'm here."

"But, sir, of course we have not produced it yet."

Then it dawned on him. They were going to make him a tuxedo in one afternoon and have it ready in time for the dinner party. He didn't know what to say. He dressed and walked back to the front. Katherine was waiting for him. Whoever these people were, they had more money than anyone he had ever been close to. Paul was dying to find out more about them. They walked out of the shop.

"Come, I want to pick up some flowers."

Paul walked alongside, feeling more and more like a puppy on a leash. He decided to see if she would tell him more about the family.

"I noticed the men in the warehouse today both had the same tattoo on their necks. It's the same as the symbol on your business card."

"You are very observant. I'm impressed."

"Does everyone in your family have this tattoo?"

"Of course not. Do you see one on me?" she said, laughing.

"No, I thought maybe just the men."

"In our family there are many functions. Some of these functions are served best if the family members are known. Most are served best when they are not known."

"So these men with the tattoos, are they soldiers or something?"

"We don't call them soldiers. We are not a war-like family. We think of them as peacemakers."

"Well, that's a nice way of putting it, but I never knew of a peacemaker who wasn't backed up by some kind of force."

"Not by force. By power."

"What's the difference?"

"You should understand this distinction. Did you not tell me you were a student of history?"

"I must have been out sick that day."

"I'm sorry, I don't understand."

"No, I'm sorry. It was just a bad joke."

"Oh, I see." She smiled at him. "It's like this. If someone is doing something to harm you or to harm your interests, and you cannot negotiate with him, you may respond with force. But this is often not effective because your adversary will likely respond with force himself, which will require greater force again by you. Normal life is interrupted and perhaps rendered impossible."

"Yes, so how is the use of power different?"

"In this case, if someone threatens you or your interests you explain to him that he may do so and you will not respond with force against him, however, if he does so he will pay a much greater price in the future. A price he is perhaps not willing to pay."

"So you threaten him."

"It is only a threat if the man does not grasp the reasonableness of your proposal. If you are successful in making him understand, it becomes simply a business decision."

"Okay. Well, last weekend I was at a bar called the Seven Seas. Do you know the place?"

"Yes, I have been there several times. It is quite interesting actually. We sometimes take guests there."

"Why there?"

"Sometimes our guests want to get a little of the flavor of the city, and we prefer to take them to a place that is, to some degree, a controlled environment."

"Well, when I was there recently, a fight started between some oil workers and a motorcycle gang. A man stepped into the middle of it and talked to both sides, and the fight was over before it really got started. That man had that tattoo on his neck."

"Once again I'm impressed. You are a keen observer, and I believe you are quite intelligent. That is good."

"I wondered if your family might have a financial interest in that bar."

"No, we have no interest, financially or otherwise, in that establishment."

"So why would one of your peacemakers get involved in that situation?"

"I cannot say for certain, but probably to protect someone he was assigned to keep from harm."

"Okay, then my question to you is, what business proposition could your peacemaker have possibly made to those bikers to make them willing to lose face and back down from a fight like that. It's not in their nature to do that."

"I don't know, but obviously they saw the reasonableness of it."

"Maybe they were told they would be cut off from their supply of drugs or whatever illegal business they were involved in."

She was silent for a few minutes, as if she were considering her words carefully. "It's good that you present these suspicions to me now, Paul. Tonight you will be meeting some people who will not be happy to answer such questions about us. I would recommend that you do not press anyone on these issues. The answers to your questions will be revealed in time if you become more involved with us. As to your question about drugs, we are not involved in any such vices whatsoever. No drugs, no prostitution, no gambling, no alcohol. We do not move outside of the law."

"It seems like in this case you were the law."

"No. You must understand that the police walk a difficult line in this city. Let me ask you, why do people come to New Orleans and, in particular, to the French Quarter?"

"Probably just to feel like they're doing something just a little risky. Something they wouldn't do at home."

"That is an interesting way to put it. Most of the people who come here and walk up and down Bourbon Street would never purchase drugs or pay for sex, or be involved in illegal gambling. On the other hand if those things did not exist here, the tourists would have no reason to visit. A certain level of these activities is tolerated for the overall financial good of the city. There is almost no crime on Bourbon Street. No serious crime. This street is protected. You don't see it because most of the police are not in uniform. The remainder of the French Quarter is permitted to operate as it always has. Unless it gets out of hand. The police here investigate crime. They do not necessarily do anything to prevent it."

"So that is where your family comes in?"

"No, not at all. We have no responsibility to prevent crime. We simply protect our interests."

"So if those bikers had not seen the reasonableness of your peacemaker's proposition, what would have happened?"

"He would have done whatever was necessary to protect his client. Even though this client may very well have not known that he was enjoying such protection."

"And if doing so cost him his life?"

"He would have done whatever was necessary."

- 9 -

The man sat on a bench on the levee by the Mississippi River. His hair was nearly white but full and it curled out from beneath his black beret. He wore a goatee and a light jacket despite the heat. His dark eyes behind wire-rimmed glasses gave him a scholarly appearance. He could have been a professor at one of the Universities. Although he had a cane lying across his lap, he sat straight with his shoulders square and his legs tucked under his body as if he were ready to stand. He had a bag of peanuts and was tempting the squirrels with them, dropping them closer and closer, until finally placing one on the seat beside him. There was a stillness about him, like a man accustomed to waiting.

After a long while, a squirrel jumped up onto the edge of the bench, tilted its head, and looked at the man suspiciously. It sniffed the air, turned its head to eye the peanut, then jumped back down again and scratched the ground, pretending not to be interested. The man watched it out of the corner of his eye, remaining perfectly still. The squirrel jumped back onto the bench, a little closer this time, but suddenly it stood up on its hind legs and darted off across the grass, scrambling up a nearby tree and beating its tail frantically. Bruce Taylor came around the front of the bench and sat next to the man without speaking. He picked up the peanut and flicked it at the tree.

"You have startled my friends, Senor Taylor. I do not think they will forgive you."

"Yeah, well sometimes you have to take a little risk to get what you want."

"Sometimes what is offered is not worth the risk."

"I am sure your friends feel otherwise."

"Perhaps, but we are also not talking about peanuts, are we, Mr. Taylor?"

"Not in my experience, Eduardo. So let's have it. What do you have for me?"

"You Americans. You have no love of conversation. To begin, the amount is acceptable, but the terms must be 100% upon delivery."

"Now, Eduardo, you know we need to cover our up-front expenses."

"I do not think your employer will have to borrow this money. No?"

"No, but let's just say we're looking for a certain commitment on the part of our business partners."

"Is it partners we are, then? Somehow I do not think so."

"We will not proceed without the buy-money. If this cannot be arranged the deal is off."

"Let us put this aside for the time being. As to the other matters, we have an agreement in principle on four of the five contracts in question. The fifth - well, let us say an urgent family matter has removed this contract from the table."

"Which contract?"

"The pipeline. It will not be awarded in your favor. However, as a concession, our friends offer the construction of the offshore pumping facility as well as an agreement to purchase the required heavy equipment for the pipeline from a distributor of your choice, at the customary markup, of course."

"I will present your friend's offer to my employer. We would like you to provide us with preliminary copies of the contracts at our next meeting. If they are acceptable, we will require signed copies at the time of the exchange. If not, we will advise you as to what changes we require. We do not wish any delay in the consummation of our agreement, Eduardo. Nonetheless, we will review the documents with great care. Once the terms are acceptable, we will let you know. And, Eduardo, we expect these contracts to be written in permanent ink. If the agreements are broken after the fact, there would be consequences."

"There is no need to worry, Mr. Taylor. In these matters, my friends have always kept their word."

"Also, we will require 50% of the buy-money before we obtain the item."

"So we return to this issue so soon."

"Do your friends imagine, Eduardo, that we will take the money and fail to deliver the item?"

"Of course not, Mr. Taylor. But equally, does your employer believe we will arrive at the transaction point empty handed?"

"So, as a compromise we will accept 50% up front and the remainder when the item is delivered."

"Except that this is not a compromise. It is what you have proposed to begin with."

"Has it occurred to you, Eduardo, that we may wish to deal directly with your friends at the Lodge and leave you to feed your squirrels?"

"Of course, there is always this risk. But the risk is also yours. We have many friends and your employer has many interests in many places."

"I don't know, Eduardo. That sounds a little like a threat to me."

"Of course it is not a threat. It is only to point out that this is a business proposition like any other.

You deal with me because it is the most efficient way to achieve what you desire. There is no other reason. If you believe someone else can negotiate for you to your better advantage, then you are certainly free to do what you want. I would simply point out that most of the foundation is now in place. If you desire to start over, you may not find the reward to be as great, and much time will have been lost unnecessarily."

"What I believe, Eduardo, is that 50% of the buy-money, invested by you, let us say in short term T-bills, could get you a handsome Mercedes and a beautiful woman to keep your bed warm."

The old man smiled for the first time. "You are a suspicious man, Mr. Taylor. But very well, I will tell our friends that you insist on the up-front money. They will weep bitterly and swear that you do not love them."

"Yeah, well, we'll throw in a box of tissues."

"How soon may we expect an answer from your employer?"

"I will contact you by the end of this week."

"And how long before the item will be available?"

"That is an unknown at this time. We will not ask for the down-payment until we have everything in place."

"Time is not our friend, Mr. Taylor."

"Time is no one's friend, Eduardo."

"Perhaps you will permit me to ask a small favor?"

"Anything for a friend."

"There is a social event next month which will take place in Atlanta. It is sponsored by a certain civically minded organization in which your employer is a prominent member. The guest speaker, I believe, is an employee of your State Department. Attendance is, of course, by invitation only. I would very much enjoy listening to this presentation."

"I'll look into it for you, Eduardo. Under the circumstances, though, I don't think my employer would enjoy the proximity."

"Of course. If your employer will personally attend, this is understood. I thought perhaps if he were not planning to be present, he would not mind if a certain prominent business man from Caracas were to attend the dinner."

"And what precisely is your interest?"

"Do not worry, my friend. It is merely an opportunity for what you Americans call networking."

"In your case, Eduardo, I think the term is fishing."

The old man smiled for the second time. Taylor put his hand on his shoulder.

"My employer is a jealous man, Eduardo. He would be very upset if he thought you were courting other suitors."

"Please let him know that he still has my deepest devotion. Besides, I am sure there would be, shall we say, someone in my pocket should I be so graciously invited."

"You can count on that, my friend. I'll let you know."

* * *

On the other side of the river, in Algiers, Ernesto sat in the backyard of the row house with Hector.

Hector had become Ernesto's teacher and tour guide. Ramón spent a lot of time with him as well, but Hector had become his friend. It didn't hurt that Hector's twin sister Anna was the most beautiful girl he had ever met. She had long black hair like threads of silk and beautiful brown eyes that sparkled when she laughed. Her body was so beautiful, Ernesto would lie in bed at night and rub himself as he fantasized about making love with her. She was constantly laughing at him when he expressed his confused ideas about life in the United States. Her laughter became his favorite music. He didn't mind that she laughed at him; in fact he liked it so much that he looked for opportunities to display his distorted view of his new home. To begin with, he could not adequately comprehend the size of his new country. He thought you could drive to New York and back in a weekend and suggested they should all go together. He also thought that Los Angeles took up most of the state of California, except for a small area where San Francisco was located.

Ramón, who was in touch with the people who had brought Ernesto on his journey, told him he should not be seen too much in the neighborhood. Castro's spies were everywhere and they might be looking for a new face. He spent hours at the house with Hector and Anna and their aunt Maria, who owned the house and treated them all like they were her children. They played dominoes and watched TV. To Ernesto it was all new. With Hector he shared the love of football, what the Americans referred to as soccer. They often went to a park away from the neighborhood and kicked the ball around. Sometimes they were invited to play in pick-up games. They were about the same size and both were mid-fielders. Although Hector was a little faster, Ernesto was more accurate with his passes and was more difficult to defend. People began to refer to them as the twins.

Ramón, who was bigger than both of them, had a bad complexion and a bit of a potbelly. He was not very athletic. His passion was automobiles and he always had grease under his fingernails. He allowed Ernesto to work with him on his car and was impressed with his skill with engines. Ernesto had never worked on a car as nice as Ramón's '58 Chevy Impala, with its huge 348 cubic-inch engine and twin Holley, two-barrel carburetors. When they went to the auto parts store together, Ernesto walked around like it was Christmas. He did not know such a place was possible. Ramón had a friend who owned a garage, and he was sure Ernesto could find work there when his mission was completed. Ernesto asked every day when he would be able to hand over what he had brought with him, and every day he was told it would be soon. It had become a terrible burden for him. He had hidden the backpack in his room, but he felt like he needed to check on it several times a day. He was afraid it would be stolen or there would be a fire and everything would be lost. In spite of the responsibility, he was happy. Maybe as happy as he had ever been in his life.

- 10 -

Katherine dropped him off at the house in the early afternoon. She asked if he was uncomfortable with Eugene. Paul told her that he wasn't used to anyone fussing over him, but he wasn't uptight about his sexual politics. She told him just to think of Eugene as a maiden aunt and that he was really quite amusing to be around. The tuxedo, complete with patent leather shoes, was delivered by five as promised. There was even a black raincoat in case the weather turned bad, which it had not. He was impressed. Eugene insisted that Paul model it for him right away. Not surprisingly, it fit perfectly. The shoes, despite being new, felt like he had been wearing them for months. Eugene gushed over him endlessly and swore he was going to telephone Esquire and have them come take pictures. When he looked at himself in the mirror, he saw a different man. It was a portrait of another kind of life. One he was feeling more and more comfortable in. He understood at once why men dressed in these things. It was only a small part about how it made you look. It was mostly about how it made you feel.

After Katherine had dropped him off, he found a florist in the Quarter and purchased an orchid for her. He felt like he was getting ready for the senior prom, but he needed to give her something. Vincent arrived with the limo at seven. Katherine came in to meet him. She looked gorgeous, as usual, and her face lit up when she saw him. She asked him to turn around.

"You look like you were born to wear it. Really, you look quite handsome."

She was dressed in a long white gown. It was cut very low in the back, which really accentuated her figure. He gave her the orchid and she looked shocked.

"How wonderfully thoughtful of you, Paul. It will look lovely with my gown. I also have something for you."

She gave him a small box wrapped in gold foil. Eugene pinned the orchid on her gown as Paul opened the box. It was a pair of gold cufflinks in the shape of the family's talisman. He wondered if it meant more than just a temporary decoration for the evening.

"Let me look at you both," Eugene said. "Oh, my God, I wish I had a camera. You look absolutely fabulous together. Well, you both shoo yourselves out of here now. You don't want to be late for the ball."

Once in the limo, Katherine filled Paul in on the upcoming event.

"The head of our family is Marc Francoeur. He's a wonderful person and I know you'll like him immediately. Don't feel uneasy with him. For a man of his importance, he is as friendly and down to earth as a person can be. I will introduce you to him first. There will be some members of the family in attendance and also some influential individuals from the community. There will be a congressman, a number of state representatives and some city officials, including an aide to the mayor. There will also be a Catholic bishop, an assortment of bankers and company presidents as well as an Air Force colonel, from your base I believe."

Paul looked uneasy at the mention of the colonel.

"There is no need for concern. We have checked into the matter and you are not violating any regulations by attending a private party. Colonel Jordan is quite friendly with Marc. It could even be good for your career, if you wish it to be. I will introduce you to him. In all, twenty-three people will be in attendance. There will be a cocktail party first, followed by a formal dinner."

"What's the occasion?"

"There is no occasion. These events occur at least every few months. It is an opportunity to exchange ideas and develop friendships with influential people in government and private businesses."

"And who am I supposed to be?"

"You are yourself, of course. You are my guest. No one will question this."

"I'm going to feel seriously out of place."

"That's why I gave you the cuff links. They identify you as a member of the family. No one will question you. No one will ask what you do. This is understood."

"Okay, but promise to rescue me if I get into a conversation with the bishop."

She laughed, and for the first time he thought he saw a glimpse of who she truly was. He realized he was hopelessly in love with her.

"I'll stay by your side, don't worry. If I'm called away for any reason, I'll arrange for someone to occupy you until I'm able to return. Honestly, Paul, there is nothing for you to fear here. Enjoy yourself. You will meet people at this dinner who can be very helpful to you."

"Why are you doing all of this for me?"

"It is not entirely for you. These events can be difficult for me if I am unescorted. My function is to act as a facilitator. The guest list is not at all random. There are guests whom we wish to put into contact with other guests and members of the family. There will be many powerful, and may I say somewhat egotistical, men in attendance. On previous occasions, a few of them have monopolized my time for the entire evening and I was unable to accomplish my tasks. It is much better for me if I am escorted, particularly by an attractive young man. It is far less likely that they will forget themselves."

"I never considered that life can be difficult for a beautiful woman like you."

She smiled at him again. "Thank you for the compliment. One last thing. After dinner, Marc would like to spend a few minutes with you. I will take you to him when it is appropriate. Other than that, you are free to enjoy the evening."

* * *

They were early. The ballroom was on the top floor of a bank building on Canal Street. Katherine used a small key in the elevator console to gain access. The elevator opened directly into the ballroom. Katherine took him over to a door at the side of the room where a waiter stood like a guard. He was wearing white gloves and had the talisman tattoo on his neck. Katherine smiled at him and nodded her head. He knocked on the door and then stood aside to let them enter. Marc Francoeur was studying a document and did not look up right away. The office was sparsely furnished. Instead of a desk, he was sitting at a mahogany Chippendale writing table. There was nothing on the table other than a gold pen set, a telephone and an appointment book. The only other furniture, aside from two Hepplewhite chairs facing the table, were a matching leather couch and chair in one corner, separated by a small table, and an Edwardian inlaid mahogany display cabinet on the opposite wall. *It was a statement,* Paul thought. *Nothing in this room sat idle for want of a decision. What arrived at this desk was here for a signature and a destination. Beyond here, there were only wheels turning.* After a few seconds, Marc stood up and came around to greet them. He hugged Katherine. It was a tender embrace, like that of a father to his daughter. Paul could not guess his age. He had piercing gray eyes, set in a rather long face with deep creases at the cheeks. He was obviously a man accustomed to being in command, but in spite of this, he gave Paul a genuinely warm smile as he shook his hand firmly.

"Well, who would have thought when we fished you out of that rain puddle that you were really a prince in disguise. Katherine is seldom wrong about these things."

"I'm pleased to meet you, Mr. Francoeur. Thank you for everything you've done for me."

He nodded to Paul by way of acknowledgement. "Katherine, there are some details I must attend to before the guests arrive. Please enjoy yourselves. Mr. Greene, I would like to spend a few minutes with you after dinner, if you would be so kind."

"Of course, and please call me Paul."

"I am looking forward to talking with you, Paul."

He was uneasy about the prospect of a long conversation with Marc Francoeur. Katherine must have sensed it, for she took him by the arm. Back in the ballroom, she introduced Paul to some members of the family and to the guests as they arrived. Paul needn't have worried about being conspicuous. Everyone was so enthralled by Katherine that they didn't seem to notice him at all. He immediately forgot everyone's name and just smiled a lot. Katherine was not only beautiful, she was able to hold her own in conversations about everything from the world economic system to local politics and the war. She did not express strong opinions, but neither did she cave in against a forceful point of view she didn't agree with. She drew Paul into the conversations by saying 'Paul and I were discussing the exact same thing the other evening' and by asking his opinion frequently. At one point she whispered in his ear.

"You're doing great, you're a natural at this."

He knew he wasn't, but it made him feel good to hear her say it.

"I need to talk to some people for a few minutes. I am going to introduce you to Evangeline. She's a member of the family who lives in Charleston. Just stay with her for a while until I get back."

Evangeline was attractive, but not in the same league as Katherine. She didn't talk about herself or what she did for the family. It seemed to Paul that she was performing her function just by keeping him occupied. He got the feeling she had been told to do exactly that. They made small talk about New Orleans and commented on some of the people at the party. She had a good sense of humor, which he supposed was part of her job qualifications.

When Katherine returned, she took Paul to meet the colonel, who was in uniform. He was a full-bird with enough decorations to cover half of his chest. He smiled warmly at Paul and shook his hand.

"I understand you're stationed at Keesler."

"Yes, sir. I'm assigned to the headquarters squadron."

"You can forget the military protocol for tonight, Sergeant. I understand you have a degree. In history, is it?"

"Yes, I concentrated in Post Renaissance European History."

"The infancy of modern civilization. The subject fascinates me, as well. Tell me, why didn't you try for a commission?"

"Well, I thought about it, but I just didn't want to commit that much time to the military. I intend to go into teaching."

"A noble profession in its own right. Well, I'm pleased to see you've found such admirable company in your off-duty hours. A lot of our NCOs just come into the city to drink and have a good time. This is a first rate organization and some of the best people I know. Stay with them, son, they do good work."

Marc gave a short speech before dinner, welcoming everyone. He made mention of a trade bill before Congress and how beneficial it would be for their mutual interests. The dinner was elegant and delicious.

Paul had never held a silver fork in his hand or even seen a real crystal goblet. Afterwards the doors were opened to a wide veranda with a breathtaking view of the city. Cigars and after-dinner drinks were provided by the waiters. It was a balmy, late-spring evening with a thin, crescent moon rising. It hovered over the dark flowing Mississippi like a crooked halo. Everything about the evening was perfect. Marc circulated among the guests. Paul could tell by watching him which conversations were of some consequence and which were merely glad handing. Throughout the evening his own people would come to him and pass along information. He would say something to them and they would dispatch to one guest or another to engage them in conversation. There was a lot going on below the surface, and Paul got the feeling that fortunes were in play.

As the crowd started to thin out, he found himself standing on the veranda with Katherine. It was the first time he had been really alone with her all evening. The warm breeze had loosened a few strands of her hair and she reached up with her hand and pulled them away from her face. He couldn't stand it any more. He leaned forward and kissed her on the mouth. She didn't exactly kiss him back, but she didn't pull away, either. She smiled at him as if to let him know it was not completely out of line.

"I had to do that."

"I know. I must tell you, though I have come to like you very much, I am not for you. Please do not involve your heart too deeply. We can be friends, good friends if you wish, but nothing more."

He wanted to ask why, but she took him by the arm and led him back into the ballroom.

"It is time for you to meet with Marc. Please don't be apprehensive. I assure you it will be a comfortable conversation. He is quite pleased with the way you handled yourself this evening. I will be here waiting for you when you are through."

As if by mental telepathy, a family member appeared and nodded to Katherine.

"Thomas will take you to him."

He felt like a lamb being led to the slaughter, but he resolved to be himself no matter what. He wasn't very good at lying anyway, and he had the feeling there was a lot at stake in this meeting. Marc was seated behind the table when he entered, and he got up again and shook Paul's hand. He motioned for him to sit on the leather couch on the side of the room, and he sat in the matching chair.

"Allow me to congratulate you on a successful evening. You fit in quite nicely, but I suspect your head is spinning just a bit by now."

"I've been trying to keep it from spinning off all day."

He laughed again. It was either a genuine laugh or he was very well practiced. "Would you like a drink or a cigar?"

"No, thank you."

"How much do you know about our family, Paul?"

"Not very much really, but I can recognize power and influence when I see it."

"That is actually a good starting point for our conversation this evening. What do you think about the war in Vietnam, Paul?"

His stomach tightened. Marc was obviously not one to waste time on niceties. Considering his obvious connections in government and industry, Paul guessed he was a major hawk. For a split second he was tempted to give him a politically neutral, non-committal lie, but in the end he decided to just say what he believed.

"I think it's a disaster and a terrible tragedy without justification on any level."

Marc sat back in his chair and looked at him for a moment, forming a tent with the tips of his fingers. Paul thought it was going to be the end of the conversation.

"A courageous answer, Mr. Greene, and one I happen to agree with."

The relief must have shown on Paul's face.

"Tell me," Marc went on, "do you believe that our government is fighting this war for the reasons stated by this administration? To protect a vulnerable, democracy-loving people from domination by a hostile, totalitarian and malevolent neighbor?"

"I think there are some in the government who believe that. There seem to be a lot of people in politics, and elsewhere, who can only see the world in terms of black and white, good and evil. Sometimes I envy their clarity, although I do not have a lot of regard for their opinions."

"Well said. But if you do not accept this justification for the war, may I assume that you believe there is some other dark conspiracy afoot? Let us say an effort on behalf of the so called, military-industrial complex to realize financial gain by encouraging the prosecution of a protracted and ultimately unwinable war?"

"I don't really believe that, either. Although I'm sure there is a great amount of money being made on this war. History tells us that human beings are, for the most part, far too incompetent to sustain a conspiracy of this magnitude for any great length of time."

Marc smiled and then looked up at the ceiling as if he were trying to recall something. "Someone once said that history consists of a series of accumulated, imaginative inventions."

"That was Voltaire. Another man with a jaundiced eye for the State."

Marc laughed again. "There is more to you, Mr. Greene, than meets the eye. I am pleased to see it. So what do you think are the real reasons we are involved in this war?"

"I think we got into it out of ideology and a desire to preserve the strategic balance of power in Asia. Unfortunately, I think no one had a firm grasp on what our objectives really were or how they could be achieved or, most importantly, how to get out. We're still in Korea after all. We seem to have an unfortunate tendency to send the cavalry over the hill without first taking a good look at what is on the other side."

"Do you believe a man in my position profits from such a war?"

"Well, I don't know anything about your business. I imagine, though, that the kind of wealth and influence I've seen here tonight was not acquired in the last decade or maybe even in the last century. I know that some men have made fortunes from war. If I were to guess, I would say that war is too unpredictable an enterprise to be a part of your business plan."

Marc leaned back in his chair. "Excellent. You are quite astute, Mr. Greene. Once again the old wisdom proves itself to be true."

"I'm sorry?"

"How do you think individuals become members of our family, Paul?"

"I hadn't really thought about it."

"We do not accept resumes, nor do we comb the world looking for people who may be of service to us. What we do is keep our eyes and ears open. The most important talent a businessman can possess is the ability to recognize and act on opportunities when they appear. This applies to people as well as to financial opportunities. We have found repeatedly that when we recognize a need somewhere in our organization, we shortly find someone with the ability, the character and the ambition to fill it. When we took you off the street that evening, Paul, we had no idea who you were, what kind of a man you were or whether we would ultimately have any interest in you, beyond a purely humanitarian gesture toward someone in obvious trouble. Since then, we have learned a great deal about you. There are a few qualities that our family values above all else. Some of the most important are courage, initiative and loyalty. We find that you possess these qualities to an uncommon degree."

"How would you know that?"

"Well, I think it is quite obvious. Let me briefly summarize the events that have resulted in us sitting together this evening, as I understand them. First of all, you are a man who resides, at least currently, in an environment that is both safe and orderly. Where many, perhaps most men, covet this kind of existence or some similar structure, you flee from it at every opportunity. You come into this city alone, not with the protection of a group or even a friend, and instead of staying safely in the company of the other tourists, you explore some of its darkest corners. You are brutally assaulted by a known killer, and are badly injured, almost losing your life. In spite of your narrow escape, you return and again risk your life in an attempt to save someone you barely know. Would you say this is an accurate portrayal?"

"I'm not as brave as you think."

"Nonsense. You say this because you felt fear when confronted by this killer. You are mistaking the presence of fear for the absence of courage. Nothing could be farther from the truth. Men who have no fear are of no interest to us. Such men are often known to crumble when they are suddenly confronted by circumstances that are not a part of the familiar paradigm of their lives. The man who fears, but is able to act in spite of it, is the kind of man we admire. Moreover, in our conversation this evening, I have found you to be a man who is not afraid to speak his mind, even if he believes his opinions are unpopular or contrary to what might be expected."

"I have no reason to pretend to be anything other than what I am."

"Precisely my point. You have shown yourself, whatever your yet-undiscovered talents may be, to be an uncommon man. We do not succeed by associating ourselves with common men. You are of great interest to us, Paul. As it turns out, there is a valuable service you may provide for us. I understand we have rendered you a favor and that you have agreed to repay us with a service. On a strictly voluntary basis of course."

"Yes, I have." He could feel his muscles clenching again.

"As it happens, you are perfectly placed to help us with a project that is both very interesting to us and potentially very lucrative."

"What do you want me to do?"

"Allow me to explain a little further. I cannot get into the finite details of this enterprise until you have agreed to participate with us. If you do agree, we will welcome you into our membership, and I will explain in detail the project we are involved in. I think you will be intrigued. There will be a small retainer involved and you will enjoy the many benefits of working within our family Of course, we will ask you to sign a non-disclosure agreement to protect any privileged information you may have access to during the course of our service to us. Okay so far?"

"So far."

"In addition to our many commercial enterprises, we work closely with various agencies of the government on projects which are, shall we say, sensitive. We are what is known as a contractor. Often, especially when our client is the Pentagon, we are paid for our services out of what is called the 'black budget', meaning the expenditures are not subject to scrutiny by the congressional budget committees. The congress, and indeed the general public, is kept in the dark on these projects because of the danger that the enemies of this country might find out about them and beat us to the punch, shall we say. These projects are compartmentalized and on a strictly need-to-know basis. Most people assume that everyone in the Pentagon knows everything that is going on. Nothing could be further from the truth. The particular project we are involved in at the moment involves the analysis of certain data by a unique group of individuals we have employed, who possess talents to a large degree not available to the military. At least, not in numbers sufficient to explore our area of interest. We are provided with this data by a project director within the military who, as it turns out, is a high ranking officer stationed at Keesler Air Force base.

"Officially, this project, for the reasons I have stated, is known only to our contacts at the Pentagon and to this officer. The project is related to his command on the base, but is not known by anyone else in his command. Our problem is in finding a secure and reliable way to transport the data from the base to our analysis group here in the city, without the risk of compromising it. The officer in question sometimes delivers the data in person, but he is in a high-profile position and it is not practical or desirable for him to make frequent trips into the city. We tried transmitting the data by commercial courier until some documents were inadvertently lost in transit. They were ultimately recovered, but it alarmed us enough to discontinue that means. Let me stress that none of the documents in question are classified or require a security clearance. When we have completed our analysis, we provide a written report, which then needs to be returned to the officer in question. Do you understand?"

"I think so."

"We would like you to act as a conduit for this information. Would you be willing to be of service to us in this way, at least as a starting point in your relationship with us?"

It was Paul's turn to sit back in his chair. The alarm bells were going off in his head so loudly it was difficult for him to formulate a response. "Why can't this officer just order one of his people to deliver the information?"

"Yes, that would seem the most logical way to proceed. However, as I stated previously, this project is known to this officer alone and, as I am sure you are aware, a high ranking officer does not normally give direct orders for an assignment of this type. It goes down through the chain of command to the appropriate level. Along the way several, perhaps many, individuals become aware of the mission even if they do not know the details. It would raise too many questions to handle the deliveries on a normal mission basis."

Paul was silent for a moment. He studied Marc's face as he tried to formulate a response. "Mr. Francoeur, in spite of my differences with my government over the war, I believe in democracy. I also believe that, despite its flaws, this is the greatest country in the world. I am not willing to do anything that would undermine this government or this democracy, at any price."

"You suspect we are doing something illegal, perhaps even an act of espionage?"

"It could look that way."

"Did you take notice of the kinds of individuals we have entertained here tonight? You told me that you believed human beings were too incompetent to manage a conspiracy of any size for very long, did you not? Do you imagine that, were we inclined to be involved in some sinister plot against the government of this country, we would be able to interact so openly with such a group of powerful individuals? Or do you suppose these officials are our co-conspirators?"

"I don't know. It could be a perfect cover for you."

"Let me ask you this then. If I were to give you, let us say one million dollars to start a business of any kind you choose, where would you start your business?"

"In this country, or perhaps in Switzerland if my profits were extremely large."

He smiled. "And why is that?"

"Because all things being considered, including corporate tax rates, I believe it would be most profitable to do here."

"Why would you not choose some other place? For instance, a totalitarian regime such as the USSR? In such a place you may well be able to, by means of certain well-placed bribes, avoid not only taxes, but also certain barriers to free enterprise such as labor and environmental laws."

Paul thought for a moment. "Well, there is an old saying: 'He who rides a tiger, dare not dismount'."

"I know this adage well. Tell me how you think it applies in this case."

"Meaning that once you begin to pay people to operate illegally, the line of people you need to pay off tends to lengthen in proportion to your success. Operating outside of the law also deprives one of its protection."

"You are correct, Mr. Greene. That is why our businesses are located strictly within the borders of this country and other democratic countries around the world even though we have interests in over one hundred nations with every type of government. You told me a few minutes ago that you did not imagine my family was making a profit from the war. That is not entirely true. We have interests in certain manufacturers whose fortunes have improved as the war has escalated. I will tell you, however, that for our long term interests world-wide, the best circumstance is one of overall peace and prosperity where goods, services, money and ideas are freely traded. It has always been this way throughout time. Wars have never been entirely profitable events for our family. Sometimes they result in improved opportunities and sometimes they are necessary to ensure opportunities continue to be available. Also, often the best scientific and engineering minds are employed by the military simply because of their ability to pay. Many advancements in commercial technology have come as a result of research originally intended to find better ways to kill people or to keep them from being killed. We have been able to benefit from these technologies when we have been wise enough to exploit them before others have done so. Like you, Mr. Greene, we appreciate democracy and in particular the brand of democracy practiced here in the United States. It is flawed to be sure, and I will admit to you that we sometimes make use of those flaws to our advantage, as many large corporations do. We, however, have never and will never act contrary to the interest of the United States and have foregone millions of dollars in potential profits because of our unwillingness to do so."

He paused for a moment to let the point sink in.

"Allow me to reiterate. None of the documents you would be handling are classified. What is sensitive about this project is not the data itself, but the attempt to make civilian use of a military technology. It is only sensitive because, until we have proven the feasibility, we, and our friends in the Pentagon, do not want to come under budget scrutiny or congressional constraints. This is a pilot project, Paul, and there is as yet no proof of its viability. None of us wish to expose the project until we have proven its worth. Finally, before you suspect us of perpetrating an act of espionage, I would ask if you are familiar with the history of espionage against this country?"

"Not in any detail."

"Everyone, without exception, who has studied these cases has come to the same conclusion. Which is that the perpetrators of these crimes have done so for what amounts to pocket change. Sometimes it is done for ego, sometimes for a grievance, real or perceived, and often by agents planted by the opposition. In terms of financial gain, however, I can assure you that this family has made more money while we have been sitting here chatting, than all of the spies in the history of the world. The project I am speaking with you about is worth billions of dollars not just to us, but to the economy of the United States as a whole. It represents an unprecedented leap into the future. But I do understand your reticence; in fact, I would have been disappointed in you had you not raised these issues. Please, do this for me. Take as long as you wish to think about it. If you decide in the end that you are not comfortable with it, we will part company and there will be no further contact between us. I would only ask that you keep our conversation tonight private. I believe you have the personal integrity to agree to this."

"Certainly."

Marc stood up and offered his hand. "I will wish you a good evening and, again, my thanks for joining us tonight. Let me just say that our need is urgent. Please inform us as soon as you are able, of your decision. If you decide to join us, I will meet with you again and give you the details of this project to the extent I am able. I assure you, you will be amazed."

Paul started to leave and then he hesitated. "Could I ask you one more question?"

"Of course."

"How do you really know that you want someone like me in your organization? After all, aside from our conversation here tonight and what Katherine has told you, what do you really know about me?"

"I can assure you, Paul, that we know a great deal about you, even the name of the dog you kept as a pet when you were in elementary school."

Katherine was waiting for him when he left the room. Paul was still in shock and it showed. She did not ask him how it went.

"I am sorry, Paul. I have some additional business to attend to this evening, and I cannot accompany you to the apartment. Vincent will drop you off. Please do not be angry with me for this. I did very much enjoy your company this evening."

"Of course," he said, trying to hide his disappointment.

"May I join you for breakfast again tomorrow morning? Shall we say at nine?"

He brightened up at the suggestion. "Sure, that would be great."

"Very well, then, I will say goodnight." She reached up and kissed him on the cheek.

* * *

After the guests departed and Paul had returned to the apartment, Katherine joined Marc in his office. It had been a good evening and they were both pleased with the way things had gone. Quickly, the conversation came around to Paul.

"So what did you think of him?"

"I was quite surprised. He is not as innocent as I supposed. I found him to be quite intelligent and well informed. I liked him actually. He obviously has courage, but I would say he is a bit reckless. I have no doubt he could be trusted to do the job, and I think he has the nerve for it."

"Yes, he is interesting, if a bit naïve."

"That has worked in our favor in this case. He is obviously smitten with you. Do you think he will agree to our proposition?"

"I think that he will. He is a searcher, and he feels stifled in his current circumstances. I believe the project will appeal to his spirit of adventure."

"Do not press him on it. As before, we should let him come to us. I believe he is attracted enough to you to take a risk. We will give it two weeks. If he has not come to us by then, we will discuss our next approach."

* * *

Eugene rousted him out of bed at eight.

"Up, up, you lazy man. How can you even think about sleeping when that goddess is going to be here in an hour? I would have been up hours ago, just fixing my hair."

Paul was starting to enjoy Eugene. Even with him, things were not really as they seemed. Paul had begun to recognize that he was playing a caricature of himself. He was sure that he was not just there to change the linens and cook. Paul played along with him.

"Well, Eugene, your hair is so much more elegant than mine."

Eugene struck a pose in the doorway. "I'll bet you say that to all the boys."

Once again Katherine arrived exactly on the hour. Paul found it a little unnerving how precise everything seemed to be with these people. Like somehow they were part of the clockwork mechanism of the universe. Nothing seemed to be left to chance. Eugene served another flawless breakfast. Afterward Paul sat drinking his coffee, content just to be sitting at the same table with Katherine. She broke the silence.

"I must tell you your conversation with Marc went extraordinarily well last night. He is quite impressed with you. He asked me to convey to you again that he would be very pleased to have you join us. I can tell you that it is not everyone who impresses him so thoroughly or so quickly. You have done well, and I'm very pleased."

"Pleased for you or pleased for me?"

"Both. I told you, Paul, I like you very much. I would feel a loss if you did not decide to join us."

"Does he really know the name of my dog?"

She laughed. "If he says he knows this name, you may be sure it is true. Marc does not make idle statements. Have you given it any more thought?"

"I have thought about nothing else since last night. I barely slept. I just wish I knew more about your organization and what it is involved in."

"I can only tell you that we do much good in the world and that we are welcomed wherever we go. Marc is the kindest man I have ever known. The family has intervened at its own expense, and on many occasions, to alleviate famine and poverty in many parts of the world."

"Do you know anything about the project he was talking about?"

"I know nothing about this, and I have no desire to know. If I did, I would not discuss it with you or anyone else."

"Why?"

"My position with the family is a vulnerable one in that I must interact frequently with individuals who are not family members. For my own protection, and for the protection of the family, I am told very little about sensitive projects we may be involved in."

"So what does it mean to be a member of the family?"

"It is wonderful, Paul. I am sure Marc explained that you will receive a stipend. Not a large one to start but still, considering your current circumstances, I am sure it will be welcomed. In addition, you will have the use of this place whenever you are in the city, although the master bedroom may, on occasion, be unavailable. If you are in need of transportation or assistance related to your project, you will have a number to call, any time of the day or night. If you are in trouble, for any reason, help will be provided."

"So what happens when the project is ended?"

"You will still be a member of the family. You will not be paid unless you are involved in a project, but you will have access to everything I have explained to you as long as you remain with us. You may be asked to participate in events like the dinner last evening or to meet with certain individuals who may be of interest to us. You will be evaluated periodically and more projects will be assigned to you as befitting your competence and performance. Your circumstance is a little different because you have a commitment to the military for a period of time. It may be that we cannot provide you with an immediate project when this one is complete, but we will attempt to do so. When you have discharged your duty, it should be possible to increase your involvement with us. I have seen individuals rise very quickly in the family. The higher you go, the better the financial rewards and opportunities. I am sure Marc explained that we are almost everywhere in the world. In every country where we maintain a presence, there are places like this one where you will be welcomed without question. Help is available nearly anywhere in the world if it is needed."

"What would I be doing exactly, I mean after this project?"

"It is hard to say. A lot will depend on your talents and initiative. You are not uncomfortable in a social situation and you seem to be able to find common ground with strangers engaging you in conversation. This is a skill of its own."

"And what about you?"

"What about me?"

"How will I interact with you?"

"I can't say for certain. It depends upon the needs of the family."

"But you will not be involved with my project?" Paul asked.

"No, I will not."

"So how often will I be able to see you?"

"Again, I can't say. I am very busy with my responsibilities."

"Don't you get any time off?"

"Of course."

"Will you go out with me now and then?"

"Of course, we can meet socially from time to time, Paul, but as I told you last night, I am not available in the sense that you mean."

"Are you his lover?"

"Who, Marc?"

"Yes."

"No, of course not. I have known Marc since I was a little girl. He is a father to me. Please do not suggest this again."

"I'm sorry, I didn't mean to offend you."

"I forgive you. But my personal life is my own. Perhaps if we get to know each other better I will tell you more, but not now." She reached out and took his hand. "Please consider the offer Marc has made to you, Paul. I would regret it if I never could see you again."

- 11 -

Ernesto could not believe how different things were in America. The people he was living with were poor. But even poor people in America had things no Cuban could even dream about. When he was allowed out, he could spend hours just walking through the stores or looking at the new cars on the street. The French Quarter reminded him of Havana but he was not permitted a lot of time in the city. Not until the hand-off was completed. He missed his mother and his sisters, but he knew he would not be going back. Not of his own free will, in any case. Also there was Anna. He had decided that Anna would be his wife, in spite of the fact that he had no job and nothing to give her. Those things would come to him, he knew. He had taken the risk, and soon would come the reward.

Finally, on a Saturday afternoon, when he returned from a soccer match with Hector, Ramón gave them the news. The hand-off would be this night.

"I will pick you up at nine o'clock, Ernesto. Make sure you are ready."

"I am coming, too," Hector said.

"No, Hector, there are only to be two of us. The instructions are very clear."

"What difference does it make, Ramón? Besides, what if you get lost or something. Ernesto does not know his way around."

"I will not get lost, Hector. You know I have done this before. You worry too much."

"Perhaps, but we three came here all the way from Texas together. I want to be with you to celebrate when the mission is finished."

Ramón looked at him for a minute, shaking his head.

"I would like Hector to come also," Ernesto said.

"Well, I suppose it doesn't matter. Still I think when we get to the place, you should stay in the car so that they do not suspect anything is unusual."

They left after dark in Ramón's car. He had the top down and salsa playing on the radio. Their spirits were high. Hector told Ernesto to stay low in the back, at least until they got out of the neighborhood, in case anyone was following. Ernesto lay on the back seat, looking up at the stars and clutching the backpack to his chest. He felt as though he were back on the boat again, where it had all started. But now he had finally reached the end of his mission, and he could at last unburden himself of this thing that had felt like a chain around his ankle since he left his island. The ride was long and, in a while, he slept.

He was awakened by a loud noise and the sound of Hector screaming. He looked up and saw Ramón had fallen over and was leaning against Hector's arm. There was blood all over Hector's face. Before he could utter a sound, the car swerved violently and flipped over several times before coming to rest against a tree. He only remembered flying through the air and landing on his back in a field next to the road. The wind was knocked out of him, and he could not speak. He managed to roll over on his stomach, but he could not stand. He looked back toward the road. In the spill of the headlights he could see some men were pulling Ramón and Hector from the car. Ramón was not moving, but Hector was struggling with them. The men were hitting him and shouting questions at him. Finally, they threw him to the ground next to Ramón, and he heard two rapid gunshots and saw the muzzle flashes.

They moved to Ramón, who was still not moving, and shot him two times as well. Ernesto wanted to scream, but no sound would come. Then the men started searching the area around the car, making wider and wider circles. Someone came toward him and his agony turned to terror. The man was sweeping the ground with a flashlight. In a few seconds he would be right on top of him. Suddenly the man stopped and stooped to the ground. As he did so Ernesto saw his face. He was an American with short blond hair and large, strong looking hands. Ernesto closed his eyes and started to pray silently. The man stood up, holding the backpack. Ernesto had forgotten all about it. He started to yell, but the sound caught in his throat. He knew they would kill him, too. The man walked back to the road. Another man approached the bodies of Ramón and Hector. He was holding a knife. He ripped open their shirts and then bent over them with the blade. Everything went black.

* * *

He awoke some time later. It was dark by the road now and the men were gone. He could no longer see the bodies of his friends. He managed to get to his feet and stumble out to the road. His friends lay dead beside the mangled car. They had something carved on their chests. The backpack was gone. He did not know where he was or how to get back to the people he knew. He sat on the road with his head buried in his hands and cried. After a few minutes, he began to think more clearly, and he thought he should get away from the area. The men who attacked them must not have known he was in the car, but they might come back, he thought. He stood up and tried to straighten himself up a little. His back hurt badly, but he was not bleeding, and he was able to walk. He started to walk down the road from the direction they had come, but then he stopped and returned to the bodies of his friends. He reached under Hector's body and found his wallet still in the back pocket of his jeans.

"I am sorry, Hector, my brother, but you will not need this now, and I must have it to survive. May God take you and Ramón to be with him in heaven."

Inside the wallet were Hector's driver's license and some money. Ernesto hoped he would be able to pass for Hector if he was asked for identification. He continued down the road, jumping into the underbrush twice to avoid being seen by passing cars. Finally, he heard sirens and he went into the woods and waited until the police cars and ambulance sped by. He stayed just inside the woods and moved as quickly as he could until he came to the edge of a small town. He walked down the sidewalk trying not to appear injured. *I must find a telephone*, he thought, although he was not sure there would be a phone number in Hector's wallet.

At the end of the first block he came to a Sinclair gas station and there was a taxicab at the pump. He walked over to the driver and asked if he was for hire. The driver asked to see his money. Ernesto showed him a twenty-dollar bill and got into the back seat. More police cars sped by with their sirens blaring. When the driver got behind the wheel, Ernesto gave him the address on Hector's license.

When Ernesto showed up alone in a taxi, everyone knew something had gone terribly wrong. They took him inside immediately. Anna became hysterical when Ernesto told them what had happened. Maria buried her face in her hands and cried quietly. He felt guilty that he had not been killed instead of Hector. Anna would not look at him. Some phone calls were made and they took him to his room and told him to rest until it was decided what to do. They offered him food and something to drink, but he could not touch anything. When he was alone in the room he slumped onto the bed. He was exhausted from the trauma and grieving for the loss of his friends. He wondered what would become of him now. After a while he heard a soft knock on the door and Anna came in. She just stared at him, crying, and he went over and held her to him.

"I am so sorry, Anna. I wish that it was me and not Hector who was killed. It should have been me. It is my fault."

"It is not your fault, Ernesto. I am glad that you were not also killed."

They sat on the bed, holding each other for a long while.

"Don't take any more risks like this, Ernesto. I could not stand to lose you, too."

"I don't know what will happen now, Anna. I must do as they tell me."

"Why? You are here now. You have done enough. What happened has happened and it cannot be changed. There is nothing more for you to do."

"We will see, Anna."

She stood and looked at him angrily. "You stupid men, with your secrets and your killing. What has it done for anyone? What good is it?"

"I have killed no one, Anna."

She looked at him angrily for a moment and then stormed out of the room. Ernesto lay down again and finally sleep took him. He was awakened later in the evening by a knock on the door. A woman he did not recognize told him to come downstairs, someone had come to see him. He ran his fingers through his hair and straightened out his clothes. There were three men whom he had never met before. Two of them were older, and Ernesto recognized right away that these were hard men. One had a long scar down the side of his face from a blow that had just missed his eye. The eyelid was pulled down from having been stitched and from the side he appeared to be sleeping. The other one did not have visible scars, but his face was like a piece of stone. They were both dark skinned and short in stature, but with strong shoulders and arms. The third stood in the doorway and was apparently there to make sure they were not disturbed. Ernesto wondered for a second if they had come to kill him for his failure. Anna and Maria were gone. The one with the scar spoke to him.

"I am Vicente and this is Arturo. You have not met us before, Ernesto, but we are they who sent Ramón and Hector to meet you when you arrived from Mexico and who arranged for your mission."

Ernesto almost broke down at the sound of their names. "I am sorry, senor, for what has happened. I don't understand it."

"It is all right, Ernesto, you are not at fault. None of us blame you for what has happened. We are happy you have returned to us. Happy that you were not killed, but also we hope you can tell us what happened. Please start at the beginning and try to remember everything you can."

He told them how Ramón had met him and Hector after the soccer game and told them that the hand-off would happen this night. How Ramón had come by after dark and picked them up.

"Why did Hector go with you?"

"I don't know. We have become friends. I think he wanted to protect me."

"Where were you sitting in the car?"

"I was in the back seat. Hector told me to stay low."

"Si. Normally we send two men only on a mission such as this. One who carries the documents and one who drives. The only reason you are not also dead is that they did not see you in the back seat of the car. Please continue."

They listened intently, and he could see the anger burning within them. When he told them about the large, blond man who had retrieved the backpack, Arturo stood up and kicked his chair across the room. Ernesto was startled.

"It was him, then. We thought it to be the pigs of Castro, but it was this Americano. The one who was to purchase the list from us. I knew he was not to be trusted. Let us find him and kill him now. We must kill him tonight."

The one with the scar spoke now and his voice was calm. "We will kill him, Arturo, but let us think for a moment what has happened. The Americano and his expensive friends do not need this list for themselves. They led us to believe they would be making the document available to the American intelligence services. Perhaps they have received a better offer. What if the DGI was willing to pay much more for the list? We can be sure they would want it badly. No?"

"But why kill us?" Arturo asked. "The money was not so great. We only wanted the names to be known."

"Perhaps because they did not want their friends from the CIA to know they had the list so that they could give it to Castro's pigs for more money."

Arturo slammed his fist against the wall. "It doesn't matter now. Let us find him and kill him."

"Be calm, Arturo. You will have your revenge, but perhaps all is not lost. You have seen the big house where the Americans live with their big cars and their fat horses. It is quite likely they will take the list there."

"So let us gather our people and take what is ours and burn them to the ground."

"You are not thinking clearly, Arturo. Would it not be better if we could find out who they are selling the list to, and perhaps have a chance to get our property back and to kill also the ones who would buy it from them?"

Arturo was silent. "Let us tie a bell on the tail of this man Taylor and see where he goes."

"We do not know if he lives at the big house, Vicente."

"This is true, but we can guess that the list has gone there this evening and will stay there until arrangements are made. If we watch the house, sooner or later Senor Taylor will appear. Once he does, we will become his sombra. I think we will not have to wait long." He turned. "Ernesto, you have done well. Are you willing to help us retrieve our property and bring justice to those who have killed your friends?"

"Si, Vicente. I will do anything."

"I want you to go with Arturo to watch the big house. We want to make sure the man you saw was this Taylor, even though we are already convinced of it. Will you do this?"

"Yes, gladly, Vicente."

"Arturo we will need two more cars and of course, the radios. You and Ernesto will wait near the big house until Taylor appears. You will only tell us which way his car goes when he exits the driveway. He must not see you, Arturo."

"He will not see me."

"He will pass one of our cars whichever way he turns and then we will alternate so that he does not see the same car behind him. Whenever he stops, one team will remain with his car and the other will follow him on foot. I will make sure we have enough people to keep fresh eyes with him. We must not lose him. Sooner or later he will lead us to who buys the list."

- 12 -

If it had not been for Katherine, he would have just walked away. Of course they knew that. Even after she had warned him that she would not be his lover, he could not turn away. The sound of the last words she had said echoed in his consciousness: "I would regret it if I could never see you again." He couldn't stand the thought of it. Everything that Marc had told him seemed real enough. This was no sinister organization hiding from public view. He considered the people he had met and what the colonel had said about the family. Anyway, he thought, he had told Marc he would not do anything illegal and if it turned out that was what they wanted, he would refuse, no matter what the cost. By mid-week he couldn't stand it any more, and he called Katherine from the base. She seemed overjoyed to hear that he had decided to accept the offer. She told him that Marc would meet with him on the following Saturday morning. She also asked when and where he would like to rendezvous with their driver. There would be no more hitch-hiking into the city. It had begun.

Paul arrived at the house on Barracks Street at eight. Eugene made breakfast for him and then departed. Paul waited in the sitting room. It was a stormy morning, which did nothing to ease his anxiety. The limo arrived and Katherine came in to get him. She seemed detached, which made him feel even worse. She told him that Marc was waiting outside, and she would catch up with him later in the day. The thought of spending the day with her made him feel a bit better. Marc was waiting in the limo and greeted Paul warmly. The car pulled away and he watched the now familiar streets glide by. Marc asked if his study of history had acquainted him with the ancient Celts.

"Not really. My recollection is that they didn't believe in writing down their history. From what I remember, they had priests who kept a verbal record of their history, and recited it at gatherings. I think a lot of what we know about them is taken from accounts from other cultures, like the Romans."

"Yes, that's true. And it is also true that history is written by the conquerors, not the conquered. The Celtic culture is poorly understood."

The car stopped at a pier on the river. A large freighter was sliding by silently, running toward the Gulf. Paul wished he were on it. The feeling inside the limo was decidedly oppressive, and he was very uncomfortable. The rain was pelting the back windshield. He had to fight the desire to open the door and run.

"So, you have decided to join us. I am pleased. You will not regret it."

Paul didn't respond. He just wanted Marc to tell him everything that could possibly go wrong and how he would magically make it right. Instead, he removed some documents from a brief case and handed them to Paul.

"Do you have questions or some reservations, perhaps?"

"I have to admit I am uncomfortable with the idea of acting as a courier of information that I know nothing about and that could potentially land me in a lot of trouble."

"I assure you that you have nothing to worry about. After I have explained everything to you this morning, I think your mind will be put at ease."

"I hope so."

"This is the nondisclosure agreement I mentioned, as well as a contract outlining your general duties and responsibilities to the family. It also includes your salary and the benefits you will be entitled to. Please take your time and read them before you sign. If you do not want to read them in the car, you may wait until we get to my office. These papers do not obligate you to do anything except to keep what you are about to learn an absolute secret. You may speak of it to no one except me or someone I may designate for you to communicate with. Can you agree to this at least?"

"Yes, I can do that."

"If, after I have explained everything to you, you decide not to accept this assignment, we will part company as friends. The employment agreement will be destroyed, but for obvious reasons you will continue to be bound by the non-disclosure agreement. It is open ended. I reiterate, you may never speak of this to anyone."

Paul took the documents and began reading them. There was the usual fine print but he didn't see anything that seemed out of line. He noticed that his weekly starting salary was more that what he made in a month as a staff sergeant. The documents specifically stated that no activities on behalf of the family would be required if they would interfere with his duties associated with his current military assignment. In any case, he wasn't worried about the terms of the agreement. He was worried that there could be something sinister going on, and he would be pulled right into the middle of it. In the end he knew there was no way for him to tell for sure. He signed the documents and returned them to Marc. They shook hands and Marc said, "Welcome to our family. A new world is about to open up for you."

At the office, Paul sat across the table from Marc. Somehow the room did not feel as comfortable as it had at the dinner party. The light coming in from the window behind Marc seemed harsh and Paul shivered involuntarily. His heart was pounding and he tried to calm himself.

"What I am about to tell you, Paul, and to some degree show you, is very sensitive information. I tell you this not to alarm you, but as further evidence that we are working with individuals at the highest level of our military and intelligence apparatus. The agency we are working for does not even officially exist. I must reiterate that the project we have undertaken is ancillary to the primary intelligence gathering function of this program. Other than our knowledge regarding what the project is and what the end product consists of, we do not have access to any classified information nor do we wish to be so involved. Do you understand?

"I think so."

Marc removed a file from a drawer in his desk and opened it. He withdrew several large, black and white photographs from the folder and placed one in front of Paul. "Do you know what this is?"

Paul studied it. "It's an aerial photograph of some kind."

"What do you see in it?"

"Well, it looks like a backyard in a suburban development somewhere. I can see a house with a pool and what looks like a garden. There is something that might be a table also."

"What if I told you that this photograph was not taken by an airplane, but by a camera orbiting in a satellite more than one hundred miles above the earth?"

"I would say that's incredible."

"Incredible indeed, but nonetheless true. There are only a handful of people who are aware of this technology. Let me give you some background. You no doubt recall the shooting down of our U2 spy plane over the Soviet Union nearly ten years ago. It represented a setback to our intelligence-gathering capabilities, but not as great as the general public, and even the congress, believed at the time. Do you recall the early Discoverer space missions? The ones that shot mice into space and were purported to be life-science missions to prepare for manned space flight?"

"Sure."

"Well, that was largely a cover story. What those missions were really designed to do was to take detailed photographs of the USSR, China and other nations to help determine their military strength and to conduct a rational risk assessment for the Pentagon. This was done, is being done, with a highly sophisticated camera or pairs of cameras with incredible resolution. The first cameras could photograph objects on the order of thirty-five or forty feet. Enough to make out ships, missile installations and large troop concentrations. The current versions can see objects as small as six to ten feet and the technology is improving almost yearly. Soon you will be able to see not only the people sitting at that table but also what they are eating."

He paused to let it sink in.

"The major drawback to date has been the need to send the film back to earth to be developed. C119 and C130 aircraft pluck these capsules out of midair upon reentry. It is an impressive display of piloting, but it is by no means a perfect system. I'm sure you have seen one or two of these missions on the television, although you did not know the real purpose, until now. We have been told that in the near future there will be a way to develop the film on board and send the images back to the earth by encrypted radio signals. The first dozen or so flights of this mission were failures, but eventually they solved all of the technical problems. The first successful mission gathered more film of the Soviet Union than all of the previous U2 flights combined. Over 3000 feet of film. That mission alone mapped more than 1.5 million square miles of the Soviet Union. Later missions recorded much more territory. It is safe to assume we now have photographs of every square kilometer of the USSR."

"That's unbelievable."

"Indeed. And there is much more information that has been gathered using this technology, but will not be revealed to us."

"Okay, but I don't understand why you would be provided with this information."

"Yes, that is the next piece of the story and, oddly enough, it involves a bit of a philosophical discussion."

"Philosophical? That word doesn't really seem to fit in this conversation."

"Ah, but it does, very much so. You see, Paul, there are differences of opinion, at the highest levels of our government, as to what constitutes national security. There is no argument that our military strength needs to be such that no nation in the world could hope to successfully challenge us. There are many, however, including myself, who believe that national security is even more dependent on economic security. The other night we talked about this family and whether we profit from war. I told you that as a rule we do not. There are, in fact, wars going on in various places of the world almost continuously. It is disruptive to commerce and occasionally economically disastrous to entire nations. For the United States to be secure requires more than a military advantage. It requires an economic advantage. The technology I have introduced you to represents not only a quantum leap in military capability. The commercial possibilities are breathtaking. I do not think I am exaggerating when I say that this technology will eventually revolutionize nearly every area of the world economy. The country that is able to exploit the commercial possibilities first will have an advantage that cannot be overstated."

"I guess I don't see how that could work."

"Don't feel badly. It requires some background and some extremely flexible thinking to see it. Let me show you some more photographs." He removed two more photographs from the folder and handed them to Paul. "What do you see in those pictures?"

"Nothing, really. It just looks like an empty field. Actually, by this stream running along the top corner, it appears to be two pictures of the same field, maybe taken at different times."

"Exactly. Now compare the photographs and tell me what is different."

Paul studied them for a while. "I don't really see anything except that maybe one shows the field before it was harvested."

"Actually, those pictures were taken about one year apart at the same time of the year. What they show is a wheat field, with and without a sufficient amount of rainfall."

"How can you be sure it is the same field?"

"You see the numbers and letters down in the right hand corner of the photographs? Those numbers indicate the exact latitude and longitude of the reference mark on the photo, as well as the date and time the image was taken. They are encrypted so that you cannot tell what they are."

"If it is the same field, why are the numbers different on the two photos?"

"A random code key is used. You need to have access to the proper equipment to decipher the code."

"Okay. So of what use are the photographs?"

"You are probably aware that the Soviet Union is the single largest importer of the US wheat crop, in years when their own crop has failed."

"No, I didn't know that."

"It is the case. The question for our agriculture industry is how much wheat will the Soviet Union purchase from us this year. Up until now it was anybody's guess. Let us say a farmer has six hundred acres. His problem is how much to sow in wheat, how much in corn, how much in soybeans, let us say. It is, for him, not an academic exercise. He must make a decision and purchase seed based on his guess. If he is wrong and, let us say, has planted entirely in wheat in a year when the wheat crop in the USSR is bountiful, there will be too much wheat on the market and prices will fall. He will not make enough money to cover his costs. Now we have a means to let him know in advance, to a much higher degree of accuracy, how he should allocate his fields."

"So all of this top secret business is about helping farmers?"

Marc laughed. "No, that is only one small example, although you should not underestimate the size of the agricultural component of the US economy. With this technology, we can see open pit mines, algae blooms in fisheries, weather systems and storms at sea, the extent of the polar ice caps, ship yards, power plants and manufacturing facilities under construction, to name just a few. Scientists are working on ways to identify mineral deposits under the ground by means of high-altitude photography. With astute analysis the information is invaluable. In the future there will be commercial satellites able to provide this information. Today, the only such assets belong to the military."

"So the military is photographing fields for you?"

Marc laughed again. "In a way, yes. As I mentioned, the first successful mission for this technology covered more than one-point-five million square miles of the Soviet Union. The satellite is moving extremely fast, around 17,000 miles per hour.

It is not possible to take one photograph of a small area of interest. The camera is turned on, and a ten-mile wide strip of geography, 120 miles long, is captured on film. Perhaps one-half-of-one percent of that film footage is of interest to our military or shows any kind of strategic or military installations. The remainder of the film is destroyed. Fortunately for us and for this country, there are those involved in this project who immediately grasped the commercial potential of this technology. There was great debate at the highest levels as to whether this aspect should be explored. The idea was largely tabled primarily because of the fear of revealing the capabilities of the technology, but also because the intelligence apparatus was not about to assign highly qualified photo analysis personnel to, as you say, look at wheat fields. It was agreed eventually that a pilot project using a trusted outside technical source, and making available only those images that did not reveal the resolution of the cameras, would be permitted."

"And you are that source?" Paul asked.

"One of our businesses has been involved in aerial photographic interpretation for many years. Many of our analysts are ex-military. As you can imagine, a lot of this expertise was developed during recent wars using aircraft of various kinds. There have been commercial applications as well. We have often taken on projects for the military that were, let us say, not of sufficient urgency to involve the intelligence agencies, but of interest nonetheless."

"So who is purchasing the analysis from you?"

"No one. At this moment, we are performing the analysis and providing reports back to the intelligence agency that has contracted with us. We receive an adequate amount of money for our services."

"It hardly seems like it would be worthwhile for you, although I guess you're gambling that this thing will take off and you'll make a lot of money from it in the future."

"An interesting choice of words. Whether or not we eventually become involved in the commercial analysis of this information as a business will depend on our cost benefit analysis of that opportunity. We are, however, already making a good deal of money on it."

"How?"

"Have you ever heard of the futures market?"

"Sure."

"Do you know how it operates?"

"Vaguely."

"Let us just say that the technology we are working with gives us an analytical tool in this market place that no one else in the world has at this time, nor is likely to have for many years. I would like to mention one other point to you, Paul, concerning this project and our family. We do not involve ourselves in projects like this for profits alone. As a family we are interested in the advancement of civilization as a whole. We seek and attempt to facilitate a transition for mankind into a new era, one in which there is no more need for war, and where goods and services trade freely around the globe. We seek the end of poverty and deprivation and the subjugation of the weak by the strong and wealthy. When we find an opportunity to advance this aim, we pursue it, even in many cases if it is not profitable for us in financial terms."

Paul was silent for a few moments. Marc returned the file to his desk and then came around and sat next to him.

"You must have some questions."

"Tell me what my part in this will be."

"It is very simple, really. You will be contacted when a package is ready to be delivered. You will be instructed where and when to pick it up on the base. Let me interject here that you may open the package at any time and examine the contents if you wish to reassure yourself that the contents are as I have described. I only ask that you do this in a safe place where there is no likelihood that someone may see the contents and, of course, that you take the utmost care not to lose or damage any of the contents. We will try to have the package ready for pickup at the end of the week, preferably Friday afternoon so that you only need to be in possession of it overnight. This may not always be possible. There will not be a package every week. When you are in possession of the package we expect that it will be kept in a secure area. Can this be arranged?"

"Well, I have a locker. No one has ever tried to break into it."

"That should suffice as long as you insure it is kept locked. Once you have received the package, you will contact us at a number I will give you. Use a pay phone; do not call from your duty station phone. You will arrange for a pickup. Since hitchhiking into the city has been your custom, you will continue to do this, however you will wait at a designated location and obviously not accept a ride from anyone while you are waiting for your transportation. At the time of your call, you will be told the make, model and color of the car that will be picking you up. It will not always be the same. The car will drive you to the apartment. You will leave the package on the seat when you exit. That will be the end of your duties unless we have a report for you to return to the base. If there is a report to be returned, it will be given to you when you are picked up at the apartment on Sunday. You will be given instructions on when and how it is to be dropped off. Do you understand these instructions?"

"Yes."

"Do you have questions?"

"What would happen if, for some reason, I were stopped with the package and required to show it to someone?"

"There should be no reason for this to happen, but should it happen for any reason, your cover story is simply that you are studying to take your pilot's exam and that part of the test involves identifying ground features on aerial photographs, which by the way it does. It is one of the more difficult parts of the test in fact. Only a very highly skilled photo interpreter could tell the difference between these photos and those taken from an airplane."

"Suppose the package is confiscated for some reason?"

"Again, I don't foresee this happening, but if it does, you will contact us as soon as you are able and advise us of the situation. You will be given instructions, depending on the circumstances. If for any reason, you are unable to get off the base as a result of your duties, you will call us. We will give you instructions to drop off the package at a safe location on the base, where it will be held until you are free to make the delivery. Keep in mind that although these materials are very important to us, we are not working under any kind of time constraints. This is only a pilot project to assess the value of this kind of intelligence for commercial use."

"How long do you expect this project to continue?"

"It is open-ended at the present time. My best guess is that we will need another six months to a year to have enough information to justify a decision."

Paul nodded.

"Do you have any more concerns?"

"None that I can think of at the moment."

"I will ask you then if you will agree to accept this assignment?"

Paul didn't answer right away. He looked Marc in the eye, trying to see if there was any hint of deceit there. He saw none. "Yes, I will accept it."

Marc reached over to him and shook his hand. "Then I will say again, welcome to our family. May it be a rewarding experience for all of us."

- 13 -

The man with the beret and the neatly trimmed goatee did not look out of place on the bus. He sat in the back and read his newspaper, occasionally glancing out of the back window. Two hours earlier, dressed in his suit, he had taken a cab from his apartment to the zoo where he spent an hour watching the children ride on the backs of the big turtles. To any casual observer, he was just a kindly old man enjoying a sunny afternoon. The St. Charles Street trolley took him back to Canal Street where he visited several stores. He purchased a pair of slacks and a light jacket and changed in the dressing room. Leaving by a rear exit, he stopped at a dry cleaner and dropped off his suit. By the time he boarded the bus, it was nearly noon. After a dozen stops, he was satisfied that he had not been followed. He exited by the rear door and, after walking two blocks, hailed another cab to take him back to the city. He told the driver he wanted the Café du Monde.

His thoughts took him back to the revolution - living in the jungle camps, sometimes even sitting with Fidel and Che as they discussed the new Cuba that would emerge after their victory. He was not too old to fight in those days, but old enough already to feel the damp ground soaking into his bones in the night. It was ironic, he always thought, that his reward for helping to create a socialist paradise had been exile to these decadent capitalist playgrounds. He did not feel guilty about it. In fact he had come to appreciate the soft beds and the gourmet meals, even if he, too, often had to spend his time in anonymity, living like a refugee.

At a small table under the awning he sat and watched the tourists walking up Decatur Street toward Jackson Square. The women in their short summer dresses with their long beautiful legs were magnificent. *What a shame*, he thought, *that we cannot remain so young. A tragedy that our experience teaches us how to love with so much more skill, at a time when our bodies begin to fail us.* After a while, he opened his newspaper to the business pages and began to peruse the stock tables. By one o'clock the café was completely full. A man came over to his table.

"Would you mind if I sit with you, sir? The café is very crowded today."

He did not look up. "Not at all, please join me."

To anyone watching he had resumed reading his newspaper, while the other man stirred his coffee aimlessly and appeared to be deep in thought.

"I trust you are well, Mr. Taylor."

"Just fine, Eduardo. And you?"

"I am also well. Thank you."

"Do you have news for me?"

"The news is good. My friends have agreed to your proposal."

"Did you bring copies of the contracts?"

"Yes. I will leave them in my newspaper when I depart. Contact me after you have reviewed them. I am sure there will be nothing to surprise you."

"And the down payment?"

"As agreed. I am ready to make the delivery as soon as you give me the word." Taylor removed an envelope from his pocket and placed it on the table. "Here is a small gift for you, Eduardo, as a token of our appreciation for your diligent efforts. It appears my employer will not be attending the function you mentioned at our previous meeting. There is an additional ticket for a beautiful woman of your choice."

"Your employer is most gracious. Please thank him for me. Perhaps he has a beautiful woman in mind to use the additional ticket?"

"Well, Eduardo, that has never seemed to be a problem for you in the past."

"Yes, this is very true. However many of my beauties lack, shall we say, the savoir-faire, to be suitable for such an event."

Taylor laughed. "In my experience, a low-cut gown trumps savoir-faire every time, my friend. Just tell her to lean over a lot."

"So, Mr. Taylor, when will your employer be ready to consummate our agreement?"

"I don't have a firm date yet. It will be soon. I will contact you by the usual means."

Taylor sat back and studied the old man. It was unusual to find someone his age still doing this kind of work. "When are you going to pack it in, Eduardo? I would have thought you would be ready for a nice little house on the beach by now."

"Soon. Perhaps after our current project is successfully completed, it will be time for the Shepherd to retire to the pasture, as they say."

"Back to the island?"

"Perhaps, although I must confess I have become a little too fond of my vices, and here I do not have to work so hard to enjoy them."

"The workers' paradise not all it's cracked up to be, huh?"

"The workers' paradise, Mr. Taylor, is for those who desire to work."

* * *

Vicente and Arturo sat in the front seat of the van parked down the street from the café. They had almost lost Taylor as he circled the area attempting to find a parking spot. As soon as they stopped they had dispatched Juan from the back of the van to follow Taylor on foot. As it turned out, Taylor went into the Café and they could watch him from where they were parked. Arturo had the field glasses and he watched as Taylor purchased a coffee. He followed him as he looked around for an empty table and then headed to a corner off by the sidewalk. Arturo studied him through the glasses, imagining how he would kill him. It would be slow. The Americano will beg for death, he swore it. Suddenly he stiffened and cursed under his breath. Vicente looked over at him.

Arturo was extremely agitated. "Hijo de puta! El Pastor, Vicente. It is him."

"Let me see," he said, snatching the glasses.

"My God, it is him! The Shepherd himself is here. I did not know this snake was among us. And here he sits calmly reading his newspaper, right under our noses. This explains many things."

Arturo opened the glove compartment and took out a large caliber pistol.

"Put that away, Arturo."

"We must take him now, Vicente. How long have we wished for this chance? I can walk by on the street and kill both of them now. In this crowd, with the panic, I can get away."

"You are not thinking, Arturo. Let us watch for a moment and see what transpires. Get on the radio and tell Juan we want to follow the man sitting with

Taylor. The old one with the beard. Make sure he understands."

Arturo picked up the radio and said something in rapid Spanish. "Juan has seen him. He is ready. He asks what about Taylor?"

"He is of no importance now. We must find out where the Shepherd goes."

Vicente continued to watch through the glasses. "The devil has not changed. You would never know how many he had murdered by looking at him. He looks like a school teacher. Wait!"

"What is it, Vicente?"

"The Americano has removed an envelope from his pocket and placed it on the table."

"It must be the list."

"Yes, this is what I think."

"What is happening now?"

"Patience, Arturo, they talk. Yes, and now the envelope falls on the floor. The Shepherd picks it up and places it in his pocket. Tell Juan to be careful he is not seen. Tell him not to use the radio until there is no chance he will be noticed."

Arturo spoke again into the radio. "He will be careful, Vicente. He knows what to do."

"Now, Arturo. He stands. The newspaper remains on the table. The payment must be in the newspaper. He is moving now, Arturo. Tell Juan he is moving."

"Juan has him. He has crossed to the other side of the street. He is standing by the curb. He is looking for a taxi, Vicente."

"Who is with Jose?"

"Only the young one, Ernesto."

"Radio Jose and tell him to pick up Juan and wait for further instructions. We will follow the cab."

"But what of the Americano, Vicente?"

"The Americano can wait a while longer for the machete. Now we have a chance to strike a blow for our countrymen. There will be dancing in the streets when they know that the Shepherd is with the devil."

- 14 -

Paul received the call the next Friday morning at his duty station. He was told to report to personnel where an envelope would be waiting for him at the front desk. He walked over at lunch and just picked it up. No questions asked. It was a normal looking, interoffice mail envelope addressed to his mail stop number. The name of the sender, from the previous user of the envelope had been crossed out, and nothing indicated where the current contents had originated. He stopped and put it into his locker on the way back without taking the time to examine the photographs. He did that in the evening after his roommate went out. It was just as Marc had claimed. He didn't see anything in the pictures except geographical features. There were fourteen photographs in all. The next morning he rose early and walked to the bank of payphones next to the mess hall.

"State your business."

"Yes, this is Paul Greene. I need to arrange a pickup."

"No names. What time?"

"Ten a.m."

"Wait at the bus stop on I-90 in front of the Burger King. Are you familiar with this location?"

"Yes."

"Look for a white Ford sedan with Louisiana plates. There will be a green ball on the top of the aerial. Do you understand?"

"Yes."

"If you are not there, the driver will return to that location every fifteen minutes for one hour. If you are not there after one hour he will terminate and return. If this happens, follow the instructions you have been given."

Paul heard a click on the other end of the line. He waited until nine-thirty and then walked out through the main gate. It took about fifteen minutes to walk to his pick-up point, and he stood by the bench feeling like everyone driving by was staring at him. The car arrived right on time, and he sat in front next to the driver. There were no introductions. Paul attempted to make some small talk, but the driver was not very interested in conversation. After a while, he gave up and just looked out the window. In spite of the now familiar scenery, he felt like he was making the trip for the first time. The thought of the envelope tucked into the gym bag at his feet was like a mosquito buzzing in his ear. There would be no peace of mind until he was rid of it.

They reached the apartment at eleven-thirty and Paul left the envelope on the front seat as instructed. He had been given a key to the place and he let himself in. To his relief, Eugene was not there. He grabbed a beer and sat out in the courtyard next to the pool. The whole thing had gone off like clockwork, and he was beginning to feel a little pleased with himself. He decided to call Katherine.

"Vincent."

"Yes, hello, Vincent, this is Paul Greene."

"Yes, Mr. Greene, how are you?"

"I'm fine, thank you. Is Katherine in this morning?"

"Hold the line please. I will see if she is available."

He waited for a few minutes, before she answered.

"Hello, Paul, how are you?"

"I'm fine. I'm at the apartment. I was wondering if you had any free time today or this evening."

"I'm afraid not. I'm sorry."

"Well, how about tomorrow? I could buy you lunch or something?"

She said nothing for what seemed like a long time. He thought the phone had gone dead.

"Actually, I am busy most of tomorrow as well, but I could come over and have breakfast with you if you like."

"Sure, that would be great."

"I'll be there at nine. I'll contact Eugene and have him prepare something for us."

"Great. I'll see you then."

He felt a rush of anticipation surge through his body. Now all he had to do was find some way to spend the rest of the day. Up until this point, a large part of the weekend had been spent just getting into the city, trying to arrange a place to stay and finding an inexpensive place to eat. Now, suddenly, he not only had all of that taken care of, but a pocket full of money as well. It was a new experience for him. One that was going to take some getting used to. He tried Spencer's phone, but he got the answering machine. He decided to walk over to Baby's and let him know about Lucky.

Baby was raising hell in the kitchen as usual, but when Paul poked his head through the kitchen doors, his whole demeanor changed. He waddled over with a big grin on his face and put his arm around Paul's shoulders.

"Well how you doin', Mr. Paul. I haven't seen you in a while."

"I'm doing great, Baby. I wanted to tell you about Lucky."

He turned serious. "I know. I heard all about it. One of the girls told me. They don't call that girl lucky for nothing. I heard she got beat up pretty bad though."

"Yeah, she was a mess when I saw her, but she is going to be okay. She just needs some time to get well."

"Nobody seems to know what happened to that bad-assed pimp, Jackie Davis, but the word is he left town. Somebody must have scared the crap out of him. In fact, I heard a rumor some tough-as-nails, young, white dude took care of him. I don't guess you know anything about that, though." A smile started to spread across his big fleshy face.

"Who, me? No, I just mind my own business, you know that, Baby."

"Uh huh, I know a lot of things." He laughed. "I also know lunch is on me today. As long as you have the special."

"Which is?"

"Which is the best damned gumbo there ever was."

After lunch he decided to try Spencer again, and this time he picked up the phone.

"Paul, oh yeah, man, where the hell have you been? Listen, I found out some stuff for you. Why don't you come over and I'll fill you in. You remember how do get here, right?"

Paul passed Spencer's girlfriend Audrey on the way up the steps. She didn't seem too pleased but she managed a smile. He hadn't made any kind of connection with Audrey. She was friendly enough, but to her he represented a side of Spencer's life that she had not yet been able to control. Paul hadn't yet approached the top of her 'to do list' though, and she remained polite but uninterested. She was a genuine southern belle, complete with white gloves and a frustrated expectation of civility. They made kind of an odd couple, but it seemed to work on some level. When they were dressed up, they looked like they had just stepped out of the last century. Spencer looked like he had just gotten up.

"You want some coffee? I'm going to make an omelet, how do you like it?"

"No, thanks, Spence, I just had lunch."

"Suit yourself, but I make a killer omelet. It's the only thing I know how to cook. Commodore Spencer Dupree, commander of the egg! Did you catch the countess on your way in?"

"Yeah, she didn't look too happy."

"She's on the rag again. Wanted me to take her shopping. Can you imagine that? Like I have time for that crap."

Paul took a seat at the counter and poured himself a cup of coffee. He started looking through the newspaper. Spencer began chopping some onions. The apartment was decorated in a combination of psychedelic and southern chic. Along with the expensive leather furniture and French ceramics, were day-glo paintings, along with framed and, in some cases, autographed photographs of Jimmy Hendrix, the Doors, the Rolling Stones and a half dozen other rock stars. There were also a lot of signed photographs of Spencer shaking hands with various people that Paul didn't recognize. There was a two-foot tall bong on the coffee table and a bag of pot sitting next to it like it was tobacco.

"Oh, hey, listen to this." Spencer went over to the stereo and put on an album. "This is Neil Young with Crazy Horse. It is some very freaky stuff. Tell me what you think."

It was good background music for the conversation.

"So what did you find out?"

"Well, first of all, I can tell you this is a serious bunch of people, whoever they are. I asked a lot of contacts who should know about a group like this and most of them didn't even want to talk about it. That doesn't happen to me unless people are nervous, you know? The ones who did have something to tell me gave me the 'you didn't hear this from me and if anybody asks me I'll deny it' routine. To make a long story short, I found out a lot just by my sources not wanting to talk about it. I can't verify any of this, but here goes. Supposedly this group, or at least something connected to this group, has been around a very long time, maybe since before Christ. I was right about the symbol, it is Celtic, but not from Ireland or Scotland. It's from central Europe. Apparently this group, or at least the ancestors of this group, kicked the crap out of the Etruscans in Italy and later laid siege to Rome. This is Rome before it started to crumble, sometime back in BC. They scared the Romans so bad that they bought them off with a thousand pounds of gold. Can you imagine that? A thousand pounds. Anyway I looked up the symbol and it is not part of the Celtic alphabet. The Celtic alphabet is called the Ogham and it has twenty letters. Each one represents a type of tree. Pretty cool, actually. The symbol you showed me is what they call a Rune. The Druids used them. The Druids were part priests, part healers and part historians. They had these little stone tiles with these Runes carved into them and they would throw them like the I Ching. The Rune you showed me is called Thurisaz. It represents the seeing of the future. Pretty wild, huh?"

"Yeah, but what do they do now?"

"Well, that's what nobody wants to talk about. From what I have been able to find out, they are into everything and nothing, all at the same time. It's really weird, man. It's like nothing goes down in this city that they don't know about, but they don't really get involved in any of it. It's like they just watch. Lots of people have seen the guys with the tattoos on their necks. They call them ghosts because they are there one minute and then they are gone. For whatever reason, nobody messes with these guys and yet no one I talked to has ever seen them do anything but stand in the shadows and watch. The whole thing creeps me out."

"Did you find out anything about the businesses they are involved in?"

"Not very much. Apparently this group is like a giant holding company that has interests in a lot of different businesses. It's not clear whether they actually own these businesses or just invest in them. The consensus is that they sit on the boards of these companies and pull strings behind the curtain. Like the wizard of Oz, man. You just might be walking down the Yellow Brick Road. I hope you don't run into the wicked witch."

Spencer scooped his omelet onto a plate and dug into it.

"Oh, yeah, one other thing. The cops will not arrest these guys. If they raid a place and one of these guys is there, they ignore him like he is a piece of furniture. One cop told me they burst into an apartment one time and found three dead guys on the floor and one of these ghosts just sitting on the couch like he was watching a ballgame. This cop was about to cuff the guy when his sergeant told him to leave him alone. He just said the guy didn't have any part in it. I thought they might be involved in some kind of protection racket, you know, keeping the pimps and dealers in line for a piece of the action, but everyone I asked said no. The closest thing to an answer I got was that this group was like a thermostat. Because they seem to know everything that is going on and have so much influence in high places, they can more or less turn on the heat if anyone gets out of line. You know, one well-placed phone call and the cops decide to come down hard on the dealers and keep their foot on their necks until they agree to play nice. The same sort of thing happens if a tourist gets killed, but then the cops have to make a show of it."

For Paul, it just deepened the mystery more. The feeling of apprehension started to return.

"I'm not one to be giving advice, general, but I don't think you should be messing around with these guys. I mean, maybe they are just a bunch of players on some major power trip, but it bothers me when everybody who knows anything about them won't talk to me unless we're standing in a broom closet."

Spencer excused himself to go to the bathroom. When he returned, he found Paul engrossed in the newspaper.

"Ah, I see you have found my writings. No doubt you are suitably impressed. Allow me to direct your attention to my byline."

"This is her."

"Who is her, and who is she anyway?"

"This picture. It's Katherine."

Spencer looked shocked. "This woman. Katherine Francoeur. She's the Katherine you told me about?"

"That's her."

"I'm astonished. You've actually spent time with this woman? This is the woman who rescued you?"

"One and the same."

"I am in awe of you, sir. Most of New Orleans would give a month's pay just to stand in the same room with her, and I would be first in line."

"How do you know her?"

"Are you kidding? She's present at every major social function in this city, and she's also a very big contributor to local charities. She's one of those civic-minded types. Supports the firemen and police. I think she might have bought a fire engine for the city out of her spare change. She's the first name on the 'A' list. I can't believe you know this woman."

"Just dumb luck, I guess."

"I'm beginning to think not. You seem to have a talent for attracting extraordinary people. I think I need to be keeping a closer eye on you."

Paul spent a few hours with Spencer. They smoked, and it helped get his mind off the family. Hanging out with Spencer when he was stoned was like taking a guided tour through an alternative universe. Spencer had an angle on everything and saw the world as his own private Easter egg hunt. He kept a pad and pencil within easy reach to record his flashes of brilliance. A lot of the time, he had no idea what the notes meant when he woke up the next day.

He promised Paul he would continue to investigate the family and fill him in if he got any more information. Paul went back to the apartment and spent the remainder of the day by the pool.

Eugene rousted him out of bed in the morning as usual and then busied himself in the kitchen. He insisted Paul go back and do a proper job of shaving. Katherine arrived at the appointed time and they went out to their usual table by the pool. She was wearing a lime-green pants suit and her hair was piled on top of her head behind a pair of white designer sunglasses. Even when she was dressed casually, she looked classy. He wondered if she ever wore jeans and a sweatshirt.

"So are you finding the accommodations suitable, Paul?"

"Of course. Although I'm still having a problem waking up in that room in the morning. I keep thinking I'm somebody else."

"It will grow on you, I assure you."

"So where are you off to today? You don't seem to be wearing your uniform."

"My uniform?"

"Yeah, you know, the evening gown with the killer stiletto heals."

She laughed. "Well, it may not look like it, but this is what I think you refer to as the uniform of the day. I will be going on a shopping trip with some acquaintances. It is the equivalent, I think, of men playing golf, although in this case instead of making deals, I will be creating pressure on the men who make the deals by reaching a harmonious understanding with their wives."

"Nothing is left to chance is it?"

"We try to be thorough."

"How did you get to be so good at what you do?"

"I don't believe I am especially good at it, as you say. People, particularly those referred to as the nouveau riche, are impressed with old wealth and great power. They are attracted to it like the moth to a flame. I think being around it to some degree validates their conception of themselves. They see me as connected to it and yet accessible. Many of them are quite insecure, actually. They need to be assured that they belong to a higher class. It is sad in a way, at least to me."

"Why?"

"I suppose because I have never associated wealth with class. I have met many wealthy people. Some of them are quite wonderful, but on the whole I have found more class in the everyday people I know. They tend to be much more honest about who they are. Marc tells me that my talent is that I am non-judgmental, which of course is not the case. I am merely accomplished at keeping my judgments close to my heart."

"You seem to enjoy it, though."

"I'm not sure that is always the case either, although I find some of what I do very stimulating. I have never known any other life, at least as an adult."

"Where are you from?"

Eugene delivered the breakfast with his usual flourish, and Katherine provided him with the required superlatives. She studied Paul over the rim of her glass, obviously deciding how far to open the door of her life to him.

"I was born on the island of Kerkira. You may know it as Corfu. It is one of the many islands that comprise the nation of Greece."

"Were your parents wealthy?"

"Quite the contrary. My family lived in poverty, but they were killed in an earthquake when I was quite small. I have no memory of it. I am told that we lived in a small house of stone and, that on the morning of the temblor, I crawled out the front door and sat looking at the house as if I knew it was going to happen. I was taken in by an aunt, but she died two years later of cancer, and I was sent to an orphanage in Athens."

"How did you become involved with the family?"

"Marc and Andrea found me in the orphanage and adopted me."

"Andrea is Marc's wife?"

"She was Marc's wife and my mother. She passed away fifteen years ago."

"I'm sorry."

"Thank you. She was very dear to me. I often speak to her in my dreams when I am in need of guidance. I keep a picture of her with me always. Even if I am not wearing it, it is with me."

She removed a gold, heart-shaped locket from her blouse and opened it. There were two small pictures inside - one of a dark-haired child with an innocent smile and snow-white skin. The other of a stunningly beautiful blond woman who looked to be in her late thirties. The picture was in profile so that she appeared to be looking at the child and smiling.

"She was very beautiful."

"Yes, more so even than this likeness reveals."

They were silent for a while. He thought he saw some sadness in her face, but it quickly passed and she smiled at him. He changed the subject.

"So is all of it work?"

"What do you mean?"

"I mean that you seem to spend a lot of time doing things that other women do when they are on a date, except that you are working."

"Yes, I guess it could be seen in that way."

"So where do you go when you are actually on a date?"

"I do not go on dates, as you put it."

"Never?"

"Not in many years. I have, on occasion, agreed to accompany someone of interest to the family to the philharmonic or the ballet when there was no agenda other than to have an enjoyable evening. Perhaps you would call that a date."

"No, I wouldn't."

"What would you call a date, then?"

"Well, I guess I would call it a chance to get to know someone better to see if there is the basis for a deeper relationship."

"In that case, no."

"Why?"

"Do you mean, am I not interested in finding a relationship with a man?"

"Well are you?"

"No, I am not."

"Well, I guess it would be pretty difficult for any guy to compete with the kind of life you have here, anyway. Pretty intimidating."

"That really doesn't enter into it. I believe that what I do is not conducive to fostering a strong personal relationship with someone. If I were to desire a relationship, I would want to be completely free to dedicate my life to it."

"Why are you not free to do that now?"

"Let's just say that at this time in my life, I choose to be as I am."

"Are you always working? I mean do you ever get any free time?"

"Of course."

"What do you do?"

"I do what everyone does, I suppose. I like to read."

"Do you watch television?"

"Almost never. I find it superficial and uninteresting."

"Do you ever go to the movies?"

"On occasion, when there is a film worth seeing."

"Why don't you let me take you to a movie some night. Just as friends, I mean."

She smiled at him, but didn't answer.

"Not going to happen, is it?"

"As I told you before, I do like you but you are a man whose heart is searching for something. Perhaps it is a woman to fall in love with. Perhaps it is something else. I am not sure you know yourself. I have always believed that people must first find themselves before they will be ready to find someone to share their life with. It would not be good for you to become involved with someone like me at this point in your life. It would only lead you to frustration. As I have told you, I am not interested in forming that kind of bond with anyone at this time."

"Maybe that's because you haven't found the right one yet."

"No, it's more than that. I have met many attractive and interesting men, but I have also observed the nature of the relationship that many men seem to want. Many men look for an attractive woman as a decoration for their lives. The more rich or powerful they are, the more they need this for their ego. I have witnessed the results of these kinds of relationships many times. Inevitably the women are diminished in their own lives by it. In time, the man finds someone more attractive or younger, and the woman becomes lost in an empty life, surrounded by things that do not bring her either pleasure or fulfillment."

"So you don't believe in marriage."

"I believe marriage requires two people who are willing and psychologically able to place the happiness and well-being of the other above their love of themselves. I have seen many marriages where only one party is able to do this and many more where both parties are so completely self-absorbed that you could hardly call it a marriage at all. I have also seen some good marriages. I believe these people are among the luckiest people on this earth."

"So you don't think you are going to find someone willing to do that for you?"

"No, Paul, I am not sure that at this point in my life, I am able to do this for someone else."

They were both silent for a while. Finally, she looked at her watch.

"I really must go. I always enjoy talking with you. You have an honesty about you that is rare in the circles I travel. I'm sure we will have many occasions to talk in the future. If you are in need of anything, you have my number."

- 15 -

The Shepherd had taken his time about it. He traveled around the city by taxi and went into several stores, also stopping at one point to eat. Vicente was proud of his people. They did not lose him, neither were any of them seen. Finally they were rewarded when the final taxi ride brought him to a house on a quiet, rundown street in the Treme. The curbs were littered with trash and abandoned cars in various stages of decomposition, like fallen trees returning to the earth. Ernesto joined Vicente and Arturo in the back of the van. Arturo's leg was bouncing up and down as if he were playing a base drum.

"I don't think there is anyone else in the house, and the Shepherd has not come out. We should move now."

Vicente held up his hand. "Let us wait for Jose. He is checking out the back of the building.

As usual, Arturo was agitated. "Let's just go and kick the door in. We have waited long enough."

"Patience, Arturo. I see him coming now."

Jose climbed into the back seat.

"What took you so long?" Arturo hissed.

"There is a fire escape in the back. I climbed it. He did not see me and he has loud music playing. I think he has been drinking. There is a bottle of rum on the table by the bed. He is there on the second floor, lying on his bed. I did not see anyone else. Also I believe the kitchen window in the back is not locked."

"You should not have taken such a risk, Jose."

"It is no problem, Vicente. I am like a cat."

"Did you get a good look at the lock on the front door?"

"It appears to be a dead-bolt. I can probably pick it, but I don't know how quickly."

Vicente thought a minute. "All right, this will be our plan. Ernesto, I want you to stay in the van with the radio and watch the front door. I will also have a radio. If someone comes to the door or if anyone tries to leave, let me know right away. If the Shepherd leaves, follow him. Do not let him see you, but you must keep him in sight. Do not try to stop him. Jose, Arturo and I will go to the back. It is important that you do not use the radio unless you have to. The sound could give us away. Arturo, I want to take him alive. I want to get him to the van and take him back to the garage where we can question him."

Arturo smiled. "Yes. I will enjoy questioning him. And then I will make him eat his own huevos before I kill him."

The street was quiet. The men left the van one at a time with a few seconds in between. Jose and Arturo had machetes hidden in the leg of their pants. Vicente had the pistol tucked in his belt. He hoped he would not need it.

When everyone was in place, Jose handed his machete to Arturo. He went up to the back window and tried it. It would not budge at first but finally it moved a few inches. It made a noise and everyone froze in place. After a few minutes, Jose pushed again and managed to lift the window. He removed his shoes. The others boosted him up and he climbed into the kitchen of the house. He crept over to the doorway and looked into the adjoining rooms. They were empty. He returned and quietly unlocked the door. Vicente and Arturo came in. They could hear the music from the second floor. Vicente opened the refrigerator door quietly, and found a bottle of soda. He poured it out in the sink and tucked the plastic bottle under his arm.

Arturo looked at him as if he was crazy, but he didn't speak. The three of them crept up the stairs. The music was loud and they could not hear anything else. On Vicente's signal they leapt into the room.

Eduardo was sitting on the side of his bed and the shock was evident on his face. His cane was leaning against the table, and he rose slowly using it to support himself.

"If you have come to rob an old man, you are welcome to whatever few things I have. Please do not hurt me."

"Jodete y aprieta el culo!" Arturo screamed, raising his machete. "We have not come to rob you, lechon. We have come to kill you."

Vicente yelled at him, but it was too late. Arturo came forward with the machete raised. Suddenly Eduardo straightened. Taking his cane in both hands he pulled on the handle and drew out the long blade that was hidden inside. Arturo came forward, a crazed look in his eye. Eduardo parried the blow from Arturo expertly and then like a fencer and, as nimble as a cat, he lunged forward and ran Arturo through, withdrawing the blade with a flourish. Jose rushed at him, but he had no chance against the expert swordsman. The blade cut him at the throat and the blood gurgled from his mouth as he fell. Vicente was standing in the doorway. He held the pistol in his right hand and with the left held the soda bottle over the muzzle. Eduardo charged him. Vicente fired once. The bottle exploded, but the sound was just a muffled thump. The bullet hit Eduardo square in the chest, and he crumpled to the floor. Vicente ran over to Arturo, but there was nothing he could do for him.

"Why did you not listen to me, Arturo?"

Arturo spoke weakly. "I am sorry, Vicente. I only wanted to frighten him. I didn't..." His voice trailed off as the remainder of his life drained away.

Vicente checked on Jose, who was also dead. Vicente removed the radio from his pocket. "Ernesto, can you hear me?"

The voice on the other end crackled and sounded far away. "Si, Vicente."

"What is happening on the street?"

"Nothing. It is all quiet."

"Ernesto, I need you to come up to the second floor. There is a can of gasoline in the back of the van. Put it in one of the plastic bags and bring it with you. Make sure no one sees you in the street. Make sure you lock the van and bring the keys. You will find the back door open. Do not run. Do you understand?"

"I will be right there."

Vicente went over to Eduardo and felt his neck. He was dead. "What we might have learned from you. But now at least you are in hell where you belong." He went through his pockets, but found nothing. Ernesto gasped as he came into the room. His face turned white and Vicente thought he would faint. "Ernesto, listen to me. Do exactly as I tell you. Find the bathroom and bring me two towels. Do not touch anything. If you need to open a door use your sleeve. Do it now."

Ernesto ran down the hall. The Shepherd's jacket was hanging over the back of a chair. Vicente went over to it and carefully removed an envelope from the inside pocket. He opened it and a confused look crossed his face as he removed two tickets.

"What are these," he asked out loud. "Where is the list?"

Ernesto returned with two towels. "What has happened, Vicente?"

"Ernesto, listen to me carefully. We must search the room and we must do so quickly. Give me one of the towels. Do not touch anything with your bare hand. Use the towel. Look in the drawers and in the closet. We are looking for an envelope or a piece of paper with names on it. It could be inside a book or in the pocket of a coat. Begin now, quickly."

Ernesto began searching the room, using the towel as he had been told. Vicente went to the bodies of Arturo and Jose and removed their wallets. He removed the pillowcase from the bed and put the wallets inside along with the envelope he had found. He took the wallet that was on the dresser using the towel. Looking through it, he found a piece of paper with a phone number and some kind of code. He put the paper in his pocket and then threw this wallet in with the others. Next he took the gun, wiped it with the towel, and threw it on the floor. He felt under the mattress all around the bed and found a Venezuelan passport with the Shepherd's photograph and an entry visa for Cuba. He put these in the pillowcase as well.

"Have you found anything, Ernesto?"

"Only this," he said, holding his hand out to Vicente.

It was a locker key.

"Yes, this may be something, but Eduardo did not go to a locker today. Not since we have been following him. Look again, Ernesto. Make sure you check all of the pockets."

Vicente looked through some books that were sitting on the dresser. He emptied all of the drawers onto the floor.

"Did you look in the shoes, Ernesto?"

"Yes. I have found nothing else, Vicente."

Vicente looked around the room one more time and noticed the neck of the soda bottle lying on the floor. He picked it up with the towel and wiped if off.

"We have been here too long, Ernesto. We must go. Take the pillowcase. Do not touch anything."

Vicente took the can of gasoline and removed the cap. He poured the gasoline over the bodies of the three men, making sure their hands and faces were doused and then he wiped his hands with the towel and lit a cigarette. After drawing a few times to get it going, he tucked it behind the remaining matches in the book. He jammed the match-pack between two of Eduardo's toes with the lit end pointing toward the floor to keep it burning. He took a towel and soaked it with the remainder of the gasoline and then laid it carefully across Eduardo's foot so that the flames would reach it as soon as the matches ignited. After putting the gas can back in the plastic bag, he and Ernesto quickly exited the room.

Ernesto went first. Vicente followed, wiping the handrail as he descended. In the kitchen he wiped the refrigerator door handle and then followed Ernesto into the back yard. He wiped the doorknob as he shut it and then threw the towel into the yard. Ernesto looked ill. Vicente grabbed him by the arm and shook him hard.

"Listen to me and do exactly as I say. Go to the van. Get into the driver's side, start the engine and then climb over to the passenger seat. Give me the pillowcase."

Ernesto did as he was told. Vicente waited a few minutes. Finally, he heard a muffled 'whoosh' and he knew the fire had ignited. He walked calmly over to the van, got in behind the wheel and threw the bundle into the back. He drove away slowly. Ernesto was silent. He was holding his head in his hands.

After a short while, Vicente looked over at him. "If you are going to be sick, go in the back. I think there is a bucket there."

"No, I will be okay. What is happening, Vicente?"

"I am in need of your help now, Ernesto. You have done well tonight. Do you think you can keep it together a little longer?"

"Yes. I can help you."

"That man back there, Eduardo, he is called the Shepherd. He is called this because he travels among the Cuban exiles in this country as if he is their friend, and then, like sheep, he leads them to the slaughter. We have sought him for many years and now at last he is dead. I had hoped to question him. There is much he could have told us, but at least he will not trouble us again. The list you carried with you from Cuba has the names of DGI agents in Central and South America. We were to sell the list to the American CIA, not just for the money, but to continue to be a thorn in the side of Castro. But we have no contacts with the CIA, so we chose this man Taylor who is known to have contacts in the security agencies of this country. Except it now appears that he has betrayed us. Until today we were not sure what had become of the list. We guessed Taylor might sell it to the DGI. When we saw him with the Shepherd today, we were sure of it. Now, however, we do not understand what has happened. We know there was an exchange of some kind at the Café, but it appears it was not the list. Something else is happening."

"So what will you do now?"

"We must find the locker that fits the key you have found, and we must do it now before anyone identifies the bodies. We will start with the train station. After that, we will try the bus station and next the airport. I will need you to check the lockers by yourself, Ernesto. They may be watched and I am known to many. It would not be the police watching them. If you are stopped, tell them you saw an old man drop the key and so you took it. I will be watching your back. Can you do this, Ernesto?"

"Si, Vicente. I can do it."

* * *

The train station was almost empty and Ernesto was frightened. He walked over to the lockers, but before he got there he turned and went back to the van.

"What happened? Why did you not go to the lockers?"

"The keys here are a different color, Vicente. This is not the place."

At the bus station, Ernesto got out again. He could not find the lockers at first and when he found them he was out of sight from Vicente. The keys seemed to match and he walked by the rows of lockers trying not to look too interested. He found the locker, but he did not stop right away. He walked over to a row of chairs and sat down. He looked around the waiting room to see if he could find anyone watching. There did not seem to be anyone interested in him, although he knew he would probably not see them anyway. There was nothing to do but to go and see if the key fit. He walked over to the locker and put the key in the lock. His hand was trembling. The key turned and his heart almost leapt from his chest. He opened the door and inside there was a brown gym bag with a white stripe on each end. Like an American football he thought. He removed the bag quickly, closed the door and walked directly to the door though which he had entered. When he got to the door he stopped and looked behind him. It did not seem like anyone followed. He walked over to the van and got in.

"I have found it Vicente."

Vicente started the van and drove to a dark area of the parking lot. He stopped and took the bag from Ernesto's lap. He unzipped it and then just stared for a moment.

"Santa Madre de dios!"

He reached his hand in and pulled out bundles of one hundred dollar bills. Ernesto could not believe his eyes. Vicente held the bag on his lap and thought about what to do.

"What does this mean Vicente?"

"I am not sure, except that this is undoubtedly to be used to purchase something. Something very important. I think it has nothing to do with our list. But it must have something to do with the man Taylor. I will need some time to think about this."

"So much money, Vicente. What will we do with it?"

Vicente appeared to think about it for a moment. He went through the bag, counting the bundles of bills and then paused for a moment, as if doing a calculation in his head.

"Each of these bundles has one hundred bills. There are fifty bundles, Ernesto. This is one half million US dollars."

Ernesto was awe-struck.

"I have never seen so much money."

"Here is what we must do, Ernesto. We will drive back to the train station. You will take the bag and place it in one of the lockers there. You must keep the key with you, Ernesto, and guard it at all costs."

"Why me, Vicente? Why won't you keep the key?"

"Because the death of the Shepherd is a serious thing. We do not know what will happen now. If they suspect us, they will come looking for me. You are unknown in this community. I want you to go back to the house of Hector. They will take care of you there. Keep the key in a safe place and tell no one about it. I will contact you when we have decided what to do. Tell no one about tonight. Tell no one that Arturo and Jose have been killed. Tell no one where you have gone. Do you understand?"

"Si, Vicente."

"You have become an important part of our organization now, Ernesto. May I rely on you do this task?"

"I will do it."

"You must become quiet, Ernesto, like a mouse."

- 16 -

May slipped into June, and with it the memory of gentle breezes and star-filled evenings along the beach. The air was heavy and there were tropical storms stirring out in the Atlantic. An oppressive heat had, again, settled in over the Gulf and there was not enough air to blow out a candle. After several document drops, Paul no longer worried about anything going wrong, but he was bored. BK. Before Katherine, had been an adventure. Coming into town, trying to work out a place to stay and someplace to hang out. How to get in. Now it had become routine. It was still better than spending the weekend on the base, but he was beginning to get restless again. During the day, New Orleans was just another city. It had its charm, but he had seen everything worth seeing. Hanging around with a bunch of tourists felt like a kindergarten field trip. He was surprised they didn't make everyone hold hands. There was nothing to keep him on the edge. No eyes watching him from the shadows. Behind it all was a lingering question about what the family was into and why. It echoed around in his head and made enough noise to make him uneasy.

He was seeing less and less of Katherine. On the weekend after their conversation by the pool, a woman showed up at the apartment. Eugene explained that she was a friend of the family from California and was in town on business. Paul had no idea she would be at the house. He found her swimming naked in the pool. She apologized, saying she had lost track of the time, but she didn't ask him to turn around when she got out of the pool; she held his eyes and smiled. Eugene made a great dinner for them, complete with wine. She was very good looking and seemed fascinated by Paul's life, but she was trying too hard. He considered it, but in the end he decided to leave her alone. He guessed Katherine had put her in the apartment to get his mind off her. Or maybe it was some sort of test, which would have been intriguing and more than a little encouraging. After dinner, he excused himself and went over to the Seven Seas. When he came home, she was asleep.

He really didn't know what he wanted. Katherine seemed to be out of his reach. It was not that he had a hard time picking up women, he just wanted more than that. Everything hinged on some future life that he was incapable of imagining. He met a few new people, mainly through Spencer, and made some acquaintances, but no real friends. Mostly he prowled the Quarter at night, looking at people, trying to figure out what they were into. He had become a regular at the Seven Seas. The ghost had shown up several times, but he never acknowledged Paul. He wondered if the guy knew he was working with the family and, if so, what would happen if there was trouble. Would the ghosts intervene for the sake of a family member who was not their assignment? In the end he decided the guy knew who he was; they were way too on top of things for it to be otherwise. And then, if they knew when he was at the bar, did they know everywhere else he went? Did they know who he knew? More noise.

Paul had learned who the various players were in the bar. He knew who was dealing pot and psychedelics and who was pushing coke and heroine. The bikers handled amphetamine and PCP. He knew a few pimps and a lot of working girls. They knew him, too. They knew enough not to bother him. To them he was the guy who saved Lucky. He could have had any one of them, no charge. The players seemed to have reached a consensus about him also. After a brief time when they thought he might be a police informant, they decided he was harmless and considered him part of the wallpaper. When he hit it off with a woman in the bar, which happened occasionally when he was in the mood for it, he took her back to the apartment, but he always called a cab afterwards and sent her home. It wasn't a seduction. It was just two people who wanted to forget for a little while and to spend their tension gasping in the dark on that big soft bed. He knew it was a pretty lush life for someone in the service. Still he couldn't get easy with it.

It was another Saturday afternoon and he was sitting out by the pool wondering what to do with the evening. The phone rang and it startled him. His spirits started to lift, thinking it might be Katherine. Instead it was Spencer.

"Paul? What are you doing right now?"

"Nothing, just hanging out. Why?"

"I'm heading down to the precinct. I think you might want to come along."

"Why?"

"Katherine Francoeur has been arrested."

"Arrested? For what?"

"I'll explain on the way. Can you be ready in ten minutes? We need to get down there before she is arraigned."

Paul was on the curb when Spencer pulled up.

"What's going on, Spence?"

"They picked her up over in one of those antique stores on Chartres Street. She was trying to leave with some jewelry she hadn't paid for."

"Shoplifting?"

"I'm afraid so. Its more common than you think."

"Katherine, shoplifting? I can't believe it. She has everything she could possibly want. All she needs to do is ask."

"You would be amazed at how many of these society chicks are into it. A shrink I know told me it isn't about the stuff they take. It has to do with needing love and feeling they have to take it or some crazy crap like that."

"What's going to happen to her?"

"If we get there on time, maybe nothing. The desk sergeant is a friend of mine. He always gives me a scoop when any of the hoity-toity get naughty-naughty. I'm pretty sure I can get the charges dropped. The shop she was in doesn't need that kind of publicity and, besides, they haven't lost anything. If they press charges against somebody like Katherine Francoeur, they might as well hang out the going-out-of-business sign. Like I told you before, Katherine is a big contributor to the police benevolent groups and PAL. I think I can talk them into letting her walk."

"How are you going to handle it?"

"When we get to the precinct, I want you to go see her. I'll get them to let you in. Try to keep her calm and don't let her make any statements. If she hasn't called her lawyer yet, tell her to wait until I've had a chance to do my thing. I might not be able to squash this thing if she gets some big name suit involved. I'm going to talk to the gendarmes and find out who's calling the shots. After I find out what's going on, I'll come down and talk to you. And, Paul, if I can pull this off, I'm going to want some invitations to a few very exclusive social functions. See if you can find a subtle way to let her know that. It would be better coming from you."

They had put her in an interrogation room rather than a holding cell, which was a relief to Paul and certainly, he was sure, to Katherine. The police apparently knew who they were holding. When he entered the room, her jaw dropped. A look of deep sadness came across her face and she looked down at the floor, refusing to look at him.

"Are you okay? Can I get you anything?"

"No. What are you doing here?"

"I came with Spencer Dupree. Do you know who he is?"

She glanced up at him, a flash of anger crossed her face. "You mean the gossip columnist?"

"He's a friend of mine. He's here to help you."

"Help me? Don't be ridiculous. It's bad enough Marc is going to find out about this. Now it will be front page news."

"That's not going to happen. Spencer thinks he can help get you off. He's promised not to write about it."

"Why would he do that?"

"First of all, because you're my friend. Secondly, because he knows your social position in the city, and he thinks you can be helpful to him."

"So, a deal with the devil."

"Look, Katherine, he really is a good guy. It's his job, that's all. What would be the harm? All he wants is to get invited to some functions he hasn't been able to get into in the past. I think he could actually be helpful to you."

"We will see."

"Have you called a lawyer?"

"No, I've been waiting to see what they want to do with me."

They were silent for a while. Paul really didn't know what to say. She looked so different sitting across from him. The shoulder strap of her dress was hanging against the top of her arm and she looked a bit disheveled. More than that, she looked vulnerable. Something he had never imagined was possible.

"Is this the first time, Katherine?"

She looked at him for a few seconds and unconsciously bit down on the corner of her lower lip, as if trying to decide what to say. She resumed looking at her shoes. "Are you expecting me to pour my soul out to you? Confess to all my sins?"

"No, I've never expected anything from you. You've given everything to me, without me asking. Everything except your time."

She looked up at him again, her face a little softer. He thought she might cry, but she didn't.

"The first time I've done it, or the first time I've been caught?"

"Either, both."

"I was caught once before, in Paris. I paid a fine."

"Did Marc know?"

"No. He mustn't find out about this, Paul. It would be very difficult for me."

"Why? What would he do?"

She didn't answer. "I started stealing when I was a young girl. Small things. I did it for the excitement, for the thrill. I haven't taken anything in many years. Please, I really do not want to talk about it."

They sat in silence for a few minutes until the door opened and a short, heavy-set man with a graying crew cut entered the room. He was wearing a bow tie and had a badge clipped to his belt.

"I'm detective Norris with the New Orleans police. I'll need to ask you to leave the room for the time being, sir, while I talk to Miss Francoeur."

"Please, Detective, could he stay with me? I would be grateful."

"Very well, but please do not interrupt, sir, or I will insist that you leave the room. Miss Francoeur, I assume you are aware that this is not a trivial matter as far as the New Orleans police and the law are concerned. The merchandize you attempted to take was worth several hundred dollars. That constitutes a felony theft offense. Are you aware of the consequences?"

"I can imagine."

"Miss Francoeur, I must tell you at this point that you are entitled to a lawyer. Anything you say can and will be used against you in a court of law. If you cannot afford a lawyer, one will be appointed for you."

"Yes, I understand."

"Do you wish to contact an attorney?"

"Not at this time."

"Miss Francoeur, we're aware of the many good works you perform in this city and that you've been generous with its public servants. We've discussed the matter with the owners of the establishment where you were apprehended and they have agreed not to press charges against you. The owners are actually quite embarrassed about the incident. Nonetheless, since the police have become involved, we may still determine to arraign you on these charges and turn the matter over to the prosecutor's office. Do you understand?"

"Yes."

"Miss Francoeur, I've been on the police force a long time, nearly thirty years. I've seen this kind of thing many times before, and I know better than to ask you why you would do such a thing. I gave up asking why a long time ago. Mostly I ask how, and when and what else have you not told us. Miss Francoeur, I do not want to see your good name ruined nor do I wish to create yet another scandal in this city. We've decided to release you into the custody of your friends. There will be no record of this arrest, however, I must impress upon you that this will be the last time we extend this courtesy to you. If you're apprehended again, we will have no choice but to allow the justice system to run its course. I would appeal to you to seek counseling if you're unable to control this problem, if it is a problem, on your own. Now, do you understand what I am telling you, Miss Francoeur?"

"Yes. Thank you, Detective. I assure you it will not occur again."

"I hope not, Miss Francoeur, for your sake. Good afternoon." He turned and left the room.

Spencer was waiting outside. He introduced himself and Katherine took his hand, giving him a weak smile. Paul took her by the arm.

"What would you like to do now, Katherine? Shall I call you a cab?"

"Can we go back to the apartment for a little while, Paul? I need to calm myself down a bit."

Spencer volunteered. "I can drive you. Just meet me out front. I'll bring the car around."

On the way back, Spencer made small talk to avoid too much dead air in the car. Katherine just looked out the window. When they arrived at the apartment, Spencer turned to Katherine.

"Miss Francoeur, I'd like to put your mind at ease. You have my word as a gentleman that this matter will not be discussed with anyone nor will it find its way into my newspaper."

"Thank you, Mr. Dupree. That is very kind of you." She reached into her purse and pulled out one of her cards. She handed it to Spencer. "Here is my phone number. If there is anything I can help you with, I will try to do so."

Spencer had scored again.

She looked tired, and there was something else. Paul studied her, wondering what it was exactly. She opened her purse and took out a cigarette. He had never seen her smoke before. She lit it with a lighter that looked like a jeweled fountain pen and then lifted her chin slightly, forcing the smoke out through slightly parted lips. She kicked her shoes off and tucked her legs up under her in the corner of the couch, holding a green velvet pillow against her stomach like a shield. He was trying not to stare at her. She glanced over at him and then quickly looked away, flicking her cigarette nervously in the general direction of an ashtray on the coffee table. It was, he decided, the lack of something he had noticed. Being around her had always been like being in the presence of a princess, imperturbable, in control.

Now, she seemed unsure of herself. It was like a door had opened. He resisted the temptation to rush in, fearing it would slam in his face and the moment would be gone. They sat in silence, measured by the ticking of a clock he had never been conscious of before. Finally she got up and went over to the bar. She filled a glass with bourbon from a crystal decanter.

"Do you want something to drink?" she asked, not looking at him.

"No, thanks."

She returned to her position on the couch. "Well, aren't you going to say anything?"

"I don't know what to say."

"Are you shocked? Do you think less of me now?"

"No. I like you even more now that I did before, if that's possible."

"Why? Because you find that I am a flawed human being like everyone else?"

"You are not like everyone else. I guess I'm just happy to see that you're real, after all."

"Do you think I was being dishonest with you before now?"

"Not dishonest, really. I think people in your social position take on a persona. I've always imagined you put it on with your clothes, like jewelry."

"So you think I have been acting?"

"No. I think after a while it becomes who you are. I just wondered if you ever remembered who you used to be."

"Used to be when?"

"When you used to carry your own suitcases and wash your own clothes."

"I have never really had to do those things."

"Never?"

"Marc has always had great wealth. I was completely spoiled as a young girl, and I am sure I was an insufferable snob as a teenager."

"So, you really are as you seem?

"Yes, to the extent that you know me. I do not pretend to be anything other than I am."

"But there is something missing."

"Why do you say that? Because of what happened today?"

"Yes."

"Perhaps. I don't know why really."

"Maybe because you are not really happy."

She laughed, exhaling a stream of smoke toward the ceiling. She reached over and stubbed out the cigarette. "What is happiness anyway? Have you ever met anyone who is happy?"

"Well, nobody is happy all of the time. But I've met people who have found some contentment in their lives."

"Yes, I sometimes wonder what it would be like to feel that, to be in a different life."

"I think most people would be willing to trade places with you."

"Yes, I am sure that is true, yet I envy them in a way."

"Why?"

"Because they have had to struggle and test themselves, perhaps reach down in times of difficulty and discover hidden reserves of strength. I don't romanticize it, I am sure it is often dreadful, but I do see the value in it."

"You think it's good that people have to struggle?"

"Yes, to some degree. I think we all need to be challenged. To overcome ourselves. What else is life for?"

"So you feel like you need to be tested?"

"Not this so much. Only to find out if there is more to me than what I have found."

"A lot of people seem to think it's about getting what you already have."

"Yes, I live a privileged life, but it is meaningless, really. I am surrounded with beautiful things, almost nothing is out of reach for me, and yet I do not really covet any of it. It is not me."

"But today you wanted to take something that you could have had for the asking."

"Yes, I can't explain it."

"Maybe it is because you can have anything you want. Maybe it isn't a challenge anymore."

"Perhaps."

"You seem so complete to me as you are. Until today I couldn't find any part of you to relate to."

"And now you feel some connection with me?"

"I don't know. I just feel like we inhabit the same world, after all."

"Do you think this will change things between us?"

"I don't know. Our relationship, if you could call it that, has always been what you wanted it to be. I don't think you want it to be anything else. I doubt that this will change anything."

"I have never allowed myself to consider a different relationship between us."

"Because I am not in your social class?"

"No, of course not. Did you think me so shallow?"

"No. I didn't think I had anything you needed."

"I have not allowed myself to consider a different relationship with you. As I have explained to you, in my position I meet many attractive men. Allowing my heart to become involved would only serve to complicate things. It would interfere with my responsibilities."

"And what were your responsibilities with me? Was it to recruit me into the family?"

"Yes, of course. Did you think it was otherwise?"

"Not really. I do think you led me on a little. But maybe that was just me wanting there to be more to it."

"No, I confess I was aware of your attraction to me. It is part of my value to the family. Men are drawn to me. I have come to accept this."

"So you were never the least bit attracted to me?"

"No, that is not true. You are so different from the men I usually meet. You are so honest. When I first met you, I thought you naïve and perhaps a bit immature, but there is surprising depth to you, and you have a very kind heart. Also you are intelligent, but you do not try to impress anyone with it. Most of all, I think you have great courage. I meet so many cowards. Perhaps because I am one myself."

"Why would you say that?"

"Because it is true. I have allowed my life to carry me along, with every decision made for me by someone else."

"By Marc?"

She looked at him for a moment, obviously considering again how much she wanted to reveal about her life. "Yes, for the most part."

"Why don't you just go off and try something on your own?"

"Because I am a coward."

"What are you afraid of? Are you afraid you would fail?"

"No, that's not it at all. I am so accustomed to the life I live. I suppose I am afraid that I could not adjust to another reality. Sometimes I feel that I am merely a creation of the life I am living, and if I were to leave it, I would somehow vanish like an image in a dream."

"You mean you would miss all of the luxury you have around you?"

"No, not the luxury, so much as the security of my life. I think that I am afraid that I could not cope with the uncertainty. I cannot comprehend how you can do what you do."

"What do you mean?"

"To come into a city like this, with very little money, no place to stay, no friends. It would be terrifying to me."

"It's just a matter of what you get used to. You learn to trust that you'll find what you need."

"Yes, exactly this. I do not have this trust."

"That's because you've never had any need for it. I believe it's there for everyone."

Katherine got up and refilled her drink. She turned and held it out to Paul by way of asking if he wanted one. He shook his head no. When she returned to the couch she sat closer to him, no longer clutching the pillow in front of her.

"Would he let you go? Does he own you?"

"Would Marc let me go? Of course."

"Are you sure? Have you ever tried?"

"Not really. In any case, I would not leave him now. Not at this time. There are too many things going on. He is in need of me."

"Why?"

"I suppose it is because he is such a powerful man. People are intimidated by him. Sometimes that is an advantage to him, but often it prevents him from getting close to people. I help him with this, among other things."

"How?"

"People know that I am close to Marc. They often tell me things that they would not say to him, knowing that I will tell him for them. They see me as a channel to him. I also often relate Marc's feelings to them, in order to give them the confidence to open up a dialogue with him directly."

"Plus you seduce young men for him."

"Let us just say that I give them a reason to want to stay close."

"Like bait."

"No, this not really a fair description. I do not make false promises. I do not pretend to have interest if I don't."

They were silent for a while, but it was a more comfortable silence. Paul was turning things over in his mind, wondering where the conversation was leading. He wanted to find out more about her before the walls went up again. Katherine broke the silence.

"I haven't thanked you for rescuing me today. I am very grateful to you."

"I was just returning the favor."

"How is it that you know Mr. Dupree?"

"We met by chance one night. I like him a lot. He's a real character."

"I can tell you that many people in my acquaintance do not think highly of him, although I have never heard anyone accuse him of being inaccurate in his reporting, or vindictive, if that is the right word."

"I suppose people in high places don't like anyone looking in their closets."

"I am sure that is true of people in all places, except that unless they are wealthy or well known, it does not constitute a news story. Will he keep his promise?"

"Yes, I believe he will. He would like you to be a friend."

"I will see if I can be of help to him."

It appeared that the bourbon was having its effect. Katherine seemed more relaxed than he had ever seen her. He decided to see if she would give up more of her past.

"Have you ever been in love?"

"Of course. Many times."

"I mean really in love."

"Yes. But it's getting late and I'm starving. Are you hungry?"

"Sure, do you want to go out?"

"No, I couldn't stand to be in a restaurant right now. Let's go see what Eugene has in the kitchen."

He followed her into the kitchen. She took a couple of dinners out of the refrigerator and read the labels. "Do you know how to use the oven?"

"You're kidding, right?"

"Yes. Here put these in. I have to call Vincent and let him know where I am. See if you can find us some wine."

"Red or white?"

"I don't care," she said over her shoulder, as she hurried out of the room. "Whatever you can find."

She was gone for what seemed a long time to Paul. He set the table and filled the glasses with a Merlot he had found in the rack. This was a new side of Katherine he was seeing, and it excited him to think something could develop out of it. He was removing the dinners from the oven when she returned. She was wearing a pair of shorts and a tube top and her hair was loose and just touching the back of her shoulders. His jaw must have dropped because she pointed at him and laughed.

"I'll bet you are terrible at poker."

"Where did you find that outfit?"

"I keep some clothes here, in one of the spare bedrooms. Just in case."

"Just in case of what?"

"In case I don't have anything to wear when I am released from prison."

"Where do you live, anyway?"

"A million miles away in a huge castle with a moat and a dungeon."

They ate in the kitchen but, when they were through, she took her wine out to the courtyard. Paul followed her. She stretched out on a lounge chair and threw her head back with her eyes closed. Her hair looked like a black silk waterfall. She took in a deep breath of the evening air and then stretched her body like a cat. He wanted to take her, right then and there, but a voice in his head was telling him to go slowly. He resisted the temptation to sit with her on the lounge chair, instead pulling a deck chair over. She looked up at him sleepily and took his hand.

"And what of you, Paul? What do you want out of this life?"

"I don't know. That's the only good thing about being in the service. You can put off thinking about your life for four years."

"But you have not stopped thinking about it."

"How do you know?"

"Because you are a seeker. It is not in your nature to do so."

"Well, I guess that's true to some degree. The thing is, I still have two more years to go. It's likely that my next duty assignment will be in Vietnam. It's like a wall I can't see over."

"Will you be in danger?"

"Not much, I don't think. I have a pretty tame job. It should keep me away from any real fighting."

"What do you do?"

"Logistics mainly. You know, the bullets go in and the bodies come out. Somebody has to keep it all moving."

"Are you fearful?"

"No, not fearful really. In a way, it's like an adventure. There is a part of me that is excited by it. The thing is, it's just so wrong. It makes me sick thinking about it. The thought of being part of it bothers me a lot. At least for the time being, I can choose to ignore it. I have this picture in my wallet of a little girl running down a road with her clothes burned off by napalm. I keep it to remind me what is really happening there."

"I've seen this picture. It is horrible, I agree."

"So, anyway, I don't do a lot of future planning. Not now."

"Yes, I can understand this, but surely you have thought about what you would like to do at some point. I am curious to know what you find interesting in this life."

"I find you interesting."

"So you have told me. But what else? What excites you?"

He resisted giving her another flip answer. It was a question he had asked himself many times, without coming up with a real answer. "I like adventure. I don't want to be sitting in an office all day. At least not while I'm young. I like to be around people, but only people I can respect. I want to do things that challenge me."

"Like a dare devil?"

"No, I don't mean taking stupid risks just for the rush. It's like you said. Having to reach down and find out things about yourself that you didn't know. I guess, practically speaking, I will probably teach. Eventually, anyway. Not very adventurous I know, but I think I could be good at it."

"Perhaps we are not so different after all, Paul. Maybe we will run away together some day."

"Any time you're ready to go."

He excused himself to use the bathroom. When he returned she was fast asleep. Instead of waking her, he went and got a blanket and covered her with it. He watched her sleeping for a moment and then he bent down and kissed her on the forehead.

Sometime during the night, he awoke and felt her get into bed with him. He turned and she put her finger to his lips.

"Can we just hold each other for a while, nothing more?"

He wrapped his arms around her and fell into a deep, contented sleep. When he woke in the morning she was gone. He wondered if it had been a dream.

- 17 -

Marc stood at the fence watching the trainer walking a magnificent black Arabian stallion. It was a spirited horse and it jerked its head and danced sideways, objecting to the bit in its mouth. The trainer stopped and rubbed the horse on its neck and flank, loosening the reins a bit to calm him down. The stallion's rich, ebony coat glistened with moisture from his recent run. A white Cadillac pulled up to the stables. Taylor emerged from the car and walked over to Marc at the fence rail.

"You have news for me, Bruce?"

"No, sir. Nothing. It's as if he's vanished into thin air."

"Come, take a walk with me."

They walked along the riding path. Marc looked out over the fields, seeming untroubled, even though he was more than a little concerned at how things had unfolded.

"Tell me again how you left things with Eduardo."

"As I told you, we met at the café. He told me that all terms were agreed upon. He left the contracts for me and I gave him the tickets. He asked if we were ready on our end, and I told him we would be shortly, and that I would let him know through the normal channels when we were ready to make the transfer."

"Did you lead him to believe it would be a lengthy wait?"

"No, sir. I told him we were nearly ready, and I would be contacting him soon."

"And how did he appear when he left you?"

"The same as always. He did nothing to make me think there could be a problem."

"And this was two weeks ago?"

"Two weeks ago, Saturday."

"And when did you first try to contact him?"

"I made the first call last Friday evening, and left the usual message. Since then I have called every day at the same time and left the same message. I used a different pay phone each time. He has not contacted me."

"I think by now we must assume something has happed to Eduardo. It could be that he has simply been injured or perhaps even had a heart attack."

"I suppose that is possible."

"But you don't think so."

"The Shepherd has a lot of enemies, Mr. Francoeur. If he has gone missing, I would tend to suspect someone has found him. Someone who would like to see him eliminated."

"What is our fall-back position, Bruce?"

"It is a bit thin, I'm afraid. As you know we have had many dealings with Eduardo in the past and he has always worked alone. We do know some people who are attached to the Cuban security apparatus. They will know him, of course, but I would be surprised and even alarmed if they knew very much about this operation. It could be risky contacting them. Eduardo was not free-lancing on this operation, but it would be known only at the highest levels of his agency. I suppose there could be other agents in the US who are aware of the operation. But we don't know who they are."

"Any other alternatives?"

"Well, the Shepherd's friends have put up a lot of money to make this thing happen. I have to assume that the money is already in the country since we were close to making the deal. They will be more concerned than we are if the Shepherd has gone missing. I suspect that sooner or later they will be in contact with us through some as-yet-unknown channels."

"What about contacting them?"

"Again, that is problematic. We do not know specifically who is involved on their end. We have contacts within the ministries that will be letting the contracts, but it is very doubtful they know why we have been awarded these contracts. It is decidedly unhealthy to ask those kinds of questions."

"And the KGB?"

"Certainly they are deeply involved. But they have gone through the Cubans to minimize their exposure. I'm not sure how much they know of the details of this operation."

"Won't they be keeping tabs on Eduardo, assuming he has the money?"

"Perhaps, but I don't think they are overly worried about losing the money. They can always get it back from their friends in Havana. It is more likely they will be watching after the item has been delivered. They will know this has not yet occurred."

Marc was silent for a while, turning the alternatives over in his head. Finally he spoke. "Is there any chance there is a connection with our recent operation to obtain the DGI agent list?"

"Extremely doubtful, sir. I'm sure they believe a pro-Castro element was responsible for the hit and they probably know of the Shepherd. But they also know that the Shepherd is much too heavy to be involved in that kind of operation. It would be like suspecting Fidel himself. Besides, these guys are just a bunch of uneducated peasants."

"And they do not suspect us?"

"No, sir. I screamed bloody murder when they didn't show up for the drop. They were very apologetic and assured me they would have more information to sell in the future."

"It's all very unsettling, Bruce. Especially now that the item is gift wrapped and ready to be left under the tree."

"Yes, sir. I am concerned about it."

"How do you suggest we proceed at this point?"

"Well, sir, we need to find out what has happened to Eduardo. I would suggest making discreet contact with some of the pro-Castro groups to see if anyone has information about him. We could concoct a cover story to explain why we are interested in him."

"What kind of story?"

"Perhaps we can have some of our people pose as members of a revolutionary group from a third country, looking for support from Cuba. Perhaps Chile or Argentina. We could claim we had been in initial conversation with the Shepherd and now he has broken off contact. We could insist on seeing him and hope they have some information about his whereabouts. It's a shot in the dark, but we don't have many other choices, except to wait it out."

"That may be worth a try. See if you can find the people we need and work out a contact scenario. Don't proceed beyond that point until we have spoken further."

"Yes, sir."

"In the meantime, we should have someone contact the local hospitals and morgues, under the guise of looking for a missing family member of Eduardo's description. Perhaps they have a body they don't know what to do with. At least then we would know with certainty that he is dead."

* * *

Vicente was a clever man. He thought long and hard about getting his revenge but he had already lost too many good people. He wanted to know if Taylor had given the Shepherd the agent list. If possible, he also wanted to prevent any deal the Shepherd had been trying to make with the American from happening. He needed a way to hurt Taylor and to put a stick in the eye of the DGI without exposing his organization to more losses. In the end, he remembered an old saying from his days of fighting in the jungle. 'If you are being hunted by two jaguars, make them fight each other for the privilege of eating you.' He called Taylor first.

"Mr. Taylor, I am an associate of Eduardo Colon. I am afraid I have some bad news. Eduardo has been killed."

"What happened?"

"It appears to have been an accident. He fell on the stairs and his neck was broken."

"When did it happen?"

"It was about a week ago. The body was not found right away."

"This is a terrible loss. He was a friend and a business associate."

"Yes, we are aware of the project you were discussing with Eduardo. The thing is, Mr. Taylor, his room has been thoroughly searched. We do not know if it happened before or after the accident. He did not keep any large sums of money with him, if you understand my meaning, but we do not know if anything else was taken. Did you, perhaps, provide Senor Colon with any documents that might have been important?"

"No. We did not. Where did this happen? I must see the body."

"I am afraid this is impossible. For obvious reasons, we could not have the police involved. Eduardo's body has been buried at sea."

"Our business agreement has been lost then."

"That is the reason for my call, Mr. Taylor. We are prepared to move forward with the arrangement as before."

"Do you have the buy-money?"

"Yes, we have it."

"Can you verify the amount?"

"I am sure you know how much."

"Yes, but if you have the money, I am sure you have counted it."

"Very well, Mr. Taylor. The amount is five hundred thousand US dollars."

"When can we meet?"

"Mr. Taylor, we feel that we must be very careful at this point. We cannot be sure that Eduardo was not murdered, even though we do not have any evidence of this. Of course you are not suspected, but we would be more comfortable having our first meeting in a very public place. I would suggest we do no more than discuss how we may continue with the arrangement."

"Very well. When and where?"

"Perhaps you know of a public place where it would also be possible to have a private conversation."

"Yes, I know a place like that. It's a place called the Seven Seas. It's on Ursulines Avenue in the French Quarter. Do you know it?"

"We will find it."

"There is a courtyard in the back where we can talk. There will be enough people around to make you feel comfortable."

"Very well, Mr. Taylor. I would propose a meeting next Saturday night at midnight."

"We will be there. How will I recognize you?"

"Will you come in person, Mr. Taylor?"

"Yes, of course."

"If you will hold a file folder in your hand, we will find you."

So far, so good. It sounded like Taylor bought the story. Next came the difficult part. He wasn't sure who Eduardo's contacts were. He had the paper with the phone number that was found in his wallet and decided to chance it. He called the number and heard a woman's voice.

"Buenos dias. Identificacion, Por Favor."

Vicente was not sure what to say, so he simply read off the code number from the paper. There was a hesitation and he had started to hang up the phone when the woman spoke again.

"One moment, please."

He hoped he was doing the right thing. It was a pay phone, and he did not think they could trace it.

He waited for at least a minute before hearing a male voice.

"Eduardo, we are happy to hear from you. Where have you been?"

"This is not Eduardo. The Shepherd sleeps, Senor."

"Who is this? How did you get this number?"

"I am an acquaintance of Eduardo. Listen to me very carefully. I know who killed him."

"Who did this?"

"It was the American, Taylor. Do you know this man?"

"Yes, we know him. We know he would not kill Eduardo."

"The man Taylor has a list of names, Senor. Names of your agents that he has purchased from your enemies. He offered this list to Eduardo at a price. Eduardo did not want to pay for this information. This was not part of the original agreement. There was a confrontation and Eduardo was killed. They have stolen a great deal of money from him. Money that was meant for something else."

"This is a lie."

"If you think it is a lie, tell me Senor, where is the Shepherd now, and where is the money he carried?"

"First, you tell me how was he killed and where."

"He was shot, in the chest, in a house in the area of the city known as the Treme, and his body burned with two others who worked for Taylor."

"How do you know this?"

"Because I was there. I also worked for Taylor, until I found out what kind of a man he is."

"I do not believe you."

"You may believe me or not. It is of no consequence to me because I will not be coming back to this place. I only called to tell you what I know. I have found out there will be a meeting this Saturday night with Taylor and some people who are very interested in the agent list."

"What group?"

"I do not have this information. I only know that Taylor will be at the meeting. He will carry the list in a file folder."

"Where will this meeting take place?"

"At a bar in the French Quarter called the Seven Seas. In the courtyard. They will meet at midnight."

- 18 -

Paul made a pick-up the following Saturday morning and got to the apartment around noon. He didn't know what to expect. All week long, he had been turning the possibilities over in his head. He knew there was a strong likelihood that he had merely caught Katherine in a moment of vulnerability. That and a little too much alcohol can make people do things they wouldn't normally do. Even people like Katherine. He hoped it had been the start of something between them, but all the same he didn't think he should call her. He spent the day at the apartment, pacing around like a caged lion. When he hadn't heard from her by six, he decided to go to Baby's and eat dinner. Baby was having his daily crisis in the kitchen, and he didn't have time to talk. Before Paul left, though, Baby waddled over to the cash register, lifted up the bill tray and retrieved an envelope. It was a letter from Lucky.

> Dear Paul:
>
> I've been wanting to write to you for a while, but I just didn't know where to start. They got me this job at an accounting company in Metairie. I am a receptionist right now, but they are training me to do some other things to help out when they do audits. They gave me these tests, and it turns out I am not so dumb after all. Who would have known? Maybe you. I can't tell you how happy I am. I just never believed there was

anything for me in this world. You changed all of that. I never would have a shot at a job like this except for you. It's a whole new life. Don't worry, I'm not going to mess it up. Not in a million years. The more I think about what you did for me, the harder it is to believe. Like some kind of a miracle. I know God sent you to help me. I don't know why he would bother. I owe my life to you and I always will. I'm not usually in the city on the weekends now, but I would come in to see you in a second if you want to have dinner with me or something. I really would love to see you. I'm all healed up now and you can hardly see the scars. If you want to get in touch with me, just go and see Baby. He will know how to find me.

Love always,

Lucinda.

It made him feel good to know she was really on her way. Still, it was like a message in a bottle, coming ashore from a previous life. He did want to see her, but nothing more than that. For now, it would only complicate things. His whole being was focused on Katherine. He walked around the French Quarter for a while, taking in the spirit of the place. It occurred to him that his connection with Katherine gave the place a new perspective. It looked a little less disreputable. A little more quaint.

Spencer wasn't at the Limbo. After a couple of a beers, Paul decided he wasn't coming by and he went back to the apartment. It was nine o'clock when he heard a knock on the door. By the time he got to the foyer, Vincent and Katherine had already come in. Vincent was carrying some packages that he took into the kitchen. Paul tried not to overreact, but he couldn't keep from smiling.

"Would you return for me at eleven, Vincent?" Katherine asked. "I have some things to discuss with Paul."

"Certainly. Good evening, Mr. Greene."

He wanted to take her in his arms and make love to her right there on the floor. She went into the living room and sat on the couch. He sat next to her.

"I thought we should talk about last weekend."

"Only if you want to."

"I do want to. Not about the incident with the police. About what happened between you and me."

"I know, it was all just a mistake. You were upset. It never should have happened."

"No, not at all, Paul. I haven't felt so comfortable with anyone in many years. It was a terrible day for me, but it was such a wonderful evening. I just don't know...

Paul pulled her close and kissed her. At first she seemed surprised, but then she began to kiss him back. All of his doubts melted away as he felt her passion rise. They made love first on the couch, and then on the floor and finally he carried her into the bedroom. The tension that had built up between them over the past months was finally released, in exquisite spasms of unbelievable pleasure. Finally, they collapsed into each other's arms, their bodies heaving with exhaustion. They lay still then, holding each other; lost in their separate worlds but no longer alone. Katherine stirred first.

"Vincent will be coming back. I have to go take care of myself."

Paul got dressed, then went out to put the living room back in order. She returned and kissed him lightly, not wanting to ruin her makeup.

"There isn't much time. We really need to talk."

"I'm sorry, I couldn't stop myself."

"No, it is good it happened this way. It was wonderful. Perhaps it will be easier now. There is danger in this for me, Paul, and possibly for you. Marc must not know that something has happened between us. It will be difficult."

"You really are afraid of him, aren't you?"

"I have never been afraid of him in the past, but nothing like this has happened to me for many years. I've explained this to you."

"What do you think he would do to you?"

"I don't believe he would do anything. Certainly not hurt me in any way. But still it would change things a great deal. I don't know what it would mean for you."

"I don't care about that."

There was a knock on the door. She kissed him again. "I have to go. I will try to come back tomorrow afternoon, so that we may talk about this. It may be later in the day. Will you wait for me?"

"I've been waiting for you for months."

He was too charged up to sleep. There really wasn't anywhere he wanted to go, so he walked over to the Seven Seas. The main bar was going full throttle and he wasn't in the mood for it. The courtyard was busier than usual also, but still not nearly as crazy as the other room. He got a beer and found a table under a tree. The evenings were more humid now, and it was just sticky enough to make everyone a little uncomfortable. You had to talk over the buzz of the cicadas. The crowd felt a little edgy. There was a group of people having a discussion in Spanish. They were pretty loud, and he changed his seat to get farther away from the noise. Something didn't feel right, but he couldn't quite put his finger on it. People came and went from the main bar. Paul became lost in his own thoughts. The vision of a whole new life had opened up for him. It was like someone had punched a hole in the egg he had been curled up in, and he could see through to a completely different world. He was intoxicated with the idea of being with Katherine, and wondering how they were going to make it work. He was so lost in his own thoughts that he didn't notice someone had joined him at the table. He turned and almost jumped out of his chair. It was the ghost, and Paul realized right away what an accurate description that was. He had what the guys coming back from the war called the thousand-yard stare. He was looking Paul right in the eye and yet it felt like he was looking through him. There was nothing close to human contact. The guy didn't seem to have the need to blink. There was no acknowledgement and no introduction.

"You have to leave this place. You have to go right now."

Paul felt his anger rising. He was startled and he didn't like being pushed around. "What are you talking about? I just started my beer."

"You can take it with you."

"Suppose I don't want to take it with me."

"Then you may leave it on the table."

"I'm not going anywhere, I just got here."

"Please do not be difficult, Mr. Greene. We have no desire to cause you any problems. We have been instructed to ask you to leave. It is for your own well-being."

"Instructed by whom?"

"I am sure you know the answer to that question."

"Why? What's going on?"

The ghost looked over to another table and nodded. A guy got up and walked over to their table. He also had the tattoo. He stood behind Paul.

"Mr. Greene, we do not wish to cause you any embarrassment. We know that you like to come here, and we don't usually have a problem with that. At this moment, however, you have to leave. If you don't leave, we will physically carry you out to the street. That is not what we want to do."

A part of Paul wanted to push it to the edge, just to see what would happen. If it hadn't been for the thought of Katherine, he might have. Instead he stood, took a drink of his beer, turned his back and walked out. There was no way he was going to ignore it, though. Something was going on, and he had to know what it was. He walked up the street and then crossed over to the other side and doubled back. He stood in the shadow of an entry stair at a building across from the bar. Everything seemed normal. He considered going back inside and staying by the door, but he thought better of it. People came and went, he could hear the noise from the bar rise and fall with the opening of the door. The ice truck came by.

It was just another Saturday night. He was about to give it up and go back to the apartment when he felt, more than heard, something change. It was like a charge of electricity moving through the air. A few people ran out of the bar, and he heard screams. Suddenly the place started to empty out. People were scattering in all directions. He waited. After a few minutes, he saw the ghost walk calmly out and stroll down the street. Shortly after that, the other one exited and headed in the opposite direction. There was another man with him. He was hunched over and in obvious pain. Paul couldn't see who he was. They were in a hurry, and they didn't look back. Paul watched the first one step off the curb. If he hadn't been staring at the guy, he never would have seen it. Something dropped out of the ghost's hand and fell into the storm sewer. He thought about going over to see what it was, but he could hear sirens in the distance, and he decided to get out of there.

* * *

There was nothing about the incident in the Sunday morning newspaper. Spencer called later in the morning.

"Were you over at the Seas last night?

"Yeah, I was there for a while."

"Did you see the bloodbath?"

Paul didn't want to discuss his own confrontation with the ghosts, and he decided to play dumb for the time being. He was curious to find out why they were involved in whatever went on. "No, what happened?"

"There was some kind of a melee. A couple of guys were killed. Stabbed to death. A bunch more were injured. I hear it was pretty gruesome."

"Who were they?"

"I don't know. I can find out if you are interested. Why? Do you think your mysterious friends had something to do with it?"

"No, I'm just curious about what goes on in that place."

"Ok, I'll see what I can find out."

The thought crossed Paul's mind that he probably knew where the murder weapon was, but it would have been a mistake to get involved. Besides, he was pretty sure the cops didn't want to know who did it. Whoever the dead guys were, they had apparently not been reasonable. Whatever the family was, it was not the benign, civically minded country club Katherine had described to him. He wondered how much she really knew. For the time being, there was no way he was going to challenge her on it, or say anything about last night.

She got to the apartment around three, carrying a book of wallpaper samples. It was her excuse for coming by. They went out to the courtyard. She kissed him, but he could tell she wanted to get down to business.

"We need to be very cautious, Paul, as I have told you. I do not want anyone to suspect that there is something between us. We cannot be together, I mean in that way, here at the apartment."

"That's going to make things a little difficult, I think."

"Yes, I wish it did not have to be this way, but it is for the best, at least for now."

"So how will I see you?"

"I have given it some thought. On most weekends, I go downtown to shop or to visit friends. Vincent drops me off, and I call him when I am finished to come pick me up. No one is aware of where I go at these times."

"Are you sure?"

"Of course. Do you think they spy on me?"

"I don't know, maybe."

"I assure you, this is not the case."

"What about Vincent?"

"Vincent is very discreet and I don't think he would ever say anything. Just the same, I would rather no one knows."

"So where could we meet?"

"I thought perhaps you could arrange a hotel room, somewhere downtown, not in the French Quarter. I will reimburse you for it, of course."

"Sure, I can do that, but I'll pay for it."

"No, it may be quite expensive. It would have to be one of the better hotels. I cannot risk being seen going somewhere that I would be out of place. I often have lunch at the Pelham when friends are visiting from out of town. It would be easy enough to explain if someone saw me going there. Paul, I don't want this to seem like some common tryst. I do not suggest this arrangement so that we may hide away and make love only. I would like very much to show you places in the city you have not seen, to be with you openly so we can enjoy and learn about each other. Unfortunately, it can't be like that. At least, for now. I hope you understand."

"I could spend the rest of my life in a hotel room with you."

She smiled and reached over to touch his hand. "Of course I will still see you here at the apartment from time to time, but we must not display any undue fondness for each other."

"Why would he keep you from being with someone? If he loves you as you say, I would think he would want you to be happy."

"Marc believes these are very critical times for the family. I am helping him with many projects that require a good deal of my time and attention. In some cases, I am the only connection between the family and people who may be important to us. He needs me right now. I believe when the time is right, he will allow me to move ahead with my life."

"When whose time is right? His or yours?"

"I know this must sound strange to you and maybe a bit selfish on his part, but he has given me so much. I feel obligated to try to help him in any way I can."

"Even at the expense of your own happiness?"

"For now, yes. But that is not the only reason. The other reason is you, Paul. Please do not be insulted, but you are not from our social class. You are neither wealthy nor from a well-placed family. Please understand this means nothing to me. Nothing at all. But it means a great deal to Marc. I am sure that all fathers want their daughters to marry well. To not have to struggle. Although he likes you, he would not see you as a suitable partner for me."

"Maybe I'm not."

"Please, Paul, don't be upset with this. We haven't even begun to know each other. It's far too early to be worrying about these things."

"I can't believe you've been without someone for so long."

"I have already explained this to you. But because I wish to be honest with you, I will tell you that there was someone once. I didn't want to speak of it before. A few years after Andrea died, I met a young man. We were very much in love."

"What happened? Didn't Marc approve?"

"No, Paul. He died in a terrible car accident."

"I'm sorry."

"I didn't want to live any longer. I wouldn't have gotten through it without Marc. I am sure it is part of the reason, at least, that I have not allowed myself to become interested in anyone. Until now."

"Who was he?"

"His name was Jonathon Lampert. He was from a very prominent family in Lake Charles. We had just become engaged a few weeks earlier. I was so happy."

"How did Marc feel about him?"

"He liked Jonathon very much. The night he died, Marc invited him to stay with us. The weather was very bad. I should have made him stay, but he insisted. He never reached home. A few days later they found his car in the bayou near the town of Morgan City. I could not bring myself to identify the body. I wanted to die."

"I'm really sorry, Katherine. I didn't mean to be callous."

"It is of no consequence. It was a long time ago. Those wounds have healed, to the extent that they ever do. But I need you to be understanding about this arrangement. You are young and you are not accomplished at hiding your feelings. I know if our relationship progresses, you will find it more and more difficult to be stifled in this way. I need you to promise me you will keep to our bargain."

"Of course I will, but you keep saying I am young. You can't be a lot older than I am."

"Perhaps not in years. But in my life, I am no longer young."

"Maybe you just forgot what it's like."

"Perhaps you will teach me."

After she left, Paul got his things together. He had a little less than an hour before his ride was to arrive. The more he found out about Marc, the less he trusted him. If nothing else, he was a master manipulator and a serious control freak. He wondered how Marc really felt about Katherine's fiancée.

He was relaxing in the courtyard when the phone rang. It was Spencer again.

"I have some information for you."

"Well, that was fast."

"Yeah, well after you got me in tight with our lovely and now mutual friend Miss Francoeur, I am at your disposal, general."

"Well, I really didn't do anything."

"Nonetheless, I wouldn't have made that connection except for you, as amazing as that may be. Sometimes I think you've been dispatched to me by some benevolent spirit, for reasons I cannot fathom."

"I hope you aren't going to harass her to death for party invitations."

"I am shocked, shocked, sir, at your suggestion. Seriously, don't worry about that. I'm a master at this game and, I might add, the very soul of discretion."

"Yeah, well let me know how that works out."

"You can count on it. Anyway the recently deceased turn out to be two Cubans named Jose Arroyo and one Juan Doe. There was no identification on the bodies, so they ran the prints. They came up dry on one of them, but Jose Arroyo was deported in 1963 after getting into a hassle with a bunch of Cuban exiles. He was working with a group called the Fair Play for Cuba Committee. It was a pro-Castro organization that was active in the city for a while. Here comes the best part. Guess who else was a member of the group?"

"Who?"

"Lee Harvey Oswald."

"Holy shit!"

"Yeah, that's exactly what I said, but don't go off on any conspiracy theories. We have a District Attorney down here named Jim Garrison. He's got that corner staked out already. The cops think this was some local dust-up within the Cuban community. This guy Arroyo was here illegally, and it was obviously not a robbery. The current thinking is that he was involved in smuggling shall we say undesirables into the country. Almost any Cuban can get automatic asylum in this country just by stepping on the beach. Unless, of course, he's suspected of being a member of Fidel's choir club. The problem is, it's hard to tell who is and who isn't."

"Well, like they say. You can find anything you want at the Seven Seas. I guess that includes a knife in your liver."

"Yeah, well, you watch your back."

- 19 -

Marc Francoeur was not a man who could abide failure. He didn't play unless he knew he would win. If you worked for him, there were no excuses. When you were given a task to do, it was your responsibility to analyze the situation, assess the challenges involved and develop a strategy that would take into consideration all contingencies. It was also your responsibility, once you had completed your assessment, to come to him with your action plan and inform him of any assets required to successfully complete the task. Once the plan was signed off on, it was your duty to produce a favorable outcome.

Taylor had never failed him in the past. If he had, he would not have continued in his position. But now he had failed the family twice and on an extremely sensitive and critical operation. Once by not having a fallback position in the event the Shepherd was unable to follow through on his end of the transaction, whatever the reason. And secondly by walking into a blind meeting without first finding out for certain who he was dealing with. These failures had sealed his fate and he probably knew it.

Marc Francoeur, however, was also a pragmatic man. There was nothing to be gained by removing Taylor until the situation was resolved. Besides, there was still a vital role for Taylor in this operation. As a patsy in the event, the whole thing blew up in their faces. As always, he concealed his true intentions behind a mask of concern.

Taylor was lying in bed, staring up at the ceiling when Marc came in. His left arm was heavily bandaged and in a sling.

"Oh, good, I'm glad you are awake, Bruce. Do you feel well enough to talk?

"Sure, I'm okay, Mr. Francoeur."

"Are you in a lot of pain?"

"Not right now. They gave me something. I guess it'll be hurting later."

"Yes, apparently you were lucky to escape with your life."

"Yeah, they caught me by surprise. I just got my hand up in time or I'd be on a slab right now. I guess I must be slipping."

"Don't blame yourself, Bruce. I don't think anyone could have anticipated something like this happening. Can you tell me what transpired?"

"Well, it's all a little confusing; it happened so fast. As you know, we arranged to meet the Shepherd's people. They sounded eager to meet with us over the phone. I don't really know what went wrong."

"Are you sure they were Eduardo's people?"

"Well, I was suspicious when they contacted me, but they knew things about the operation that only the Shepherd would know. I guess it makes sense that the Cubans would have a fallback position if something happened to Eduardo. Also, they claimed to have the buy money. They knew how much it was."

"So what happened?"

"Well, they insisted on meeting in a public place. I'm sure they were spooked by Eduardo's death. I thought it was understandable under the circumstances. Besides, it was only supposed to be a quick meeting. Something preliminary."

"And did you meet them?"

"Not the way you mean. They asked me to carry a file folder so they would recognize me, which I did. There were a lot of Cubans at the bar, so I didn't pick them out until they were on top of me."

"They attacked you?"

"Yes, out of the blue these two Cubans came up to me. One of them spit on me and tried to grab the folder. He was cursing at me in Spanish. While I was trying to fight him off, the other one lunged at me. He was going for my heart, but by then our people jumped in and, before I knew it, they were on the ground dead."

"Could you make out anything they were saying to you?"

"Only that they were calling me a thief and a murderer."

"Did anyone recognize you at the bar? Was there anyone there you knew?"

"I didn't recognize anyone. Our people did a good job of getting me out of the place in a hurry. Of course, I can't be sure someone didn't know me, but I doubt it."

Marc was silent for a moment. He stared at the floor, puzzled. Finally he spoke. "There is something going on here that we don't understand."

"Maybe we should just walk away, Mr. Francoeur."

"Well, let's examine where we are. Eduardo is apparently dead. We thought we had made contact with his organization, but either it was not his group or, for some reason, they suspect us of foul play. Perhaps, from the sound of it, they think we killed Eduardo, although I don't follow the logic there."

"So now we don't know who we can trust."

"I think at this point, Bruce, it is safe to say that we cannot trust any of the Cubans. There are too many unknowns; it could take forever to sort it all out."

"So what do you think we should do?"

"Well, I think we have two choices. We can walk away as you suggested. Destroy the item, dissolve the network, wash our hands and go on to other things."

"Or?"

"Or we can contact the Russians directly and try to close the deal. Everything is in place. I think it could be done quickly. This is a very important project for us on many levels. If it can be salvaged, it is worth some additional risk."

"The thing is, sir, the buy-money is apparently gone. We don't have a clue where to start looking for it."

"That is a problem for the Soviets. We know they want the item very badly. If they do not already know the Shepherd is dead, they soon will. I doubt very much that they would suspect us of stealing the money. It would not make any sense for us to do that."

"Yes, sir, well I guess it is a question of whether it is an acceptable risk at this point."

"Well, let's examine the risk. There is apparently at least one Cuban group that seems to think we either were responsible for, or complicit in, Eduardo's death. That is a fact we will have to deal with, but the problem exists whether we contact the Soviets or not. It is a security issue, and we know how to deal with that."

"What if they tip somebody off?"

"Like the CIA for instance?"

"That's what I was thinking."

"Well, one thing I am very sure of, is that Eduardo told no one what the item is. He was no fool, and there was absolutely nothing for him to gain by disseminating this information. The true nature of this operation was known at only the highest levels of the Cuban security services. I am positive no one else in this country knows about the item."

"But they know there is something going on."

"What do they know? They know that Eduardo was doing business with us, and that he was prepared to purchase something from us, and perhaps that it was something of great value. Do you think they would be fools enough to go to the CIA with that?"

"I guess not."

"No. They will no doubt try to make trouble for us in some way, but I am not very concerned with that. None of these groups wants to get involved with the CIA. Just to be sure, I will get a communication through to the DGI in Havana, notifying them that Eduardo has been eliminated by persons unknown, and that we are unable to proceed. I will ask them to put their foot on the throats of their dogs and make them back off."

"So we contact the Soviets?"

"Yes, I am a little concerned about that option, but I believe we have no other if we want to proceed."

"How do we know who to contact?"

"Exactly, that is the problem. We know some individuals in this country who are being handled by the KGB, but I wouldn't trust them enough to divulge anything about this operation."

"What else can we do? We can't just march into their embassy and ask to speak to the head spy."

"No, of course not. We do not want to be seen, for any reason, to be communicating with the Soviets. There are other ways. A few on our Council have had direct or indirect contact with KGB operatives in the past, in various parts of the world. I am sure they may be trusted to make discreet inquires as to whom we should be in contact with."

"What would you like me to do next, Mr. Francoeur?"

"For now, Bruce, I just want you to rest and heal. It appears we will be in a holding position for a while at least. You may stay here at the house for as long as you wish. That way Douglas can keep an eye on you. I'll have Charles send someone to pick up anything that you need from you residence. When you feel up to it, I think you should examine all of our security procedures and talk to our people about situational awareness. I will keep you informed as to our progress. I think it would be wise to put some additional security in place here at the house and also at our office down town. I will see to that for you."

"I would like to apologize, Mr. Francoeur, for these setbacks. I'm sure we will succeed after all of this is sorted out."

"Yes, Bruce. There will be a good outcome for the family. You may be assured of it."

* * *

The study was not the sterile, austere monument to power that his formal office was. There were stacks of books everywhere, with handwritten notes indicating passages of interest. Papers were piled up on his desk and on the credenza behind it. Maps, marked in various colors were strewn across a table, making it look like the navigation room of a ship.

There was a sextant hanging on the wall, along with a barometer and a set of clocks each labeled with a different time zone. It was the place that more closely then any other, revealed the inner workings of the man who occupied it. Few were ever admitted.

He had a file on each of the council members, which provided a detailed history of their operations going back ten years. He was reviewing reports of previous KGB encounters to determine which of the council members would be best able to help. There was a knock on the door.

"Come in."

Charles stuck his head in. "Miss Francoeur is here to see you, sir."

"Yes, Charles. Please tell her to come up."

After a few minutes, Katherine entered the room. Marc did not get up to greet her. He remained at his desk and continued to go through his files. She waited patiently for a few minutes before speaking.

"You asked to see me?" she said finally.

He put down the folder he was reading and walked slowly around the front of his desk. Katherine remained by the door, no expression on her face. He raised his head finally and looked at her. "Do you want to tell me about it?"

"What are you talking about, Marc?"

He struck her across her face with the back of his hand, nearly knocking her to the floor. She staggered, and then reached out and grabbed the back of the chair. Tears streamed down her cheeks.

She would not look at him. When he spoke, there was no anger in his voice, but it was cold as if he were talking to a criminal.

"You have betrayed me, betrayed this family. What could possibly make you stoop to such a thing? Have I not given you everything you could ever want?"

She didn't answer.

"To engage in behavior like this, to drag my good name into the gutter, to steal like a common thief. Why have you done this?"

She remained silent, putting her hand up to her cheek.

He grabbed her by the shoulders and shook her. "Answer me, damn you."

Her voice trembled and was barely audible. "I don't know why. I just did it."

"You just did it. At this time, when our negations on the hospital wing are at their critical stage. With all that is going on. Have I not told you how important the next few weeks would be?"

"Yes," she said weakly.

He stood looking at her for a long time. Katherine stared at the floor.

"What am I to do with you, Katherine? How can I rely on you now? I have involved you so deeply in my affairs. Perhaps I was wrong to have done so."

"I am sorry, Marc. I don't know what to say. I don't know why I did it."

His demeanor changed and he put his arms around her. "You know how much I love you, Katherine. You know I want only the best for you. There must be something troubling you for this to happen. What is it? How can I help you?"

"I don't know."

"Is this some kind of obsession? Have you been doing this all along?"

"No, Marc, this was the only time."

"Perhaps you need to talk with someone, a counselor of some kind."

"I don't know."

"Fortunately for all of us, my friends on the police force have been very discreet. There will be no public scandal. Look at me, please."

She raised her head and finally was able to look him in the eye.

"I must know now, Katherine. I must have your assurance now that this will never happen again."

"It will not. I swear it."

"Please, Katherine, if you need to talk to someone, tell me. I will arrange it for you right away."

"I don't think so, Marc. I will think about it."

"Please do. Now go and get yourself cleaned up. We will be having guests for dinner."

- 20 -

It was a space designed to provide the illusion of opulence. There were Renoir and Monet reproductions on the walls. The bed was plush and covered with an elegant bedspread with gold threads running through the fabric. The carpet was thick and soft under his feet and there were two monogrammed bathrobes hanging next to the shower.

A telephone hung on the wall next to the toilet, for those who understood the true value of time. There was also a bidet, which he operated a few times as if he were preparing for a test on its proper use. Paul took it all in with a shrug of his shoulders, wondering again why people needed these things to feel good about themselves.

He had planned to talk with her for a while, hoping to find a way to discuss his doubts about the family. When she arrived, they kissed and held each other and then their passion carried them away. They made love desperately at first and then more slowly and deliberately, exploring each other, losing their inhibitions, his doubts lost for a while in the intoxication of his growing love for her. Afterward they lay together, tenderly, not needing to speak. Finally he pulled back, looking in her eyes for the love he hoped to find there. What he saw was sadness. She looked as if she were about to cry. It was then that he noticed a bruise mark on her cheek. She had tried to cover it with makeup.

"What happened to you?" he asked, suddenly startled out of his contentment.

She buried her head against him, and he felt her tears against his neck. He pulled back again. Her eyes were moist, and she would not look at him.

"Please, tell me what happened."

"He found out."

"Marc? Found out about what? The police?"

"Yes."

"But how? I know Spencer wouldn't have done that."

"It wasn't him. Someone at the police station."

"He hit you? The bastard hit you?"

She buried her face against his neck again and cried softly. His mind filled with rage. She must have felt the tension rising in him, and she pulled back.

"You must not say anything about this. You must not do anything. There is nothing you can do about it. It will not happen again."

"You have to get away from him."

"How? How can I do that? Where would I go? I know no one outside of the family."

"You know me."

"Yes, but you are not in any position to help me. You are a captive also in your own life." She reached out and caressed his cheek. "Promise me, Paul. Promise me that you will not do anything about this."

"I'll promise you I won't do anything about it for now. If he ever touches you again, I'll break both of his arms."

"It will not be a problem. He is already quite contrite about it. I have made up my mind to leave him, but it is going to take some time. A way must be prepared. It will be difficult. You were right when you suggested he owned me. I have the illusion of freedom, nothing more. I was not entirely honest with you when I told you he would let me go. I think he will never let me go willingly."

"What about when you were going to get married? You said Marc liked your fiancée. He would have had to let you go then?"

"Yes, he did like Jonathon, but he was not in favor of the marriage. He wanted Jonathon to move here, but we had other plans. Jonathon intended to join his father's law firm in Lake Charles. Marc was very unhappy about it. He offered to give us part of his estate and to build us any house we wished if we would stay in New Orleans. I think if things had not worked out the way they did, Marc would have disowned me completely."

"There has to be a way."

"It is all right for now. I will be careful with him and with my life. Now I have you to fill the emptiness inside of me." She pulled him to her. "We must be careful. I don't know what he would do if he found out about us."

"I don't understand. Why would he treat you this way?"

She looked at him for a moment. He could see the struggle going on inside her. He didn't know what to say, so he just held her. Finally she began to speak, and at first he didn't realize what she was telling him.

"It was shortly after Andrea died. I was sixteen years old. It was a horrible time. Marc was devastated, and I felt like I had lost both of them. I tried to comfort him. I felt so alone. One night he came to me in my bedroom. We talked about Andrea and held each other. He had been drinking. He started to caress me and then to touch me. I was afraid of losing him. I was too afraid to stop him. He took me that night and then many times after. I loved him. I told myself it was all right because he loved me. It went on for nearly three years, long after I had realized how wrong it was. At first he refused to stop, and so I did the only thing I could do. I became passive. I let him do what he wanted, but I did not participate with him. Finally he stopped coming to me in the night. He has not touched me since, in that way, but he has always been possessive of me."

Paul continued to hold her, saying nothing, his hatred for Marc growing inside him. She rolled over on top of him, kissing his neck and then his chest passionately, as if to erase the memory from her mind. They made love again until all of the anger was washed out of him. He knew that there was no way he was going to walk out of the family now. Somehow he had to find a way to help Katherine get free of it first. To get free of Marc. He wondered just how far the bastard would go to keep her.

"I must go now, Paul. Please do one small favor for me."

"Of course, anything."

"Remain here for another half hour or so after I am gone. In case I am recognized by anyone."

* * *

Paul lay on the bed trying to make sense of it all; his thoughts racing. He was convinced that Marc would resort to anything to stay in control of her, and he wondered what he might have done already. It was still early, and he decided to see if Spencer was home. The walk helped to clear his head. Spencer was just locking his door when Paul came up the stairs.

"Hey, general, how goes the battle?"

"I'm outnumbered, as usual."

"Anything I can do to help?"

"Maybe. Would you be able to get information on an accidental death that happened about ten years ago? It was an automobile accident."

"Sure, I can look in the Times archives."

"Well, the thing is, it didn't happen here in New Orleans. It happened in a place called Morgan City."

"How come you want to know?"

"Just call it curiosity."

"There's something you aren't telling me, isn't there?"

"Well, if it turns out to be anything, I'll give you all the details. Okay?"

"Anything for a close personal friend of Katherine Francoeur. What is the person's name?"

"Jonathan Lampert."

"Lampert, as in the Lake Charles Lamperts?"

"Yeah. I mean he was from Lake Charles."

"Well, if it is those Lamperts, I can tell you they're a well-known family in this part of the world. Let me see what I can find out. I don't have any contacts at the Morgan City PD, but I'll do some digging for you. It may take a while."

Paul decided to go back to the base early. With so much chaos happening, it felt suddenly comforting for a change to be in an environment where everything was as it seemed to be and had a label to prove it. The uneasiness he had felt when he first got involved with the family had returned, but he couldn't see any way around it. There was no way to get out of it without losing Katherine. It might even be worse for her if he walked away. He wondered if Marc already suspected anything. He received a call at his duty station on Friday afternoon. It was Spencer.

"Hey, I'm sorry to be calling you at work, but I'm going out of town for a few days and I wanted to give you the information you asked me about. Is it all right to talk?"

"Sure."

"First of all, are you sure you don't want to tell me why you are interested in Jonathon Lampert?"

"Not at the moment, if you don't mind."

"Hey, whatever floats your battleship, admiral. Anyway, I didn't want to wait until I got back because this stuff is pretty interesting. Are you sure you aren't some kind of a spook or something?"

"No. I guess I just like to stick my nose in things."

"Nose, hell, you jump in with both feet. Ok, well, here goes. Jonathon Lampert did die in a car accident on Highway 90, three miles outside of Morgan City on May 18, 1958. He was twenty-one years old and the eldest son of Charles and Margaret Lampert of Lake Charles, Louisiana. Charles Lampert is a lawyer with the firm Lampert, Boudreau and Smythe. They are corporate attorneys and the Lamperts are extremely well-healed, as we say. I told you I was familiar with the family name. The police report listed the cause of death as an automobile accident resulting from the combination of excessive speed and dangerous road conditions. However, the case was kept open for a while pending toxicology results. They usually do that in these kinds of cases to rule out alcohol or drug involvement. When the test results came in they were clean, except that there was a small amount of a drug called Acepromazine Maleate in his system. I had never heard of that one, so I did some digging. Apparently it's a tranquilizer they use with horses when they need to be trailored for long distances. There were no known cases of this drug being abused by humans at that time, which raised some questions.

"The Lamperts were upset, to say the least, at any suggestion that their fair-haired son was using drugs and they quietly demanded an investigation. The investigation revealed that Mr. Lampert had spent the weekend at a property near New Orleans, which among other things, houses an impressive stable of Arabian horses. Mr. Lampert and his fiancée had been riding earlier in the day, and the theory was that he somehow came into contact with the drug in the stables and it found its way into his system. A prescription for the drug had been written months previously by a veterinarian. They found a bottle of the stuff in the trainer's office. Apparently, it's possible this drug can be absorbed through the skin. Do I need to tell you the name of Mr. Lampert's fiancée?"

"No. I'm sorry, Spence. I didn't want you to get stuck in the middle of anything."

"Perfectly all right, admiral. In any case the investigation was closed. Let's just say it was in nobody's best interest to suggest that the death was in any way drug related and there was not enough proof to charge anyone. Also, since the body had been immersed in the Bayou for a few days, it was difficult for them to determine whether there had been enough of the drug in Mr. Lampert's system to cause him problems. The fact that they found any of the drug at all suggests to me there had to be a lot more before he went for his swim, but what do I know? Anyway, the whole thing went away quietly."

Paul was silent for a few minutes.

"Are you okay, man?"

"Yeah, sorry, Spence. I was just thinking."

"Well, let me give you one more thing to think about. There are people who do not want this case discussed by anyone. I asked for a copy of the autopsy report, but I was told in no uncertain terms that not only was that not going to happen but, if I was smart, I would forget I had ever heard the name Jonathon Lampert. I kept getting asked 'who wants to know'. The guy I was talking to was whispering. Do you get what I'm saying?"

"Yeah, look I'm really sorry, Spence. I didn't want to get you in any hot water."

"Think nothing of it. In my business, hot water is an occupational hazard. That's why my paper has lawyers. Anyway, here's the good news. I got in touch with a friend of mine in Lake Charles, and he got me a copy of the report anyway. It came to my office today. I'll show it to you when I get back, but you can't let on that you know anything about this."

"Don't worry about that."

"Yeah, well, if you keep insisting on poking a stick into every beehive you find, you're going to get your ass stung. Why don't you relax a little and take up bowling or something? Maybe it would satisfy this need you seem to have for big balls."

* * *

On Saturday morning Paul made the pickup arrangements as usual. It had started to rain, and he was rushing to get to the pick-up point when a blue sedan pulled up in front of him at the curb. The door opened and a man in a suit holding a gun and some kind of identification told him to get into the back seat. He had little choice. As the car sped off, the man in the passenger seat turned around and faced him.

"Are you going to be a good boy, or do I have to cuff you?"

"Who are you? What do you want?"

"I'm agent O'Brien with the FBI. This is agent DePetro and agent Landis. What time are you meeting your contact?"

He was so sick he felt like he was going to lose it all over the car. "I don't know what you're talking about."

The agent in the back yanked his bag away from him and opened it. He pulled out the envelope and gave it to O'Brien.

"We're talking about these."

"Those are just aerial photographs I'm studying to take the pilot's exam."

"Listen, Sergeant Greene, if you want to make things hard for yourself we can do that. We know about your involvement in this operation. There are a lot of people who want to burn you down over it. They believe you have willingly committed espionage. I don't think you are a traitor. I just think you're incredibly stupid. If you're helpful to us, I think I can prevent you from being hanged. I may even be able to keep you from going to jail for the rest of your life. What happens next is up to you. If you cooperate, and I mean starting right now, I'll do what I can for you. If not, you're going away for this, if you're lucky. Now I'll ask you again, what time is your pick-up?"

"Ten thirty."

"You have a number to call?"

"Yes."

"Jim, pull over at that pay phone. Now I want you to dial the number and tell them you can't make the pick-up. Tell them you've been delayed at the base by a surprise inspection. Tell them you'll call them and arrange a different time. You don't know if it'll be today. Can you do that without shitting yourself?"

Paul nodded.

"Go with him, Jim. Make sure he says what I told him."

They took him to an office in a nondescript building along the shore highway in Gulfport. There was no identification on the door. They put him in a room and left him there for a long time. He felt like a dead man. Finally, O'Brien and the one named Landis came into the room. Landis had a tape recorder.

"Saturday, July 12, 1969, 10:36 Am. Subject is Air Force Staff Sergeant Paul Greene. Also present at the interrogation, Senior Agent Walter O'Brien and Agent Stephen R. Landis." He switched off the recorder.

O'Brien sat down across from him. "Look, I know you're scared shitless. I really do want to help you. Do you think you can keep it together to talk to us?"

"I think so."

"Can I get you a cup of coffee?"

"Yeah, that would help"

"How do you take it?"

"Black and one sugar."

O'Brien nodded to Landis and he went out to get it.

"When Agent Landis returns, I'm going to ask you some questions. Your answers will be recorded. Sergeant, the only hope you have is to be completely honest with us. You've become involved with some very dangerous people, and at this moment in time are in possession of classified US Government Documents without authorization. We have reason to believe that you have already transferred documents of this type to unauthorized individuals whose intent it is to do damage to the security of the United States. At the very least, you're an accessory to espionage."

Landis walked in with the coffee. He turned on the tape recorder.

"Now, Paul, I want you to tell us in your own words just how you came to be involved with this group and exactly what you have given them to date. Please be as detailed as possible. I must warn you we know a lot about this operation already. If you lie to us, we'll terminate this interview, and you'll be transferred to a holding facility pending the disposition of this case."

The anger was growing inside him. Anger at the family, but most of all anger at himself. The stupidity of it all had come crashing down on him. More than anything, he wanted to believe that Katherine was not part of whatever was going on. He knew he might never see her again. He told them everything. Everything except Katherine.

"Like I explained, I was told I was carrying non-classified photographs. I looked at all of them. None of them were marked classified. None of them had any kind of military installations on them. It was just photographs of fields and geological formations."

"Did it occur to you that if this had been a legitimate and sanctioned government project, there surely would have been some above-board means of transporting this data you thought you were carrying?"

"Yeah, and I was worried about that, but they were really convincing. They told me there was a lot of disagreement in the government about the project. It seemed plausible to me. That was the reason they had to act cautiously. Like I said, I didn't think there was anything classified on these photographs. They even introduced me to a full bird colonel who was involved with them."

O'Brien consulted his notes. "Would that be a Colonel Jordan?"

"Right, that was his name."

"I know this will come as a shock to you, Sergeant Greene, but there is no Air Force colonel with that name. At least not anywhere near New Orleans. The man you met was undoubtedly an actor, hired to help reel you in. These people are extremely thorough."

The shock must have shown on his face. He didn't know what to say.

"Come with me, Sergeant."

They went into an adjoining room. O'Brien opened the envelope with the latest set of pictures.

"Are these typical of the photographs you have been transporting?"

"Yes, they all looked pretty much like these."

"Well, you're partly correct about the images on these photographs. There is no classified information on the images, although the mere possession of these images is illegal, owing to the fact that they were taken by a top-secret piece of technology. That isn't what we're concerned about. Do you see the line of numbers at the lower right? Take a look at the punctuation, the period between the first set of numbers and the second?"

"Yeah, what about it?"

O'Brien reached over and slid some type of viewing device in front of Paul. It looked like a microscope, only bulkier. He positioned the photograph and then told Paul to have a look. What Paul saw made his heart stop. He looked at O'Brien, and he felt the blood rushing out of his face. He felt like he was going to pass out.

"That, Sergeant Greene, is what is known as a microdot. It can contain an entire document the size of the one it's affixed to and yet it's too small to be noticed without magnification. In this case, the dot contains one page of the technical data for the design of the camera that took these photographs. It's one of the most highly classified technologies in the military inventory. The cover story you've been given has some element of truth. They are involved in a photo interpretation project. But its actual importance is as a red herring to conceal their operation. Very clever, I might add. Do you understand now what kind of trouble you are in?"

Paul put his head in his hands. He didn't know what to say. O'Brien put his hand on Paul's shoulder.

"When we picked you up, I told you I didn't think you knew what you were involved in. After hearing the story you told us, I'm convinced of it. First, let me tell you what is going to happen, and then I'll explain how you can help yourself. The people involved in this plot will be arrested and tried for espionage sooner or later. We have a pretty complete assessment of those involved in New Orleans. We have not yet identified the foreign agent they are working with. What we need to know is how deep this leak goes at the Pentagon and in the Intelligence agencies. Our primary mission is to stop the transfer of State secrets and, if possible, to retrieve what has already been compromised. Of equal importance is to uncover everyone in the government who is involved and to apprehend them. We frankly don't know at this time where the leak is ultimately coming from. We know many of those involved, and we are close to uncovering their co-conspirators but it is going to take some more time. So you see we have a dilemma, Paul. We don't want to show our hand until we can nail whoever is running this operation, yet the longer we hesitate, the more sensitive information will be in the hands of the enemies of the United States. In addition, it is important for this case that we have direct evidence linking Marc Francoeur to this conspiracy. We must be able to prove that he knowingly has or had custody of these documents. Otherwise, he might be able to claim it was someone in his employ, and that he had no knowledge of it. It could be difficult for us to prove otherwise. That is where you come in."

Paul sat up, feeling for the first time since he had been picked up, some small glimmer of hope.

"First let me explain what I can offer you. If you agree to help us and are successful in what we require of you, you will not be charged with espionage. You may be brought up on a misdemeanor charge of some kind and the charge will most likely be dropped. You will not do any jail time. Of course your career in the Air Force is over. I believe we can get you a general discharge for some medical reason. In short, we are prepared to pretty much let you walk on this entire business. Do I have your attention?"

"Yes, what do you want me to do?"

"First of all we want you to continue to do what you are doing. The photographs you receive in the future will be altered. The micro-dot will be switched. The replacement will show some diagrams of a non-classified piece of technology of no value to them."

"Won't they know?"

"We don't believe so. Our information is that they are accumulating this data until they have all of the critical documents. In this way there need be only one single hand-off to the foreign agent they are working with and only one cash payment. The substitute documents we provide you with will be very convincing to nearly anyone who may examine them; that is until they are studied by the scientist who will be working with this data on the other side. We have one major problem, however. You have already turned over some extremely critical design data. Even without the remainder of the documents, this information alone could possibly allow the enemies of this country to replicate the camera on their own, although it would take them some time to do so. We need you to retrieve these critical documents and replace them with copies we have created which will be of no use to them. We can't afford to have these documents in their hands, even for a short time."

"How can I do anything about it?"

"That is something that is going to take a great deal of planning and, for your sake, a little luck."

"How do you know I can pull it off?"

"We don't."

"If I fail, won't your operation be blown open?"

"If you are caught with either the originals or the substitute documents in your possession, we will be prepared to move against all of those we have identified at a moment's notice. It's not the outcome we want, but we will move if we have to."

"Where are the documents kept?"

"We have reason to believe they are in the safe in Marc Francoeur's downtown office. You'll be provided with a list of reference numbers. Those will be the documents you need to switch."

"How do you expect me to get into a safe? Don't you have people who can do that kind of stuff?"

"Keep in mind we can't arouse any suspicion, or the documents may be moved or destroyed before we can act. If that should happen, our case would be difficult to prove in court, to say the least, and we may never find out who our mole is. As you are aware, this group is very cautious and they have excellent security. It's no accident they're located in a bank building. We could certainly get into the building and into the office at night without leaving evidence. It could be done as a burglary, but this isn't our first choice. As far as opening the safe, it's easy enough to do if you don't care who knows you've done it. To do it without leaving any trace is another story. In spite of what you've seen in the movies, opening a good safe, and this one is a very good safe, without drilling it or blowing off the door, is much more difficult than is generally believed."

"Well, then, how do you expect me to do it?"

"We don't. We expect you to enter the safe, switch the documents, and get clear of the office during a social function. We've had that office under surveillance for quite some time from a vacant building near by. For a man as thorough as Marc Francoeur, it's surprising that he doesn't bother to close the drapes to his office. Observation has told us that he generally leaves the safe unlocked when he's in the office and locks it when he leaves in the evening. With a little better luck we would have gotten the combination, but the angle we have causes the front of the safe to be blocked from view when it's being opened and locked."

"I can't just walk into his office and go into his safe."

"You can, and we'll show you how. This is your only option, Paul, unless you want to spend the rest of your life in jail."

"Let's say I pull this off. How long before Marc is arrested?"

"That is unknown at this time. As I mentioned, we first want to be assured that we've identified everyone involved in the operation. Beyond that, there are many in the agency who are in favor of keeping this operation going for a while. By feeding our enemies cleverly altered information, we may be able to keep them from trying to develop this technology on their own and cause them years of delays in producing a successful program."

"So if I do this, what happens? Do you just hand me my discharge papers and send me home?"

"Yes, it might be as simple as that. We may arrange a transfer to another base whereupon you will be discharged and allowed to walk. You will, of course, be required to testify once this case goes to court, and we'll want to keep tabs on you until that happens. But we're getting way ahead of ourselves here."

"Wouldn't he be suspicious if I were suddenly transferred?"

"We would make sure it was handled in such a way as to not arouse suspicion. Do you understand everything I've told you?"

"Yes, I think so."

"I want to make one more point perfectly clear to you, Sergeant Greene. I don't think you're a stupid individual. I just think you made a stupid choice. I've seen the woman. Men have done worse things for less. I hope by now you understand that your only sane option is to cooperate with us fully. There should be no reason for you to retain any vestige of loyalty to these individuals. They've lied to you and put your career and your life in jeopardy. In addition, they are attempting to put the security of the United States at risk. If you make any attempt, through the woman or otherwise, to tip them off, it will go very badly for you. Do you understand?"

"Yes. But can I ask you just one thing?"

"Sure."

"Is the woman…is Katherine involved in this?"

"We don't have any information on that either way. She's certainly embedded in this organization up to her eyebrows. We have no reason to believe she isn't involved, but we also have no proof to the contrary. All of that will be determined by our investigation after the operation is shut down. Certainly this is a very large organization and our assumption is that only a few individuals know this is going on. Most of the members of the group no doubt think they are involved in legitimate enterprises. The woman may fall into that category. We just don't know at this time. For your own sake I would advise spending as little time as possible with her until this matter is resolved."

"Look, I have a personal relationship with Katherine. If I suddenly stop seeing her, she's going to want to know why."

"Well, you're going to have to play that the best way you can. But if you tip her off either intentionally or not, it will go badly for you. Do I make myself clear?"

- 21 -

For Ernesto, living in the house with Anna was like a dream. Except for Anna's aunt, who ran the house with an iron fist and seemed determined never to let them have a minute alone together. Whenever they had time to sit together in the same room, Maria would find something for Anna to do. It became a kind of joke between them, and he had to admit it made the chase more exciting. There had been so much sadness after Hector and Ramón were killed. For a while he thought that Anna would never smile again. After a time though, she seemed to be at peace with it. Ernesto could tell that Anna liked him by the way she would look at him when Maria was scolding her. Soon they were making a game of it. Making excuses so that they would end up in the same room alone, even for a few minutes. Often, Anna would ask him to help her carry the laundry basket outside or to help her with moving the furniture when she was cleaning.

"You are spoiling that girl, Ernesto," Maria would say. "When I was her age I could carry a calf in my own arms."

"Perhaps that is why you now look like a cow," Ernesto said, but not loud enough for her to hear.

Anna laughed so hard she had to run to the bathroom. The first time he kissed Anna, he knew he was in love. Vicente insisted that he avoid being seen in public and he was beginning to feel like a prisoner, but he had to admit he liked the jail. Anna and Hector had both been born in the United States. Their mother was pregnant when she arrived on a fishing boat with Maria and half a dozen others.

Their father had been a soldier in Batista's army, and he was killed during the revolution. They were both US citizens because they were born in the United States. It was the last gift their mother would ever give them. She died from a hemorrhage giving birth to them. Maria had raised them as her own, and Anna loved her like a mother. Still, Maria was very strict and she did not understand what it was like to be young and living in America. She kept to the old ways. Although Anna laughed at him a lot, Ernesto had begun to believe she was falling in love with him. Maria suspected it too, and she watched them like a hawk.

* * *

Vicente visited Ernesto after the incident at the Seven Seas to give him the news.

"Our plan worked well, Ernesto."

He wanted to say it was not his plan, but he liked the way Vicente included him now and he felt he was becoming an important person in the organization. "Was the Americano killed?"

"No, I am sorry to say, he was only wounded, but two of Castro's pigs will never breathe again and now there is no way for the American to complete his deal, whatever it was. No one will trust him again."

"So what will we do, Vicente?"

"For now, we must wait. The Americano will be laying low somewhere and licking his wounds. We will continue to watch the big house. Sooner or later the time will come."

"And when it is time?"

"When it is time, Ernesto, we will kill the Americano, to avenge the deaths of our friends. You and I will do this together. Can you do this with me?"

"Yes, I will help you kill him."

"Good, then I will let you know when the time is right. Is everything okay for you here, Ernesto? Do you need anything?"

"No, I have everything I need, but when will I be permitted to go outside more, Vicente? I am not used to spending so much time in a house."

"You must be patient for a little longer. They will be watching our community even more carefully now and looking for unfamiliar faces."

"Yes, I understand."

"I do have something for you, though," Vicente said, as he handed him an envelope.

"What is it?"

"Open it and see for yourself."

Ernesto opened the envelope and found a document and some money.

"This is a copy of your birth certificate that was sent to us by our people in Havana before you left. It is all you will need to claim asylum in the United States. The money is not what was promised, because we were unable to sell the document as we planned, but it is a couple of hundred dollars to help you get by until it is safe."

"I don't know how to thank you."

"You do not need to thank me. You did everything we asked of you. What happened was not your fault. You can help me with a small job tomorrow night, though. I think we should go and make sure the money is still safe. We should move it to a different location. You are keeping the key in a safe place?"

"Yes, I have hidden it well. What will happen to the money, Vicente?"

"I have not told anyone about the money as yet. A find such as this is very difficult to keep quiet and the more people who know, the more chances there will be for others to find out we have it. It could be very dangerous for us if that happens. So far, only you and I know about it, and as I have said, you must tell no one."

"I have given you my word."

"Yes, I know you will keep it. I am glad it was you who was chosen for this mission, Ernesto. You have proven yourself to have courage and intelligence. I know I can rely on you."

* * *

The limousine pulled into the traffic along Canal Street and headed northwest toward the airport. Peter Thomas sat in the back with Marc.

"Thanks for the lift, Marc. I didn't expect to see you again so soon."

"I trust you have had a pleasant and profitable visit to our city."

"Yes, I have indeed. But since you don't normally chauffeur me to the airport, may I assume you have something you would like to discuss."

"Yes, there is something I hope you may help me with, Peter. I seem to recall a couple of years ago you were engaged in some kind of operation that indirectly involved a KGB operative in Istanbul."

"Yes, that would be Vasili Larionko. An amusing little cutthroat. Always had two women with him, in case one wore out, he said. The only Russian I ever met who preferred Jack Daniels to Vodka."

"What was involved exactly?"

"Well, we were having problems with pirates, of all things, operating in the Black Sea. They were intercepting our cargos and demanding protection money to allow free passage. It was a thorny problem for a while because these particular pirates had day jobs in the Turkish government. We needed some muscle, but we couldn't be seen leaning on these guys ourselves for fear of losing our contracts."

"So Vasili helped us."

"Well, it turns out these same boys were running hashish by the ton up into Odessa, and the Soviets were very interested in finding out who they were. We suspected they were mainly interested in, shall we say, levying an appropriate tax on the shipments, rather than stopping them. I knew of Vasili through a friend, and we got together and worked out a mutually beneficial solution."

"Does he trust you?"

"He doesn't trust anyone, but since we have good history, he will talk to me, especially if the price is right."

"Are you still in contact with him?"

"Not for more than a year, but I am sure I can find him if I need to. Do I need to?"

"Well, not necessarily Mr. Larionko, specifically. We have a situation in which we cannot involve our friends in Virginia. As you know we have been scrupulously careful about avoiding any KGB entanglements in the United States, and yet it seems now we need to have a conversation with them."

"Are we talking about muscle, an operation of some sort?"

"No, nothing like that. For obvious reasons, I do not want to get into any details."

"Of course, what would you like me to do?"

"I wondered if you could get in touch with Vasili and find out if he knows anyone in the US who might be willing to talk to us. We are looking for someone senior, if at all possible."

"Sure, I can do that."

"Can you rely on Mr. Larionko to be discreet?"

"As long as there is nothing to be gained by talking out of school. In this case he would have no useful information to tempt him. What type of time frame are we looking at?"

"Yesterday would not be soon enough."

- 22 -

After the FBI released him, Paul went back to the barracks and slept. He awoke in the night with a start and, although he only wanted to sleep, he could not bear to be still. He dressed and walked out to the flight line. His legs felt dead. The runways were marked with blue lights laid out in a grid of no discernable pattern when seen from the ground. It appeared to him as some giant, cosmic battlefield upon which he was now a pawn, waiting to be moved by forces outside of his control. He could not deny that he had put himself in harm's way, but it was not with intention. It was more that he had wandered onto a minefield by failing to read the warning signs.

The signs had certainly been there and had registered with him, but he had been blinded by the bright glare of his own desire. He wanted more than anything to talk to his sisters, but he wouldn't have known what to say to them. He would not be able to lie to them even if he wanted to. He wanted to talk to Katherine, but that was not possible. Not now. He sat in the grass alongside a runway and buried his head between his arms.

The fear washed over him, with a force so engulfing that he didn't hear the roar of the fighter jet racing in front of him until he felt the hot exhaust of its engine. He stood up without having made a conscious decision to do so. A feeling of determination surged through him. He watched the strobe lights of the jet climbing up through the night sky. The battle was joined. He resolved not to spend another minute in self-recrimination. Not to allow one thought of failure. Not to give in to fear. This was the challenge that now lay in front of him, and there would be nothing else to distract him. He had never been able to imagine his future, anyway. Now at least he could see the mountain he had to climb over to get to it.

He called for the pick-up the next morning. There was no time to see Katherine and he wasn't ready to talk to her, in any case. He left a message that he had been delayed and would have to return to the base that afternoon. He was convinced that she did not know the sinister nature of the operation, but if he was wrong, he could not afford to tip them off. At least not until he had switched the documents. He wasn't sure how she would react when she found out what the family was involved in. At some point he knew he would have to lay it all out for her. At least now he could think rationally about it. What had started as an infatuation had become something real, and he was convinced in his soul she was in love with him.

The safest thing would be to say nothing at all, and just let the investigation determine that she was not involved. The problem was that she might not be able to prove her innocence, and could be brought down with Marc because of it. He wasn't going to let that happen. He may have been a fool to let her lead him into it, but he was ready to risk everything to make sure she didn't get hurt. In spite of her desire to get out from under his control, Paul knew Katherine had a deep-seated reliance on Marc that would be hard to break. The more he thought about it, the more he was convinced Marc was behind the death of Katherine's fiancé. He needed to get a copy of the autopsy report on Jonathon Lampert. He was sure if he could convince Katherine that Marc had been responsible for Jonathon's death, she would turn on him. The report didn't prove anything, but she had been there. She would know whether Jonathon could have been exposed to the drug by accident. It was his only hope.

He tried Spencer's number several times during the week, but kept getting the answering machine. Paul went into the city on the following Saturday and went immediately to Spencer's apartment. Spencer's girlfriend Audrey was there. She was obviously upset, and she hugged him when she opened the door. The apartment was torn apart.

"What happened? Where's Spencer?"

"He's in the hospital. Somebody broke in. They beat him." She leaned on his shoulder and began to cry.

"Is he going to be okay?"

"Yes, but just barely. He has a concussion. His face is all swollen. He looks horrible."

"Can I see him?"

"I'm not sure. They let me see him last night, but not for long. I'm going back over this morning, if you want to come."

Paul was hoping it didn't have anything to do with the information Spencer had gotten for him. A voice in the back of his head was telling him otherwise. He felt guilty for getting his friend involved. This was the second time he was going to visit someone he cared about in a hospital room. Both times it was because of him. But this time the family was the enemy, he was convinced of it. The nurse let Audrey spend some time with Spencer, but she kept Paul out for a while. She finally agreed to give him a few minutes after Audrey came out. He was shocked to see how bad Spencer looked. He had a bandage around his head, and there were some bloodstains on it. Both of his eyes were black and his jaw was so swollen he could hardly speak. He was groggy, but he recognized Paul and lifted his hand weekly to him.

"What happened, Spence? Who did this to you?"

"It was them. It was dark, but I saw the tattoo on one of them. I think they came to get the report. They tossed my apartment. They tried to make it look like a robbery, but I know that's what they were after. They told me if I wanted to stay healthy, I'd better mind my own business."

"Christ, I'm really sorry, Spence. I never should have gotten you involved in this mess. Is there anything I can do for you?"

"No, I'm going to be okay. You know what? It didn't hurt, not after the first shot, I mean. I couldn't feel it. My head just went somewhere else. I just need some time." He squeezed Paul's arm weakly. "You need to get away, man. These are some very bad people. You need to get back to Biloxi and stay there. They might be coming for you, too."

"Did they find the report, Spence?"

"I don't know. I had it on my bookshelf, down at the bottom, inside of my modern art book. It's a big book with Fish Magic on the front cover. You know, Paul Klee. Tell Audrey to look for it."

The nurse came in and asked him to leave. Paul promised he would be back the next day. He and Audrey went back to the apartment, and he helped Audrey straighten up the place. The bookcase had been emptied and the books were strewn all over the floor. Paul found the art book but there was nothing inside of it. He stayed the rest of the day and then took Audrey over to Baby's for dinner. She had calmed down quite a bit, especially now that she knew Spencer would recover. She was really in love with him. Paul wondered if Spencer knew. He guessed he did, but didn't want her to know it.

"Whatever is going on here, Paul? Do you know? Please tell me honestly."

He felt guilty lying. "I really don't know, Audrey. Maybe it was just a burglary that went bad."

"I don't think you really believe that, Paul. I think someone wanted to harm him, and I think you know why."

"Well, you know Spencer is always poking his nose into things. It's his job."

"Of course I know about that. But could it be something you both were involved in?

I know you have become close friends. Was he looking into something for you?

"Nothing I can think of. He was doing some research on the Celts for me."

"The Celts? Whatever for?"

"It's just an area I'm interested in. Kind of a family thing." He cringed at his own choice of words.

"Well, I do wish Spencer would find another line of work. He's so talented. I hate what he does. It all seems so tawdry sometimes."

"He seems to love it, though."

"I know, but I'll never understand why. He's so sensible in other areas."

"Well just hang in there with him, Audrey. I know you're very important to him, even if he doesn't show it all the time."

"Do you think so, really? Honestly, I never really know with him. He can be so horribly brusque sometimes."

"That's just his way of protecting his freedom. You know that."

"Yes, well, I can put up with it, as long as it doesn't last too much longer."

It was the first time he had seen her smile all day. In a strange way, helping Audrey deal with the crisis had served to calm him down inside. He was angry. But a feeling of deep hatred and the need for revenge were gradually replacing it. Somehow, getting Marc convicted for espionage was not enough. He wanted to settle with him personally. When he got back to the apartment, he called Katherine. Vincent answered and told him she was out, but would contact him at the apartment when she was able. Paul was awake half of the night trying to figure out how to handle it all. The most important thing was still Katherine. He had to convince her. He didn't know how.

* * *

She called him at the apartment in the morning and gave him an address where he could meet her. It was in the Garden District on Magazine Street. He took a cab. The apartment was on the second floor of a two-story building, much like those in the French Quarter, with a wrought iron balcony and large, shuttered windows on the second floor. He walked up the wide central stairway, lit by converted gas lamps and knocked on the door on the landing. Katherine opened it and stepped back to let him in. He was a bit startled. The apartment was almost empty, except for a couple of wooden chairs, the carpet on the floor and an old, banged-up looking television set, with a coat hanger for an aerial. There was a bottle of red wine and two glasses on the kitchen counter. The odor of fresh paint permeated the rooms.

"It has been leased by some friends of mine who will be returning to America from Paris next week. They gave me the key to let the movers in."

"I really like the way it's decorated," Paul said, putting his arm around her waist and pulling her to him.

They held each other tenderly for a moment and then stood back a little, peering in each other's eyes.

Paul broke the silence. "How have things been with Marc?"

"Everything has been well, as is always the case when he becomes cross with me. He overcompensates, and I pretend that I have already forgotten it. And with you?"

"I'm fine, but Spencer has been hurt."

"Oh no, what happened to him?"

"Someone broke into his apartment and roughed him up. He's in the hospital."

"Is he badly hurt?"

"He has a concussion and some bruises...he's pretty shook up."

"Was it a burglary attempt? Perhaps they thought he was not at home."

"Spencer doesn't think so. Nothing of value was taken. He thinks someone was sending him a message."

"Does he suspect anyone?"

Paul didn't answer right away, searching her face for a moment. He concluded it was an innocent question. "He has some suspicions, but you know he has information on a lot of people in the city. Maybe he got too close to something."

"That has been known to happen here. Please pass along my condolences when you see him again. Let me know if there is anything I can do. I'll have some flowers sent over."

"That would make his day. Believe me." Paul didn't want to stay on the subject too long for fear he might give something away. There was no way he was going to mention the autopsy report unless he could get his hands on it. More than anything he wanted to be close to her now. He just wanted to forget about everything for a while. He needed to reassure himself that her feelings for him were real.

"I am afraid I neglected to bring a cork screw," she said, finally.

Paul went to the counter and picked up the bottle and glasses. He carried them to the sink and removed the foil with his penknife. "This is a little crude but it generally gets the job done." He pushed the knife through the cork to make a vent for the air to escape and then with some difficulty managed to push the cork down into the bottle with his thumb. There were bits of cork in the glasses when he poured it, but Katherine seemed pleased with it. They sat on the floor of what would be the living room and sipped their wine.

"So, Paul, please furnish this space for me. Tell me what you would buy first?"

"First, a bed. A big, king-sized bed with a mahogany headboard."

"I agree, a bed first. But we will argue about the headboard. What next?"

"I don't know. A table, I suppose, and chairs. Maybe a black iron base with a glass top."

"A good choice but perhaps not black. And then…?"

"A big sofa and two lounge chairs with hassocks by the fireplace. Leather, maybe."

"No. Next must come the paintings. You cannot pick out the furniture without first making a statement about the space. Perhaps some Matisse, and in the bedroom, Goya. Perhaps Chagall in the dining area."

"Whatever you want."

"No, of course we will pick these out together, but only after a big argument and desperate love-making with the rain coming in through the window."

He smiled at her. "I'm afraid I won't be much help in that area. I don't know much about art."

"Nonsense. You just have to trust your soul. It will tell you what it likes. You will agree with it after a time."

"I'm not used to having expensive things around me."

"Expense is of no importance. In fact, I believe it is an unnecessary impediment. When something has beauty, it does so by its own nature. If it is also very expensive, then it becomes something else entirely. It becomes its equivalent in a medium of exchange.

People admire its value in money and no longer see its beauty as it should be seen. I could decorate these rooms for less money than a few dinners at Galatoires."

"But still, I think you would miss the luxury you have now if you were forced to live a more normal life."

"No, I would not. I can enjoy great art in a museum when I feel the need to feed my soul. I can find luxury in a hotel if I find the need for it. To live with it every day dulls the senses. I believe I have lived with it too long."

"So what would make you happy?"

"Do you mean, how would I wish to live? You will be surprised at my answer."

"Why?"

"Because I would choose a small house, with only a room for each of the children. The street will have many tall trees and the neighbors will come over to sit with us on the porch in the evening and watch the children play in the yard."

"That's really what you want?"

"It is what I have wanted since I was a child. I feel as though I have been on an endless vacation in places that are foreign to me. I want to go home."

"You're right, I am surprised."

"When I told you a while ago that I have met many men, but have not let anyone get too close, it was because of this."

"Because of what?"

"Because I could not see any of them sitting on that porch with me, holding my hand and watching the children play."

"So can you see me there?"

"You are there."

He kissed her then and they began to make love. She stopped him and took the wine glasses to the sink. On the way back she let her dress slip to the floor. He wrapped his arms around the small of her back and held her close to him, pushing his face into her firm, lean stomach, kissing her and feeling her move with him. The bright open space of the apartment seemed to set her spirit free. She made him chase her from room to room, breaking free in the middle of their love-making and escaping again, making him take her anew each time. She rolled across the carpet with him, laughing and pretending to resist him until he needed all of his strength to subdue her. At last they found release, collapsing together like two people who had fallen out of the sky. They lay together, breathing heavily, each lost momentarily in a universe of their own making, until her hand reached across the void and brought him back to her. She looked in his eyes and smoothed his wet hair with her hand. Kissing him not with passion now, but with the tenderness that comes from the knowing of her lover.

"And what about you? What is your dream?"

"I've never had a dream. I mean I've never been able to visualize a future for myself."

"Never?"

"Not that I can remember."

"I cannot imagine that. How have you been able to direct your life?"

"I don't know. I think along the way I've seen a lot of things that I didn't want to see. It's kept me from sitting still for very long. For the most part, I just do whatever is in front of me."

"Yes, I have recognized this about you. And what about now?"

"Now, I see myself in your dream. I don't want to be anywhere else."

She kissed him again. "But what about your work?"

"I'll teach, I think. There's not a lot of money in it, but I think it will make me feel like I'm doing something worthwhile, and it makes me feel good when I can engage someone's mind."

"I can imagine you a teacher. I think you are a man who needs to find the reason for things. The connections and the consequences."

"I guess so. It's always fascinated me to see what drives people to do the things they do. That's what I like about history. It isn't the civilization-altering events that have occurred throughout time. It's the forces working below the surface that make men and nations do the things they do."

"And women."

"Yes, I'm sorry. The women, as well. They're some of the most interesting stories, because they have had no political standing throughout most of history, and yet they've often played pivotal roles in many great events."

"I have some money, Paul. It is not a great fortune, but it is enough. We can make a life together if that is what you want to do."

"Is it what you want?" Paul asked.

"Haven't I not told you so?"

"I still have two years of my hitch to go. I'll be away from you and probably in a war."

"There is fate, certainly. No one can escape this. But one must live believing that fate will be kind, don't you agree? Otherwise, there is no reason to dream."

"Still, a lot can happen in two years."

"Two years can be a long time in terms of events, it is true. But in the life of the soul, it is nothing. It is merely the pause between two heartbeats. Perhaps a small holding of the breath."

He kissed her and they held each other in silence for a time. He fought against the urge to tell her everything. If anything happened to prevent him from getting the document, there would be no life at all for them. He had to find a way. He looked at his watch. "Does that television work?"

"I don't know. You want to watch television?"

He didn't answer. It was an old black and white set and the picture was grainy. He moved the coat hanger to different positions to try to make the picture clearer. She came over to join him.

"What are you doing?"

They looked at the screen and saw Neil Armstrong standing on the surface of the moon.

- 23 -

It was the same dinner party. Only the faces were different. Paul didn't recognize any of the guests. Katherine was working the room, making the wives jealous. She made eye contact with him a few times and he felt her warmth, even from across the room. He was desperate to be with her, but they avoided any sign of familiarity. He tried to look relaxed, but it wasn't working. He got involved in one or two conversations, but it was just small talk. Mainly, he tried to look inconspicuous. In particular, he didn't want Marc to take too much notice of him. He hadn't originally been invited to the party. The only reason he knew about it was that the FBI had told him, and they were not talking about how they got their information. It made him wonder if they had a mole on the guest list. He didn't want to come out and ask to be invited, so he called Katherine and told her it was driving him crazy to be sitting around in the city doing nothing when he wanted to be with her. He didn't let on that he knew about the dinner party. She called him at his work number later in the week and told him she had asked Marc to allow him to help out at an upcoming function. She made it clear that he would not be her escort at this particular gathering. So far, so good. His heart was racing and he felt like he might pass out, but he managed to keep calm on the outside, at least.

They planned it to happen just before dinner. They wanted to have everyone standing so they could be moved out in a hurry. At 8:20 there was a muffled thump that rattled the windows. The room went dark and then the emergency lighting turned on. It was a surreal scene. The fire alarms went off, followed shortly by the elevator doors opening. A security guard appeared, looking concerned. A small amount of smoke was coming in through the ventilation system. It hung by the ceiling like a thin cloud. Marc went to talk to the guard and then turned and addressed the crowd. He announced that there had been a minor explosion in the utility room in the basement and there was a small fire, nothing to be overly concerned about. They had been asked to evacuate the building by means of the fire stairs. Marc started for his office but then the guard spoke to him again and Marc nodded. He asked everyone to be calm and to follow him.

Paul slipped aside, and hurried to the bathroom. He stood on the seat, stooped over, with the door slightly ajar. If anyone were going to check he figured they would look under the door for feet, rather than take the time to look in every stall. No one came. He waited for a few minutes. The fire alarm was driving him crazy. Finally he walked quietly over to the door and pushed it open just enough to listen. He couldn't hear anything except the alarms. There were also sirens in the street now and the reflection of the emergency flashers was strobing against the darkened ceiling. He stepped into the ballroom. There didn't seem to be anyone around. He walked quickly across the floor to the office door on the opposite wall and, taking one last look over his shoulder, went in and quickly closed the door behind him. Part of him was hoping the safe was locked, but when he tried the handle it opened. He had the file folder under his shirt, tucked into his trousers at the back and taped at the top to keep it flat against his body. He removed it, leaving it open on the floor. He removed a penlight from his inside pocket and clicked it on, placing it between his teeth.

There were several folders in the safe and in the dim light it was difficult to tell what was in them. After thumbing through four folders he found it. He was sweating profusely and it seemed like everything was happening in slow motion. He removed the file and started flipping through the pages to find the matching code strings, which he had memorized. He found all but one of them. He exchanged them with the duplicates. He folded the originals and put them in his inside pocket. The last document did not appear to be in the folder. He told himself to calm down and carefully read each one again. It wasn't there. The anxiety was starting to build inside of him. Where the hell was it? He went back into the safe and removed the other folders one at a time. The thought crossed his mind that he was probably looking at information that would be worth a fortune to someone.

At the bottom of the pile was a file labeled Lake Charles ME. Paul opened it. It was the autopsy report on Jonathon Lampert. His mind started to race. If they found it missing, they would know someone had been in the safe, but it was the proof he needed to convince Katherine that Marc was involved. He put it aside. He had to succeed in switching all of the photos or it wouldn't matter anyway. There wouldn't be much of a chance for a relationship with Katherine if he were living in Leavenworth.

He went through the folder with the photographs one more time, but he knew it wasn't in there. He was taking too much time. He examined the safe again, but didn't see any more files. He took the files he had piled on the floor and put them back, hoping that Marc didn't have them in some kind of order. He was about to close the door and get out when he noticed some white business envelopes in a compartment at the top of the safe. He quickly flipped through them. Most were addressed and sealed. Two were unsealed and marked only with some numbers and the word Abred. One contained a document, which he didn't have time to read. The photo was in the other one. A surge of relief ran through him. He quickly removed the photograph and put it in his inside pocket. He removed the duplicate and folded it like the original. He placed it into the envelope and put it back on the shelf with the others. The empty folder was still lying on the floor. He put it back in his waist band, not bothering to tape it and then checked all around the floor to see if he had left anything. There was only the Lampert file.

He held it in his hands for a few moments, trying to decide what to do. He knew he was running out of time. It was what he needed to convince Katherine that Marc was a murderer, but if Marc noticed it was missing it could blow the FBI's investigation and potentially put him away for the rest of his life. He thumbed through the report. Finally it dawned on him that all he needed were the toxicology findings. He found the page and removed it from the folder and then put the report back in the safe. He closed the safe, removed a handkerchief from his pocket and wiped down the handle and the door. Now all he had to do was get out. He walked quietly over to the door, opened it and looked out.

The ballroom was still empty. He had just started to step out of the office when he heard conversation and saw the fire stair door open on the other side of the room. The beam of a flashlight stabbed across the floor. He quickly closed the door. Panic started to overcome him, but he fought against it. He guessed it was Marc coming back to lock the safe. He thought for a second about hiding in the room, but there were no obvious places and he was afraid that the alarms would be reset and he wouldn't be able to get out. He went to the window and unlocked it. He lifted it and a gust of wind hit him in the face and blew some papers off the desk. He fought the urge to stop and retrieve them. The ledge was only a foot wide. He stepped out onto it and flattened himself against the building. With his left hand he tried to push the window down. It was difficult to do from the side and he nearly lost his balance. Just as the window closed, the door of the office opened and Marc came in accompanied by a fireman.

The wind ripped at Paul's clothes. He felt the pressure against his body. Even though it was a warm evening, it pushed through his sweat-soaked shirt and he felt suddenly cold and very alone. He stood trembling next to the window. He looked at the tops of the fire engines ten floors down. He heard Andre's voice. Don't look down. You're on a sidewalk. You could walk a mile on a sidewalk that wide and not fall over if it was on the ground, even in a hurricane. It's all in your head, man. Just do it. He thought about all of the times he had walked out on ledges like this one with Andre. It had never been this high. His legs began to stiffen and he fought against it. He was partially in shadow, but he was afraid with all of the fire engines, someone would look up and see him. He had to move. He inched his way along the ledge, trying not to look down.

* * *

In the office, Marc walked over to the safe and was about to lock it when he noticed the papers on the floor. He went over and picked them up, a puzzled look on his face. His gaze scanned the room, looking for anything else that might be disturbed. He walked over to the window and noticed it was unlocked. The fireman insisted that they go. He looked through the window briefly and then closed the lock and returned to the safe. He opened it and took a quick look inside, briefly running his fingers across the folders. Finally he latched it and gave the dial a spin. He glanced around the office, still looking puzzled and then left with the fireman.

* * *

Paul had made it to the corner of the building, but as he tried to ease himself around it, the wind hit him and nearly blew him off the ledge. His hands were soaked with sweat. He clutched onto the stone and fought back the panic. There was a gap between the building and the one adjacent. The wind was blowing through it like a tornado. It didn't matter anyway. The ledge only extended about three feet around the side of the building. There was nowhere to go. Fortunately the ledge was a little wider where it wrapped around the building and there was a slight recess where the decorative stone corner work protruded beyond the brick structure making up the side wall. He pressed his body against the side wall with his shoulder tucked behind the corner stones. The gaps in the corner stones gave him a place to wedge his hand. At least he was now in complete shadow and had some support. He closed his eyes and tried to calm himself. He had no idea how he was going to get down. Andre's face came back to him then. They had been up on a ledge like this one, not so high, but high enough. Andre was like a cat. He was walking along the ledge like it was a highway, but the building was old and weathered. When the ledge gave way, Andre had just turned around to tell him to hurry up. Andre gave him his big, toothy smile and waved him along like he always had. To Paul it didn't seem like he fell. He just vanished right before Paul's eyes.

* * *

On the street below, Marc spoke to the guests who were gathered in a group on the sidewalk. He explained they would not be allowed back into building any time soon and he had no choice but to cancel the remainder of the evening. He circulated through them, shaking hands and assuring them that they would be invited back soon. When they had dispersed he walked across the street and looked up into the darkness at his office window. His gaze moved across the face of the building.

* * *

Paul saw the man staring up at the building. He couldn't make out the face from his vantage point, but he knew who it was. At one point he felt like Marc was staring right at him. He pushed himself harder against the wall. Finally, Marc crossed back over and ordered his car be brought around.

All but one of the fire trucks had left and the crowd had dispersed. Paul knew he couldn't stay where he was for much longer. His legs were starting to throb, but at least he had managed to calm himself. He knew there was no way he was getting back through any of the windows. The alarms would have been reset, and he was sure security would be back in the building. For a moment he considered just giving himself up. It was a choice between losing his freedom and losing his life. In the end, he decided it would be better to die than to fail. He was standing at the base of his mountain. The one he had to climb over if his life were going to continue. The wind pushed against him, and he just wanted to be some place safe. The only way out was up.

The granite corner stones ran up the side of the building like a ladder. They protruded about two inches from the brick face. There was a six-inch gap between them. He fought the wind and wrapped his leg around to the front ledge, straddling the corner. Now it was just a matter of keeping three-point contact and lifting himself up the wall one limb at a time. It was tedious work. He rubbed his hands on his coat but he couldn't make them dry. He concentrated on the wall in front of him, forcing himself not to think about where he was. It was darker now that most of the emergency vehicles had left, and he wasn't particularly worried about being seen. He was worried about losing his grip. The mortar on the stones was flared into the brick face and he found it difficult finding purchase on the smooth granite blocks. Already his fingers were bleeding. Concentrating on the climb helped him keep his fear under control.

He only had to go up one floor to get to the roof but there was a decorative cornice at the top. It was a bit wider than the ledge he had been standing on. It looked strong enough, but he didn't know how old the mortar was. He also wasn't sure he could get a good grip on it. He reached up and out, running his free hand across the top. His fingers ached and he felt like he was going to lose his grip. There was a small groove about four inches in, along the length of the cornice. His muscles were beginning to tremble from the exertion and he knew he had to move. He pushed his fingers into the seam, and then reached up with his other hand and gripped the top of the cornice in the same way. He took a deep breath and then let his feet swing free. He was now hanging by his hands from a slab of stone, dangling like a puppet one hundred feet above the street.

The wind pushed against him and his body started to sway back and forth. The file folder had worked itself free and it fell. There was nothing he could do about it. He hoped the photographs were still in his pocket. His arms were burning. He pulled himself up and tried to lift one elbow over the top but he couldn't hold it. He let his arms extend again gathering his strength for one final try. He pulled himself up again, straining with every ounce of remaining strength. This time he managed to get his elbow over the top. He extended his arm and found a good handhold further in, where it met the wall. He swung one leg up and over and then pulled with his remaining strength until he was lying flat across the top of the cornice. He felt like he was going to pass out. He rolled over and fell onto the flat roof of the building. His chest was heaving from the exertion, and he couldn't feel his fingers.

He lay in the dark gasping for breath and trying to get some strength back in his arms. He knew he wouldn't be safe until he got off the roof, but he needed some time to collect himself. After a few minutes he sat up, and looked around. He saw what he thought to be the access stair over in the opposite corner. He walked over to it and tried the door. It was locked. Trying to force it open would probably be futile and anyway it would make too much noise. There was a strong possibility they would come up to check the roof. He walked around the perimeter, hoping to find a fire escape. There was none.

He looked over the side at the adjacent building. It was only there or four stories high. He would never survive the drop. There was an alley running along the back of the building. The veranda was in the back, but that would mean having to go back through the ballroom and setting off the alarm. That left only the side where he had climbed. He walked back over to the edge and peered across the gap. It looked to be about twelve feet but it was difficult to tell in the dark. The building on the other side was the same height.

It was a jump he could normally make with no problem. The only difficulty was that the outer wall brickwork where he was standing was higher than the level of the roof by about two feet. He would need a running start to make the distance. It meant that he would have to get up to full speed, land one foot on the brickwork, which he could barely see in the darkness, push off and leap across the gap. There was no way of knowing what was on the other roof. If he overshot the wall long or short he would go over the side. The fear had started to overtake him again. He just wanted to roll up in a ball and sleep. He sat down on the roof. There was a war going on inside of him. The part of him that wanted to surrender was beginning to win. He had started to drift off when he heard a noise. Someone was coming up the access stairs. A surge of adrenaline coursed through his body. He stood up, took one look behind him, and ran. His right foot planted firmly on the brickwork and he launched himself into the air.

Time had paused as his body hung in the insubstantial air, and his mind ran through the images of his past, perhaps searching for something to hold on to as he left this world. It settled on the memory of Katherine standing on the veranda under a crescent moon, with just those few vagrant strands of hair caressing her face to prove that she was real. He would have been content to stay there forever, but gravity pulled him back into his life. His body tumbled forward beyond his control until it collided with something he could not see. His mind screamed out in pain, but his will prevented the sound from escaping his lips. He lay, curled in a ball of agony, as he watched the flashlight beams sweep across the adjacent roof. The pain gradually drained out of his body, taking with it the last of his energy. He lay on his back and stared up into the black sky, utterly spent and beyond caring.

He wasn't sure how long he had been out of it but he awoke shivering. His body was soaked with sweat from the exertion. He forced himself up into a standing position and tried to walk. His right knee was throbbing, and he could barely put his weight on it. There did not appear to be an access door. He hobbled around the perimeter of the roof looking for a fire escape, but didn't find one. Finally he found an access hatch in the center of the roof, but it was locked from the inside. There was a large air conditioning unit next to the hatch and he sat down in front of the exhaust vent, grateful for the escaping heat. There was nowhere else to go. He supposed someone would find him there in the morning. He imagined the look on their faces as they tried to figure out how a man in a tuxedo had ended up on their roof. He decided he would tell them he had fallen out of a passing airplane. At least there were no more decisions to be made. What happened now was out of his hands.

He was lost in thought when he heard noise coming from beneath the hatch. There was nothing he could do but wait. The hatch opened and a head appeared in the middle of a shaft of light. A flashlight beam swept the roof, finally settling on his face. He shielded his eyes and waited.

"I found him," a voice said.

A man climbed out of the hatch, followed by another. Paul couldn't tell who it was. The flashlight beam settled on his face again.

"For Christ sake, Jim. Get that light out of his face."

It was agent O'Brien. "Are you all right?"

"No. I screwed up my knee. I don' know how bad it is."

"Can you walk?"

"Not very well."

"You've got more balls than brains, kid. That was the damnedest stunt I've ever seen, and I've seen a lot," Landis said. "We would have extracted you from the roof if you had given it some time."

"Yeah, well, they would have had me before you got there."

"We weren't expecting the Spiderman routine. Did you get them?"

"Yeah, I got them."

He took the photographs out of his pocket and handed them to O'Brien. He and Landis passed a look between them, as if they hadn't believed he could pull it off.

"One of them was in a separate envelope. I almost didn't find it."

"It was probably going to be used as proof that they actually had what they claimed they had. They no doubt already checked the microdot on that photograph. Our timing appears to have been perfect. That was a nice piece of work in there, Paul. Now we just have to figure how you can explain yourself if they have noticed you missing. Especially now that you've sustained an injury."

"Yeah, well, I almost got caught. I don't know if he suspects anything. I tried to make sure everything went back in the right place, but I don't know. Some papers blew off the desk when I opened the window."

"We'll just have to wait and see. As long as nothing is missing from the safe he probably won't suspect anything. He doesn't have any way to prove you were involved. We just need a way to explain how you got hurt."

Landis put the light on him again. "Not to mention, you look like you've been hit by a truck."

"That's actually not a bad idea, Jim. Lets get down off this roof and we can talk about it."

Paul needed some help on the ladder, but once on the landing he was able to limp along. O'Brien took his arm and put it across his shoulders for support. He wasn't looking forward to humping down ten flights of stairs.

"No, this way. We have control of this building. We can take the elevator."

When they got to the lobby, they walked to a rear exit. There was a car waiting for them. They covered Paul's head and upper body with a raincoat, in case anyone was watching.

"Okay, this is how we are going to play it. You've just been in a hit and run accident. You were walking home and not paying enough attention. When you stepped off the curb a car clipped you. We're going to take you to the emergency room to be checked out. We'll make sure there is a police report filed. Do you think you can handle that story?"

"Yeah, I think so. What happens now?"

"Well, we can't afford for anything to change right now. You need to go on doing exactly what you were doing. Drop off the packages just like before. We'll handle the rest. As I mentioned, we may want to let this thing go on for some time until we have a handle on all the players."

"What about our deal?"

"We're going to keep our deal. But you need to hang in there with us until this thing plays out. You can relax. You've been a great help to us, providing, of course, that this microdot checks out. The rest should be easy."

It was a Saturday night and the emergency room was packed. He sat for two hours before anyone saw him. He kept getting bumped down the list by people coming in on stretchers. The technicians took some x-rays. The doctor who examined him didn't see a fracture. He thought it was probably just a deep bruise. He told Paul they wouldn't be able to do a complete examination until the swelling subsided. They fitted him for a pair of crutches and gave him a prescription for some pain medication. He was to make an appointment in about a week. He called Katherine.

"Paul, where are you? We have been very concerned about you."

"I'm at the hospital. I was in an accident. I wonder if someone could come and get me."

"Of course. What happened?"

"I wasn't paying attention, I guess. I stepped off a curb and a car hit me."

"Oh, my god! Were you seriously injured?"

"No, I was lucky. I just banged up my knee a little. The tuxedo didn't hold up so well though. I think it went to its last party."

"Don't worry about that. I will be there shortly."

Just before the limo arrived, Paul remembered the toxicology report. He was relieved to find it had not fallen out of his pocket. Something told him to find a safer place for it. He folded it and put it into the toe of his shoe. Katherine was alone in the limo, but because of Vincent she did not show any affection toward him. On the way back to the apartment, he told her he had left the group shortly after they had been evacuated, thinking they probably would not be returning.

When they got to the apartment he was alarmed to see Marc sitting in the living room along with someone he had seen at the party, but didn't know. He was a large man with blond hair, and his arm was in a sling. The thought passed Paul's mind that this must be Marc's personal bodyguard and by the looks of things, he had recently earned his pay. He struggled to keep the anxiety from showing. Katherine was holding Paul's coat and the bodyguard took it from her. She looked puzzled for a moment, but she quickly turned to Marc and began giving him a recap of what had happened. Paul could see the bodyguard going through the pockets of his coat. He was trying to be subtle about it, but they obviously suspected something. Paul's anxiety level was rising, and he struggled to keep himself calm. Whatever Marc was thinking he didn't let it show.

"So how are you feeling, Paul?"

"As well as can be expected, I guess."

"We seem to have made a habit of finding you injured and in need of assistance."

"I'm really sorry."

"You should have told someone you were leaving the gathering."

"Yes, I know. I just thought it was over, and I wasn't feeling well."

"Are you all right?"

"Yeah. I'll be okay"

"In the future please make sure we are no longer in need of your services before you depart a function." His demeanor changed a bit. He stood and put his hand across Paul's shoulder. "You seemed very distracted this evening. It's not like you to be so careless. Is there anything wrong? Anything you would like to discuss with me?"

"No, I'm okay. Just a little tired."

Marc stared at him for what seemed like a long time. Paul did his best to look him in the eye. Finally Marc continued.

"I'm very pleased you weren't seriously injured. You are very important to us, Paul. We need you to be careful. Let us know if there is anything further we can do for you."

Marc left with his bodyguard trailing behind like a trained pit bull. When they were alone, Katherine hugged him.

"Can I get anything for you? A cup of coffee or something to eat?"

Paul felt suddenly exhausted and he just wanted to sleep. "No, I think I just need some rest."

She kissed him on the forehead. "Do you need help?"

"No, I can manage."

"Why don't you give me your tuxedo, Paul. I'll see if it can be salvaged. Otherwise we will have it replaced."

He went into the bedroom, put the tuxedo on the chair and removed the report from his shoe. He quickly stuffed it under the mattress and climbed into bed. Katherine came back in with his coat and put everything in a bag. She kissed him goodnight. He was too exhausted to enjoy it. When he awoke in the morning, his knee was still throbbing, but he found he didn't need the crutches. He left a message with Vincent that he was returning to the base.

- 24 -

It was a relic from another age. Newer motor lodges with swimming pools and family restaurants now guarded the exit ramps along the interstate, collecting tourists like flypaper, and leaving the Blue Bayou motel for those who rented by the hour. The white Cadillac pulled into the parking lot, moving slowly, like a cat in an unfamiliar room. There were two rows of freestanding bungalows, with a parking lot in between. The only light came from a small alcove with an ice chest and some vending machines, and from the flickering neon sign over the office. It was after midnight and traffic was light out on the highway. The only noise was the muffled sound of a television coming from one of the cabins. Bruce Taylor was at the wheel and he was accompanied by one of the ghosts. He pulled around the back and parked. A few seconds later, the tail car came in from the opposite direction and parked at the end of the row. No one exited.

Taylor and his man walked down the row of cabins, following the declining numbers until they came to number five. Taylor knocked on the door. He saw the light in the peephole flicker and a skinny, nervous-looking man with hollow cheeks and a pitted complexion opened the door. He had thinning, black hair plastered across the top of his head and was wearing a suit with wide lapels and padded shoulders that looked two sizes too big for him. He was doing his best impression of Al Capone, complete with a cigarette dangling out of his mouth. There was an older man sitting next to the bed. He was completely bald and his bushy white eyebrows made it seem like he was looking out at you from a cave. His wrinkled white dress shirt was open at the neck and a pair of over-wide red suspenders divided his ample girth into equal thirds. When he stood up, his pants hovered around his waist as if he were standing in a barrel. They man at the door moved aside for them, but when he had closed the door, he indicated silently that they should raise their hands so he could search them for weapons. Taylor sneered at him.

"That's quite all right. I am sure that will not be necessary," the other man said.

Taylor's expression became a little less murderous and he addressed the one sitting next to the bed. "Are you Alexi?"

"I am indeed."

"Can I see some identification?"

The man smiled. "If you wish, Mr. Taylor. However, I am sure you know I could show you a completely convincing passport proving I am J. Edgar Hoover."

Taylor reached out his hand. "Let's see it anyway."

Alexi opened a suitcase that was sitting next to him on the bed and removed a West German passport in the name of Johann Adler. It was Alexi's picture. Taylor thumbed through it, and handed it back to him.

"And may I see some identification as well, please?" Alexi asked.

Taylor handed him a picture ID with a corporate logo embossed on it. Alexi glanced at it and handed it back to him.

"Now that we have told each other the requisite lies, may we proceed, Mr. Taylor?"

Taylor just grunted and pointed his thumb toward the other man.

"My associate must, I am afraid, remain unidentified. Let us get down to business, shall we. I do not want to spend any more time than necessary in this hovel."

"All right. Did you bring the viewer?"

"Yes, it is right here in this suitcase. It will take just a few seconds to set it up, but before we proceed, we need to have a discussion about the terms of this transaction."

Taylor gave him a hard look. "We were told the terms would be the same."

"That is true, but there is the issue of a certain sum of money which was to be used as a down payment. This money has apparently vanished. We have been in contact with some friends of our unfortunate comrade, who was known to you as the Shepherd. There is the suspicion that your organization may have been involved in our comrade's untimely demise and that you may be in possession of this money."

"That is an absolute lie. We do not do business that way."

"Don't be upset, Mr. Taylor. We believe you. We were hoping, however, that you might have some idea as to what occurred and who might have this money now."

"Right now, we don't have a clue. It's possible he just got careless and was taken out by some cowboys who had no idea what he was carrying."

"Yes, that is always a possibility, however our friend was quite cautious and very good at his profession. We believe that scenario is highly unlikely."

"Well, that may be, but we don't have any other ideas at this point. We still think it was some kind of an inside job. In any case, we don't see this as our problem. We were ready to hold up our end of the deal. The buy-money is your problem."

"We will continue to look into it, you may be sure. In the meantime, may I have a look at the document?"

Taylor removed an envelope from his pocket with his one good arm and dropped it onto the bed. Alexi opened a flap on the suitcase and revealed a microscope, which he slid into the top of a black rectangular base. He uncoiled a power cord and plugged it into the socket next to the bed. There was a toggle switch at the base of the assembly and he reached in and turned the unit on. A bright light filled the suitcase. He opened the envelope and placed the photograph into the viewing area of the reader. Peering into the instrument he adjusted the focus and then concentrated on the image. After a few seconds he laughed, finally looking up at Taylor with an amused look on his face.

"What's so funny?"

"Have you examined this document, Mr. Taylor?"

"Not personally, no."

Alexi's eyes narrowed a bit and he looked down as if he were carefully considering his words. Finally he spoke. "Mr. Taylor, your organization comes highly recommended to us. I am sure you did not come here to waste our time, nor do I suspect you are stupid enough to try to deceive us. I can assure you that you would not get as far as your automobile if that were the case. Therefore I must assume that you have been deceived by someone else."

"Why? What's the problem?"

"Well, Mr. Taylor, this is indeed a marvelous and extremely high-tech piece of equipment. It is not, however, what was promised. It appears to be the design for a very elaborate, zero gravity toilet."

Taylor's jaw dropped. "What the hell are you talking about?"

"See for yourself."

Taylor stepped over to the bed and looked through the viewer. His face grew red with rage.

"At least your provocateur has a sense of humor, don't you think?"

The man at the door pulled a pistol out of his pocket and pointed it at Taylor. The ghost moved forward, but Taylor held up his hand and stopped him.

"Of course the other possibility, Mr. Taylor, is that you are agents of your government and this entire, unfortunate exercise was merely a clumsy attempt to expose myself and my associates. If that is the case, I am afraid our meeting tonight will end badly for you."

"Look, I don't know what's going on here, Alexi, but I assure you we are who we say we are and our only interest is in completing this transaction."

"I believe you, Mr. Taylor. Just the same I will require that you and your friend remain here in the room until we have had the time to get to our vehicle and depart. This building is being watched. Should anyone attempt to prevent us from leaving, you will pay dearly. Do I make myself understood?"

"Perfectly."

"It would appear that this operation has been sabotaged by persons, at the moment, unknown. It does not fill us with confidence that you will be able to deliver what you have promised. All is not lost, however, and our interest in the item remains unchanged. When you are able to show us the document in question, you know how to reach us."

Alexi started to leave, but Taylor stopped him.

"We are also not alone, Alexi. I would suggest you allow me to signal my people so that you are not to be interfered with."

"Do so, Mr. Taylor. But do so very carefully."

- 25 -

Paul's time on the base was becoming unbearable. He felt like one of the little green plastic solders he had played with as a boy, putting them in foxholes and dropping stones on them to his best imitation of exploding artillery. He couldn't concentrate, and he had become short-tempered with everyone. It got him a stern reprimand, and he had been threatened with an article fifteen. No matter what happened now, his days in the Air Force were numbered, and he just didn't give a damn.

Katherine called him during the week to see how he was doing. Paul told her he still had a slight limp, but there was a lot less pain. He had considered not going into the city that weekend unless there was a pick-up. He still wasn't sure how to approach her about the death of her fiancé. She seemed anxious to see him, though, and she asked him to arrange for a room at the Pellham.

She was an hour late and Paul was starting to get worried. Finally he heard a knock on the door. When he opened it, she hurried in, looking back down the corridor to see if anyone was watching. She sat on the bed, obviously upset.

"What's wrong?" He sat next to her and placed his hand on her back.

She looked into his eyes for a few moments as if to ask a question and then opened her purse and took out a small envelope. She opened it and removed a cufflink. It had the Family's talisman on it. He knew right away it was his.

"I am very confused, Paul. I need to understand what has happened. It is yours, is it not? There was one missing from your shirt after the accident."

"Yes, I suppose it is. Where did you find it?"

"It was given to me by the manager of our building. It was found on the roof of the building this week. How could this have happened, Paul?"

"Does Marc know about it?"

"I don't believe so. At least he has not said anything to me about it, but he has been agitated this week, and he has arranged for someone to review the security of the building. He had all of the locks changed as well. How could this have gotten on the roof?"

"Katherine, I have something to tell you. I wasn't sure how I was going to do it until now. I have something to show you, also." He went over to his suitcase and took out the toxicology report. He handed it to Katherine.

She studied it for a few minutes, not really comprehending what she was looking at. "This is about Jonathan. How did you get this? What is the meaning of this?"

"I don't think your fiancé had a simple accident, as you were told. That report shows that there was a small amount of a tranquillizer in his system when he was found. It's something they give horses to calm them down when they are being transported. Do you have any idea how that could have happened?"

"What are you saying?"

"Did Jonathon use drugs of any kind?"

"Of course not. Why are you doing this?"

"Because I believe you fiancé was murdered, and I think Marc did it because he didn't want to let you go."

She pulled away from him and stood up. She began to cry. "How could you say such a thing? How could you hurt me like this?"

"Katherine, I'm not trying to hurt you. I'm trying to warn you. Marc is not the man you think he is. He's involved in some very sinister things. I went into Marc's office during the fire last weekend. Spencer got that report for me. I asked him to see what he could find out about your fiancé's death. After what you told me, I was suspicious that Marc might have been responsible. This is why they broke into his apartment and attacked him. I knew it was Marc. I had to prove it."

"But why would you even suspect such a thing?"

"Because I know things about him. Things that you don't know. He's evil and that report proves it. I found that report in Marc's safe. It proves he was responsible for the break-in at Spencer's apartment and for the beating they gave him. I was nearly caught. I went up onto the roof to get away. That's how I got hurt. There wasn't any automobile accident."

"But even if it were true and Jonathan were drugged, why would you assume Marc was behind it?"

"Why else would he send his people to take the report from Spencer?"

"How do you know it was his people?"

"Because Spencer told me at least one of them had the tattoo on his neck. He saw it."

She stood like a statue in silhouette against the window. She was staring at the report, but not reading it. Paul couldn't see her face.

"Things are going to happen, Katherine. Bad things. I know you're innocent. You need to get away from him. You need to get away as soon as you can."

She didn't respond.

"Do you understand what I am telling you?"

"No, Paul, I don't understand. I don't understand why you would take the kind of risk you have taken. I wonder now if you are the person you claim to be. If this is true, surely it is a matter for the police. Did someone put you up to this? Is there something you are not telling me?"

"I did it because I love you, Katherine."

She walked over to the bed and picked up her purse. He reached out for her hand, but she pulled away.

"I need some time, Paul. I need to think about this. I'm sorry, I must go now."

"Katherine, you have to believe me. I am only trying to help you."

She looked at him for a moment, turned without saying anything, and then she was gone. He resisted the urge to run after her. There was nothing more he could say. He would have to wait for her.

* * *

They came for him after he had fallen asleep. It was what always happened in the dream he had been having, but now he was awake, and afraid for his life. It was Marc's personal thug Taylor, with his arm still in the sling, and two of his ghosts. He didn't recognize them. They told him to get dressed and they waited in the room with him. None of them would look him in the eye.

"What's this all about?"

Taylor responded by hitting him hard in the stomach. He wasn't prepared for the blow and he doubled over in pain. They frog-marched him out of the apartment and pushed him into the back of a white Cadillac. At least they had not given him a real beating. Not yet. He guessed that would come later. He was trying to figure out how much they knew and whether he could dance around it well enough to save his life. There was a part of him that didn't care anymore. One of the first thoughts that entered his mind as they were waiting for him to dress was that Katherine had betrayed him. It was the last tenuous string joining him to any future worth having. If it had snapped, he really didn't care about anything else. In the end, he did what he always did when he was waiting for bad things to happen. He took himself back to a lagoon he knew in Puerto Rico, where the water was blue and clear and alive with life, the jungle fragrant and singing in the hot sun, and the brown girl beside him beautiful and oiled on the bone-white beach.

They turned off the road into a long driveway lined with trees. There was a man standing just inside the entrance, but they didn't stop. At the end of the drive was an enormous house, lit up like a palace. They passed an imposing portico with Doric columns and some kind of Greek inscription on the frieze. The lamps on either side of the door flickered like torches. They continued around to the back. *So this is the castle of the king,* he thought. They marched him to a plain, windowless door, and down some steps to the basement. Their footsteps echoed against the dimly lit stone. He could make out only vague shapes of things piled against the walls. They came to a room. He expected to see manacles and a rack, but it was empty except for a couple of chairs and a table against one wall. There was a single light bulb hanging from the ceiling. The dim light didn't reach into the corners. They turned and left without uttering a word. The sound of the door slamming shut reverberated through the room, and he shuddered involuntarily. He heard the bolt slide closed on the other side.

There were no windows in the room. It felt damp, but it was not particularly cold. He walked around the perimeter to see if there was anything he could use as a weapon or a tool, not that it would do much good. Finally, he sat on one of the chairs and just waited. There was nothing else to do. He was startled when they came again. It was Marc Francoeur this time, with Taylor and the same two ghosts as before. Marc stood over him as if he were a schoolboy about to be punished for misbehaving.

"I have no desire to put you through any pain, Paul. I have become quite fond of you over the past few months. I was hoping to find a place for you in my organization. Unfortunately, some very troubling events have occurred, and we believe you are involved in them. I would like you to tell me everything you know about these events and identify any others who have been involved with you. If you tell us everything you know now, I may be able to find a way to save your life. If you do not, you will never leave this place alive."

"I don't have any idea what you're talking about."

"To begin with, someone broke into my office and removed some documents from my safe. What can you tell me about this?"

"I don't know anything about it."

"Come now, Paul, that story you gave us about being hit by a car. The suspicious fire, your unexplained absence after the evacuation. You didn't seriously think we believed you."

"I already told you what happened."

Marc straightened up and looked at Taylor. "I'm afraid Mr. Greene is not convinced of the seriousness of his situation. Please do not do anything that will prevent him from speaking to us after he has been made to understand."

He turned and left the room. Paul tried to prepare himself for what was coming. He assumed they would cuff him, or tie him the chair before they went to work, but they apparently wanted to make it a little more sporting. Or at least they wanted some entertainment. After the door closed, Taylor went over to him and gave him a backhand across the face, knocking him to the floor. His leg was still giving him a lot of pain and he had lost a lot of his agility, but he rolled and ended up on the balls of his feet. One of the ghosts came at him, but Paul sprang forward and rammed his head into the man's face. Blood flew from his nose, and he staggered backward. The other ghost and Taylor came at him together. He caught Taylor in the throat with his fist and he crumpled over, momentarily unable to breathe, but by then the other two were on him and he couldn't remember if he got any more shots in. It took a while for him to pass out. He was slammed into every wall in the room, and kicked when he fell. They concentrated on his body and he remembered seeing sprays of light, like a Fourth of July sparkler before everything turned black.

He was awakened by a bucket of cold water flung in his face. They lifted him up and put him back on the chair. He didn't know how much time had passed. He started to fall forward and one of them held him up by his hair. Marc entered the room again.

"All right, Paul, you have done what you felt you must. You have demonstrated your courage, but we had no need to be convinced of that. There is no need for you to prove anything further. Surely you can see the impossibility of your situation. There is no one to rescue you. No one knows where you are, nor do they care. This can go on for as long as we choose. Sooner or later, you will talk to us or you will die. Please save yourself further agony and tell us what you know."

"I know you're a traitor and a scumbag and a coward who beats women."

"Excellent, that is a beginning. Mr. Taylor, please get Mr. Greene a glass of water. I am sure he is thirsty."

"I have nothing more to say to you. Go ahead and do what you want."

"I know you have become quite fond of Katherine, Paul. Perhaps you have deluded yourself into thinking she has feelings for you. You are not the first naïve fool who has fallen victim to her charms. It is immensely amusing to watch."

"Yeah, well, apparently she's been charming since she was sixteen."

Marc stiffened. He drew his hand back as if to strike, but he caught himself. There was a long pause before he spoke again. "I know about the cufflink, Mr. Greene. I know you were in my office and that you have interfered in my affairs. What I don't yet know is the extent of the damage you have caused."

"I'm not stupid, Francoeur. You're going to kill me whether I talk or not. Why should I tell you anything?"

"Why, Mr. Greene? Because it is the only chance you will ever have to tell me to my face what you have done to thwart my plans. I think you need that satisfaction. It will be your only reward from this entire unfortunate episode. You are correct, Mr. Greene, I cannot afford to let you live, but you always were merely a pawn in this game. Do not blame me for that. Remember that you volunteered."

"Not for what you are involved in."

"Perhaps, but you could be back in the safety of your anonymous life on your base. It is in your nature to take risks, Mr. Greene. We recognized this about you from the beginning. That is why we chose you. You have taken a risk with us, and it has gone badly because of the choices you have made. That, as they say, Mr. Greene, is life."

"Okay, I'll tell you what I've done. You're right. It will make me feel better knowing you're going to have to sit now and wait for the hammer to fall. They know about you, Francoeur. The FBI knows about your operation and now, thanks to me, they have the proof. They busted me. More than a month ago. They showed me what you were really doing with those photographs, and what was hidden in the microdots. Now they have what they need to bust you wide open. You can kill me. But I'd rather be dead than spend the rest of my life locked up in a cage, which is what's going to happen to you."

"That, Mr. Greene, is highly unlikely. You have no idea how deeply entrenched we are in your government. You may have successfully thwarted this operation, but by no means have you done any permanent harm to us. If you were alive to witness it, you would see that this entire episode will disappear like so much dust."

"How does a man like you live with yourself? All of your talk about being patriots and loving democracy. You're just a bunch of two-bit spies selling our country down the river for a profit."

"That is where you are wrong, Mr. Greene. On several levels. I have heard all I need to from you, and I will be leaving you momentarily. But, just to show you what a fool you are, I will explain some concepts to you that are beyond the imaginings of your parochial mind. As for being a patriot, that is exactly what I am. Eight years ago, this planet was close to being annihilated by two governments made up of paranoid bureaucrats whose vision does not extend beyond the borders of their respective states.

"The United States and the Soviet Union have taken this childishness to the brink. The world cannot allow itself to be held hostage to this kind of insanity. We realize what those governments do not. You cannot make the world safer by building ever more terrifying weapons. The only sane course is to reduce the numbers and the power of these weapons, until there exists an understanding and a manageable risk. Why has this not been done? Because of fear, Mr. Greene. Because of mistrust. You now are no doubt aware of the technology we are attempting to provide to the Soviet Union. Was it some new and more powerful weapon to be used against the United States? No, Mr. Greene, it is a camera. A camera that could, and ultimately will, be used by both sides to ensure and to verify the reduction of these weapons and their delivery systems. The United States government would never agree to hand over this technology, even though they know it is in the best interest of all nations that this ability is shared. I will tell you, Mr. Greene, that we are not alone in our conviction that this must happen. Those who have helped us obtain the documents in question feel as we do, and I assure you they do love their country."

"It's still espionage, no matter how you dress it up."

"Call it what you will, Mr. Greene. But there is a second concept that is no doubt just as foreign to your limited field of view. Your country, the Soviet Union, China, Europe, continue today to function in a nineteenth-century mindset. It is a mindset that asserts the power of the nation-state and believes security lies in the ability to defend that state and perhaps to project power preemptively. It is a failed conception. You do not see it, but this model is beginning to falter. It will take a few decades, but I tell you it is inevitable. Security no longer results from an indomitable military force, as necessary as this is at this stage of political development. Security, at its core, is a function of the economic strength of a country. Those nations that are able to adapt to the new paradigm will grow and thrive. Those which do not, will decline, as surely as Rome declined. Victims of their own arrogance.

"Transportation, automation, the advent of the computer, and education, Mr. Greene. These things will ultimately make the nation-state irrelevant. In the not-too-distant future, corporations will manufacture where they can find the cheapest labor. They will cut the ties that bind them to the United States or Europe or anywhere else in the world. They will become nations unto themselves, existing in a world with no barriers to the movement of goods, and the ability to manufacture in the most advantageous environment. It will represent a giant leap for mankind and the end to war.

"This family is preparing now for this inevitability. We believe in democracy because it is good for business. We are not enemies of the United States or of any state. Our interests are not political at all. Our mission is to insure that our business interests are provided with the best competitive advantages possible, and secondly, in doing our best to ensure that the small minds of this world do not destroy it for all of us before they sink into irrelevance.

"I feel sorry for you, Mr. Greene, I really do. You have a good mind and an excellent grasp of history. I am sure, if you were to give it some thought, you would begin to agree with our position. Had you made it possible for us to bring you along, you might some day have been a valuable, and well-rewarded, asset for us. But now you will be just another corpse. A sacrifice to the inevitable tide of history. Good bye, Mr. Greene."

"What makes you think you have the wisdom to manipulate nations? What gives you license to commit murders? Who gave you the right?"

"Wisdom, Mr. Greene? Perhaps we are not the wisest group of men who have ever walked this earth, but look at your government. Look at the government of the Soviet Union. Do you see wisdom in these governments, or in any government that currently exists on this planet? At least we have a vision of the future. One that does not threaten the wholesale annihilation of our species. As to murder…everyone dies, Mr. Greene. Some, sooner than later. There is no tragedy in death, only in life lived with stupidity."

With that, he turned and walked out of the room. Paul prepared himself for a bullet in his brain. Instead they left him alone, without hope, to ponder what he had done with his life. He wondered why they didn't kill him right away. He was experiencing some vertigo, but he forced himself to get up and to move around the room. After a few minutes, he felt clearer. He could not stand up completely and he felt weak, but there didn't seem to be any serious damage. His last hope was to jump them when they came back. If they had a gun, maybe he could turn it on them. The door was thick, and he couldn't hear anything. He leaned against the wall, forcing himself to stay awake. He started to nod off a few times, and he limped around the room again and flexed his arms to get his circulation going. In the end, he could not stay awake any longer. He stretched out on the floor and slept.

When he awoke, they were already in the room. There were only two of them this time. One of them was carrying a tray, and he put it down on the table. The other one cuffed Paul's hands in the front and then took him out into the basement to another small room, which turned out to be a toilet. They kept the door open. He looked like he had aged ten years, and there was blood in his urine. He threw some water on his face and ran his fingers through his hair. They waited until he was finished and then walked him back to the room. Once inside, one of the ghosts held him while the other removed the handcuffs. As usual, neither of them said a word. They pushed him down on the chair and left. Paul felt a ray of hope pass over him. Maybe they had decided not to kill him after all. The tray contained some soup and bread, a glass of water and a cup of black coffee. He drank the entire glass of water and then took a spoonful of the soup. As soon as he tasted it, he realized how hungry he was and he finished all of it, wiping the bowl with the bread. The hot soup made his teeth ache and he wondered if they had been cracked. His jaw was sore and swollen on one side. He sipped the coffee, wondering why he was still alive and trying to figure out what to do. He expected them to come back at any minute, but nothing happened. He paced the room, tried to stretch out some of his painful muscles and did another search of his cell, looking for anything that could help him escape. The only thing useful for a weapon was the tray and the chair. His strength was returning, and he decided the next time they came in, he would make his move.

After a while, he slept again. He had no concept of time. He awoke to a faint sound at the door. The adrenalin surged through him, and he hobbled over and flattened himself against the wall. The door opened slowly and he crouched, waiting for the first man to step through. A solitary figure entered the room, and he leaped out of his crouch and thrust the heel of his hand forward. At the last second, he stopped. He couldn't believe his eyes. It was Katherine. She threw her arms around him and began to cry.

"I thought they had killed you."

Paul gained his composure. "I'm surprised to see you, after you threw me to the wolves."

"What are you talking about? I have come to get you out of here."

"Marc told me he knows about the cufflink."

"And you believe I told him?"

"That's what he led me to believe."

"The building manager told him, after they had given it to me. How could you think I would betray you, Paul, after all that has passed between us?"

"I'm sorry, Katherine. Everything's become so confusing."

"I had to make Marc believe you meant nothing to me. Otherwise there would be no chance of getting you out."

"I'm sorry I doubted you."

"There is no time. We must leave now. I have a car out back. Are you badly hurt? Can you walk?"

"I can walk. I'm just a little unsteady. I don't understand why they haven't killed me already."

"I believe they are hesitating because they are not sure if anyone is searching for you. Marc has left for the day. He has sent Taylor to see what he can find out. I think they will make a decision when Marc returns tonight. That's why we must go now."

"Go where?"

"I have a place in mind. I have packed some things, and I've brought some money. I can't pretend any longer. The sight of him disgusts me now."

"How long have I been in here?"

"It is Sunday and it is already evening. We must hurry."

- 26 -

It was Maria's habit to have Sunday dinner early so that she could attend her sewing club in the evening. Ernesto and Anna were looking forward to being alone for a few hours. Maria was an excellent cook, and Ernesto always looked forward to her Sunday dinners. Anna was worried. Maria had gone to see her Babalao, a Santeria priest, for a consultation. He had thrown the bones for her and said that there was much turmoil and death around her. More than anything, Anna wanted Ernesto to stay away from Vicente and not do any more dangerous things. She wanted to go away with him somewhere where they would be safe, but it was not her place to ask him. He had his papers now and he could claim asylum. She had hinted many times that he should do no more for Vicente, but he would not listen. It was a matter of honor, he said. She did not understand how men could be so stupid.

* * *

They had just sat down to eat when Vicente came and walked into the house without bothering to knock. Maria looked annoyed, but she offered him a plate.

"No, thank you, Maria. I must speak to Ernesto."

They walked through the kitchen and into the back yard.

"The pig has finally shown his face, Ernesto. Our people saw him leaving the big house about an hour ago. He was alone. I believe our chance has come."

"What should we do?"

"Finish your dinner. I will be parked out front. We will go to the big house and wait for him. When he appears, we will kill him."

"But how do you know he is coming back?"

"We don't know for certain. But we will wait and see."

Ernesto couldn't eat. He had never seen so much violence and death when he was in Cuba. He wondered if this was how life was in America. As much as he wanted to avenge his friends, he wasn't sure he could actually kill anyone. He thought about Ramón and Hector, and the anger began to build inside. Anna looked at him with concern. He knew she was afraid for him, and the more he fell in love with her, the less he wanted to risk his life. He wondered if God would forgive him if he killed the Americano, even though he had killed Hector and Ramón. The Americano was evil. There was no question. But perhaps it was not up to him to take revenge. Still he had promised Vicente, and he could not back out now.

"What is wrong, Ernesto? Something has upset you."

He didn't know what to say. "I'm sorry, Anna. I must go with Vicente for a while. I will return later."

She gave him a disappointed look. "Please don't go. You know how I worry about you."

"I will be fine. Do not be afraid for me."

"Finish your dinner, Ernesto," Maria said. "Vicente can wait."

"I am sorry, Maria. I don't have much of an appetite today."

Vicente was waiting for him in the van. They drove for a while in silence. Finally, he spoke. "Open the glove compartment."

Ernesto did as he was told and saw a pistol inside.

"Take the pistol."

He removed it and held it in his hand. It felt cold and heavy. He was a little afraid of it.

"Have you ever fired a pistol before, Ernesto?"

"No, never."

"That is a forty-five automatic. Push the button on the side of the handle."

Ernesto did so and the magazine fell out onto his lap.

"Now pull the slide back to expose the chamber. It is the long part on the top of the pistol. Check to make sure it is empty."

Ernesto pulled the slide back as far as it would go, but it slipped between his fingers and snapped back into place.

"That's okay, Ernesto. If there had been a round in the chamber, it would have expelled when you pulled back the slide. So now you know the gun is empty. Now put the magazine back into the grip."

Ernesto pushed it back as he was told. It clicked into place.

"Now pull the slide back again, just enough so you can see inside the chamber. Always point the gun away from you when you do this. And not at me," he added, smiling. He watched as Ernesto repeated the procedure. "Now there is a round in the chamber and the gun is ready to fire. Do you see the lever on the left side near the trigger?"

"Yes."

"That is the safety. When it is back, as it is now, the gun will not fire. Push the lever forward with your thumb. The red dot you see means the gun is ready to fire. Put the safety back on for now."

Ernesto pushed the lever back. He didn't like holding the gun.

"That is a very powerful handgun, Ernesto. It can kill a man even if you do not hit him in a vital place. All you need to do now is push the safety off with your thumb, point at your target and pull the trigger. It will fire every time you pull the trigger, until there are no more bullets. Do you understand?"

"Yes, I understand, Vicente, only..."

"You are worried you will not be able to do it?"

"Yes, or perhaps I will miss."

"That is normal, Ernesto. Think about what this man has done to your friends and do not worry. If you fail to shoot him, I will do it for you. As for missing, you will be very close to him. Hold the gun in both hands, with your left hand covering the fingers of your right. Keep your thumb away from the slide, because it will kick back when the gun fires. Show me how you will hold it."

He pointed the gun at the floor.

"Move your left thumb a little lower. That is good. Hold your arms straight out in front of you, but do not lock your elbows. The gun will kick back and upward when it fires. If your elbows are locked, it could knock you over."

"But how will we make the American stop? Must we follow him all the way to the house?"

"No. Juan is already waiting on the south side of the house near the driveway. He has a radio. I will park on the north side. We will leave the engines running. As soon as one of us sees him pass, the other will speed forward and block the entrance to the driveway before he can reach it. The other car will come up from behind and keep him from backing up. You will be waiting next to the stone pillar at the end of the driveway. There are large bushes there, and you will not be seen. The Americano drives a white Cadillac. When you see the car stop, walk out to the driver's side and empty the gun through the driver side window. Do you understand, Ernesto?"

"Yes, I understand."

"Do not worry, Ernesto, you can do this."

When they arrived at the house, Vicente drove by slowly. "Do you see the stone pillar, Ernesto? That is where you will wait. If he has not come by one hour, I will come and get you."

"Which one, Vicente? There are two pillars."

Vicente laughed. "It does not matter. Pick the one you love the most."

When Vicente had parked the car, Ernesto got out and walked cautiously toward the end of the driveway. He was very frightened to be carrying a pistol. He didn't know what to do if the police came or if someone found him waiting. When he reached the stone pillar, he peered cautiously around it. The driveway was dark, and he did not see anyone. He stood in the shadow of the pillar, with his back pressed against a bush. He didn't think anyone could see him. He felt sick inside, and he was sure something would go wrong. To keep himself calm, he thought about Anna. *After this, there will be no more*, he said to himself. *After this there will only be Anna.* Everything was quiet. He listened to the crickets and looked up at the sky. It was cloudy, but he could see the moon trying to shine through. He hoped he would not fail. He told himself that he must do this to be free.

He had seen so much death, but to kill a man with his own hands was not something he wanted to do. Even if it was an evil man. It seemed to him that this was the price of his freedom. His life had been standing still, but it seemed the only way to move into the future was to kill someone. It was like a price paid to the devil. He asked why it had to be this way. Did God not wish him to be a good man? Did God not say it was wrong to kill? Yet why had God not shown him another way? The question haunted him. He was afraid. Afraid for his life, and afraid that God would punish him for what he must now do.

- 27 -

Katherine helped Paul into the car and hurried around to the driver's seat. She started the engine and drove slowly around toward the front of the house. As she turned the corner, she checked the rearview mirror and saw two men emerge through the cellar door. They ran after the car. One was talking into a radio. Katherine sped around the front of the house and onto the driveway. Her eyes were wild with panic. The car picked up speed. Paul was looking behind them to see if they were being pursued. Suddenly a man stepped into the driveway in front of them and pointed a gun at the windshield. He was yelling at them to stop. Katherine hesitated a moment. She looked over at Paul with a frantic look on her face, and then she stomped her foot down on the accelerator.

Paul screamed. "Wait, Katherine."

It was too late. The car surged forward. The man fired twice into the windshield before they slammed into him, and he was thrown up and over the back of the car. Paul turned in time to see the man roll off the back and hit the driveway. When he turned back to Katherine, she was slumped over the wheel, her foot still jammed against the accelerator. Before he could react, the car veered off the road and crashed into the stone pillar at the end of the drive.

* * *

Ernesto had heard the car coming and flattened himself against the pillar to avoid being seen. He heard the gunshots and then the pillar behind him seemed to explode forward, knocking him to the ground. He was not hurt, but he had dropped his pistol. It was dark. He searched around on the ground with his hands, but he couldn't find it. He crawled back to where he had been standing and looked around what remained of the pillar. He saw a car with its front end smashed in and steam coming out of the radiator. A woman was lying on the ground next to the car. Blood was pouring out of her head. An injured man was kneeling beside her. He was holding her hand and screaming. He did not think such a sound could come from a man.

A feeling of pity filled him. His instincts told him to try to help, and he stood and started to walk toward them. He forgot about why he was there. Suddenly, behind him a car screeched to a halt, blocking the end of the driveway. Seconds later the white Cadillac drove up. The driver hesitated for a second, and then quickly threw the car into reverse. Just as he did so, Vicente came up behind in the van, cutting off his escape. Ernesto froze. His head was spinning, and he couldn't think what to do. He had no gun. Juan got out of the car and ran toward the van. The American leapt out of his car and fired at Juan, who fell to the ground and didn't move. He turned and saw Ernesto standing still, like a rabbit in the headlights, and he pointed his gun at him. Behind him, Vicente jumped out of the van and the American heard him. He spun and at the same time dropped into a crouch, firing twice. Vicente flew backward against the van and his gun fired into the air. He crumpled to the ground. The American turned back toward Ernesto and walked up to him pointing the gun at his head. Ernesto fell to his knees. He was frozen in fear and with the shame of his failure. He waited for his death. A shot rang out, and he fell to the ground in terror. He felt nothing. A few seconds passed, and he opened his eyes. The man who had been with the injured woman, was standing next to him holding his gun. The American lay dead on the ground in front of him. There was nothing left of his face.

"Are you all right?" the man was saying to him. "Are you hurt?"

Ernesto could see his lips move, but he did not understand. Behind them, some men were running up the driveway, shouting. The man turned and fired at them until the gun was empty. He grabbed Ernesto by his arm and pulled him toward the van. He was limping badly. Vicente was lying against the front wheel, accusing him with his dead eyes. He had failed him. The man pushed him in through the driver's seat and then forced him over to the other side. He pulled the shift lever into reverse. The tires screamed and smoked as he backed up the road. He swerved onto the shoulder and then shifted into drive. The van lurched forward and sped off down the road. Ernesto could not move. He held onto the dashboard with both hands and just stared into space, but he saw nothing.

* * *

Paul didn't know where he was going. He didn't care. He had Katherine's blood all over his hands and his clothes. His mind had become strangely calm. She was dead and nothing else mattered. He drove because it was the only thing left to do.

"Are you shot, Senor?"

Paul turned to him and realized he had no idea who he was and what he had been doing at the house. He only knew that Taylor was going to kill him and that was enough.

"Are you shot, Senor? There is blood all over you."

"No, I'm not shot. Who are you?"

"My name is Ernesto. You have saved my life."

"What were you doing at the house?"

"We came to take revenge on the American. He murdered our friends."

"He won't be killing anyone else."

"How can I repay you for saving my life?"

It was the same question he had asked Katherine, all of those months ago. He could no longer hold it back. He pulled the van over to the side of the road and wept. His hands gripped the wheel and his body shook with grief. After a few moments, he pulled himself together and began to drive again.

"Where are we going, Senor?"

Paul didn't answer right away. He wiped his eyes with the sleeve of his shirt and looked in the rearview mirror. Finally he spoke.

"Listen, I'm going to drive us to a place I know in the city, and I'll be getting out there. From there on, you're on your own. You need to get rid of this van as soon as you can and then get out of this city. Those are evil people back there and they'll be looking for you."

"Yes, I think this is good advice. You are an enemy of these people?"

He didn't answer right away. Finally, he looked over at Ernesto. "They've taken everything from me."

"You still have your life, Senor. They have not taken that."

"No, I gave that away on my own."

"The woman, you were in love with her?"

Paul stared out at the road; he was having difficulty concentrating. Finally he spoke. "She wasn't like those people. I tried to get her away from them."

"And this you have done, Senor. She is with God now, where they can no longer do her harm."

Paul pulled the van up to the curb. He looked down at the pistol, still sitting in his lap. He pulled out his shirttail, wiped it down and then offered it to Ernesto.

"You might want to keep this in case they come after you. It needs to be reloaded."

"No, Senor, I do not want it."

Paul dropped it on the floor. "If you don't need it, throw it in the river as soon as you can."

"Yes, I think so."

Paul looked over at the man sitting next to him. He could not save Katherine, but somehow he had saved this man who was a stranger to him. In that instant, some kind of bond had been forged between them, which he didn't understand. It was as if her soul had moved on, and the life she no longer needed had been given to this stranger. He wanted to know why, but he knew there could be no answer to that question. Paul reached across and put his hand on Ernesto's shoulder, searching for words and finding none. It was as if this man was his last connection to

Katherine. Ernesto smiled sadly and nodded his head as if he understood.

"What is your name, please?"

"It's Paul. Paul Greene."

"Something good will happen for you, Paul, for what you have done."

"Be careful, Ernesto. Remember what I told you." He stepped out onto the street.

"May God be with you," Ernesto said. And then he got behind the wheel and drove away.

Paul was in pretty bad shape. He couldn't walk very well, but he stumbled over the to door and pushed it open. When the waitress saw him, she screamed. Baby came running out of the kitchen.

"Oh, my God, it's Paul. What happened to you?"

"Can I wait here for a little while, Baby? Some people are looking for me."

"You can stay here as long as you want to. Come on, let's get you to the back. Do you need a doctor?"

"No, I think I'll be alright. Is there a place I can lie down for a little while? I just want to sleep."

"Sure there is. Come on, let me help you and then I'll fix you something to eat."

* * *

Ernesto had been in the city a few times and he knew at least how to get back to Maria's house. As he drove he thought about what to say. He kept looking in the mirrors, expecting to see someone chasing him. When he crossed the bridge, he took the pistol and flung it out the window into the river. He had to remind himself to drive carefully and stop at the lights. He was relieved when he finally pulled up to the house. He ran inside. Anna was sitting in the living room alone. Ernesto walked over to her and knelt down in front of her. Anna started to laugh, but when she saw the serious look on his face her expression turned to one of concern.

"What is wrong, Ernesto?"

"Vicente is dead, Anna. Juan is dead. Everyone is dead."

She covered her mouth and gasped. Tears came to her eyes.

"Anna, please listen to me. I know this is not the proper way to say this to you, but I have no choice. I love you, Anna. I want you to be my wife. It is no longer safe for me in this city and I must leave. I have to leave right away. I know this is so sudden and I will not ask you to go with me now. I only ask if you will wait for me until I can come for you."

She looked at him for a long time and Ernesto thought she was going to be angry with him. Finally, she spoke. "You are not leaving here without me, Ernesto. I will not permit it."

She threw her arms around him and they fell to the floor together, kissing passionately. Finally, Ernesto pulled away.

"We don't have much time, Anna. If you are coming, you have to pack your things now and please hurry."

They both ran upstairs. Ernesto threw what little he had into a shopping bag. He rushed into Anna's room. A suitcase was open on the bed, and she was throwing things into it.

"Just pack what you can fit, Anna. We can have Maria send the rest to you."

She stuffed the suitcase full and ran into the bathroom. She returned with her arms full of bottles, brushes and combs.

"I don't have enough room, Ernesto."

He held open his bag and she threw everything inside. He took her suitcase and ran down the stairs. Anna followed, looking flustered. He headed for the door.

"Wait, Ernesto, I cannot go without leaving at least a note for Maria."

"Quickly, Anna."

She opened a drawer and took out a pen and some writing paper. Ernesto thought she was writing her life story, but he kept his mouth shut. His feet were dancing under him and he looked nervously toward the street, expecting someone to drive up at any moment and find him. Finally, she finished and he grabbed her by the arm and pulled her out the door. They got into the van and drove away into the night.

"Where are we going Ernesto?"

"I'm not sure, Anna. Is there someplace you would like to go?"

"I don't care, as long as I am with you."

He turned and smiled at her. "I have always wanted to see Miami."

"Then we shall go to Miami, Ernesto."

"And when we get there, Anna, the first thing we will do is find a priest who will marry us." She reached over and kissed him, almost pulling him off his seat. He laughed. "Anna, you are going to make me crash." He drove to the bus station. "I have to leave the van behind. It is not safe. Those who killed Vicente will be looking for it."

"Why, Ernesto? What has happened?"

"I will explain everything, Anna. Only not at this moment. We will have to travel by bus. I am sorry, but I don't know what else to do. I do not know how to drive to Miami, anyway. Does it bother you to take the bus?"

"No, I don't care. I only wish I had put on some nicer things." She turned the rearview mirror and began playing with her hair.

"Don't worry, Anna, you could not look more beautiful."

She waited while Ernesto purchased two, one-way tickets to Miami and then they went over to the benches.

"Wait here, Anna, I will be right back."

* * *

Anna sat back. Thoughts were rushing through her mind. She had never been so excited. She was in love and going on a journey to a beautiful warm place. There could not possibly be anything better in the entire world. Finally, she had found the man she loved and she would have a new life. Ernesto would be safe now. She was still sad about Hector and about Ramón and the others. So many had been killed. She was also sad about Maria. She didn't like to think about her being all alone, but it was time for her now to make a life for herself. She pushed everything else out of her mind. After a few minutes Ernesto returned.

"Ernesto, if you were going to buy a bag, you should have taken me with you. That is the most ugly bag I have ever seen."

"Yes, it is ugly, Anna. But it is filled with dreams."

- 28 -

Agent O'Brien almost tripped over the box of Christmas decorations sitting outside his door. It was the only time of year that the office was permitted a little bit of cheer and his secretary was pushing it to the limit.

"Sorry, sir. Let me move that for you. Hey, I have another small tree. Would you like it in your office?"

"No, thanks, Ellen. It isn't even Thanksgiving for another week."

"Are you sure? It's already decorated, lights and all."

"No, that's okay. See if Landis wants it."

He wasn't much in the mood for the holidays. In August, Hurricane Camille had slammed into the Gulf coast, devastating the entire area. New Orleans itself got though it with just some minor flooding, but their field office in Gulfport was annihilated. They had lost a considerable amount of evidence, relating to several high profile cases. They were still looking for a safe that had completely vanished. Everyone in the office was working overtime to try to reconstruct the cases but it looked like they were going to have to start over with most of them. The mood in the office was pretty sour and tempers were short.

He sat at his desk and read the overnight report, stopping periodically and writing notes in the margin. The phone rang and he picked it up absently, still reading.

"Agent O'Brien." The pen dropped out of his hand. "Where are you?…Here, in Baton Rouge?" He looked at his watch. "Sure, where?…At the riverfront?…I'll be there in fifteen minutes."

The bleachers at the little league field were empty except for a lone figure sitting behind home plate as if he were expecting a game to start. O'Brien parked his car and walked over him. He reached out his hand.

"It's good to see you, Paul. I have to tell you we all thought you were dead. I'm happy to see we were wrong. Why didn't you contact us?"

"I was in pretty bad shape for a while there. Physically and mentally. It took me a while to recover. Anyway I came to tell you I'm ready to keep my end of the deal."

"You already did that. As far as the agency is concerned, we're square. When you didn't turn up after the blood bath at Francoeur's estate, well, let's just say we turned over a lot of stones looking for you. In the end you were listed as a missing person. We had the Air Force process an honorable discharge for you, and we closed your file. I'm sorry about Miss Francoeur, Paul. I know you cared for her."

"Thanks." He was silent for a moment. "Anyway," he said finally, "I wanted to tell you I'm ready to testify as soon as you need me."

It was O'Brien's turn to be silent. He looked at Paul. "We aren't going to need you to testify, Paul."

"What do you mean? What about Marc Francoeur?"

"Let me tell you what's transpired. First of all, and most importantly, we prevented any classified information from getting into the wrong hands, thanks in part to your efforts. We've been able to plug the leak on the other end and several individuals in one of our intelligence agencies will be going away for a long time. You'll never hear about it because the agency doesn't officially exist. As a result of our surveillance, we were able to identify and expel several foreign nationals who were spying for their intelligence apparatus. Taylor and his primary contact, a Cuban known to us as the Shepherd are both dead, along with several of their co-conspirators. All in all, we consider the entire operation to be a major success."

"But what about Francoeur?"

"Our case against him, despite your efforts, had a lot of holes in it. Predictably, he claimed that his man Taylor was freelancing on this one and we did not have any paper trail or audio surveillance to prove otherwise. Some of our evidence was being held at our office in Gulfport. The office was destroyed by hurricane Camille and a lot of it has apparently been lost. With Taylor dead, there is no credible witness to link Francoeur to the classified data. Even though we could prove the documents had been in his safe, we didn't have enough evidence to prove, beyond a reasonable doubt, that he knew about the classified information on the microdots. Also, as a demonstration of his loyalty, he was able to provide us with some very helpful information on the Cuban intelligence organization. It turns out that his associates also have some very detailed information on Soviet agents operating world-wide and he is currently cooperating with the CIA to help identify them."

"But he was responsible for this whole operation. You have to believe that."

"No question. We know he was running it. But what we know and what we can prove are two different things. In a case like this, we have to look at the overall outcome. This was a major success for us."

"So he gets to walk. He gets away with murder."

"If it makes you feel any better, we would have prosecuted him if we had the evidence, regardless of any information he provided for us."

Paul just shook his head. "I can't believe that bastard is going to walk."

"For now, anyway. But we'll be keeping our eye on him. I don't like this any more than you do." He paused for a moment, trying to gauge Paul's reaction. "I'll tell you what we would like, Paul," he said finally. "We would like to know what happened that night at the estate. The crime scene was thoroughly investigated, and we seem to be absent at least one shooter and at least one weapon. Can you help us with that?"

"No, I wasn't there."

O'Brien was incredulous. "You weren't there?"

Paul just looked at him.

"You know I could take you in with me right now and hold you as a material witness."

Paul just shrugged his shoulders. "I really don't care what you do to me at this point, Agent O'Brien. I don't have anything left to lose."

O'Brien studied him for a few moments. "All right, Paul. I know what you've been through. You've been a great help to us, and showing up here today to offer to testify is enough for me. I'm going to pretend this meeting never took place. You have your discharge and an opportunity to start a new life. Let's just leave it at that."

They stood up and shook hands.

"Just one other thing, Paul. I know how you feel about Marc Francoeur, and I can't say I blame you. If you're considering any kind of revenge, I would caution you to forget about it. Considering what you could be facing, I think you came out of this thing pretty well, in spite of your loss. Do yourself a favor. Walk away this time."

* * *

He could not live with it. He could not let her murder go unpunished, no matter what the price. It became his obsession. He knew his life could not continue until it was done. It was a chilly evening in early March and there was frost on the ground. The estate was quiet and things had returned to normal after months of turmoil and seemingly endless investigations. Men still guarded the house, but after so many months, they did not expect any more trouble. Katherine's blood still stained the driveway in spite of their efforts to remove it. He had seen it himself. He had come back many times, sometimes just sitting in the shadows and watching. It was the last place he had seen her alive. It pulled at him.

Clad in black, Paul emerged from behind the stables and made his way toward the house. He ran soundlessly, in a slight crouch, scanning the area for guards he might not have accounted for. His face was painted and he wore black climbing shoes and gloves. His clothes were tight fitting and a black knitted hat covered his head. He knew exactly where he was going. The house had once been featured in the Times Picayune, complete with a layout of the rooms. The back issue had been located and provided to him eagerly, by someone else who had mourned the loss of Katherine. He remembered the photograph of the great man, looking through the bedroom window above his pasture at his stable of magnificent horses.

"They are the first thing I see, when I rise in the morning," it had said.

He could not allow himself the luxury of anger now. He needed all of his faculties to be clear. A guard stood under the portico in the front and another patrolled the grounds adjacent to the mansion, circling the house every few minutes. He crouched behind a bush and waited for the guard to pass around to the back of the house and then ran silently across the driveway to the corner of the building, where the cast iron drain pipe ran up to the roof. He climbed quickly and silently, pausing in the shadow under the eave until the guard came around again and made his way to the back. He could have killed him easily and without a sound, but this was not his enemy. Not unless he tried to interfere.

At the top of the gable above the large central window was a wooden beam that ran back diagonally from the gabled roof and secured itself to the wall just above the window. He inched himself across the face of the wall, clinging with his fingers and toes to the fissures between the irregular stones. His body was healed now and the traverse was not difficult for him. When he reached the beam, he leapt across to it, clutching it with both hands and at the same time releasing his feet from the wall. He curled his body upward and looped his legs through, letting go with his hands. He hung inverted like a bat with his head now level with the center of the window and his arms folded across his chest. He was in no hurry. The guard passed by again, twenty feet below his head, oblivious to the danger above him. They had grown complacent. It would be their undoing.

When the guard turned the corner again, Paul reached into a pocket on his thigh and withdrew a thin strip of metal. He slid it between the frames of the casement window and raised the catch. He opened half of the window outward, then removed a small knife from his pocket and quickly cut the screen. By the time the guard passed below again the window was closed and he was in the room. He stood in the shadows for a moment and listened to the sounds of the house as he slowed his heart rate and prepared himself for what he must do.

He crept noiselessly over to the bed and looked down at the man sleeping there. Marc looked older than he had remembered. Paul's anger and hatred threatened to boil over. He wanted to wake him and beat him to death with his own hands. But that would not be the way. From his pocket, he removed a piece of paper. He unfolded it and placed it on the pillow next to the sleeping figure. The knife strapped to his leg was long and razor sharp, with a bone handle and a serrated edge. Paul hovered over the bed with the knife clenched in one hand and the palm of the other on the top the handle to guide the downward thrust. He hesitated, standing like a statue, looking at the man's exposed throat. Marc stirred in his sleep and mumbled something. Paul hesitated momentarily, staring down at the face he hated more than anything on the earth. Finally, his shoulders slumped almost imperceptibly and then, in one sharp thrust, he rammed the blade home. Marc never made a sound.

He removed an object on a thin metal chain from his pocket and looped it over the handle of the knife. Taking one last look, he quickly returned to the window and looked down, waiting for the guard to pass by. In less than thirty seconds he was back on the ground. Before the guard came around again he was back behind the stables and free. He came over the wall a few yards from where the car was waiting with its engine running, and quickly jumped into the passenger seat. The car moved slowly forward with its lights out, picking up speed as it entered the roadway. He removed his hat and gloves and began to wipe his face clean with a handkerchief.

"Is it done with now, baby? Can you leave it alone now?"

"Yeah. It's done. Let's go home."

* * *

Charles climbed the stairs to the master bedroom, holding the tray in both hands. When he got to the door he balanced it above his shoulder. He knocked once and pushed the door open. He looked over at the bed and gasped. The tray tipped and everything on it fell, smashing on the hardwood floor. Marc sat up with a start, looking at Charles. Charles pointed, and he turned and then leapt out of bed. A bone-handled knife protruded from the pillow next to him. Around its handle was a gold locket. It was stained with blood. He reached down and took the locket.

His fingers trembled as he opened the clasp. His head fell to his chest. Charles walked over and pulled the note away from the blade, handing it to Marc. He stared at it for a moment and then let it fall to the floor. The message would stay with him for the remainder of his days.

> From this night forward, you will never again sleep in peace
> There is no place I cannot reach you
> I will return, at a time of my own choosing
> To make you pay for what you have done
> There is no tragedy in death
> Except for a man who has sold his soul

ABOUT THE AUTHOR

Wallace Brown lives in suburban Philadelphia Pa. He is a graduate of Villanova University with a degree in English. After a career in business which involved constant travel in the company of a good book, he has written his first novel, entitled *The Shepherd Sleeps.* His favorite authors are Alan Furst, John LeCarre and Somerset Maugham. Wallace would enjoy hearing from his readers. You can find him at www.wallacefbrown.com.

Keep track of Wallace's work on his author page: http://www.readerseden.com/manufacturers.php?manufacturerid=432

Dead By The Sea by Dan Donoghue (Murder Mystery)

Jim Groggan was bored. He was so bored that when a brutal murder occurred on the beach where he was staying, he took too great an interest in it. He even volunteered to drive a police officer down along the beach to interview Hippies in a seaside camp. There he met a girl, and unwisely went to her aid. Suddenly, he was mixed up in a turmoil of drugs, guns, and murder, and boredom seemed a very desirable state indeed as he and the girl became the target of ruthless gangsters, while the police seemed more interested in using them as bait than in protecting them.

When a police officer told Jim not to shoot as it was becoming a massacre, he wasn't fooling, and he knew only the half of it.

http://www.readerseden.com/product.php?productid=94&cat=9&page=1

Fanged Justice by Patricia Lucas White (Mystery)

A funny thing happens to Albert Weston, mystery writer, on his way to his wedding in Reno. Driving across the high desert, he comes upon a wrecked auto and two terrified women. Good Samaritan that he is, Albert gives them comfort, a bit of first aid, and a lift. Then, a wild tale of murderers on the prowl, a flash flood, and a dead man later, Albert is stranded in an isolated land brimming with snakes. His bride waits in Reno, he hopes, but Albert is in dire jeopardy and just might not live long enough to tie the knot.

http://www.readerseden.com/product.php?productid=477&cat=9&page=2

The Gauntlet by Michael Hobren (Futuristic Thriller)

Russell Williams is a hard-drinking, unemployed computer analyst with no family and no prospects. But Williams has one thing going for him - his genotype. At the Trade Winds Lounge in scenic Daytona Beach, Florida, a stranger plants the notion in Williams' head that the key to all his problems is in his blood. Williams has no idea that he is being maneuvered by a group of power brokers who seek to toss him into the judicial ring to establish behavioral genetics as the newest, lucrative legal defense strategy of the decade.

But when Williams is forced through an intersection during a high-speed chase that results in the death of several vacationers, he is charged with three counts of DUI Manslaughter. A firm of ambitious lawyers, and their unprecedented Genetics Defense, seems to be Williams' only hope of escaping death row. Only veteran homicide detective Ezra "Cane" McCoy suspects that there's more to the case than a DUI.

http://www.readerseden.com/product.php?productid=253&cat=9&page=5

Retribution by John Schembra (Murder Mystery)

There's a vigilante killer loose in San Francisco, and when the justice system fails, he doles out his own brand of justice.

Homicide Inspector Vince Torelli has handled some of The City's worst murders, but this case has him baffled. It seems no matter what he does, the killer manages to stay one step ahead of him, anticipating his every move. Hell, the false clues and trail the killer leaves keeps Vince chasing shadows as the body count rises.

Will he discover the killer's identity? And will he survive long enough to bring him to justice?

Winner of the 2007 Silver Medal Award by Military Writers of America.

http://www.readerseden.com/product.php?productid=320&cat=9&page=4

Made in the USA